Marcia Willett was born in Somerset, the youngest of five girls. After training to become a ballet dancer, she then joined her sister's Dance Academy as ballet mistress. After marriage in 1969 to a naval officer, she moved around the naval ports of Britain and her son was born in 1970. In 1980 she was in need of a job and joined a firm of market researchers. Her very first interviewee was to become her second husband!

Rodney Willett, an author of non-fiction books, encouraged Marcia to write. Since then she has had three novels published by Headline, THOSE WHO SERVE, THEA'S PARROT, and THE COURTYARD.

Marcia Willett lives in Devon with her husband and their Newfoundland Trubshawe.

The Dipper

Marcia Willett

HEADLINE

First published in 1996
by HEADLINE BOOK PUBLISHING

First published in paperback in 1996
by HEADLINE BOOK PUBLISHING

10 9 8 7 6

ISBN 0 7472 5202 5

Typeset by CBS, Martlesham Heath, Suffolk

Printed and bound in Great Britain by
Mackays of Chatham plc, Chatham, Kent

HEADLINE BOOK PUBLISHING
A division of Hodder Headline
338 Euston Road
London NW1 3BH

To Kathleen and Reg

Chapter One

Phyllida Makepeace was dreaming. She muttered in her sleep and flung out an arm. Warm skin in contact with icy sheet woke her and she huddled under the quilt, letting consciousness flood in upon the slowly fading images. Reality was disappointing. In her dream, Alistair had telephoned. The submarine had developed a fault and they'd be alongside for a few days, he'd told her, and she'd been dashing round preparing for his arrival.

Phyllida tucked the quilt more firmly under her chin. The large high-ceilinged rooms of the Victorian villa were almost impossible to heat but she loved the house with its sheltered walled garden and the views across to Dartmoor. She lifted her head to peer at the clock on the bedside table and realised that four-year-old Lucy would be waking soon but she lay a little longer, preparing herself for the chilly dash to the bathroom. The sudden remembrance of the very new life within her caused a little shiver of joy to warm her and she flung back the quilt and slid out of bed. She looked an odd figure in one of Alistair's old shirts and a pair of his warm thick white submarine socks. At twenty-six she was still young enough to find comfort in wearing his clothes in his absence and she clutched his shirt to her as she hurried across the landing.

Shivering in the unheated bathroom, she remembered that it was St Valentine's Day and she wondered if Alistair might have arranged for her to receive a card. He was very thoughtful about special days like anniversaries and birthdays and made great efforts to see that cards and presents arrived when he was away at sea. She loved him so much but, though he made it quite clear that he loved her in return, it still baffled her as to why he had chosen her from amongst all his girlfriends to be his wife.

Her elder brother, Matthew, had brought Alistair home for a weekend just after she'd qualified from Norland, the nursery training college, and was completing her nine months' probation. She'd fallen in love with him at once, accepted his proposal of marriage three months later and immediately put all thoughts of a career behind her. Blessed with a happy open disposition, she'd plunged into naval life with enthusiasm and made friends quickly. Alistair, at twenty-nine, was just taking command of a submarine and his brother officers' wives were rather older than Phyllida. They were charmed by her friendly yet diffident approach, flattered by her awe of their experience and wisdom and unthreatened by her appearance. Although she was six or seven years their junior, her looks were not the kind which aroused envy. Phyllida's brand of beauty was not the obvious type. It was a simple understated attractiveness rather than the eye-catching, head-turning variety; the pure oval of her face, her wide grey eyes and the warmth of her ready smile. She was taken under the Wardroom wing and made much of and the fact that she was the Captain's wife did her no harm at all.

It was obvious that Alistair adored her and his family and friends heaved sighs of relief that he was ready to settle down at last. The general opinion was that he'd played the part of Romeo for far too long but the more cynical – and rejected – looked at Phyllida and wondered how long it would be before Alistair's roving eye began to wander yet again. What, they asked each other, did he see in her? He'd had so many gorgeous glamorous women in tow and, although she was sweet, she was hardly in the same class of beauty as his usual girlfriends. At this point, eyebrows were raised and shoulders shrugged. The more charitable – and those who were taken by Phyllida's own particular charm – pointed out that dramatic good looks weren't everything. Alistair, thickset and barely above average height, was hardly conventionally handsome but there was something in his blue eyes and in his smile which tended to make most women in his vicinity pull their stomachs in and feel irritated that they hadn't bothered to wash their hair.

Eighteen months after the wedding Phyllida produced a daughter who, like her mother, was brown-haired, grey-eyed, and blessed, also, with a sunny disposition. As Phyllida returned to her bedroom on this Valentine's Day, wondering if she would get a card from Alistair, she could hear Lucy singing to herself across the landing. She paused, as she always did, at the window. The high granite tors of Dartmoor were bathed in sunshine although the nearer ground was in shadow but, despite the clear pale blue of the sky, there was no doubt that winter still held the land in its grip. Even as she gazed, a shower of hailstones struck the window and she shivered and ran to pull on warm clothes.

Clad in cords and one of Alistair's Norwegian sweaters, Phyllida dressed Lucy in her warmest oldest clothes, for today was playschool day, and they went downstairs together. The postman arrived whilst Phyllida was making toast and she hurried out into the long hall to gather up the letters. Yes, Alistair had remembered. She couldn't prevent a grin of pure pleasure and she opened the envelope quickly, standing there in the hall, and drew out the card. On the front was a comic drawing of an extremely ragged weary-looking knight in armour astride an equally dejected very shaggy dog. 'Be my Valentine' was inscribed below them. Phyllida opened the card and her grin grew wider. 'Surely you can't turn away a knight on a dog like this?' was written inside and underneath, in Alistair's distinctive hand, 'Guess who?' She examined the local postmark and wondered which of their friends had posted it for him. Although she'd had plenty of opportunity to get used to his long absences she still missed him dreadfully and the card gave her a warm feeling.

The feeling was still with her when, having dropped Lucy at the village hall, she went on to have coffee with Prudence Appleby, a naval widow. Although Prudence was nearly fifteen years older than Phyllida they'd taken to each other from the first meeting, almost four years before, just after Stephen Appleby had died in a car accident. Prudence lived in a Victorian house in the moorland village of Clearbrook, and Phyllida always enjoyed a session with her in the big muddly kitchen. This morning, however, Liz Whelan's car stood at the gate and Phyllida's heart sank a little. Liz was Prudence's contemporary but she was very different from the

4

kindly Prudence. She was a small brown woman with a sardonic, rather bitter air and Phyllida felt slightly uncomfortable in her presence.

She parked her car and went round the side of the house to the back door. Beating a quick tattoo with her knuckles, she opened it and stuck her head inside.

'Hi! It's me.'

The door opened straight into the kitchen and Prudence got quickly to her feet to greet her but Liz remained sitting at the table, merely raising her eyebrows and giving a little nod in reply to Phyllida's smile.

'Phyllida!' Prudence gave her a quick kiss. 'Come and get warm. What a morning! And snow's forecast, I hear.' She took Phyllida's coat, her conversation shooting off at tangents as she went to make more coffee. Prudence always talked nineteen to the dozen, skipping from one subject to another, which could be amusing or irritating depending on one's mood. 'So now, tell me. How is Lucy? My goodness!' She shook her head. 'How that child grows!'

'She's fine.' Phyllida sipped gratefully at the hot coffee. 'And the little dress is lovely. She's thrilled with it. She wanted to wear it to playschool this morning.'

Prudence had been trained as a tailor and was a genius with her needle. She worked hard to supplement the naval widow's pension she received and had many clients. Her daughter worked in an advertising agency in London and her son was hoping to qualify as a doctor. Once the bills were paid, every extra penny she made went towards her children and she scrimped and saved in all possible directions. She was thin because she worked too hard, didn't eat enough and worried too much. Her warm, dark, hazel eyes peered anxiously from behind tortoiseshell spectacles.

'She looked charming in it,' she agreed, smiling in recollection, 'and I'm delighted to say that I received several orders as a result of that party she wore it to. Bless you, Phyllida.'

'It wasn't me, really. The dress sold itself. Every mother there wanted one for her little girl. You're really very clever, Prudence.'

'I've got lots of orders coming in.' Prudence looked pleased with herself. 'If I go on like this I shall need an accountant. How about it, Liz?'

'Just say the word,' said Liz. 'Special rates for you, of course.' She looked at Phyllida. 'And how's Alistair?'

Phyllida sensed Prudence's cautious look and she frowned a little as she answered.

'Fine, as far as I know. He's at sea. But I had a Valentine card this morning.' She couldn't prevent the little smile that crept into her eyes and lifted her lips. 'Did he ask you to post it, Prudence?'

'Yes, he did,' admitted Prudence. 'He's really very thoughtful,' she added somewhat defiantly, aware of Liz's amused contempt.

Liz snorted and Phyllida felt awkward and embarrassed. Liz always implied that Alistair's caring was either a sham to cover up bad behaviour, and to be suspected, or something rather sickly to be despised. Yet somehow she always contrived to bring his name into the conversation no matter how assiduously Phyllida or Prudence attempted to distract her.

'Valentine cards!' she said now, as if there was something sinister as well as ridiculous behind the old custom, but before the other two could defend Alistair or his Valentine card, Liz finished her coffee and stood up.

'I must go,' she said. 'I'm meeting a friend for lunch. See you, Prudence. Thanks for the coffee. 'Bye, Phyllida.'

The kitchen door closed behind her and Prudence cast an anxious glance at Phyllida.

'Why does she do that?' asked Phyllida crossly. 'She always manages to imply that I shouldn't really trust Alistair and that he's trying to hide something.'

'Oh dear!' Prudence looked distressed. 'You know, poor Liz is a very bitter girl and it would be unwise to pay too much attention to her. She had a bad time with Tony and the divorce was a painful affair. She really loved him, you know. Well, you can imagine . . .'

'I know all that,' said Phyllida, unmollified by the explanation. 'But I don't see why she has to unsettle other people. I know about Alistair's reputation. I ought to! Everyone wanted to tell me about it.'

'The sad thing is that Liz is still in love with Tony.' As usual Prudence attempted to soothe without being unkind. 'He only married her because of the baby and he was never faithful to her.'

'I know.' Phyllida smiled at her. 'It's just that she always unnerves me. Let's forget it. I've got some news.' Prudence looked at her expectantly, already half prepared and Phyllida grinned back at her. 'You've guessed, haven't you?'

'I think I have.' She sounded cautious.

'I'm pregnant! Isn't it great? Due at the beginning of

September. Lucy will be just five.'

'It's wonderful!' Prudence came round the table to give her a hug. 'Does Alistair know?'

'Not yet. I wanted to be absolutely certain. He's been away so much I thought we'd never get the chance to start another one. He'll be delighted. I shall wait till he gets home now; it's only another three weeks to go. I want to see his face when I tell him.'

'Of course you do. How exciting! Have you told Lucy?'

Phyllida shook her head. 'I'm deciding how to do it but I want to wait till after the weekend. My brother, Matthew, and his wife are coming with their two and I don't want anyone to know before Alistair. Lucy's bound to say something and it will mean explanations all round.'

'I quite understand. I shan't say a word to a soul.'

'I just had to tell someone but keep it to yourself. Especially don't tell Liz!'

'As if I would! I shan't breathe a word. But you really mustn't let her upset you. It's probably just old-fashioned jealousy. Tony never reformed the way Alistair has.'

'Reformed!' Phyllida began to laugh. 'Thanks, Prudence! You make him sound like Bluebeard! I'm beginning to feel really nervous!'

'Oh, honestly,' began Prudence, distressed by her tactlessness, 'I didn't mean anything of the kind . . .'

Phyllida pushed back her chair and stood up. 'Only teasing,' she said. 'I've simply got to dash. I must shop before I fetch Lucy.'

As she drove back towards Yelverton, however, Phyllida felt a twinge of the anxiety that had caused her discomfort in the early days when she'd been introduced to Alistair's previous girlfriends. Some of them had been friendly but several were resentful. They took care to emphasise their relationships with him – reminding him of private jokes, behaving intimately with him, ignoring her – and her confidence had been sorely tested. Again and again she'd wondered why he'd chosen her when he could have had someone so much more beautiful, more poised, more experienced. Alistair's conduct had been irreproachable. He'd made it clear to these few determined women that the past was finished with and his loyalty and love now belonged to Phyllida. He'd done his best to be firm without causing too much offence and gradually the situation was accepted and Phyllida began to relax. Now, six years later, strong in his love, these fears only occasionally caused her alarm but this morning the twinge became a sudden stab of terror. Liz's cynicism had undermined her security and she allowed herself to wonder if Alistair had ever been unfaithful. Perhaps, given his reputation, she'd been too foolishly trusting; too ready to believe that he'd put his past so readily behind him. After all, there was so much opportunity. Her heart knocked erratically as she imagined him in tempting situations and she gripped the wheel tightly, willing away the images that crept into her mind.

Remembering how destructive these fears could be, and determined not to let her trust be undermined, she deliberately brought her mind to bear on the coming baby. Her spirits rose a little and a measure of confidence returned.

Blast Liz! she thought, parking the car and making a dash for the shops as hailstones again descended suddenly and painfully from an apparently clear blue sky. She seized a trolley, dug out her shopping list and, pushing the remembrance of Liz and her insinuations resolutely away, she concentrated on her requirements for the coming weekend.

Chapter Two

It was whilst he was making his breakfast that Quentin Halliwell noticed the shaft of sunlight shining on Clemmie's pot of polyanthus on the deep windowsill. It was the first time this year that the sun's rays had crept into the kitchen and his heart gave a little upward bound of pleasure as he stood for a moment, gazing at it with quiet gratitude. He made a deep reverence within his soul that he should be spared to see the beginning of his eightieth spring and treasured up the moment to recount to Clemmie when she should wake. His numerous aches and stiff joints ensured that Quentin's nights were seldom free from pain and he was always ready to rise early in the morning and allow Clemmie to sink into peaceful sleep, undisturbed by his restlessness. He felt guilty each time he woke her up with his twisting and turning and she, in her turn, would often lie awake, scarcely daring to breathe, until at last he fell asleep and she immediately needed to go to the loo. They laughed about it together and discussed the solution that single beds offered – each in a terrible anxiety lest the other might find it a sensible idea – and had both been tremendously relieved when neither had been ready to entertain it.

'We've shared a bed for fifty-five years,' said Clemmie, holding his hand tightly for a moment. 'I can see no reason to change the arrangement now.'

As he ate his porridge and watched the sunbeam move across the kitchen wall, Quentin remembered his relief. It was impossible to imagine going off to sleep each night without Clemmie curled into a ball against his back. Whilst he waited for his toast to cook on the top of the Esse's hotplate he opened the back door and looked into the courtyard. The old granite house was L-shaped which gave the courtyard two of its walls. The third, which faced south, was a stone shed which Quentin had converted to a long summerhouse and the fourth wall had a high door to the garden in the centre of it. The sun was still too low to penetrate the courtyard but it would not be long now before Clemmie could sit once again in the summerhouse, enjoying the sunshine and watching the robin feeding on the crumbs she threw down for it.

Quentin ate his toast, reviewed a few phrases that might suitably note this memorable morning in his journal, and realised that it was St Valentine's Day. A happy thought struck him and, when he had finished his toast and shared the crusts between the robin and Punch, the black retriever, he took down his coat from its hook and let himself out by the garden door. Outside the shelter of the courtyard the wind blew fresh and keen across the moor. He paused for a moment to fasten his coat against it, drew his tweed cap from his pocket and set off across the lawn with Punch at his heels. A belt of twisted, stunted trees did their best to protect the property from the prevailing south-westerly gales and the tors rose steeply to the north but Quentin, seeking a more protected environment, climbed the stile set in the dry-stone wall at the edge of the lawn and walked briskly down to the woods below.

Once in the shelter of the trees he slowed his pace until he came out on to the path that ran beside the river. He strolled along between the smooth boles of the beech trees, the dead leaves making a thick carpet beneath his feet, until he found the primroses he'd noticed during an earlier walk. Bending his creaking knees he tenderly gathered just a few, selecting the pale blooms carefully and placing them gently in his handkerchief. He passed on behind the high banks of rhododendron and laurel which hid the river from his sight so that it was merely a flash of brightness, a dazzle of reflected sunlight, glimpsed between their branches. A little further on where the path opened out again, above a short length of shingly beach, he found some violets and added several of these to his tiny bunch. Some twigs of early catkins completed his lover's posy and, free now to let his gaze wander further afield, he stopped to watch the turbulent water, peat-brown after weeks of heavy rain. To his joy, he caught a glimpse of the dipper, bobbing on a smooth boulder near the far bank and beneath the grey stone bridge which took its name from the blackthorn that grew beside it. Quentin watched, delighting in the bird's regular movement, rounded brown back and the pure white of its breast. How well it was camouflaged against the grey-brown water with its frothy white waves! Suddenly it plunged into the river, disappearing completely, whilst Quentin peered for it in vain. A few moments later it regained the rock where it spent some moments preening itself before flying off upstream, straight and true, only inches above the water.

For years the dipper had been a symbol of hope and good luck to Quentin and Clemmie, and Quentin could never see one without a soaring of spirits, followed by a private prayer of joy and gratitude, and his heart was light as he turned for home.

From her bedroom window Clemmie saw him coming up the moor above the wood, his booty cradled tenderly in his hands and Punch toiling in the rear. From this distance, with the cap covering the pure white hair, he might have been the young Quentin, returning from the walks he'd taken in this beloved landscape for the last fifty years. They'd moved to this house when her mother had died and left it to them, twenty years before, at which time Quentin was very ready to retire from the Chambers where their son, Gerard, continued to practise as a barrister.

How swiftly those twenty years had fled and how happy they'd been! They'd spent so many holidays at The Grange that the final move had been merely like a homecoming and they'd settled in gladly. For Clemmie it was as if she'd hardly been away and the memory of the middle years in London started to fade a little until it seemed as though all their life together had been spent here. Even Quentin's mother – once his father died – had come with them to The Grange on the twice-yearly holidays, at Christmas and in the summer, and Gerard, in his turn, had brought his wife and children. The Grange was a family home but lately, with the grandchildren flown from the family nest and settled in far

14

parts of the world and Gerard widowed and now remarried to a woman with her roots in the north, the visits were becoming fewer and many of the rooms remained unused.

Clemmie shivered as hailstones rattled suddenly against the window. She watched Quentin's tall broad figure hurry across the lawn below her and disappear from her view. Crossing to the bed, she climbed back in and drew the quilt up round her ears. Thank God they'd both survived the winter! Each of them feared the day when they might have to consider leaving The Grange. For some time, friends and family had been shaking their heads and telling them that it would be much wiser to live in the town. They pointed out the advantages of being able to walk to the shops and the library or to the health centre, unable to understand that for Clemmie and Quentin none of those benefits could outweigh the glory of the views that they had from their windows or the walks that they took from their door. But Clemmie's heart was troubled. Despite the exercise he took, Quentin suffered with arthritis quite dreadfully and she, only a few years younger, was beginning to stiffen up alarmingly.

'It's not much wonder,' scolded the same friends who advised the move to the town, 'with all that rain up there on the moor and that cold draughty old house.'

But we love it, thought Clemmie, drawing up her knees with difficulty and staring out at the wooded valley that ran down to the river and the high slopes of the moor beyond it. Why can't people understand that? We'd die in a town.

The fact was that, as people grew older, concern centred on their physical well-being and their spiritual needs moved into second place. Even the closest and most loving of friends seemed to imagine that comfort and convenience were all that mattered. The young were more ready to accept that the balance was still essential, probably because they had no experience of aching joints and sleepless nights. Clemmie thought about Quentin's godson, Oliver Wivenhoe. Oliver's grandfather, General Oliver Mackworth, had been a close, well-beloved friend and his death had come as a severe blow to the Halliwells. A strong relationship had developed between Quentin and the young Oliver, who looked so like his grandfather and had inherited his insight and his kindly caring ways. Oliver was one of the few who could understand how they felt about leaving The Grange and, despite the fact that he was sharing a flat in London with an old friend whilst he tried to find a job, he always made time to come and see them when he was home visiting his family just across the moor. Clemmie shook her head a little, thinking how odd it was – and how sad – that Quentin should have more in common with Oliver than he did with his own son.

She was still musing thus when the door opened and Quentin came in with her morning tea. He smiled to see her tiny form huddled in the quilt with her bright brown eyes just visible and the fluffy grey hair standing up like a halo. He placed the tray on the bed beside her and she saw the little posy in the miniature vase and gave a cry of pleasure.

'First primroses,' said Quentin proudly, bending to kiss her. 'Happy St Valentine's Day.'

'Oh!' Clemmie looked distressed as she lifted the vase to sniff at the violets. 'I quite forgot it. Oh, my darling, I'm so sorry.'

'So did I,' admitted Quentin. 'We had the sun in the kitchen this morning for the first time this year and it made me think about the date. Spring's coming, Clemmie!'

'So it is.' They beamed at each other, both feeling that sense of victory at having survived the winter. 'Oh, Quentin! If the sun's in the kitchen then it'll soon be into the courtyard and we'll be able to have our morning coffee outside.' She poured the tea, feeling cheered. 'It must've been lovely down in the woods.'

'I saw the dipper.' He gave her a quick almost triumphant glance before pulling up a basket chair and taking the cup she held out to him. He always waited to have his second cup of tea of the day with her. 'He was on the boulder under the bridge. The river's running high.'

'Hardly surprising. I thought it would never stop raining.' Clemmie sipped her tea. 'I'm glad you saw the dipper. It's been weeks since we saw him.' She touched the violets with a gentle finger and smiled at him and a secret look passed between them that needed no words. 'What's the agenda for today?'

'If it stays dry there are a few jobs I'd like to catch up with outside and then I thought we'd take the library books into Tavistock and get any shopping we need. Better keep well stocked up. If we're going to get any snow it'll be in the next few weeks.'

Once, the idea of being snowed in had been exciting and winter something to be accepted, welcomed even, and beaten at its own game. The larder was stocked up and the log shed filled, paraffin lamps stood at the ready in each of the main rooms and candles were scattered about with boxes of matches to hand. Three years before, they'd been cut off for several days and had emerged to find that a prisoner had escaped from the prison at Princetown but this winter there had been, as yet, no severe weather apart from the normal quota of gales and storms. Nevertheless, Quentin was right. There was plenty of time for it yet.

'I'll make a list while I have my breakfast,' agreed Clemmie. 'And you could check the paraffin.'

They finished their tea companionably and Quentin prepared to take the tray away. Clemmie pushed the covers back.

'Dress up warm,' he advised her from the doorway. 'The sun might be shining but it's bitterly cold outside.'

Clemmie pulled on her usual winter uniform: woollen stockings, a thick Harris tweed skirt and a Guernsey. She went downstairs and into the kitchen. Quentin was already outside and from the window she could see him at the end of the garden. Her anxiety returned and she wished that they could afford someone to help them in the garden occasionally. There wasn't that much to do. It was too exposed to be able to grow anything except the most hardy of shrubs. Nevertheless . . . Clemmie sighed and turned away from the window. She must concentrate on breakfast and the shopping list and stop worrying.

Quentin pulled away the rotten branch that had been brought down in the last gale and looked at the damage it had caused to the dry-stone wall near the stile. It wasn't too serious, nothing he couldn't cope with, but it was very important to keep the boundary walls in good repair otherwise the sheep and ponies wandered in off the moor and trampled the lawns and the few shrubs that Clemmie had encouraged to grow. As he lifted the stones back into place, with many groans and pauses for breath, he wondered where all the years had gone. He remembered clearly how he had felt when, at sixty, they had moved down to The Grange; how strong and fit and full of energy. The years had seemed to stretch endlessly ahead and he felt as if he would live for ever. His old friends, now dead, came fresh into his mind: William Hope-Latymer, Oliver Mackworth, James and Louisa Morley. They were all gone and their children were grown up with children of their own. Young William was running the Hope-Latymer estate and Henry Morley had taken up the reins at Nethercombe while Oliver's grandson, Oliver Wivenhoe, still spent many happy hours with Quentin exploring the surrounding woods and moors. He wished that Gerard had some interest in carrying on the family tradition at The Grange but he suspected that Gerard would find it an encumbrance and sell it as quickly as possible. Of course, The Grange was not an estate which could provide a living but, even if it had been, he couldn't see his son accepting the responsibilities of land and tenants as William and Henry had done so readily. He knew that Gerard was an urban animal to whom country life had little appeal. Nevertheless he would have been happier if he could have believed that Gerard would keep The Grange – perhaps for holidays – until it could be passed on to his own children. It would be a sad day indeed when the house fell into the hands of strangers.

Quentin shook his head and heaved the last stone into place. It didn't bear thinking about. He straightened his back and stared down the valley. He thought of all the seasons he had seen; watching the bare branches mist over with green and, in due course, become heavy with glossy leaves which, in time, turned slowly brown and orange and red and, at last, fluttered and whirled away until the branches were bare again. How terrible it would be to have foreknowledge of one's own death; to know that this was one's last spring or autumn.

Quentin remembered his earlier joy over the sunbeam and the primroses. He knew where to look, as the seasons moved gently forward, for the early anemones by the river, the welcome haze of bluebells deep in under the trees and where to catch the first astringent whiff of wild garlic. He thought of Housman.

> And since to look at things in bloom
> Fifty springs are little room,
> About the woodlands I will go
> To see the cherry hung with snow.

Well, there were those who said that Housman was obsessed with death but perhaps he'd been obsessed with life and the brevity of it. Even twenty springs had seemed for ever to Quentin but, if one were lucky enough to live at The Grange, for ever would be too short a time to watch the passing seasons and praise God for His blessings.

Quentin walked slowly across the lawn, dragging the dead branch behind him, and left it beside the woodshed door to be sawn into firewood. Without warning, hailstones clattered down and he made a dash for the courtyard door and so into the kitchen.

'Goodness!' He brushed the sizeable balls of ice from his old tweed jacket and grimaced at Clemmie who sat at the table eating toast and marmalade and jotting notes on to a piece of paper. 'It's certainly not spring yet.'

'But it's coming, my darling, and we shall see it together.'

He looked at her quickly, wondering how she had divined his thoughts and she got up and went to him, putting her arms about him.

'Be my Valentine?' he asked ridiculously and she burst out laughing, reaching on tiptoe to kiss him.

'Well, you're certainly not going to have anyone else if I've got anything to do with it,' she said. 'Coffee for you, my boy, before we go out. You're frozen stiff.'

He leaned with his back to the Esse, grateful for its warmth, and smiled at her.

'Since it's Valentine's Day,' he said, 'what about a sandwich at the Bedford after we've done the shopping?'

'Splendid!' she said, giving him a mug of steaming coffee. 'And I'll buy us a glass of wine each out of my pension. I can't say fairer than that.'

Chapter Three

Claudia Maynard had no fears that her husband, Jeffrey, would forget St Valentine's Day. Jeff could always be relied upon to bring flowers on her birthday, book a table at their favourite restaurant for their wedding anniversary and perform all those boring little tasks – brushing up the hearth, wiping down the working surfaces, putting his dirty clothes in the laundry basket – which, though unimportant in themselves, when continually neglected can be the irritants which spark off many a matrimonial row. In addition, he was extraordinarily good-looking in a dark dramatic way and all Claudia's girlfriends coveted him. There was a great deal of satisfaction to be had from this and she made the most of it. At social occasions, however much he was pursued and besieged, he was always aware of Claudia's wellbeing and could never be long distracted from her side, much to the said friends' annoyance.

Nobody was particularly surprised by this. Claudia herself was beautiful in a fine-boned, elegant way and was as fair as Jeff was dark. Her hair was always smooth and clean, her nail varnish was never chipped and her clothes always looked newly laundered. Their detractors – and they had a few –

said, amongst other things, that they were simply too proper to be true and wasn't it odd that, despite their beauty, neither of them was the least bit sexy? It was quite true. Jeff was amusing, witty, polite, but he never flirted and Claudia took everything too literally and too seriously and was too intent on making a good impression to make a good partner for some light-hearted fun. It was also true that they had no very close friends. Neither of them possessed the gift of relaxation and both tended to hold people at arm's length. Jeff, who was an accountant, seemed quite happy with this state of affairs but Claudia, who was beginning to feel the pressure to become more open and 'one of the gang', was almost relieved – if somewhat surprised – when Jeff suggested a move from Sussex to the West Country. He'd even gone so far as to apply for a job with a firm in Tavistock and had been asked to an interview. When he was offered the position, the Maynards sold up and moved down to a small but delightful Georgian town house and Claudia was aware of a strange sense of freedom.

It wasn't that Claudia was a private person but rather that she had a secret. In the early days, the fact that Jeff seemed content to make love to her only rarely was frustrating but not worrying. He was a very unemotional, quiet man who showed his love by caring and thoughtfulness rather than by physical demonstrations. Claudia, who until she'd met Jeff had been a rather undemonstrative person herself, tried to reason his indifference away and it was only when she began to become more friendly with the group of young wives who lived near her that she realised that such behaviour was not the norm. First she became anxious and then she became obsessed; for Claudia had another secret. She was very aware that it was she who had pursued Jeff quite relentlessly until he had proposed marriage and her fear was that he did not truly love her. She might joke about his devotion and imply, by raised eyebrows and a teasing silence, that he was a tiger in bed but she lived in terror of one of those inquisitive, prying girls discovering the truth.

Despite the extreme frustration of having to sacrifice an exciting new opening in her own career as a dress designer, she'd been only too pleased to get away from them and into a new environment and, to her delight, Jeff had become more passionate since the move to Devon. She'd read – for by now she'd made quite a study of it – that men who were very preoccupied by their work were often too tired to perform satisfactorily in bed and she wondered if there had been rather too much pressure. He'd certainly been pushing his way up the ladder, always ready to take on more work, rising early, working late. Now, in this calmer, slower atmosphere he seemed to have shed some sort of mental load and Claudia felt full of hope.

He was still quite adamant, however, on the subject of children. He said he simply wasn't ready to become a father and Claudia, who was not particularly maternal, was quite prepared to shelve the subject for the time being and enjoy the present state of affairs. Ever since she'd left college she'd worked at the design studio in Brighton but now she decided to take a little holiday. Even if she'd wanted to work there was precious little around. The West Country was in the grip of the recession and the Maynards were glad that, having sold their Sussex house at a good price, they were able to take full advantage of the depressed housing market and make quite a good profit to be tucked away.

They'd both been delighted when Jeff came home with the news that he'd been given the account of an estate on Dartmoor. As a newcomer it was quite a feather in his cap and they went out to the Elephant's Nest, their favourite pub, to celebrate. He told her about the Hope-Latymers, the family who had been there for centuries in their Elizabethan manor house, parts of which dated back further to the thirteenth century. Claudia was fascinated and felt tremendously proud of him. He looked so handsome as he sat describing it all to her, flushed and excited with this new challenge, that she ceased to hear his words and saw only his mouth and his hands as they gesticulated. With a rare gesture, she reached out and captured one of those square, long-fingered hands and he stopped and smiled at her.

'Am I going on too much?'

'No. Oh, no.' She shook her head. 'It's terribly exciting. It's just . . . Oh!' She gave a little shrug. 'You know. I love you.'

She leaned forward to whisper it, so that the other diners should not hear and he, surprised by this unexpected show of emotion, squeezed her hand in return and gave it a little kiss before releasing it. She felt weak with love for him and longed for the moment that she would have him to herself but, when they got home and she'd arrayed herself in her most seductive nightdress, it was some time before he appeared.

'Good,' he said. 'You're all ready for bed. Go ahead and hop in. I've got some stuff I want to mug up on. Big day tomorrow! I'll probably sleep in the spare room so as not to disturb you. 'Night.'

He'd dropped a kiss on her head and disappeared, leaving her to sit on at her dressing table fighting back hurt, humiliation and desire. She'd still been awake hours later when she'd heard him come upstairs and go into the spare bedroom but pride prevented her from calling out to him. He must never know that she needed him: it was too humiliating. She lay awake rationalising his indifference. This account was important to him and tomorrow – or rather, today – he was to meet William Hope-Latymer. Naturally he was worked up, nervous, tired. It was useless to expect too much and things were definitely better . . . Finally she fell asleep.

Now, some months later, Claudia arranged the dozen red roses in a vase and smiled at the little note. No, Jeff would never forget St Valentine's Day. The smile faded a little. Sexually, things were no better. The passion of those early weeks in Devon had slackened until it was practically non-existent and Claudia felt frightened. Her fears that Jeff didn't truly love her began to take hold again and she found herself watching him. If he gave attention to a woman she felt jealous and miserable, however harmless it was, and she paid an unexpected visit to the office so that she could check up on all the girls who worked there. There weren't many and one of them, Liz Whelan, had already become a friend. At least Claudia had nothing to fear from Liz. Since her divorce she seemed to have no time for men and Claudia was able to relax in her company. They occasionally lunched together and it was during one of these sessions that Liz introduced her to Abby Hope-Latymer. Claudia was impressed with Abby's casual friendliness and was delighted when she joined them at their table. Liz had obviously known her for years and they chatted about their children – Liz had a daughter in her mid-teens – and their mutual friends. The names – Wivenhoe, Barrett-Thompson, Lampeter – meant nothing to Claudia who sat listening attentively and smiling at Abby whenever she glanced at her. She hoped that an invitation to coffee perhaps, or lunch, might come out of it but, when they parted, Abby merely raised a hand in farewell saying, 'Tell your husband to keep up the good work,' and drifted off.

Now, on this St Valentine's Day morning, when Claudia entered the Bedford Hotel where she was meeting Liz for lunch, the first person she saw was Abby sitting with an elderly couple in the corner. Claudia smiled and waved her hand in greeting and had the humiliation of seeing Abby frown a little, nod rather coolly and continue with her conversation. Embarrassed, Claudia sat down and picked up the menu. Could it be possible that Abby hadn't recognised her? A few minutes later, Liz arrived and received a much warmer reception from the table in the corner. Claudia wondered if, now that Abby must have put two and two together, she might make some friendly gesture but, when Liz finished chatting and came over to Claudia, Abby merely turned back to the elderly couple.

Claudia pretended indifference but inwardly she was upset. From what Liz had told her of these people, they sounded like a little group of friends that she would be very happy to join but, so far, apart from introducing her to Abby in the first place, Liz had made no effort to encourage it. She had imagined that Jeff would have been invited out to the Manor but apparently everything was done at the office and Claudia realised that if there were to be efforts made towards friendship she would have to make them herself.

'Are they Abby's parents?' she asked casually.

'No, no.' Liz studied the menu. 'The Halliwells are close friends of William's father. Clemmie's family has been on the moor for centuries, like William's. She and Quentin moved into the family home when he retired shortly after her mother died. They used to play bridge with William's father and General Mackworth. They're godparents to Abby's children and Quentin's godfather to the General's grandson, Cass Wivenhoe's eldest boy, Oliver. He was the General's aide during the war. Quentin, I mean. Everybody's interrelated one way or another round here, you know. You have to be very careful what you say. What are you having? Let's have a drink while we're deciding.'

While Liz was ordering at the bar, Claudia studied the little group again. She was beginning to be obsessed by them and she was thinking of forcing the pace a little but Liz forestalled her.

'Actually, I want to introduce you to a friend of mine,' she said as she sat down again, passing Claudia a glass.

'Really?' Claudia's heart beat fast. 'Who is it?'

'Her name's Phyllida Makepeace. She's a naval wife, on her own a lot. Her husband's rather older than she is and he's got a bit of a reputation. I think he's another Tony and that she shouldn't trust him an inch but she's the trusting sort. I can't help feeling sorry for her.'

'Poor girl,' said Claudia feeling pleasantly superior and

wondering if this might be a way into the inner circle. 'You must bring her over.'

'I might do that. Or I might give her your number if that's OK with you. I'm not one of her favourite people, mainly because her husband and I don't hit it off.'

'Fine.' Claudia glanced into the corner. 'Actually, I was wondering whether to give a little party now we're settled in and I've got the house right.'

'Sounds fun.' Liz picked up the menu. 'Do you know enough people yet for a party?'

'Well.' Claudia was a little nonplussed. 'It wouldn't be a very big party. Perhaps,' she took her courage in both hands, 'perhaps you could introduce me to a few people. Other than this Phyllida.'

Liz looked a little surprised. 'I suppose so. I don't know too many people myself. Now that I work full time again I don't have much time for socialising. I suppose there are one or two in the office but you must have met them already.'

'Oh, yes. Yes, I have. I was thinking more of . . . well . . .' she hesitated. 'Well, you must know a lot of naval people,' she finished lamely.

'Oh, I know them,' said Liz bitterly, 'but when the blow came I lost most of them to Tony. That's what made me think that Phyllida might find a few civilian friends useful. Just in case.'

'Yes, I see.' Claudia was unwilling to be distracted by the problems of the unknown Phyllida who seemed, after all, not to be a member of the magic circle. She threw caution to the wind. 'Perhaps Abby and William might like to come. I know William and Jeff have met at the office. And I've met Abby.'

Liz looked instinctively at the group in the corner and back at Claudia with a half-embarrassed, half-pitying expression on her face.

'I think it's unlikely,' she said bluntly. 'It's a bit of a closed shop, to tell you the truth.'

Claudia felt as though she'd been snubbed.

'Jeff said that William was charming to him,' she said defensively.

'I'm sure he was.' Liz pushed her glass aside. 'William's manners are impeccable but you'll just have to take my word for it. We're the Hope-Latymer's accountants and you'll find that that's as far as it goes.'

Claudia remembered Abby's frown and cool nod and she felt humiliated but she was determined not to let it show.

'I thought that sort of snobbery went out with the ark,' she said lightly.

'Did you?' Liz looked at her sharply. 'Maybe it has upcountry but I can assure you that down here the class barriers are where they've always been.'

'But you're friends with them and you're an accountant.' Claudia couldn't let it go.

'But I wasn't always.' Liz's voice was clipped now and Claudia could almost see those barriers rising between them. 'I was an admiral's daughter and then a naval wife. It was only after the divorce that I finished my accountancy exams. There's a difference.'

'And what makes you think that I'm not an admiral's daughter,' said Claudia in a light-hearted attempt to reinstate the previous status quo.

Liz stared at Claudia, realising that her attempt to deflect her hadn't worked but for once her usual forthrightness, which had become so much part of her character since the divorce, deserted her. She shook her head.

'Let's leave it, Claudia,' she said. 'After all, what does it matter? Abby Hope-Latymer and her cronies aren't the only people in this area. They just happen to have been here the longest and so it's a difficult ring to break into. The old farming communities are just the same. Don't rush things, that's all, and perhaps it will happen in its own time. Let's order, shall we?'

When she made her way to the bar Claudia watched her, feeling resentful and disappointed, rather like a child who'd been put in its place by an impatient adult. As Abby and the elderly couple got up to go Claudia tilted her chin and stared blindly at Liz's back, determined not to look at them. When Abby, having stopped for a quick chat to Liz, waggled her fingers at her on the way out, however, Claudia found herself beaming back and was aware of a quite disproportionate sense of pleasure.

Chapter Four

The snow came in early March. The high peaks of the moor were etched white and clear against clouds dark and heavy with more snow and Quentin shivered as he came into the kitchen, having taken his morning walk down as far as the bridge. Even Punch had refused to accompany him, taking one look outside before returning to his warm bed by the Esse.

'Definitely more to come,' Quentin announced, hanging his coat behind the door and kicking off his boots. 'Good job we stocked up.'

'The postman's got through,' said Clemmie. She waved a letter at him and went to make him some coffee. 'We've been invited to lunch.'

'Gracious.' Quentin took the letter and leaned against the Esse. 'Whoever . . . ? Oh, it's Cass, bless her. Just to have a few friends round for lunch to celebrate Oliver's birthday.' He turned the card. 'Can they really want old crumblies like us?'

'Well, I wondered that, too,' admitted Clemmie, pushing a mug of hot coffee into his cold hands. 'And I thought . . . Well, they don't have to ask us. But, after all, you are his

33

godfather so I decided that they really did want us and that it would be fun.'

'Good.' He smiled at her, remembering a time when she'd hated and feared social functions and feeling the old familiar twinge of guilt that accompanied those memories. 'We'll go then.'

'It'll be lovely to see them all.' Clemmie took the sheet of paper from him and glanced at it again. 'Oliver's twenty-three.' She shook her head. 'It doesn't seem possible. Where have the years gone, Quentin?'

He looked at her sadly, wondering if any person ever came to the end of his or her life totally content with the sum of the years.

'Wherever they've gone, they've gone too fast,' he said and then put melancholy away with an effort. 'Well, this gives us something to look forward to, doesn't it? Let's hope the weather's better by then.'

'Oh, bound to be. It's just after Easter, more than four weeks away. This won't last long, you'll see.'

'Well, it's another afternoon by the fire for us.' Quentin was warm enough now to leave the Esse's heat and find his shoes. 'Got plenty to read? I'm going to get my journal up to date.'

'Could you stock up the log basket?' She smiled at him, and as he turned away to do as she asked she was visited with a sense of sadness. She'd noticed his melancholy and knew the cause. If only that faint but remaining shadow could be dispersed before either of them should die.

Claudia was quite determined to give her party. She generally got her own way by using the simple expedient of deciding what she wanted and sticking to it. Protests and obstacles alike were simply pushed to one side or quietly steamrollered. It wasn't that she was insensitive to the needs or requirements of others but she assumed that people thought and reacted exactly as she did and ignored any manifestation of behaviour to the contrary. Meanwhile, she wanted a party and she wanted Abby and William at it. Here she had an enormous stroke of luck. She'd gone to meet Jeff from the office one lunch time and, since Liz had come out with him, the three of them walked along together, practically bumping into Abby as she emerged from Crebers, the delicatessen in Brook Street. Naturally Liz stopped and, as soon as she'd finished introducing Jeff to Abby, Claudia had plunged into an enthusiastic account of her longing to see the Manor. It sounded so beautiful, she'd said wistfully – whilst Liz bit her lip in anger and Jeff looked embarrassed – was it ever open to the public?

Abby, caught between her friendship with Liz and the necessity to be polite to William's accountant, smiled briefly and said no, certainly not, but if she was that desperate to see it, she must come for coffee one day with Liz.

Claudia was delighted, ignoring the tepid nature of the invitation, and continued to press Liz until she gave in at last and took her to coffee at the Manor. Abby and Liz between them had arranged it for a day when Abby had a lunch engagement and it was all kept as short as possible. Claudia was a tiny bit disappointed that none of the other friends, of whom she'd heard so much, was present and she was slightly put out at the speed with which she was dispatched but she accepted it when Liz explained how busy Abby was. She managed to introduce her visit into the conversation whenever she saw anyone she knew, elaborating and embroidering until she almost believed her exaggerations herself, the pretence of belonging increasing her confidence.

By this time she'd met Phyllida whom Liz had introduced in the hope that it might deflect Claudia's interest in Abby. To begin with, Claudia felt a slight sense of resentment and behaved rather patronisingly towards Phyllida once she discovered she wasn't on intimate terms with any of the inner circle. She was annoyed that there were no further introductions to Liz's special friends and was inclined to look upon Phyllida as someone who was being forced upon her to keep her quiet. Moreover, since she was still anxious that no one should suspect that her marriage wasn't wonderfully happy, she couldn't resist bragging about Jeff's virtues, feeling comfortingly superior in the light of Liz's disclosures about Alistair. It didn't take Phyllida too long to see through Claudia's show of pomposity and she decided that the best way to handle it was to remain unmoved and hope that Claudia would eventually be able to relax. She discovered that, behind the prickly exterior, there was a genuinely kind person and, after a few meetings, things became a little easier.

Meanwhile, Claudia found Phyllida's simplistic approach to life both soothing and flattering. She wholeheartedly admired the charming Georgian house, complimented Claudia on her beauty and elegance and told her how gorgeous she thought Jeff was without making the least attempt to flirt with him. She was impressed by stories of Claudia's experiences in the designer world and, though she sympathised at her career being disrupted by the move to the west, she didn't question it. Phyllida was used to living with a man whose job had to be put first and she accepted that Claudia felt the same about Jeff.

Claudia, who'd been busy justifying her decision to put Jeff's career before her own, felt enormously relieved but immediately became anxious to defend her position regarding children. She didn't want Phyllida to suspect that she was not maternal but she didn't quite know how to explain Jeff's absolute veto without it sounding unnatural. It was still necessary to present the perfect image.

'I just don't feel Jeff's ready for fatherhood,' she said, watching Lucy having her bath one evening. She'd come for tea and stayed longer than she intended, knowing that Jeff was going to be late home. 'He works so hard and carries so much responsibility.'

'There's plenty of time, isn't there?' asked Phyllida easily. 'After all, Alistair was thirty-one when we had Lucy. He's much more patient with her than a lot of the young fathers I know are with their offspring.'

She swung Lucy out of the bath and into the large towel across her lap. Claudia looked at them both – they were ridiculously alike with their short tousled brown hair and wide grey eyes – and experienced an unusual feeling of peace. Phyllida wouldn't require her to take part in the bedtime scene, accepting without question that Claudia, who was not yet able to forget herself sufficiently to romp or read stories, would be happier having a drink downstairs until she reappeared.

'Go and pour yourself a drink,' she said, as if on cue. 'I'll be down in a sec. Don't dash off yet.'

Downstairs in the comfortable, untidy sitting room, Claudia wandered, a glass of wine in her hand, peering at silver-framed photographs, picking up books and toys. Despite the untidiness and the shabby furniture and hangings that were rented with the house, she felt relaxed here and wondered why. She almost wished that she could be as indifferent to her own appearance as Phyllida was; content to dress in comfortable old clothes and live in a muddle. Although she made no attempt to pry into Claudia's private life, Phyllida had made it clear that she and Alistair were very happy and Claudia suspected that it was this security that gave Phyllida the confidence to live as she pleased, unworried by other people's opinion. She was still brooding when Phyllida appeared looking harassed and ready for a drink.

'I'm always torn at this point,' she said, sinking down on to the sofa. 'Part of me is delighted that Lucy's in bed and I can relax but part of me wishes she could stay up and keep me company. The evenings seem so long.'

'It must be awful.' Claudia tried to imagine such a strange way of living. 'It's such a waste of time in a way, isn't it?' She couldn't control a note of complacency when she thought of her own organised and well-regulated life.

'Well, I think so. Still, it's no good complaining. You can't marry a sailor and then moan when he goes to sea.'

'I suppose not.' Claudia picked up Lucy's baby doll and sat her in the corner of a chair. 'You must get used to it, after a bit.'

'The winter's the worse time.' Phyllida rumpled her hair

and yawned hugely. 'Sorry. I'm a bit tired. She was a bit troublesome this evening. I think she's got a cold coming. I've got a feeling it's going to be one of those nights. That's what you miss, really. Someone to share the load. Clear up the toys, do the washing-up, make a cup of tea. You know?'

'Mmm.' Claudia nodded, thinking of how good Jeff was at pulling his weight. 'Of course, I always worked so we got used to taking turns with the chores. Cooking meals or doing the washing, that sort of thing. Jeff's wonderful. I suppose I take him for granted a bit. He doesn't do so much now I'm home all the time. It must be a bit lonely having to cope all on your own.'

'It was worse before I had Lucy.' Phyllida kicked off her shoes and tucked her feet under her, ignoring the tendency to patronise that Claudia still couldn't occasionally resist. 'I was terribly lonely then. Sometimes I quite like it. I don't have regular meals to worry about and masses of ironing. I can please myself a bit.'

'You'll miss Lucy when she goes to school, though,' said Claudia understandingly. 'Will you get a job?'

Phyllida hesitated but the desire to share her good news was too strong.

'I'm expecting another baby,' she told her and Claudia gave an involuntary cry of surprise. 'It's great, isn't it? I was beginning to think Lucy would be too old. I don't think it's a good idea to have too big a gap between children. But it should be OK.'

'Of course it will be.' Claudia quelled a stab of envy. 'Probably better than having them too close and quarrelling all the time. Lucy's old enough to be sensible about it.' She sounded very positive as she raised her glass. 'Congratulations.'

'Thanks.' Phyllida smiled into the fire. 'I can't wait to tell Alistair. By the way, don't tell anyone. Only you and Prudence know yet.'

'I'm really looking forward to meeting Alistair,' said Claudia, who had a very different picture of him now. 'I'm glad he'll be home for my party.'

'It'll be fun.' Phyllida grinned at her. 'Help yourself to some more wine.'

'Not for me. I must be going.' Claudia sounded regretful. 'Jeff'll be home soon. I must go and organise some supper. Sorry to leave you on your own.'

'Don't worry, I'm quite used to that,' said Phyllida cheerfully. 'Drive carefully. It's beginning to freeze again.'

She'd just closed the front door behind Claudia when the telephone rang. It was Alistair to tell her that the boat's programme had been changed and he wouldn't be home for a further two weeks. Her disappointment was acute. During her six years as a naval wife she'd become accustomed to the uncertainty of service life and realised that a positive approach was the only chance of survival but this time it was very hard to adopt her usual philosophical attitude. She'd been so looking forward to seeing Alistair's expression when she told him about the new baby but now she decided that the telephone would have to be the next best means of communication.

'I'm so sorry, Phylly,' he said when he'd explained about the delay. 'It's rotten luck. Still, at least when we do get in I shall be around for a bit. How are things?'

'Everything's fine,' she told him, trying to sound cheerful. 'Well, Lucy's got a bit of a snuffle, actually, but it's nothing serious. Matthew and Clare were down and both theirs had colds. There is something though . . .' She hesitated.

'Spit it out,' he said encouragingly. 'Been breaking the bank? I shouldn't worry about it.'

'No, it's not that.'

He could hear the smile in her voice and smiled too, imagining the small figure at the other end. 'What are you wearing?' he asked, seized with an almost unbearable longing to have her in his arms.

'One of your jerseys,' she answered with a chuckle. 'It's freezing here. We've got snow.'

'I love you,' he said and her heart seemed to dissolve in her breast at the change in his voice.

'I love you, too,' she said shakily. 'Oh, Alistair. We're going to have another baby.'

There was a complete silence and Phyllida held her breath until, fearing that they'd been cut off, she spoke his name anxiously into the receiver.

'Oh, Phylly. Yes, I'm still here. It was just the surprise. Oh, darling, it's wonderful news.'

'I wanted to wait until I saw you,' she explained, 'but now it's been postponed I couldn't wait any longer.'

'I'm glad you couldn't. Does Lucy know?'

'Not yet. I wanted you to be the first.'

'Oh, darling . . . Damn!' His voice changed. 'I'll have to go. Look, I'll write to you tonight and post it before we sail. Take care of yourself and love to Lucy. Love you.'

The line went dead and Phyllida stood quite still, clutching the receiver. She sighed as she put it back on the rest. She was glad that he knew and at least she could now look forward to his letter, providing that he didn't decide to celebrate first and get pissed before he got a chance to put pen to paper. Nevertheless, there was a decided feeling of anticlimax about the whole thing and Phyllida was briefly resentful.

She wandered over to switch on the radio wishing that Claudia could have stayed. The unmistakable sound of the husky voice of Nina Simone singing 'If I Should Lose You' filled her with a poignant sense of loneliness. It was one of Alistair's favourite tracks from a well-played tape and she was almost overcome with a terrible longing to feel his arms round her. Before she could become really miserable, she heard Lucy's voice calling to her. Depression gave way to anxiety; she'd been restless all day with this impending cold and Phyllida wondered how long it would take to get her back to sleep. Cursing the fact that small children were always at their most worrying at night, or at the weekends when surgeries were closed, Phyllida collected up various toys that might bring comfort and ran lightly up the stairs to Lucy's bedroom.

Liz, with her fifteen-year-old daughter, Christina, was having lunch with Abby in the large kitchen at the Manor when Claudia telephoned to invite Abby and William to her party. Abby, taken by surprise, could only thank her and say that she would have to check William's diary – otherwise she couldn't see why not. She slammed down the receiver with a muttered imprecation and Liz looked amused.

'Whoever was that?'

'Claudia,' said Abby crossly. 'Inviting us to some party. Why can't she accept that I have quite enough friends and I don't need any more?'

'She's OK,' said Liz. 'I think she's lonely.'

'Well, that's not my problem. Why doesn't she get a job or something?'

'She designs clothes.' Liz shrugged. 'Can't imagine there's a lot of demand for that around here. To be honest, I can't see why they left Sussex. Or, at least, why they came to Tavistock. They're simply not country people.'

'Perhaps they've been down on holiday,' suggested Christina, who was only half listening to the conversation whilst she attempted the crossword puzzle in Abby's *Daily Telegraph*. 'Lots of people move down just because they've spent their summer hols in Devon and fallen in love with it.'

'And move back again after the first long wet winter,' agreed Abby cynically.

'If you find her a nuisance, why don't you invite her to serve on one of your committees?' said Liz idly. 'That would keep her busy and she'd think she'd been accepted and might stop bothering you.'

Abby stared at her. 'That's brilliant,' she said. 'I'll co-opt her on to the Red Cross committee. We always meet here which would please her and she can persuade Jeff to do the accounts for nothing. Aren't you clever?'

'Think nothing of it,' said Liz. 'By the way, I've got an additional guest for your lunch on Sunday.'

'Heavens!' Abby arched her brows. 'Don't say you're bringing a man?'

'Well, I am but not the sort you're thinking of. Uncle Eustace has decided to grace us with his presence for a week or so.'

'Great!' Abby clapped her hands with pleasure. She had known Liz's uncle for many years and, like most of their friends, had grown to love him and look forward to his visits. 'He always makes a party go.'

'Doesn't he just,' agreed Liz morosely. 'It's like having an enormous bossy little boy to stay.'

'Oh, Mum!' protested Christina. 'He's not a bit bossy. He's really fun and not a bit like an old person. I love him.'

'Don't we all,' said Abby. 'I know I do.'

'Oh, honestly! He's the archetypal male chauvinist pig. How Aunt Monica coped with him I simply don't know.'

'She adored him like the rest of us.' Abby began to lay the table. 'He misses her dreadfully.'

'Of course he does,' said Liz caustically. 'No one to wash his socks, cook his dinner, run round him . . .'

'Don't be so bitter and twisted,' said Abby lightly, winking at Christina who'd grimaced reproachfully at her mother. 'And you haven't told me what you think of Jeff. Pretty dishy, I thought.'

'Who's Jeff?' asked Christina, moving the newspaper out of Abby's reach.

'He's very good-looking,' admitted Liz. 'But he's terribly proper. D'you know what I mean? His manners are so perfect, he's almost too good to be true.'

Abby burst out laughing and shook her head. 'There's just no satisfying you, is there?' she asked. 'Never mind. I'll get us some lunch and we'll take turns to invent the perfect man! Put that crossword away, Christina, and make yourself useful.

Chapter Five

When Abby telephoned Claudia to say that she and William would be unable to come to the party, she hurried quickly into her suggestion that Claudia be co-opted on to her Red Cross committee. Claudia's protests were silenced by the surprise of such a request and Abby, throwing caution to the winds, explained the form, urged her to think about it and told her that, if she liked the idea, they could get together for a chat. For Claudia, it made up for everything. A party would only last for a few hours but to be on one of Abby's committees meant an on-going relationship with her, meetings at the Manor and a definite link with the group which she had so set her heart on joining. Even as she replaced the receiver with promises to get in touch, she was imagining how this new development could be woven into her conversation and what an opportunity it was for wonderful throwaway lines which would give people an idea of her social standing, thereby boosting her confidence.

Claudia's heart swelled with pleasure and pride and she prepared for her party in high spirits. Thanks to Liz there would be quite a number of people coming and she was already composing little phrases to be dropped casually at opportune moments throughout the evening.

'What a pity Abby and William couldn't come . . . Yes, the Hope-Latymers. D'you know them? . . . Oh, yes. Very well indeed. I'm on one of Abby's committees . . . She works so hard but she's great fun when you get to know her.'

Claudia sighed with pleasure as she sat at her dressing table screwing on her earrings. Jeff stood behind her, bending his knees so as to be able to see himself as he tied his tie, and she smiled at him through the looking glass. It occurred to her that he'd been rather quiet these last few days and she looked at him more carefully.

'Are you OK?' she asked him and swung round on the stool so that she was face to face with him.

'Of course.'

He smiled at her and she had the feeling she so often had with Jeff; that he was a charming stranger. She wondered if it had anything to do with their indifferent sex life and pushed the thought away. She had no desire to examine that well-worn, inconclusive route, especially on the eve of their party. He looked very attractive in his dark suit. Despite his sedentary job, his skin always kept its tan and his hair – very short as Claudia liked it – was thick and shiny. She felt a warm weakening wave of desire for him beginning to curl over her and she got up quickly.

'You look very smart.'

She went close to him but he merely lifted her hand to his lips and kissed it; a gesture he often made.

'And you look beautiful. Mustn't mess you up though.'

She knew that he was tacitly acknowledging the fact that she needed more than this gallant gesture and was excusing its inadequacy but she wished that he would seize her, drag her clothes off and ruin her carefully applied make-up. For a dreadful second they stared into each other's eyes; he knowing her desire and she knowing that he was horrified by it. Quickly, instinctively, they jointly attempted to hide their knowledge.

'I'm going to hurry down and pour us a drink,' said Jeff. He smiled with a terrible gentleness into her eyes. 'We're probably both a bit worked up. I know I am.'

'Of course.' She gladly accepted this excuse. 'The first party in a new house is always nerve-racking. Go on, then. I'll be right behind you.'

When he'd gone, she sat down again and stared at herself in the glass, her old fears returning. She simply didn't turn him on. Yet she was pretty, slim, and she made certain that she was always newly bathed and sweet-smelling every night. Their surroundings were attractive and the bedroom was always spotless and tastefully decorated. The whole house was perfectly decorated, everything in keeping with its period, and it would be lovely to show it off to all their new friends. She shook off her fear and deliberately recalled the joy of Abby's invitation. It was simply being silly to worry so much and she was getting the whole thing out of proportion. Sex wasn't that important. All she needed was to be busy again, to get back a sense of proportion. After all, there might be other committees, lunches . . .

Claudia went downstairs, excitement creeping back. Jeff appeared from the kitchen to give her a glass of wine and, as she took it from him, he saw that her smile was unshadowed and the dangerous moment had passed. She went into the lovely Georgian drawing room to check that everything was in order and with a sigh of relief he watched her go. His guilt was quite overwhelming at times. He knew that he should never have married her but she had pursued him so relentlessly that, in the end, it had seemed the easiest as well as the wisest course to take. He'd been in love once – totally, desperately, passionately – and had been loved in return. Then quite suddenly it was all over and, even now, the remembrance of the rejection and the pain caused Jeff to go quickly into the kitchen and stand quite still, silently fighting back despair. He'd resolved never to chance his heart again and Claudia was a shield and defence against temptation but he knew she was unhappy. If only he could be capable of lust without love then he might at least satisfy her natural desires but, for Jeff, the two went together and the harder he tried the more impossible it became.

He refilled his glass. If only Claudia could be easier and more relaxed, less desperate and premeditated. The mere sight of her, perfumed and powdered and so inexorably ready for sex, was enough to destroy any stirrings he might have. Jeff took a great gulp of wine and shook his head. It was quite disgusting of him to blame her. The whole awful burden lay squarely on his own shoulders and he knew it. The doorbell rang and he straightened up and set the glass down. His hands went automatically to his tie and he moved out into the hall, the famous 'Jeff smile' crinkling his eyes, to meet his guests.

Everyone seemed to turn up together: several naval couples who were all friends, a couple from the local riding school where Jeff rode, Phyllida and Prudence with Liz close behind them. Claudia was only able to talk about Abby's committee when she was quite certain Liz was out of earshot, nevertheless she was enjoying herself. She basked in the general approval of house and food, raising her eyebrows, pulling her mouth down at the corners and giving a tiny shrug at each compliment, as if to imply that it was all perfectly natural to her and only what she'd always been used to but that she was glad they were able to appreciate it. It was a splendid performance and only Liz was amused. The others were too busy drinking and talking and enjoying themselves to care much one way or the other. Most of them hardly knew Claudia and Jeff and were rather surprised to have been invited to this house-warming, as Claudia had decided to call it. Since many of them were Liz's friends and always ready to go to a party, they'd accepted the invitations assuming that Claudia and Jeff were a friendly couple who wanted to settle into a new area as quickly as possible. And why not? Most of them knew Prudence and drew her and Phyllida into their group and Phyllida, worrying about Lucy who had now developed a rash, tried to relax and enjoy herself.

The party was in full swing when the doorbell rang and Liz, who was coming down from the loo, answered the door. Claudia was made aware of the new arrivals by the expression on Jeff's face. He stood transfixed, a plate in either hand, staring towards the door. Claudia swung round sharply. A girl stood there, a look of bright expectation mingled with faint anxiety on her face. Her short blonde-streaked hair stood out from her small vivacious face like a halo. As she moved into the room, Claudia saw that she wore the shortest of miniskirts and her excellent legs were shown off by black tights. Claudia felt an immediate and violent reaction against the unknown girl and looked again at Jeff. He looked mesmerised by her but, before Claudia could speak, Liz was leading her towards them through the crowd.

'This is Jenny,' she said. 'She's been transferred from our Bristol branch. This is Jeff. I know you two haven't met yet. And this is Claudia.'

'We were coming with Sue and Jerry,' explained Jenny in a rather breathless little voice. 'Only they had some bother with the car and they telephoned to tell us to come on ahead.' She smiled at Claudia, still anxiously. 'It seemed a bit rude but they told us that you'd said to come along.'

'So I did.' Jeff's voice seemed almost as breathless as Jenny's and he turned to set down the plates so that he might take her outstretched hand. 'Liz told me you'd arrived and I thought it would help you to get to know a few people.'

'It was really kind.' Jenny sounded grateful. 'It's going to be a bit of a culture shock after Bristol. I can see that. Only I wanted to get away. Oh!' She gave a dismayed squawk. 'I'm ever so sorry. This is Gavin. He lives in the flat above and he's been helping me move in. He's been great.'

I bet he has, thought Claudia sourly, noticing for the first time the lean young man who lounged easily behind Jenny and now moved forward. He grinned at them, white teeth flashing in a brown bony face. His dust-coloured hair was cropped untidily short and his eyes, uptilted like a cat's, were a shallow light blue. He wore a T-shirt and jeans and seemed quite unmoved that he looked so completely out of place in this elegant room amongst well-dressed people; rather like a tiger in a cage of pretty domestic cats. Jenny looked equally out of place. She reeked of the big city with her moussed-up hair and glittering make-up. Her silk shirt was deeply revealing and her small feet were encased in black suede pixie boots.

'Get Jenny a drink, Jeff, for goodness' sake,' said Claudia abruptly, desperate to shake him out of his preoccupation, and looked away as Gavin grinned at her. There was something almost complicit in his smile, as though he recognised Jeff's reaction and her own dismay. 'And Gavin too, of course. What would you like?'

'Got any beer?' His voice was casual with London overtones.

'I think there's some in the kitchen.' Jeff's eyes were fixed on Jenny.

'Well, why don't you two go and get some beer and I'll find Jenny some wine.' Claudia was determined to separate them. She made herself smile at the girl. 'Come with me, Jenny. We'll find you something to drink and then I'll introduce you to the rest of the mob.'

'Thanks.' Jenny flashed a smile at Jeff and Gavin and followed Claudia through the crowd.

'Well then.' Gavin raised his eyebrows and pursed his lips and after a moment Jeff smiled briefly in return. 'That just leaves you and me, mate. Where's this beer, then?'

When Phyllida discovered that both she and Lucy had contracted German measles from Matthew's two children, life seemed to stop in its tracks and she was incapable of any emotion but despair. Her GP, a kind young woman in her thirties with children of her own, was tremendously sympathetic but made it clear that the effect on the unborn baby could be catastrophic. She offered her a termination of the pregnancy and suggested that she should think it over and discuss it with her husband.

When Alistair arrived home a few days later, full of excitement, he was almost as devastated by the news as Phyllida herself. Both of them managed to maintain a brave face in front of Lucy but, as soon as she was in bed, Alistair poured them both very large drinks and then pulled Phyllida down beside him on the sofa. She turned to him at once, burying her face in his jersey and weeping as though she would never stop. He sat quite still, holding her, his face set in bleak lines and making no attempt to comfort her until she'd had her cry out. Presently she sat up and he mopped her face tenderly with his handkerchief.

'I keep doing that,' she said, her voice trembling. 'I just can't get over it. It's so terrible. It'll be like . . . like killing our baby.'

He held her tightly and his eyes were bright with tears although his voice was quite steady.

'It's not as if you're getting rid of a perfectly healthy baby because you don't want it. The whole thing's tragic but you wouldn't want to risk it really, would you? You have to think about the baby.'

'We can't be certain that it'll be affected.'

'I know.' He stroked her hair gently. 'But the odds are terrifically high. It wouldn't be fair. To either of you.'

He put her into the corner of the sofa and gave her the glass. She took it, holding it with both hands, and sipped. Alistair watched her. He realised that his own shock and disappointment were nothing compared with hers and he thanked God that this had happened at a time when he had a few months ashore. There was no doubt in his mind that the pregnancy should be terminated but he could see that, as well as sadness, Phyllida would continue to feel guilt and when she spoke she confirmed his suspicions.

'If only I hadn't invited Matthew and Clare,' she said, wiping away another tear as it slid down her cheek. 'If only I'd been inoculated. Mum thought I'd had it when I was little.'

'It's not your fault.' He shook her knee gently. 'You simply can't blame yourself. We must be positive about this, Phylly. There's plenty of time to have more children. As soon as you've recovered and you're feeling up to it, we'll try again.'

He blotted away another tear and tilted her face to his. She tried to smile at him and nodded.

'I know.'

'And it's such fun trying.'

She knew that he was doing his very best to comfort her and she made an effort to match his courage.

'I'm so glad you're home. It'll be more bearable with you here.'

'I'm glad too. I should have hated to be away with this going on. I've got two weeks' leave before I go to Greenwich so the best thing is to . . . to deal with it at once. I can look after Lucy and you can have a good rest . . . afterwards.'

She nodded and drank deeply and he sighed with relief. He'd been quite anxious for a short while that she might insist on carrying the baby to its full term and had been terrified that he might have to get tough. He kissed her and she managed a smile. They'd get through it somehow, he felt quite certain about that. Meanwhile, she needed all the support he could give her.

'It could be ages before I get pregnant again. Look how long it's taken.' She looked sad. 'I wanted to have lots of children.'

'Well, we still can.' He tried to keep it light. 'We'll just have to try harder, that's all. Good job I shall be weekending, I shall need the weekdays to recover!'

She smiled then and he slipped his arm round her and gave her an encouraging hug.

'I know you're right really, it's just so awful.'

'I know.' Alistair took their empty glasses and went to refill them. There was no real comfort to offer her and it seemed the only positive thing he could do.

Chapter Six

Oliver Wivenhoe, having found that a good degree from Cambridge was of little help when applying for jobs, accepted an offer from his old school friend Giles Webster. Giles was running a photographic studio in London and suggested that Oliver join him on a very temporary basis, in return for a minimal wage and lodging with Giles in his flat.

Work being rather slack, Oliver had taken the opportunity to spend some time with his family and, as he came out of the Book Stop in Tavistock and rounded the corner into Bedford Square, he saw Abby standing on the corner waiting for an opportunity to cross the road.

'And where are you off to?' he murmured in her ear.

'Oliver!' she exclaimed. 'You made me jump. I didn't know you were home. Come and have a cup of coffee with me.'

'Why not?' He took her arm and they crossed the square together. 'I gather we're heading for the Bedford?'

'We are indeed. Quentin and Clemmie are coming in to the market and I've arranged to meet them. They wouldn't come back for lunch so we're having coffee instead.'

'So why do you need me?' enquired Oliver as they

went up the steps of the hotel. 'Not that it won't be nice to see them.'

'The thing is,' said Abby, glancing round quickly and choosing a table in the corner. 'I'm being pursued.'

'Good Lord!' Oliver's eyebrows shot up. 'Does William know?'

'No, no.' Abby fished for her purse in her large leather satchel. 'It's a woman. Her husband works with Liz. He's William's new accountant and she is quite determined to become a bosom friend. She's on my Red Cross committee and I hear that she goes about the place talking about "my great chum Abby Hope-Latymer".'

'"Jane Fairfax and Jane Fairfax!"' murmured Oliver. '"Heavens! let me not suppose that she dares go about Emma Woodhouse-ing me."'

'What on earth are you talking about?' Abby was staring at him. 'Her name's Claudia Maynard.'

Oliver burst out laughing. 'I didn't believe that rumour that you never learned to read,' he said. 'But perhaps it's true after all.'

'Oh, don't show off with me,' said Abby. 'Just because you've been to a posh university. Go and order some coffee and if a slim blonde girl approaches the table, I rely on you to see her off.'

Ignoring the money she was trying to push into his hand, Oliver strolled up to the bar. Abby searched for her cigarettes and sat back, watching him. As he got older, the likeness to his maternal grandfather grew stronger. Now, slightly turned away from her, silhouetted against the brightness from the window behind him, the resemblance was startling. It was there in the set of his broad shoulders and the turn of his head as he joked with the girl behind the bar. His fair hair was longer than the General's had ever been but his eyes were the same dark blue and Abby smiled at him with tremendous affection as he set the tray on the table.

'Flirting so early in the day?' she enquired affably. 'I saw you.'

'I thought you'd given up smoking?' countered Oliver, ignoring her remark and sitting down.

'Oh, don't you start,' said Abby, pouring coffee. 'I have William at it all day long. Oh!'

Oliver swivelled quickly in his chair but it was Liz whom Abby had seen. She had a girl in her mid-twenties with her and Oliver turned back and raised his eyebrows questioningly at Abby who shook her head. Liz came over and the girl followed, looking faintly uncomfortable.

'This is Phyllida,' Liz said, 'a friend of mine. Husband's Navy and away. This is Abby Hope-Latymer and Oliver Wivenhoe, Phyllida. We met in the market so I've dragged her along for some coffee.'

'I'll go and get some more,' said Oliver smiling at Phyllida who smiled back, murmured something and disappeared in the direction of the ladies cloakroom.

'Sorry to butt in.' Liz grimaced and sank into a chair. 'The poor kid had a miscarriage a couple of months ago and she's still a bit under the weather. I thought I'd try to cheer her up a bit and it might be easier with a few more people around. D'you mind?'

'I gather that this is not Mrs Elton?' enquired Oliver and Liz looked puzzled.

'Who?'

'Take no notice,' advised Abby. 'He's been showing off just to prove that he's had an education. I was telling him about Claudia Maynard and he started droning on about some people called Jane Fairfax and Emma something.'

Liz stared for a moment and then burst out laughing.

'Yes, of course. I see. Certainly not! Phyllida's no Mrs Elton, I promise.'

'Oh, don't you start,' said Abby disgustedly. 'As long as she's not a Claudia, that's all I care about.'

'I really can't see why you're so set against her,' said Liz as she sat down.

'Neither can I, to be honest,' admitted Abby. 'I suppose I just don't like being dragooned into a friendship I don't particularly want. Ah! Here come the others.' She waved to Clemmie and Quentin and sat back in satisfaction. 'That's good. I do love a great big party. And now, even if Claudia does show up, there won't be any room for her!'

By the time summer arrived, Claudia had persuaded herself that her nightmares had become reality and Jeff had fallen in love with Jenny. At the beginning, he'd become very withdrawn. His charming attentiveness to her small comforts and needs – which had gone such a long way to making up for his physical inadequacies – became absent-minded and mechanical. She'd come upon him staring out of the window while the kettle boiled unheeded beside him or he would forget to execute small commissions for her. Then, a few weeks after their own party, Jenny invited them to supper. Claudia, already suspicious, decided to test the water.

'Do we have to go?' she asked in a rather weary tone, when Jeff told her about the invitation.

She was sitting in the evening sun on the little terrace at the back of the house with a glass of wine in her hand. She'd been to the Manor for a meeting in the morning and she'd begun to copy some of Abby's ways and her manner of speech. Jeff remained in the doorway, leaning against the door jamb, his feet crossed at the ankles, hands deep in his pockets.

'Don't you want to?' His voice was quite neutral but Claudia sensed that he was watching her and, although his pose was casual, his body was tense.

'Do *you*?' She managed a smiling frown of faint disbelief that he should want anything so undesirable.

'Well.' Beneath her lowered lids, Claudia saw him shift and move a little. 'It will look a bit odd if we don't go.'

'Why?' asked Claudia sharply and she took a sip of wine in an attempt to calm herself.

'It's always difficult when it's people you work with, isn't it?'

'Is it?'

Jeff moved forward and sat down beside her and Claudia registered the fact that he'd been so full of the invitation that he hadn't changed out of his suit, which was usually the first thing he did when he arrived home each evening.

'In a small place like this it is. Anyway, it helps to oil the wheels. Don't you like her?'

Taken aback by such a direct attack, Claudia's pride reasserted itself. 'I can't say I've given her a thought,' she said indifferently. 'She's so absolutely not my sort of person that I can't say that I like or dislike her. I certainly don't want to encourage her.'

Jeff stared down the garden. It was long and narrow with high stone walls against which espaliered fruit trees grew. It was all as neat and tidy as the inside of the house and he felt a strange despair creep over him.

'We won't go if you don't want to,' he said.

Claudia looked at him quickly. 'Obviously you want to go,' she said.

'I might pop in,' he said and sat up in his chair a little. 'Yes. That's it. I'll pop in for a few moments. That way she can't take offence and you needn't be bothered.'

Claudia's heart beat fast and she forced herself to take another sip of wine before she answered.

'Oh, if you feel that strongly,' she said and shrugged a little, 'we'll both go.'

'Honestly.' He turned to look at her and she knew at once that he didn't want her to go now that he'd realised that he could go alone. 'There's absolutely no need for you to go . . .'

Claudia got up quickly. 'Oh, for heaven's sake. It couldn't matter less either way. I can't imagine why you're making such a big deal of it. We'll both go. I'll just check on the dinner.'

She went inside and stood for a moment, still clutching her wine glass, her heart knocking furiously against her breast. Presently she stood the glass down, checked the casserole and went upstairs. She sank down on her stool and stared at herself in the looking glass. She was looking her best. Her well-cut shining fair hair had been cleverly streaked to make it look sun-bleached and her skin was a warm honey brown after hours of careful sunbathing. Her cotton shirt and linen shorts were fresh and fashionable and gold bracelets circled her narrow wrists. How could he possibly prefer that tarty little piece with her dyed hair and thick make-up?

Claudia put her elbows on the dressing table and dropped her head into her hands. Ever since the party he'd been unlike himself. She remembered how he'd stared at Jenny when she'd arrived in the doorway with Gavin lounging behind her and Liz leading her in. It was as if everybody else had ceased to exist for Jeff at that moment and Claudia knew that her fears had been justified and he'd fallen in love with Jenny as he had never done with her. He was behaving like any lovesick boy. His appetite appeared to have deserted him, he was absent-minded and he went off to the office each morning as though he were going to a party. He might try to hide it but Claudia was not deceived. When he returned in the evening she questioned him lightly about his day but he never mentioned one person more than another. She heard that some of them had started going to a nearby pub at lunch times but closer questioning revealed that Liz was usually amongst this number and that Gavin, who was accepted by now as Jenny's boyfriend, worked behind the bar.

In fact, the evening of Jenny's supper party was great fun for everyone except Claudia. Jenny and Gavin were allowed to use the little garden at the back of the flats and they'd set up a barbecue. There were quite a few guests that the Maynards didn't know who were all very free and easy and prepared to be friendly. Gavin, deeply tanned and wearing old shorts and a frayed T-shirt, was doing the cooking whilst Jenny, skittering about pouring drinks and giggling, wore a very brief sundress which made no attempt to disguise the fact that she was wearing only the briefest of knickers beneath it.

Claudia cloaked the panic in her heart with an icy exterior. She managed to convey her distaste with the whole scene by adopting a look of amused disdain and making it clear to Jeff, whenever he glanced anxiously at her, that she was bored stiff. Jenny, scurrying about, attempting to make sure that everybody was happy, and making good-natured ripostes to remarks about the briefness of her dress, sensed Claudia's antagonism. She was used to arousing married women's jealousies and stopped to chat reassuringly to Claudia, telling her how smart and elegant she looked and asking her where she got her hair cut. Getting only the shortest of replies in response, and suddenly annoyed by Claudia's air of insufferable patronage, Jenny threw caution to the wind and when Gavin put a tape on his hi-fi she seized Jeff and made him dance with her. Casting humorously helpless glances at the disgusted Claudia he allowed himself to be persuaded into the applauding circle and, when Gavin plonked Jenny's sunhat on his head and pushed a can of beer into his hand, Jeff suddenly decided to enter into the spirit of it all and began to respond to her burlesqued advances.

It was all so obviously harmless that Claudia's reaction surprised even herself. The sight of the proper, unemotional, formally behaved Jeff letting himself go was shocking to her. Biting her lips, her eyes bright with mortification, she turned her head away and looked straight at Gavin. Once again he gave her that amused glance which implied complicity, showing her that he knew exactly what she was thinking and how she felt. She was humiliated that she'd given herself away so completely and stared haughtily at him for a moment before turning to look elsewhere. Almost immediately it was all over. Jeff clapped Jenny's hat back on her head, bowed deeply to her and made his way to Claudia's side.

'Well,' he said breathlessly. 'That's my effort for the evening.' He took a deep swig from the beer can and Claudia saw Gavin raise his own can to him and grin.

'Well then,' she said icily, 'if you've finished making an exhibition of yourself, perhaps we can go home.'

As the summer settled in to a warm dry spell there were more invitations. Since these were always to join a group of people and Gavin was always at Jenny's side, nothing concrete could be picked on to bolster up Claudia's suspicions. Nevertheless, she knew there was something. Her fear took the form of anger and, since her pride forbade direct accusation, she took to sneering obliquely at Jenny hoping to denigrate her in Jeff's eyes. He remained silent. He neither agreed with her nor defended Jenny and she felt frustrated and puzzled.

With Abby, too, Claudia was getting nowhere. Abby smoothly and politely fielded all Claudia's efforts to move their acquaintanceship into friendship and, as the summer passed, she felt that she was being held by an unseen hand in some sort of limbo.

Phyllida was faring better with her new friends. Having heard through Prudence how bravely Phyllida was facing up to the loss of her baby, Liz attempted to help smooth her path. She told Abby, in the strictest confidence, what had happened and Abby decided to take Phyllida under her wing. She introduced her to the little group of people that Claudia so longed to know and included her in many invitations, one of which was a visit to The Grange. Abby often went to see the Halliwells and one morning she took Phyllida with her.

Phyllida was very taken with the old granite house and its warm sheltered courtyard where they had their coffee. Lucy was soon perched on Clemmie's knee with the toys that the old lady had kept to entertain her grandchildren when they were small and it was Clemmie who suggested that Quentin take Phyllida down to the river. Abby was only too happy to sit and chat with Clemmie and Lucy was too absorbed in the toys to want to move, so Quentin and Phyllida set off together.

To begin with she felt that there was some restraint on his side and she wondered if he'd have preferred to stay in the warm sunshine chatting with Abby, but presently his reserve vanished and soon they were talking with the ease of old friends. It was lovely in the woods. The thick canopy of leaves allowed only bright fingers of sunlight to penetrate the cool shade and she wandered along the sandy path feeling strangely at peace, soothed by the murmur of the river and the distant chuckle of the yaffingale. Presently they reached the bridge and wandered on to it, stopping to stare down into the water below.

'I love these old bridges,' said Phyllida, stroking the warm crumbly stone. 'What do you call it?'

'It's called Blackthorn Bridge,' said Quentin. 'There's the tree beside it. It grows all along the hedgerow and it's a mass of white blossom in the early spring. Quite breathtaking. There was a ford here in olden days before the bridge was built. Just a shallow one I imagine, but deep enough to make a bridge necessary when transport became more sophisticated.'

'I think it's fascinating to find out how these old names came into being, don't you?' Phyllida stretched out a finger to touch the sharp black thorns on the bough beside her. 'Some are such a long way from the original that you simply can't work them out at all. I like the idea of a ford being here first and old carts creaking through it and people having to wade across.'

'It was probably impassable in winter,' said Quentin. 'Hence the bridge. The dipper builds beneath it most years.'

'I don't think I've ever seen a dipper,' said Phyllida, leaning over and peering down. 'This would be a terrific place for Pooh sticks.'

'We used to play Pooh sticks here—' began Quentin and stopped. 'Shall we go back? Or would you like to cross the bridge and walk up the lane?'

'No, no.' Phyllida had heard the change in his voice and knew instinctively that some shadow had crept across their friendship. 'We ought to go back.'

She smiled at him, anxious to see him happy again and feeling drawn to this courtly, gently spoken old man. He smiled back at her and followed her off the bridge.

'And was that what we saw earlier?' She went ahead of him along the path, her chin on her shoulder as she talked to him. 'A dipper?'

'No. That was a wagtail.'

'Oh, yes. I remember now. You called it grey although it was yellow.'

Quentin smiled to himself. 'It's very confusing,' he admitted. 'But if you were to see a yellow one you'd understand. They are a very bright yellow underneath and they have yellow faces with green backs.'

'So what's this dipper like?'

'It's very well camouflaged,' he said and described its colouring and behaviour as they paused for a moment to look for the elusive bird. 'They're not at all easy to spot.'

He realised suddenly that he didn't want to see the dipper whilst he was with her. He decided, as he tried to analyse his feelings, that it would feel like a sort of disloyalty to Clemmie to see her particular, special bird whilst he was with this stranger, charming though she was. Perhaps it was because he found her such delightful company that the idea of loyalty had come into his mind. He was relieved that it had been Clemmie's suggestion and not his that he should bring Phyllida into the wood but he felt that it was important that they should not linger. Phyllida, aware that some element of tranquillity had vanished, turned once more for The Grange.

'I hope that Lucy isn't being a pain,' she said as they climbed the stile into the garden and crossed the lawn.

Quentin opened the door into the courtyard upon a peaceful scene. Lucy had fallen asleep on a long deck chair and Clemmie looked ruefully at Phyllida.

'I hope that this isn't going to ruin some important routine,' she said. 'One minute she was playing and the next she was fast asleep.'

'Not at all.' Phyllida smiled at Clemmie as she sat down.

'She's not sleeping too well at the moment. It will do her good.'

In the tiny silence that followed, Phyllida knew quite surely that Abby had told Clemmie about the baby. She was surprised at how little she minded and when she looked again at Clemmie she saw a very odd expression on her face.

'Stay to lunch,' Clemmie said quickly. 'Do stay. It's such a shame to wake her when she's sleeping so soundly. Can you, Abby?'

'Fine with me.' Abby stretched her legs out and tipped her face to the sun. 'For once I've got a whole day all to myself.'

'Well then.' Clemmie looked hopefully at Phyllida. 'How about it? Just a quick early lunch. We won't hold you up.'

'I should love to,' said Phyllida. 'If it's no trouble. It's so lovely here. So peaceful.'

Clemmie looked at the wistful expression on her face and took Quentin's hand to assist her to her feet.

'That's wonderful then. You two sit here while Quentin and I rustle up some food.'

Phyllida watched them go into the house and settled herself with a sigh of contentment.

'Aren't they sweeties?' she said to Abby, shutting her eyes against the sun. 'And I do love it here.'

Chapter Seven

As autumn approached, Liz was not entirely delighted to receive a telephone call from Uncle Eustace proposing another visit to the West Country. Liz suspected that, since Monica's death, he was far more lonely than he was prepared to admit and she hadn't the heart to refuse him. He and Aunt Monica had always been great favourites, not only with Tony and Christina but with most of their friends too. Easy-going, amusing, larger than life, they crossed the age barriers with no difficulty at all and friends had fought over them; asking them to suppers and lunches and drinks parties when they came on their twice-yearly visits to the Whelans.

When she and Tony had divorced they had both been very kind to her but she guessed that Uncle Eustace's sympathies were with Tony. She imagined that he expected her to turn a blind eye to Tony's infidelities and, in the years since the divorce, her growing bitterness had built a barrier between them. Eighteen months before, Monica had died from a protracted painful illness and Eustace was left alone. There were no children from the marriage to comfort and console him and Liz wondered whether her suddenly increased popularity was due to the fact that, since there was no other male in her household, he could expect to be made much of. Christina made a tremendous fuss of him and, despite her air of antagonism, Liz was very fond of him.

She met him from the train at Plymouth, noting with a cynical eye that two boys in their late teens were carrying his luggage.

'Hello, darling,' he said in his gravelly old voice, which was the expensive product – as he put it – of thousands of cigarettes and good malt whisky. 'How are you? These dear boys are helping with my gear. Car close by?'

She raised her eyebrows at the boys inviting their tolerant resignation, even irritation, but they beamed back at her and she felt a familiar annoyance at his ability to instil, even in complete strangers, this desire to oblige him.

'I'm in the car park, just opposite.' She led the way out and across the road. 'This is it.' She unlocked the car and opened the boot. 'If you could put it all in there. Thanks.'

'I've told them to come out and see us,' said Eustace, watching the proceedings. 'They're at the college. They've come back early to settle in to new digs and they're going to get a friend with a car to bring them out. Such fun for Christina, I thought.'

Liz swallowed her exasperation at Uncle Eustace's generosity with her hospitality. 'I'm sure he's given you the address,' she said sarcastically to the boys who were grinning cheerfully at the prospect. 'Perhaps you should have the telephone number, too. It would be such a pity if you came all that way and we were out.'

'They've got it,' said Eustace, who knew exactly what Liz was thinking. 'Nothing to worry about. If the worst comes to the worst, we'll all go round to the pub. See you later. Thanks for your help.' He waved a hand and folded his tall, well-built frame into the car.

They drove out through Plymouth and up on to the moor. The hint of autumn in the thin crisp air made Eustace think of wood fires and crossword puzzles and hot toddies after long walks and he sighed with pleasure.

'Lovely to be back,' he said. 'Oh, look at these dear ladies.' Liz was slowing down to overtake some stately cows who were meandering all over the road and Eustace wound his window down so that he could chat to them as they passed. 'That's it, my darling,' he said, giving the last one a pat on its broad flat flank and winding the window up. 'She's nearly as big as the car, dear old thing. Goodness, I'd kill for a decent cup of tea.'

Liz parked outside her cottage on the edge of Whitchurch and helped carry the luggage up to Eustace's room. This was the spare room which looked out over the moor; it was large, austere, clean and impersonal but, by the time Eustace had unpacked and put out a few belongings, it looked as if he'd been sleeping in it for years. He closed the locks on his empty case and felt in his pockets for a cigarette. Liz watched. She'd deliberately omitted to put an ashtray by his bed.

'Make yourself at home,' she said pointedly and then felt mean. 'I'll make some tea. Come down as soon as you're ready.'

He watched her go, shook his head a little and strolled over to the window which he opened. Perching sideways on the window seat, with his arm resting on the sill so that the smoke could drift out into the quiet air, he let his thoughts wander. A businessman with a finger in many pies, an insatiable curiosity and a great passion for life, he'd viewed the years of his old age with a certain amount of alarm. With Monica gone his anxiety had increased. They'd been alike in their needs, enjoying the good things, treating friends and relations with a tolerant if cynical generosity and turning a blind eye to the failings and weaknesses of each other. He'd kept up certain business interests after he'd retired and they'd bought a house in Shropshire, where they'd spent many happy times with friends who'd settled there some years before. Eustace would have preferred Devon but Monica already had her eye on her own needs: her bridge group, her golfing cronies, coffee mornings and a great fondness for the market town of Ludlow. So it was settled and if Eustace found the little clique of elderly people with their regular routines a touch stifling, he didn't say so. They both enjoyed their visits to Devon and when Tony left they'd done their best to ease Liz's pain.

Now, with Monica gone, Eustace was drawn back more and more to this glorious corner of Devon and to his unhappy niece and her delightful daughter. He realised that, in his clumsy attempts to soften Liz's bitterness, he often did more harm than good. Nevertheless, he felt that it was right to try to show her the lighter side, to keep her sympathetic of others' failings and to maintain a sense of tolerance. Liz was like her father, his older brother: sensible, cautious, ready to make judgements, disapproving of weakness in themselves and other people. It made them uncomfortable to live with and difficult to help. Only once had Liz veered from her strict code of morality and that was with Tony. Eustace remembered his brother's rage and winced, even now, sixteen years on. They'd rarely spoken since that day when Eustace tried to make her father see Liz's transgression with a more humane and understanding eye. The divorce had come as an even greater blow and there had been a certain amount of relief all round when Liz's parents had decided to retire to their property in Provence.

Eustace, who had always been the *enfant terrible*, shook his head sadly and wished it could have been otherwise. His attention returned to the scene before him and the expression on his handsome old face softened.

'Beautiful,' he murmured, gazing out on to the misty slopes that stretched away, fold after fold, lying tranquil and remote in the late afternoon sunshine. 'So beautiful.'

He threw his cigarette stub out of the window, picked up his holdall and peeped inside. The silver flask reposed comfortingly amongst the muddle and he smiled serenely, patted his pockets to check for cigarettes and followed Liz downstairs and into the kitchen.

Phyllida sat in the corner of her sofa, her feet curled up beneath her and Lucy's teddy clasped in her arms, watching the television. It was a Friday evening, Lucy was in bed and Phyllida was dreading a long weekend alone. Alistair's course at Greenwich was over and now he was in Scotland. She'd always found the weekends, traditionally a time for families to be together, lonelier and more drawn out than weekdays, and she missed Alistair more then than at any other time. Phyllida thought about him and felt a tiny twinge of guilt. Whilst he'd been at Greenwich he'd been able to get home every weekend and she'd leaned on him heavily since she'd lost the baby. At first she'd been terribly depressed, only just able to bear up through the weeks until Alistair arrived home on Friday evenings. People had been wonderfully kind but she'd felt obliged to show a brave exterior and it was only with Alistair that she'd really broken down.

She made a little face to herself. It couldn't have been easy for him. He'd been upset, too, but he'd recovered quite quickly. After all, as he explained in justification to her unspoken criticism, it wasn't as if they'd known the child. It was all over and they must put it behind them.

Easier said than done, thought Phyllida.

She put the teddy down, uncurled her legs and stood up. Making supper would give her something to do but her thoughts accompanied her into the kitchen. The most positive thing that had come out of it was the growing friendship with Claudia. Her ready sympathy and understanding had taken Phyllida by surprise; she'd seemed so disinterested in the idea of children and, although she was sweet with Lucy, she wasn't in any way maternal. Nevertheless, Phyllida had been grateful for her support especially as she suspected that Claudia had problems of her own. Not that she'd ever so much as hinted that everything wasn't perfect . . . The telephone bell made her jump and she hurried to lift the receiver.

'Hello, Phylly.' It was Alistair.

'Hello!' Her heart leaped with pleasure. 'How are you?'

'Fine. Just wanted to make sure you're OK. Not moping?'

'No, honestly I'm not. Really.'

'Good. Lucy OK?'

'She's fine.' Phyllida chuckled. 'She did a huge drawing for you at school today which she insists I post to you. Don't be surprised when it arrives.'

'Thanks for warning me. Look, I must crack on. This was just a quickie to say I love you. I'll give you another buzz over the weekend.'

'I love you too. Take care.'

She replaced the receiver and stood for a moment, willing back the weak tears which seemed to spring so readily to her eyes since the loss of the baby.

'Don't be so wet!' she told herself fiercely and jumped again as the bell trilled out.

'Hello,' she answered it, swallowing back her tears. There was a silence and she said, 'Hello,' again, more strongly.

'Is that Phyllida?' It was a woman's voice.

'Yes, it is.'

'It's Clemmie Halliwell.'

'Oh, how are you?'

'We're both well, thank you. We were hoping that we might be able to persuade you to come to lunch on Sunday. We should so love to see you again. And Lucy too, of course. If you could manage it?'

The voice tailed off a little uncertainly and Phyllida spoke quickly.

'We'd like that very much. How kind of you.'

'Not a bit. Shall we say about midday then? You remember where we are?'

'Oh, yes. Thank you. We'll look forward to it.'

Phyllida replaced the receiver. Perhaps the weekend wouldn't be so long and empty after all. As she went to prepare some food, the telephone rang yet again. This time it was Liz.

'Hello, Phyllida. How are you? Good. Yes, I'm well, thanks. You remember Uncle Eustace, don't you? Yes. Well, he's down for a while and he'd love to see you again. I wondered if you'd like to come to lunch tomorrow? Bring Lucy. Prudence is coming and a few others. How about it?'

'I'd love to,' said Phyllida with heartfelt pleasure. 'It would be great. Thank you.'

'Fine. Say around twelve, then? Good. See you then.'

Phyllida returned to her contemplation of supper, her spirits lifting a little. She poured herself a tumbler of wine and thought again of Alistair and heard his voice saying, 'I love you.' How lucky she was and how good he'd been! She suddenly felt positive and much stronger, especially now that she had a very busy weekend to look forward to instead of two long days stretching emptily ahead. She raised the glass to herself and determined that by the time Alistair arrived home the next weekend she would have put the loss of the baby behind her and be her old cheerful self.

'She says she'd love to come,' Clemmie told Quentin who was setting out the Scrabble racks and the tiles on the low table before the fire. 'She sounded rather strange when she first answered. I think she'd been crying.'

'Poor child.' Quentin cleared his throat and spoke more firmly. 'It must be a very lonely life.'

Clemmie looked at his bent head. It had been a very awkward moment when Abby had told her in confidence about Phyllida's baby. It was more as an explanation as to why she'd brought Phyllida along than anything else but she'd had no idea what ghosts she was raising. She imagined that Clemmie was silent because she was remembering her own lost child. After they'd gone, each time Clemmie thought of speaking about it she feared that Quentin might think it was an oblique reproach for his one brief affair connected with their daughter's death. How foolish that they should still be so sensitive after all these years! She knew that Quentin's reluctance to accompany Phyllida into the wood was lest Clemmie should in any way resent it, plagued even now by habitual and irrational jealousy. Suddenly she had known that this was the moment for which she'd been waiting. She felt with absolute certainty that an opportunity had arisen which, if taken, might remove the shadow for ever. She didn't yet know how; she just knew that it was here.

When she'd looked at Phyllida's sweet face with its wide grey eyes, she'd felt the old pain like an echo in her own breast. She knew what she must be suffering and her first desire was to attempt to alleviate it a little. She'd sent them down to the bridge, hoping that Quentin would realise that she felt no fear, and she'd seen the way Phyllida had relaxed during her walk in the woods. Nevertheless, she couldn't explain to Quentin just yet. Old prejudices and fears cannot be done away with overnight and she could hardly expect him to react instinctively, as she had done.

Clemmie touched his head lightly and he smiled at her as she sat down opposite.

'It must be dreadful to have a sailor for a husband,' she agreed, accepting his suggestion for Phyllida's unsteady voice on the telephone. 'Now. Whose turn is it to start?'

* * *

Phyllida was delighted to meet Oliver again at Liz's lunch party the next day. He greeted her as though she were an old friend and when she introduced him to Prudence they discovered that they had several naval friends in common. Uncle Eustace was in very good form and talked of coming down again for Christmas. Liz looked at him sardonically, aware of his cunning. She could hardly refuse him in front of so many friends. Christina slipped an arm round his portly waist and hugged him, obviously delighted at the thought. Liz shrugged a little, accepted with as good a grace as possible and turned away to speak to an old friend with whom she'd been at school and who was down for a fortnight's holiday in the area.

'Damned ugly woman, that,' murmured Uncle Eustace in Oliver's ear. 'Thought she was a man to begin with. Dashed embarrassing.'

'Unk!' Oliver looked shocked. 'You can't go around saying things like that any more. Politically incorrect.'

'What d'you mean?' demanded Uncle Eustace, He stared fixedly at the old school friend. 'But she's ugly! No two ways about it! What would you call her?'

'Aesthetically challenged,' replied Oliver promptly. 'Just as you are not "old" but "chronologically gifted".'

'I'm not old,' protested Uncle Eustace. 'Dammit! I've only just turned seventy.'

'Would you prefer "experientially enhanced"?' Oliver grinned at him. 'I can see that you've got a lot to learn, Unk. I shall have to lend you my handbook.'

Phyllida joined them and the older man beamed at her.

'He's educating me,' he explained. 'Tells me I can't call people old or ugly any more. Did you know that?'

'I've heard rumours,' admitted Phyllida. 'It's very confusing.'

'Let's have another drink,' he suggested, brightening a little. 'Might come easier, then. I suppose I'm not allowed to get drunk either?'

'Chemically inconvenienced,' murmured Oliver and smiled at Phyllida as Uncle Eustace disappeared in search of some more wine. 'I hear I shall be seeing you at The Grange tomorrow?'

'How nice.' Phyllida looked pleased. 'Isn't it funny? I was dreading this weekend and it's turning out to be great fun.'

Oliver looked at her, wondering whether to ask why she should have been dreading it but deciding against it. He'd been surprised at how pleased he was to see her again but, before he could analyse his feelings further, Uncle Eustace was back to announce that lunch was ready.

Chapter Eight

In September Alistair was promoted and given command of a Polaris submarine. It was something of a pierhead jump but Alistair was delighted by both the promotion and the command. He went away to Faslane on a course before taking over, having first come down for a weekend. Phyllida was very pleased for him although disappointed that he would be going back to sea so quickly. They discussed the possibility of a move to a married quarter near the base, agreeing that it was tiresome that this had happened just as Lucy had started at Meavy School and was settling in very happily.

'Think about it and we'll talk again when I come back,' said Alistair as she drove him to the station. 'I should be able to fit in some leave before we sail.'

On her way back to Yelverton, Phyllida decided to drop in on Prudence and tell her the news. It had happened so suddenly that she hadn't had the opportunity to discuss it with anyone. She saw Liz's car outside but the old feelings of discomfort had gone. Liz had been much less prickly with Phyllida since she'd lost the baby. Beating her usual quick tattoo on the back door she opened it and stuck her head inside.

'Can I come in or shall I be interrupting?'

There was a moment of silence and Phyllida knew at once that both women had been talking about her. Prudence, who'd been standing with her back to the Rayburn, came to give her a hug but she looked embarrassed and upset. She chatted away as usual whilst she made some more tea but Phyllida had the feeling that, this morning, she was doing it to cover up the awkward moment or, perhaps, to prevent Liz from speaking.

She sat down at the table, accepted a mug of tea and glanced at Liz who was watching her with an almost calculating expression that made her feel uneasy. It was evident that Prudence felt the same. She sent Liz a very severe glare accompanied by a brief shake of the head before turning her attention once more to Phyllida.

'I haven't seen you since Liz's lunch party. How's Lucy?'

'Fine. I really dashed in to tell you the news. Alistair's been promoted. He's going to drive *Ruthless*. The captain has been taken ill so it's a bit sudden but he's delighted, of course.'

'Of course,' said Prudence quickly. 'That's wonderful. Give him my congratulations.'

Liz stirred. She didn't seem particularly excited by the news.

'Shall you be moving to Faslane?' she asked and Phyllida sensed something more than casual interest lay behind the question.

'I can't decide,' she said. 'Lucy's settled so well at Meavy but I suppose she'd adjust to the move. I don't think that I particularly want to go. I've made so many friends here, but I feel I must support him. Don't you agree?'

Prudence nodded but her eyes were fixed on the other woman and she made an involuntary gesture as Liz pushed back her chair and got up.

'I've got something to tell you,' she said to Phyllida.

Prudence got to her feet, too. 'No. Please, Liz. We've discussed this and I've asked you not to.'

'Why shouldn't she know? Why should she be made a fool of, like I was?' Liz turned abruptly on Prudence. 'I wish someone had told me when Tony started to play around again. She's got a right to know.'

'Wait!' Phyllida stared at each of them in turn. 'Please. What is all this? A right to know what?'

'Alistair's having an affair with a Wren,' said Liz brutally, 'and I don't see why you should be the last to know about it.'

Prudence, who had instinctively turned her back as if to disassociate herself from Liz, turned round almost immediately and went to Phyllida. She laid a hand on her shoulder and stared at Liz over Phyllida's head.

'All I can say is that you'd better have your facts right.'

'Oh, don't be foolish, Prudence,' answered Liz impatiently. 'It's like me and Tony all over again. I was always the last to know and it's bloody humiliating. Everyone sniggering behind my back and nobody with the guts to tell me. Why should Phyllida give up her life here to go to Faslane to support him? Can you imagine the gossip and the speculation? Why shouldn't she be able to fight back on her own terms? At least she should know the facts.'

'Please,' said Phyllida, struggling up from beneath Prudence's hand and from the crushing blow she had just received. 'Please don't speak about me as if I'm not here. And anyway I don't believe a word of it. Alistair had a reputation before we got married, I know that, and it's always clung to him. People love to gossip.'

'Quite right,' said Prudence after a moment. She stared at Liz, daring her to utter another word, and Liz stared back.

'OK,' she said and gave a mirthless little laugh. 'I felt like that to begin with, too. Anything's better than the truth, if it hurts. But eventually you have to look it in the face. Personally, I prefer to know where I stand, but perhaps you don't. It's OK, Prudence. I'm going. You can stop glaring at me. I shan't apologise, Phyllida. Whoever says that ignorance is bliss is a bloody hypocrite. Think carefully before you make sacrifices, that's all! Thanks for the tea, Prudence. See you.'

She went out. Phyllida continued to stand quite still but Prudence hurried to fill the kettle.

'More tea, I think,' she said, casting a distressed look at Phyllida. 'Look, I've told you before, you simply mustn't attach too much—'

'She said "with a Wren",' Phyllida interrupted. 'That means that people are definitely saying things.'

'Oh, my dear. People are always saying things. You know that.'

'Did she say which Wren?'

'No,' lied Prudence uneasily. 'No, certainly not. It's just malicious gossip. Oh, it's so unfair.'

She refilled Phyllida's mug and pushed it into her hand. 'Sit down and drink that and forget all about it. Goodness! Do you have so little faith in Alistair that you believe the first thoughtless gossip you hear? Where's your loyalty? And he's been so good since you lost the baby.'

Phyllida tried hard to bring her whole mind to bear upon this rather than on an image of Alistair making love to another woman. It was a tremendous effort and Prudence watched her anxiously.

'Yes,' she said at last. 'Yes, he has.'

'He rushes down every weekend,' pointed out Prudence, 'phones most evenings, writes to Lucy. Does that sound like the behaviour of an unfaithful husband?'

Phyllida summoned all her strength and smiled at Prudence. She had a terrible fear that it might be exactly how an unfaithful husband would behave and her stomach churned and her hands were icy.

'I'm sure it isn't,' she replied and noticed with a hitherto unused, watchful corner of her mind that Prudence's relief was out of all proportion if she did indeed believe in Alistair's innocence.

'Then let's forget all about it. I'm sure it's just some malicious rumour.' Prudence cast about for something to distract Phyllida from her fears. 'I want you to see some new material I've found in Dingle's . . .'

But Phyllida was drinking her tea as quickly as she could. It was imperative that she should be alone to think about what Liz had said and to examine her own reactions. She felt frightened and miserable and she needed to assimilate the shock and decide how to behave.

'I must go,' she said, pretending regret. 'It really was a quickie to tell you the news. Don't worry. I'm fine.' She smiled brilliantly into Prudence's worried eyes and nodded reassuringly. 'I promise I shan't get things out of proportion. I'm quite used to living with Alistair's reputation, you know.'

She managed such a confidently rueful grin that Prudence gave her a kiss and let her go, albeit reluctantly. Once behind the wheel, however, Phyllida found that she was trembling and, having driven carefully until she was out on the open moor, she pulled into the side and switched off the engine. She knew, without any doubt at all, that Liz had told the truth. She had no idea how she was so sure but, somehow, she knew it with a deep conviction. From the beginning there had been those who, jealous that Alistair had preferred her, had made quite certain that she knew of his reputation. In her happiness and confidence in his love she had borne it all and put it away from her. Now she realised with a sickening tightening of the stomach muscles that love and trust are not enough. She may have been subject to the occasional twinge of insecurity but in her innocence she had never really believed that anyone who behaved with such love and tenderness and continual caring would be capable of such a betrayal of trust.

Phyllida stared out over the bright windswept landscape and felt both terror and despair. She simply had no idea how she should go forward. How could she live from day to day until Alistair returned and she could discover the truth? And why did she feel so sure that it was the truth? Was it because Liz had no axe to grind? She was not one of Alistair's old girlfriends and surely, having suffered so much herself, she was hardly likely to inflict such pain needlessly on anyone else? Moreover, since the loss of the baby, Liz had been so much kinder to her, less abrasive, more friendly. Surely she must have very good grounds for speaking out? Phyllida tried to imagine confronting Alistair. How would she do it? Lightly, as though it were a joke at which she expected him to laugh? Seriously, as though he were expected to defend himself and prove his innocence?

She realised that she couldn't imagine the scene at all and knew that, whatever the outcome might be, everything would be changed between them. Even if he denied it and she felt tempted to believe him, she knew that never again would she be able to live in that safe bright world of trust. Liz's words had shattered it and let in the shadows of doubt and nothing could ever be quite the same again.

Claudia picked up her tapestry frame, set her workbox on a low stool and sat down by the fire. The October day was cold and dreary. The wind blew handfuls of rain against the window and daylight was fading fast. Unwilling to put up with the ashes and dust that a wood fire produces, Claudia had insisted on a gas fire being installed and the flames flickered on the imitation logs most convincingly. She sat beside its cheering glow but the tapestry frame remained idle on her lap and her eyes rested unseeingly on the flames.

During the autumn, there had been an indefinable change in Jeff's behaviour. He'd ceased to be absent-minded and, instead, had become over-solicitous in his attentions to her. He did all the things he'd always done for her but there was a kind of desperation behind his actions now which did nothing to allay Claudia's fears. It was as if he were trying to prove something but whether to himself or to her she wasn't quite sure. Perhaps it was to both of them. Claudia spent hours trying to analyse his behaviour. To begin with she'd felt certain that he'd developed an infatuation for Jenny which, though humiliating and infuriating, might have died a fairly painless death. This change was more worrying. She feared that his feelings for the girl had developed into something much stronger and that Jeff was fighting hard against them. When she could hold her panic in check, she'd almost convinced herself that it was a kind of summer madness that would pass with the silly season. Jenny was so obviously not his type that it could only be a crazy infatuation. To back up this belief, Jeff's behaviour was so adolescent. Whilst he was in Jenny's presence he acted like a schoolboy, which was so utterly out of character for the sensible quiet Jeff she'd always known. The dancing at the barbecue had been just such an example and, on these occasions, Gavin egged him on and laughed as much as anyone. Yet he and Jenny were always together, accepted as a couple and invited to parties as such. Surely, if there were anything to suspect or resent, Gavin – who was not at all the type of man to sit back and be made a fool of – would not be nearly so complacent?

Knowing how sensitive and unbalanced she could be in these situations, Claudia tried to reason with herself. If Gavin saw nothing to fear, why should she? Things were not that simple, of course. Jenny, to do her justice, made no real attempt to attach herself to Jeff. Her friendly light-hearted jokiness was the same with everyone she met and she seemed genuinely fond of Gavin and he of her. No, it was not that Jenny might be pursuing Jeff that worried Claudia but that Jeff might feel for Jenny all the things he'd never felt for herself. That he might prefer another woman was unbearable. That it should be a painted, sexy little idiot was more than flesh or blood could stand. To Claudia, it was an insult.

She was incapable of talking the matter over with Jeff or approaching it in any way other than with blind anger. Her only defence was attack. She usually managed to hang on to her pride so that her observations were always directed at Jenny, never at Jeff. She pretended that she assumed that he must feel as she did and she would sneer disdainfully whilst attempting to appear indifferent.

'She really is such a common little thing . . . I can't imagine why she's bothered to put that dress on, can you? She simply has to display everything she's got . . . I can't help feeling she must be so insecure, poor thing. This need to have all the attention!'

When these little comments brought no reaction, rage pushed her nearer to the point.

'The trouble with people who don't mind behaving badly is that they drag others down to their level . . . Of course, men are so easily taken in, aren't they? They can't resist a chance to have their egos boosted . . . It's really so pathetic. They think it's so clever and yet they look such fools. Of course, that's what women like Jenny adore. They love the triumph over wives and girlfriends who wouldn't dream of being so cheap . . .'

Jeff never reacted. He listened and was silent and Claudia fumed inwardly. So it had been all summer and through the early autumn. Now this change was reason for fresh alarm. She must think of ways to bind him to her. At least during the winter months the social occasions might be fewer. Even so, he saw her every day at the office . . .

Claudia's hands clenched on her tapestry as she saw all

the opportunities for little exchanges and jokes, not to mention lunches at the pub. She'd taken to going along at lunch time but it was clear that the others thought it odd that she should be there, although Jeff always appeared pleased to see her. She began to fear that they might suspect her visits and sometimes she caught Gavin's sardonic eye from behind the bar. She'd given up going in the end, her pride making it impossible, but she seethed impotently at the thought of those informal jolly gatherings.

The pealing of the doorbell broke into her thoughts and she put the tapestry aside and went into the hall. Gavin stood outside the door. Claudia gaped at him in surprise and then felt an absurd thrill of fear. He stood smiling a little at her and she had the usual feeling that he was privy to all her imaginings.

'Come in,' she said and turned away and went back to the drawing room.

He followed her in, alert yet easy, his eyes summing up the room in his casual, bold manner. Despite the chill October day he wore only a sweatshirt with his jeans but his vitality seemed to radiate from him and he looked completely out of place in the delicate, tidy room. After he'd looked around and summed it all up, he turned to her and smiled. Claudia stared at him. She'd planned to sit down and take up her tapestry in an effort to make him feel awkward, implying that she could see no reason for his visit and that, as far as she was concerned, he had no business in her house. Instead, she stood staring at him as he smiled at her.

'It looks as if you've just moved in,' he observed. 'Everything so neat and clean. Doesn't look as if you actually live in it at all.'

'Not everybody likes to live like a pig in a sty,' she answered, her temper rising. It seemed that far from being impressed or cowed he was actually criticising her. She thought of Jenny's muddled, untidy flat – they'd never been to Gavin's – and her anger increased. 'What do you want?'

He laughed outright then and she felt her face flame.

'Poor old Claudia,' he said and the genuine sympathy in his voice made her spirit writhe. 'I've had the feeling that things aren't going too well for you so I decided to pop in on my way back from the pub and see if there's anything I could do.'

Insult upon insult! The mere idea that he should presume that he could do anything for her was so preposterous that she nearly laughed in his face.

'I have no idea why on earth you should imagine anything of the sort,' she said icily. 'And now, if you'll forgive me . . .'

'Oh, don't put on that lady of the manor stuff,' he said and even his contempt was friendly. 'It's just not you, is it? Stop pretending that you're a bit better than the rest of us. Why don't you unbutton a bit and try to enjoy life?'

She gazed at him speechlessly. He'd struck her in a very sensitive spot and she felt quite suddenly that she might shatter into tiny pieces and utterly collapse. Gavin saw that moment of weakness and pounced. He took her arm and his warm firm grasp made her shudder.

'I'll tell you something,' he said softly, almost tenderly. 'The unhappiest people in this life are the people pretending to be something they're not. It's so exhausting. You daren't let down the barriers for a second once you start along that road. You can fool some of the people some of the time but you're never going to take in all of 'em. A few of 'em will be taken in – that's nice, you can show off to them and it'll make you feel good. The ones you're trying to imitate will see through it and despise you and you'll never be at ease in their company, in case you show yourself up. And the rest? Well, the rest just won't care. They'll be too busy living their own lives and enjoying themselves. Is it worth it? You're not fooling anyone, you know.'

There was a silence. She couldn't look at him and suddenly he took her chin in his fingers, jerked her face up and kissed her. In ordinary circumstances she would have fought; hit him, struggled. As it was, with her carefully erected barriers kicked so brutally away, she found herself quite limp in the circle of his arm, his fingers biting into her jaw, but when his tongue touched hers she felt galvanised with a violent shock of desire. She leaped away from him – though not before he'd experienced her response – in an attempt to hide this second humiliation.

'Please go,' she said and her voice shook. 'How dare you . . . ?'

'You see?' His voice was still calm, amused even. 'Still pretending. Why not simply unwind a little? Accept yourself for what you are? You're a very beautiful girl, Claudia. Very attractive. You can't blame me if you turn me on. You must have guessed it by now.'

If he'd said anything else she might have coped, controlled her emotions and sent him away, but this particular flattery, coming on top of such a shock, undid her.

'I don't believe it. That's absolute nonsense,' she said weakly. 'I think you should go.'

Behind her, Gavin smiled to himself.

'I think you do believe it,' he said softly. 'You've seen me look at you. You're not like Jenny. Obvious. If you've got it flaunt it. No. You're cool. Much more sexy. Lucky old Jeff. I just hope he deserves you, that's all. Seems like a bit of a cold fish, to me.'

The pause went on far too long and Gavin's smile widened.

'No,' said Claudia faintly, at last. 'No, he's not . . .'

'Well,' he was close up behind her now, 'you know best, of course.' His arms slipped round her, his lips were against her ear. 'But I should have thought—'

The shrill of the telephone bell caused them to leap apart. Gavin swore softly under his breath as he watched Claudia tremblingly pick up the receiver.

'Hello? Oh, Abby. Hello.' Nothing could have so surely pulled her together than Abby's voice. 'Hang on a sec. Just saying goodbye to a friend . . .' She laid the receiver down and smiled with false brightness at Gavin. 'Better go. I'm afraid this might take a while.'

He grinned at the loud, consciously refined tones and the terrified eyes, took her face in his hands and kissed her again.

'See you,' he said and went out. The front door slammed.

Shivering violently, Claudia picked up the receiver again.

'Sorry, Abby . . . No, not at all. He . . . they were just going. Now, what can I do for you?'

Chapter Nine

Phyllida had begun to think that the weeks until Alistair's return would never pass. She hadn't appreciated how happy she'd been until now, when each day dragged past in a fog of misery. Sometimes she almost managed to persuade herself that Liz was mistaken and the report of Alistair's infidelity was nothing but a malicious rumour. Deep down, however, the doubt persisted and before long the misery would return, taking possession of her heart which seemed to expand and swell with it until even swallowing became difficult and speech almost impossible. She wondered, now, why she had so lightly dismissed the warnings that she'd had. Even her brother Matthew, a good friend to Alistair, had thought it right to point out the dangers. Confident in a new exciting overwhelming emotion, she had found it impossible to believe that Alistair would ever hurt her and, even when she'd experienced uncomfortable twinges when she'd met – or had pointed out to her – his girlfriends from the past, his publicly declared love for her had carried her over these moments.

Now she found herself remembering these girls and imagining, with a painful clarity, Alistair making love to them. She felt ill with the misery of it and was grateful that she had Lucy, attempting to distract herself with the child's company. She grew to dread the long empty evenings. She found that she couldn't even bring herself to write to Alistair and spent the hours until bedtime huddled in the corner of the sofa staring mindlessly at the television. Once in bed, sleep eluded her and she wept for those happy days of innocence. In the morning she was heavy-eyed and listless and found herself avoiding the company of her friends. At last, Alistair was due home and Phyllida was relieved to hear that he would be arriving back on an afternoon when Lucy was at a friend's birthday party.

He'd hitched a lift from a brother officer and Phyllida, watching from a bedroom window, saw him get out, slam the car door and hurry up the drive. Her heart beat erratically at the sight of him and she realised that all her carefully rehearsed speeches would be useless in the presence of a flesh and blood Alistair. She heard the door close and his footsteps in the hall but was quite unable to move. She hadn't been prepared either for the wave of love that she felt when she saw him again or for the dark undercurrent of anger at how he had betrayed her love and ruined their relationship. She heard his voice calling her name and forced herself to go to the door, opening it as Alistair arrived at the top of the stairs. He crossed the landing, his face bright with joy at the sight of her, and swept her into his arms.

'I wondered where on earth you'd got to,' he exclaimed between kisses. 'God! I've missed you! Did you get my letter? I haven't had anything from you for ages and you sounded so odd when I telephoned.'

It occurred to him that her reception was not the joyous

welcome he was used to and he looked closely at her, keeping his arm round her. He saw the shadows under her tired eyes and the pinched look around her lips and his arm tightened.

'Are you all right?' he asked. 'You look fagged out. What have you been up to? Is Lucy OK?'

She turned her eyes away from the love and concern in his eyes and attempted to free herself.

'I'm fine. We're both fine. Lucy's at a party. Let's go down, Alistair. I want to talk to you.'

She looked at him again as she spoke and saw the knowledge and the guilt spring together into his eyes and his arm dropped from her shoulders. She stared at him aghast and it was he, this time, who looked away.

'So it's true,' she whispered and felt that she might fall down if she were not supported. She knew now just how large a part of her had counted on his denial.

'Who told you?' he asked and she took hold of the balustrade for support.

'Liz.' Her heart felt as though it would burst with anguish. 'It was Liz Whelan. I didn't want to believe her . . .'

'But you did. That's why I didn't get a letter.' His voice was curt and she guessed that he was hiding his own hurt at her readiness to believe ill of him.

For a moment she felt guilty, as though it were she who had betrayed him, and caught quickly at her own pain. After all, had he not admitted his guilt? She turned to look at him, her arms behind her back, her hands clenched on the wooden rail.

'I couldn't think what to write,' she said. 'Liz was so certain. She said that you were behaving like her husband

and that I ought to know the truth.' They stared at each other across the shadowy spaces. 'It seemed unbelievable and yet somehow I knew that it was true. And it was.' Her lips trembled. 'Wasn't it?'

He nodded. 'But it wasn't anything like Liz experienced with Tony. Oh, I know.' He raised his hand in acknowledgement of her unspoken retort. 'But there *is* a difference. Tony married Liz because he made her pregnant. He never loved her. He was in love with Cass Wivenhoe and when she threw him over he married Liz. I love you, Phyllida. You know that!'

'Then why?' she cried and her voice was hoarse with pain. 'Why? You've destroyed everything, can't you see? Was it worth it?'

'Have I?' He stretched his arms out to her and his eyes were full of fear as she made a fierce gesture which utterly repudiated his plea. 'It was nothing.' He thrust his hands into his pockets and hunched his shoulders. 'Oh, Christ.'

'Liz said it was a Wren.' Phyllida had regained a certain amount of composure but her hands, hidden again behind her back, were trembling.

'Yes.' Alistair sighed deeply, glanced about him as if seeking inspiration and looked back at her. He felt as if he were confronting a stranger. 'I've known Janie for ever. We had an affair for a while but I was never in love with her. She knew that.' His voice which had been strong in an effort to convince became flat. 'She was there when I was at Greenwich for those few weeks. I was upset about the . . . the baby and she was very understanding. She had a spare ticket for the opera and it didn't seem too much of a big deal to go along.

There was a party of us and we went back to her place afterwards . . .' He paused for a long moment but Phyllida made no attempt to help him out. 'There's always a danger,' he said at last, as if he had just discovered the fact, 'in resuming friendships with people with whom one has been intimate.'

Phyllida stirred. 'You,' she said. 'Not "one". You. Don't try to impersonalise it.'

Alistair bit his lip. 'OK,' he said, nodding. 'You're right. I meant it as a generalisation but you're quite right. There's an easiness, a resuming of old habits. Somehow it doesn't feel so wrong as chatting someone up deliberately.'

'I can't see the difference.'

'I'm sure you can't and I'm not trying to excuse it—'

'Oh, good.' Phyllida marvelled at the cynical coolness of her tone. It could have been Liz's voice. 'So does that mean that every time you meet one of your old mistresses – and let's face it, there's no shortage of them – that I should accept that you're likely to hop into bed with them? Just for old times' sake?'

'No. No. I don't.' He was angry now. 'It's only been once and you can believe that or not, as you please. It was once with Janie and I regretted it immediately. I should have known that after you it couldn't ever work again. I was a bit low and worried about you and we'd had a few drinks. She realised it was a mistake. We were both at several other social events during those weeks and that's how the rumours started. But I only went to bed with her once.'

Those last words had a curious effect on Phyllida. Her terrible suspicions and fears had been named and could now be imagined. She had met Janie very briefly several years before but could picture her quite clearly: a long-legged girl, with brilliant brown eyes and a mass of dark hair. A great surge of jealousy engulfed her and the pain squeezed her heart unbearably.

'It might as well have been a hundred times,' she cried. 'It's ruined everything and I shall never be able to trust you again. How could you? How could you destroy everything we had?'

He stared at her, white-faced. 'I love you,' he repeated. 'Please, Phyllida. Please try to understand. I promise—'

'No!' she screamed at him. 'You promised things before. How could I ever believe you again? Don't touch me!' She struck at his outstretched hands. 'I'm going to fetch Lucy.'

She slipped past him down the stairs and out through the kitchen. The back door slammed and he heard the car's engine as she backed down the drive and, after that, silence.

Alistair's long weekend was unbearable. For Lucy's sake, Phyllida was quite unable to behave towards him with sustained coldness. She couldn't bear that the child, who adored her father and was used to loving harmony between her parents, should be upset or made to feel insecure and Alistair, naturally enough, had made the most of his opportunities. Nevertheless, once they were alone, Phyllida had held out against his pleadings. She said that she needed time to think but was completely unable to come to any rational decision. The choice was plain enough. Either they parted – Phyllida shrank from this thought and her heart was faint with despair as she considered life without him – or they started again, putting his infidelity behind them. But how was that to be done? He attempted to make love to her and she resisted him, feeling sick and inadequate, sure that he was comparing her unfavourably with the gorgeous Janie. On the last night – after a party at which she'd drunk more than usual in an effort to keep up her spirits lest anyone should suspect – knowing how miserable he was, how bitterly he was regretting his action and unable to crush down her own desire, she'd allowed him to take her in his arms. His passion and remorse swept aside her inhibitions and his lovemaking had left her trembling.

In the morning, however, all the old horror and bitterness returned and she simply could not go forward as Alistair clearly imagined would be the case after such an act of love. His disappointment was so acute that she nearly relented but, in the clear light of day, she saw again Janie's face and form and she wondered whether she would ever be able to trust him, despite his promises and very genuine despair. She saw her response to his lovemaking, now, as humiliating and regretted her loss of dignity. He went back to Scotland, frustrated and unhappy, leaving Phyllida to attempt to sort out her emotions.

Prudence had been deeply distressed when Phyllida told her all about Alistair and the Wren. The idea of divorce was abhorrent to Prudence and only in extreme cases could she accept it as a solution. She urged Phyllida to believe Alistair's story and try to trust him when he vowed that he would never do it again.

'It's easier said than done,' said Phyllida, watching whilst Prudence sat at the end of her kitchen table sewing a seam in a tiny garment. 'Part of me longs to, but the other part can't get rid of the idea of him with that woman.'

She stared at Prudence, the horror still there at the front of her mind, and Prudence nodded with sympathy apparent in her face.

'Oh, I can quite see that,' she said at once. 'Naturally. But do think carefully, Phyllida. Divorce is such a huge step and there's Lucy to consider.'

'Do you think I haven't thought about it?' cried Phyllida. 'Good God! I never think about anything else these days. I've decided that I shan't go to Faslane, though. I need time. I couldn't cope with the strain of living in quarters and knowing that everyone's talking about us.'

'Oh, Phyllida—'

'Yes, they will be. You know that. Look how quickly Liz heard about it.'

'And you don't think,' ventured Prudence, 'it would be wiser for you to be with him?'

'No.' Phyllida frowned with distress. 'Can't you see, Prudence, I can't be like that? Behaving like a watchdog. His good behaviour dependent on whether I've got my eye on him. How horrid! In the end I'd have to go with him everywhere, wouldn't I? Afraid every time he meets a pretty woman, or dances with one of those girls he used to go out with. Can you imagine it? And what happens when he goes away?'

Prudence watched her, distressed, her work cast aside.

'So how do you see it?'

'It must either work properly or not at all.'

'But how?' Prudence asked after a moment.

'That's the trouble. I haven't got that far. You see, if I stay with him, then it's not really a matter of trust, is it?'

'Isn't it?' Prudence looked puzzled. 'I thought that's exactly what it's all about.'

'Oh, Prudence.' Phyllida sighed impatiently. 'Try to see it from my point of view. How can I trust Alistair again? I think that once something like that gets smashed, it's impossible to make it like new again. You can bodge it up but it's always going to be terrifyingly fragile. Isn't it?'

'Well, yes,' agreed Prudence, trying to concentrate. 'But if you're saying that you can never really trust him again – and I totally accept that point of view – how could it work?'

'That's what I'm getting to,' explained Phyllida. 'I've thought and thought and it all comes down to whether I can love Alistair enough. Absolutely unconditionally. No reproaches, no suspicions, just love.'

'That's a very tall order,' said Prudence at last.

'I know.' Phyllida looked sombre. 'I'm not saying I'm capable of it. I'm just saying that, for me, that's the only way I see it working.'

'What about Alistair?'

'Alistair will agree to anything as long as it isn't divorce. He loves me, I know that. And there's Lucy.' Phyllida put both elbows on the table and massaged her forehead with her fingers. 'That's why I'm not going to Faslane. It's like a testing time for me. I'll see how I feel when he comes home for leaves. How I react. Whether my suspicions are too great and things like that.' She looked at Prudence. 'What d'you think?'

'I think it's a very good idea,' said Prudence. She was

filled with admiration for Phyllida's courageous attempt to save her marriage along such generous lines and moved by the thought of the loneliness ahead for her. 'Can you stay on at your house in Yelverton?'

'I hope so. And Lucy's so happy at Meavy School. I'll try and find a job or something . . .' She sighed and dropped her head into her hands.

Prudence stood up.

'Lunch time,' she said. 'And a glass of something. Very cheap, I'm afraid, but it takes the edge off things. Of course, I'm delighted you're not going.' She put a glass of wine beside her and squeezed her shoulder. 'Drink up.'

Phyllida tried to smile and picked up her glass.

'At least we've got Christmas to look forward to,' she said and took a long swallow. It was going to be very difficult to keep cheerful enough to make it a joyful time for Lucy.

Chapter Ten

Clemmie crossed the meadow below The Grange, relying more heavily than usual on her stick. It was a mild afternoon overarched by a pale grey sky and, as she approached the wood, the stillness of the day began to be filled with the sound of rushing water. The lush undergrowth of summer had died back, the last of the leaves had fallen, and the whole wood looked as though it had been painted over with a sepia wash. The tints were all muted greys and browns and the glowing scarlet berries of the holly tree that stood at a bend in the path were a visual shock in this gentle landscape. The branches stretching up with twiggy fingers made a sharp, dark intricate tracery against the soft, pale cloud beyond and the water, tumbling and splashing along in its rocky bed, was brown with the moorland earth it carried with it down to the sea. Clemmie looked for the dipper and felt the shock to her heart as she saw him almost at once, bobbing on a low bough of an overhanging tree on the opposite bank.

It wasn't until she'd met Quentin that Clemmie endowed the bird with almost magical properties. She remembered the first time quite clearly. She'd met Quentin at the Manor at a party given by the present William's father. Quentin and

William had been at Oxford together, become friends and stayed in touch after they'd graduated and now Quentin had been invited down for the party and for a few days' holiday.

Clemmie had fallen in love with him immediately. The formal black dinner jacket suited his dark, lean, good looks wonderfully and he'd been such fun. He had a keen wit and a ready humour and spent as much time as was proper with the shy, young Clemmie, pretty in her long frock. They'd seen a great deal of each other in those few days; Quentin and William coming to tea at The Grange, and a group of them going on a hike to Sheepstor. When Quentin returned to London, Clemmie wandered by the river. Her heart beat fast when she thought of him, wondering if he would write to her as he'd promised.

'If I see the dipper,' she told herself, 'there will be a letter from him tomorrow.'

She'd walked on, her eyes darting to and fro, watching for the elusive bird, so cleverly camouflaged against his surroundings. She was on the bridge when she saw him, skimming low above the water below her. He came to rest on a large rock downstream and she watched eagerly as he preened himself and bobbed a little, before walking into the water and disappearing. She went home, laughing at herself a little. How silly! She was like a child relying on certain formulae to hold misfortune at bay. But when the letter arrived in the morning and Clemmie read the words '. . . and I was seized by a sudden need to write to you this afternoon . . .' she was certain that it was whilst she had been watching the dipper that he'd felt her own longing to hear from him. From that time forward the bird had become symbolic.

'If I see the dipper he'll propose tonight . . . come back alive from the war . . . this child I'm carrying will be a boy . . .' There were so many occasions when the dipper had given hope and the promises had been fulfilled. She remembered, too, the evening when, with a heart heavy with despair, she'd watched the midges hovering in a dazzling golden cloud above the slow-moving water, low now after a long hot summer. The sun shone between the boles of the beech trees and the stones of the bridge had been warm to her touch. 'If I see the dipper then Pippa will live' had been her thought and she had waited and watched until the sunshine had vanished and the shadows were thick beneath the trees. Still she stayed on, her eyes probing the water, until the light had gone and she left the bridge and hurried home to The Grange where her small daughter, struck down by poliomyelitis, was being nursed by her grandmother. Pippa had died and Clemmie had remained at The Grange, sunk in grief, until a letter from an old friend warned her that Quentin was finding his own comfort elsewhere. She'd fled back with her son, miraculously untouched by the illness, to find Quentin, miserable, lonely, grieving at the loss of his darling daughter, seeking consolation in the arms of a divorced friend.

Now, forty years on, Clemmie still felt the thrust of jealousy, dulled by the years but still there. Coming so soon after Pippa's death, his unfaithfulness was a crushing blow and she still wondered, even now, how they'd struggled from beneath it to rebuild their lives together. How nearly she'd left him then! Sick with grief and humiliation, she'd felt it to be impossible to start again but Quentin, ashamed and desperate, had beseeched her to forgive him. She'd come to The Grange for the half-term holiday and, walking by the river, had put her future to the usual test. 'If I see the dipper I'll go back to him.' As she'd made her vow she saw the bird perched on the boulder beneath the bridge and Clemmie knew then that she must try to forgive Quentin, for how else could it work? So she'd gone back and she'd tried to forgive and forget and, occasionally, believed that she had. She never trusted him again and it had been a shadow that had lengthened with the years, flinging its darkness across the sunshine of their happiness together.

They both knew it. Quentin hugged his guilt to himself, longing for the word or gesture that would at last release him from its burden and Clemmie watched helplessly, unable to provide it. Gradually they'd resumed their loving, happy ways but Clemmie had never quite been able to stifle her fear. She grew to dread social occasions, unable to control the stab of jealousy when she saw him with another woman, however innocently. Quentin understood her feelings and did everything he could to restore her confidence. Never in all the ensuing years had he given her a moment's cause for anxiety yet he knew that she still mistrusted him despite all her efforts to overcome it.

The dipper took flight suddenly. Straight and low he flew downstream and out of sight round the bend in the river. Clemmie came back to the present with a start and wondered how long she'd been standing watching him. She shivered a little and walked on, remembering her conversation with Abby a few days before. She'd told Clemmie about Alistair and the Wren and it had come as a tremendous shock to

Clemmie to realise how closely Phyllida's situation mirrored her own. She'd been deeply distressed and found herself thinking about her more and more. She longed to help her but wondered how she, who had so signally failed, could help anyone else in the same predicament.

Phyllida and Lucy had come over for Sunday lunch not long afterwards and she'd experienced, yet again, the uncanny sensation that, through these two, she could come to terms with her own fears. There had been no opportunity for any private conversation with her but, when Phyllida and Lucy had gone, Clemmie sat by the fire, watching the flames curling round the logs. The house seemed silent and she was aware of the great echoing spaces around and above her; of empty rooms and corridors.

'Tired?' asked Quentin, coming in with a cup of tea and putting it down on the table beside her.

She turned to look up at him. 'I'm getting so fond of Phyllida,' she told him. 'And little Lucy.'

'Yes.' Quentin sat down opposite. 'She . . . she's a sweet child,' he said cautiously.

Clemmie regarded him serenely. 'They both are,' she said. 'I feel that Phyllida's like Pippa would have been had she lived and Lucy reminds me of Pippa as she was but I know that's foolish really. I'm getting strange fancies in my old age. I already love little Lucy and I feel strangely close to Phyllida.'

'Perhaps . . .' Quentin hesitated and then spoke bravely. 'Perhaps that's because you know she's having to cope with the same problems that you had.'

Clemmie looked at him quickly. 'How did you know?'

she asked. There was no point in pretending to misunderstand him.

Quentin sighed. 'Abby told me. She mentioned it in passing and seemed surprised that you hadn't told me.'

'I'm sorry.' She felt distressed. 'I should have said something, I suppose. It just seemed . . .'

She hesitated and he nodded with a resigned understanding which roused her sympathy.

'Don't worry,' he said. 'I know it's a sensitive subject.'

'Well, it shouldn't be!' she cried. 'Not after all these years. It's simply silly. To be like this at our ages is ridiculous. When I met Phyllida and Abby told me about the baby I felt this was going to be my chance for finishing it once and for all. Does that sound foolish? It seemed that through her I could finally come to terms with it. I can't describe it any better than that. This latest thing brought it all back and I really feel for her. Of course I do. But she seems to have so much more courage than I had. Much more sense.'

'Nonsense.' He spoke strongly. 'You can't say that. You've no idea what she's like when she's on her own. It's easier to put on a front in company. You did.'

A shadow crossed Clemmie's face. 'I realise that,' she admitted. 'I just feel that she'll be able to come to terms with it so much better than I have.'

'Oh, Clemmie.' Quentin looked wretched. 'I would give anything to wash it right out—'

'No, no.' She stretched a thin hand to him. 'Don't. Please. The last thing I want is to resurrect it again. It's over. It's been over for forty years and should have been decently buried. God knows you've done everything you could to put things right. It's not you but I who have kept disinterring it over the years. I had to keep going back and digging it up to look at it. I think that Phyllida will do better than that.'

He took her hand between his two warm ones but he couldn't look at her. 'I love you,' he said and her fingers tightened on his own.

'I know,' she said. 'And I love you. I can never decide whether it's best to love too much or not enough. If I'd loved you less I wouldn't have cared so much and if I'd loved you more I could have forgiven you more readily.'

He smiled a little. 'Trying to view it from its most positive angle,' he said, 'there's something very flattering in having your wife feel twinges of jealousy about you when you're old and ugly. Even,' he hastened to add, 'when they're totally unjustified.'

He was relieved to see that she was smiling too. Time was when he would never have dared to joke about it.

'I know I've been ridiculous,' she admitted. 'I was never very confident, you see. A little country mouse. And you were so confident and clever and all those women you knew . . .'

'Ah, Clemmie.' Quentin shook his head in distress. 'That had nothing to do with it. You know that.'

'I do really,' she agreed at once. 'It was Pippa. I should have come back and we should have mourned together. We both know that. I was as much to blame as you. I stayed here drowning in my own grief and never thinking of how you were coping.'

'You were exhausted. Worn out with nursing. I have no

excuses for what happened except the usual plea for the weakness of humanity.'

'Confidence is a strange thing.' She still held his hands tightly. 'It can help you to achieve so much but if it gets destroyed you can slip down and down and it's so hard to climb back up. I've taken longer than most would, that's all, despite all the help you've given me. We've been so happy, my darling. Let's not forget that.'

'That tea's cold.' He got to his feet. 'I'll get you some more.'

He took the cup and went away and Clemmie gave a deep sigh. She'd been right. The shadow was being dispelled at last and she felt wonderfully at peace. Her thoughts went back to Phyllida, who had been the unconscious instrument of this release, and she wondered how she could help her in return. How amazed she would be to know that two old people were still suffering the pangs of jealousy and remorse after forty years.

The trouble is, thought Clemmie now as she leaned on the bridge watching the water slipping away, we don't feel old inside. Inside we get stuck somewhere along the line and we're not so dulled to passion or pain as the young imagine. It just looks ridiculous, that's all, when you're bent double and all wrinkled.

She remembered the young Quentin carrying Pippa upon his shoulders with Gerard running at his side, and how her heart had beat at the sight of his tall strength. She smiled and shook her head at her foolishness and, taking up her stick, she left the bridge and started home.

* * *

Christina, travelling home from school on the train, was delighted that Uncle Eustace was coming for Christmas. He added a new dimension to the atmosphere of the little cottage with its utter lack of male influences. She wondered how she would react if Mum ever decided to marry again. It was extremely unlikely. As far as she could see, the only men of her mother's acquaintance belonged to other people nor did she seem to be aware of any lack in her life. Nevertheless, Christina knew that such unexpected things happened; she'd seen it with her friends at school whose lives had changed almost overnight. Some had welcomed the new man, others were jealous, and Christina tried to imagine what she might feel in similar circumstances. It was difficult to picture Mum in such a situation. She simply couldn't see her even being affectionate, let alone passionate. She was too reserved, too contained.

Christina stared out over the wintry countryside. She liked men, even old ones like Unk; they fascinated her and she liked to watch them and listen to them. She loved her father, despite the fact that she knew it upset her mother. She couldn't help it, she just loved him. He was easy-going, cheerful, amusing and, though she sometimes felt ashamed of loving someone who had hurt her mother so much, she needed him. Fortunately, he never tried to justify himself to her nor did he try to undermine her love for her mother. He accepted that he was weak, that he'd behaved badly, but that it was too late now to put things right. His love for Christina had never wavered or altered and she felt secure in it.

Christina watched the people piling off the train at Exeter and, once the journey continued, found herself looking out at the familiar landscape with the usual feeling of excitement. The tide was sweeping up the Exe estuary and the light of the setting sun was reflected in golden slivers on its choppy surface. The beach at Dawlish was empty, the sand washed smooth by the cold grey water of the encroaching sea. Across from Teignmouth the lights of Shaldon were twinkling in the gathering dusk and Christina was aware of a sense of homecoming.

She thought about Christmas with a tingle of pleasure. There would be parties and, most exciting of all, she would see Oliver again. Although she'd known him all her life, it was only in the last holiday that she'd really become aware of him as a man rather than a childhood friend. Her heart knocked a little faster as she thought about him; his broad shoulders, his long legs, his blue eyes. If only she were a little older . . . Christina sighed, put in her earphones, switched on her Walkman and settled down to a nice long fantasy.

Chapter Eleven

Phyllida had a happier Christmas than she could ever have imagined. Alistair was to be at sea and, when she heard this, Phyllida couldn't decide whether she felt relief or disappointment. In fact, she experienced something of each. Christmas being such an emotional time she was almost afraid that, if he were at home, she might be swept off her feet by it all and commit herself to things for which she was not yet ready. Her feelings for Alistair were still very confused. There were moments when she was convinced that her love for him was enough to overcome that one lapse but when he came home on leave she realised that the edge of resentment which had made things so difficult before was still there. It just wasn't going to be that simple. She couldn't get Janie out of her mind and her sense of inadequacy and hurt kept a barrier between them. How could he do such a thing, she asked herself, and still truly love her?

Gathering up her courage, she'd told him exactly how she felt and what she hoped to achieve and he was so relieved that she was prepared to give their marriage another try that he was only too ready to agree to her terms. Although it was a long way down to the West Country from the west coast of

Scotland, the travelling to and fro would be a small price to pay. After all, the boat would be at sea for a great deal of the time and he would be on courses in between, so he was prepared to make the best of it. He would have given everything he owned to turn back the clock and cancel out his night with Janie. What a fool he'd been! When he saw Phyllida's forlorn face and the reservation with which she treated him, he could have wept with misery and frustration at his stupidity.

Sometimes he did cry a little; a few tears when he longed for the tenderness and sharing which had been between them and which he had so lightly tossed away. He never let Phyllida see him weep. He avoided any device that would arouse her pity. Apart from anything else it would have seemed like cheating. He accepted her terms and did everything possible to restore the trust that had been between them.

He was quick to see that she was grateful to be spared scenes and he redoubled his efforts to build on her own hopes. She wanted it to work again, she wanted her love for him to outweigh any other feeling and that must be enough to start with. Enough! It was far, far more than he deserved and he knew it. He guessed how humiliated she was by the rumours that had travelled so quickly through the naval grapevine and writhed with shame at the thought of how he had exposed her. Whilst making no demands upon her, he made it as clear as he could that he wanted nothing more than to create a new life together. He knew that there was no question of restoring the old one. With one thoughtless act he had destroyed it and now he must start again. He was deeply touched by the mature way she was dealing with it.

After that first terrible scene she had approached the whole thing with a steady, constructive maturity which he would have thought was beyond her. She'd always been so sweet, so pliable, eager to please, ready to be advised, so much younger than his friends, that they'd grown used to treating her like a little sister, to be teased and looked after and, although he saw much deeper and knew her so much better than they did, even so, this thoughtful strength that she was showing took him by surprise and he was even more determined not to lose her.

Disappointed not to have achieved more, but refusing to despair, Alistair went back to Scotland trying to think that it was a good thing that he was at sea whilst Phyllida was attempting to come to terms with things. He knew that she longed – but couldn't quite bring herself – to make the big step across the chasm that had opened between them. At least she'd let him make love to her after they'd been to Prudence's pre-Christmas party.

There had been a point when things could have been made very much worse. Despite his gratitude that Phyllida was giving him a second chance, there had been a moment at Prudence's party when he'd felt a reaction against it. He had no doubt whatever that Prudence had heard the gossip. There was a certain reserve in her greeting to him and, when he saw Liz watching him from across the room, he guessed at once how the rumours of his fall from grace were continuing to circulate. She'd never liked him, he knew that, and she merely stared at him coldly and gave a brief nod when he smiled at her. All at once he felt an enormous resentment against womankind and Liz in particular. He knew that she was a very bitter woman and realised that she'd felt it her duty to warn Phyllida and, no doubt, inform several other people as well. He was aware of one or two glances and a few heads bent to whisper and, even whilst he felt a stab of guilt for what Phyllida must be suffering, he turned away from them all and made his way to Uncle Eustace.

'Hello, my boy.' The tall familiar figure, standing by the fire, seemed pleased to see him. 'And how are things with you?'

'Hello, Unk.' Alistair accepted a glass of punch and raised it to him. 'Happy Christmas. I'm OK. No need to ask you. I can see that you're younger than ever.'

'No flattery is too gross for me, dear boy.' Uncle Eustace beamed at him. He lowered his voice a little. 'I hear you've blotted your copybook.'

'Oh, honestly.' Alistair looked disgusted. 'Not you, too. I thought I'd be safe from gossip with you.'

'And so you are, dear boy. So you are. No reproach shall fall from my lips.'

'I should think not!' said Alistair, with a show of spirit. 'Don't tell me you went through life pure as the driven snow, Unk, because I simply shan't believe you.'

'And quite right, too.' Uncle Eustace nodded with simple pride. 'I'm not one of your New Men. We knew how to enjoy ourselves in my day.'

'Yes. Well, we're not allowed to do that any more,' said Alistair bitterly, resentment still strong within him. 'No sex, no smoking, no drinking. The water's poisoned and the air's polluted. If something tastes good it's sure to be bad for you. We mustn't do anything enjoyable and certainly nothing dangerous. We're so damned precious these days, so busy holding off death, that we've forgotten how to live.'

'You sound liverish to me.' Uncle Eustace cocked an eye at him. 'What you need is a sensible drink.'

'Can't do that!' said Alistair with exaggerated horror. 'This one'll have to do. I'm driving.'

'Dear me.' Uncle Eustace shook his head. 'You're in a bad way. Mustn't get bitter, dear boy. Committed the unforgivable sin. Have to take your med'sun.'

'You mean I should be down on my knees? *"Mea culpa*, Father, I have sinned"?' Alistair drank his punch in one angry gulp. 'It was only once, for God's sake!'

'Well,' admitted Uncle Eustace, 'I wasn't thinking so much of your, er, well, little dalliance. I was thinking more of your getting found out. That was the unforgivable sin in my day.'

He drooped a commiserating eyelid at Alistair who stared at him for a moment and then burst out laughing.

'You old devil,' he said. 'OK. You're on. Find me a decent drink and to hell with the rules and regs!'

Remembering that conversation, as the train rattled its way north, Alistair smiled to himself. He knew that it was a combination of his own resentment and Uncle Eustace's partisanship which had given him the courage to make love to Phyllida that night. He'd realised that a show of strength might be no bad thing. After all, it was unlikely that Phyllida would be capable of swallowing her pride to the extent of making any physical overture to him. If he forced the pace a little she could always comfort herself afterwards with the solace that she'd been the passive partner. The simple, releasing act of love between them might very well do some good. On the last occasion it hadn't been very successful but all this pussyfooting about could go too far and they might find themselves stuck with an impasse; he, too nervous to approach, she, too proud to ask.

Alistair felt certain that it had been a sensible move. It was important that she knew how desirable he found her and how much she moved him. Afterwards, he'd held her tightly, sensing that she might feel that he'd taken an unfair advantage, and trying to keep anything but a tender gratitude out of his reaction. She mustn't feel that he was experiencing any sense of triumph over her and was relieved when she fell asleep fairly quickly. Uncle Eustace's humour had given his own resentment a sense of purpose and his malt whisky had given him the courage to carry it out. Still smiling to himself, Alistair turned over in his bunk and settled himself to sleep.

Phyllida was glad to have some time to recover. Alistair had been quite right to take the initiative. Oddly, Liz's obvious antipathy towards him, far from making Phyllida feel the injured party and grateful for moral support, had given her a sneaking feeling of sympathy towards Alistair. When he'd turned away from them and made his way to Uncle Eustace, she'd felt a strange sense of loss. Her loyalty to him had been roused and, whilst she realised that she ought to be experiencing quite different sensations, she longed to go across to him and publicly declare how she felt about the whole situation.

Her courage had deserted her. She'd seen the dark look on his face and, sensing his anger, watched Uncle Eustace turn it away with laughter and then disappear only to return moments later with some dark gold liquid in a tumbler. There had been between them a complicity of understanding that she simply didn't dare to interrupt and she'd felt a longing to be one with Alistair again. Her relief when he'd made love to her was enormous. He'd given her no chance to make gestures nor embarrassed her with pleas which her pride might have been forced to reject. He just took her with a tenderness and passion that made all those other emotions look simply petty.

Phyllida had been missing him far more than she could have imagined. She'd suspected that knowing what she knew would, in some way, help her to miss him less, that her anger would sustain her; for she did feel angry, despite her attempts at a rational approach. Alistair's own attitude during his leave had gone a long way to encouraging her, however. He'd tried so hard to make amends that her heart had softened towards him but she was determined to make no false moves. There was a very long way to go and each single step must be sure and certain. She felt guilty that, by refusing to go to Faslane, she was depriving Lucy of a certain amount of her father's company but common sense told her that it was better to make sacrifices now. After all, Lucy was used to a father who was at sea and who came and went at irregular intervals. Meanwhile she was taken up with a whole new world of school and, as long as she did not suspect that anything was wrong between Phyllida and Alistair, no harm would be done.

When Alistair had gone back, she took a deep breath and thought about Christmas. She knew that she wasn't strong enough to face her own family, fearing that her mother, with that sixth sense she had, would detect something was amiss and probe until she discovered the truth. She needed time to adjust. Once her friends heard that she was to be alone, invitations poured in: from Prudence, from Abby, from Clemmie and Quentin. She was touched by the fact that people cared enough for her and Lucy to want to include them in that most personal of all times but she was determined that they should have their own little Christmas, too. Christmas Eve and the morning of Christmas Day she kept strictly to themselves. They decorated the tree and then went to make mince pies for Father Christmas with Lucy standing on a kitchen chair, cutting grubby circles of pastry with immense concentration. Phyllida, who could see that her supper would consist of these lovingly made delights, deflected her from making enough for the entire team of reindeer and watched her set the generous plateful beside the fireplace. She braced herself to explain just how this very large person was going to squeeze himself out into the small Victorian grate and was deeply relieved when the problem didn't present itself to Lucy who had decided that, if the reindeer weren't to get mince pies, then they might like some carrots. She bustled away to the larder and brought back a good handful, which she put beside the plate, and then remembered that Uncle Eustace had told her that she must be sure to leave Father Christmas a glass of port with which to warm himself. Substituting sherry for port – Phyllida didn't like port – she stood the glass with the other delicacies and Lucy took a deep breath of satisfaction.

'He'll like that, won't he, Mummy?'

'He'll love it.' Phyllida smiled at the small round figure, bunchy in her cosy red dressing gown, the glossy hair in two fat plaits. 'He'll have a lovely rest in the armchair while he's eating his goodies.'

'Will you see him?' Lucy's eyes were huge with the thought of it but Phyllida pursed her lips and shook her head.

'Doubt it. He comes very late, you know. I expect I'll be asleep.'

'I wish I was a mummy,' said Lucy, obviously disappointed at Phyllida's lack of enterprise. 'I'd wait up to see him. I wouldn't care how late it was.'

'Well, when you're a mummy you shall do just that.'

Phyllida swung her up into the air and then hugged her. Lucy clasped both arms round her mother's neck and gave her cheek a smacking kiss.

'How will he get down the submarine to Daddy?'

Yes, well! thought Phyllida. And I thought I'd got away with the chimney question!

'Straight down the hatch,' she said cheerfully. 'Nice ladder all ready for him. Much easier than chimneys. He can park Rudolph and the boys on the casing. No problem at all. No need to worry about Daddy.'

'Will the sailors make him mince pies?' Lucy gazed into her face anxiously.

Phyllida was quite certain that, should Father Christmas appear in the Wardroom of one of Her Majesty's submarines on Christmas Eve, he'd get more than mince pies but she considered the question carefully.

'Probably not mince pies,' she said at last. 'It's not everyone who knows how much he likes them, you know.'

'Oh, good.' Lucy wrapped her legs tightly round Phyllida's waist and they danced out of the door and into the hall and up the stairs.

Lucy's stocking was already hanging up and Phyllida tucked her into bed and kissed the rosy cheek.

'Sweet dreams,' she said. 'Not a sound or you'll frighten him away.'

Lucy, thumb in mouth, nodded solemnly and Phyllida smiled at her and turned away.

'Mummy.' Phyllida paused, her hand on the door handle.

'What is it, sweetheart?'

'I wish Daddy was here, don't you?'

'Yes,' said Phyllida, after a moment. 'Yes, of course. But it's not his fault, you know. His job is very important. He'd rather be home with us but sometimes other things have to come first.'

'Perhaps he'll see Father Christmas.'

'Perhaps he will. Good night, Lucy.'

She closed the door and went downstairs. She felt a tremendous urge to burst into tears and howl loudly but went instead to the larder and poured herself a drink. She must be cheerful for Lucy's sake if not for her own. She stood by the fireplace, sipping her wine, and her eye fell on the parcels beneath the Christmas tree. Alistair had bought presents for them both and wrapped them before he left and she saw now that one of her parcels had a card tucked into the ribbon. Standing her glass on the mantelpiece, she crouched down and removed it. She perched on the edge of the armchair and opened the envelope. The picture was a reproduction; an evening scene of a cottage from which lights streamed out

126

over the snowy landscape. A single star hung low in the deep blue of the sky and, in the distance, a solitary figure trudged towards the cottage. It was entitled 'The Homecoming'. Inside, Alistair had written a message opposite the words 'Happy Christmas'.

> When I saw this picture, I immediately identified with the figure who is returning to his home and loved ones. A fixed, stable place in an uncertain, changing world. That's how I think of you, Phyllida. You're all that matters to me and, without you, the world is an empty place and life a pointless existence. You will say, and fairly, that I should have thought about that before betraying you and our relationship. I can't keep saying I'm sorry. Although I am, in the end the words become meaningless and lose their value. Like the words 'I love you' which we scatter round mindlessly until we find the one person for whom they should have been saved. I love you, Phyllida. Only you. Always.

She stared at the words until they blurred before her eyes and, turning sideways, she leaned her arms on the side of the chair and burst into tears.

Chapter Twelve

When Jeff agreed to spend Christmas and the New Year in Sussex, staying in turn with each of their families, Claudia was overcome with relief. She'd expected that he might want to spend the holiday at home which would have certainly meant parties and socialising, with no chance of avoiding Jenny or Gavin. She couldn't decide, now, which one she most wished to avoid. Ever since Gavin had turned up and kissed her, Claudia's mind had seethed and boiled with confusion. Desperately she told and retold herself how much she had hated it, convincing herself that her treacherous response had been a form of shock. Fearfully she allowed herself to dwell on Gavin; his lean, relaxed frame, the dry, dust-coloured hair, the knowing eyes. It was quite impossible that she should have the least flickering of desire for such an uncouth man.

She watched Jeff as he moved amongst their relations and became aware of an odd feeling of resentment. His shiny hair was neat and clean, his skin smooth, his clothes smart and well matched. His manners were perfect; he was all things to all men – and women – from the youngest to the oldest and they all told her, solo and chorus, how very lucky she was to have him. Her resentment deepened. It was his fault, she told herself angrily, if she'd felt a response – even a tiny one – to Gavin's advances. If Jeff performed in bed only a fraction as much as everyone imagined such a handsome, desirable man must, then there would have been no temptation. She was only human, she reminded herself, and he'd put her in an unforgivable position. Through his inadequacies, she'd been exposed and made vulnerable. It was only when they were on the way home that she realised that she was looking forward to seeing Gavin again. At some point during the holiday, her resentment had moved her to such a degree that her view had altered.

As they drove down the A38 she sat silently beside Jeff, who rarely talked when he was driving, and examined the feeling of excitement that was churning her stomach and making her heart thump. She'd conveniently forgotten Gavin's insults about pretending to be something she wasn't and remembered only the kiss and his voice. '. . . You're a very beautiful girl, Claudia . . . You can't blame me if you turn me on . . .' Claudia wriggled a little and cast a sideways look at Jeff. Gavin had obviously sussed him out. '. . . Seems like a bit of a cold fish to me . . .' Well, he was. All these years she'd thought there was something wrong with her and now she was beginning to see that it was Jeff's fault. Gavin obviously fancied her . . .

But Gavin probably fancies anything in a skirt, said an unwelcome voice in her head. Jeff's just fastidious, that's all.

Fastidious! Claudia gave a snort of disbelief and Jeff glanced at her curiously. She gave him a brief smile, sniffed rather ostentatiously once or twice and, opening her handbag, she took out her handkerchief and blew her nose vigorously. Fastidious! The way he behaved with Jenny proved that he couldn't be anything of the sort. Maybe, after all, it was simply that he wasn't in love with her and wasn't turned on by her. It was the old fear. The excitement began to dissolve and despair crept round her heart. Perhaps she'd been too obvious from the beginning and he naturally took her for granted? She tried too hard to please him. Perhaps . . .

The idea that occurred to her was so shocking that she almost stopped breathing. Maybe it was her turn to play hard to get, to flirt and play around a little? Perhaps if she fooled around with Gavin as Jeff did with Jenny, Jeff might get jealous himself? She'd never in all their life together given him the least cause for anxiety. She'd been the one begging for favours, grateful for the least attention. Now it was time to try a different approach. Gavin had already showed that he wanted her, so why not use him to test this theory? Certainly she felt no compunction in using him. His behaviour had negated any need for consideration, as far as Claudia was concerned. The excitement was beginning to return and she settled more comfortably in her seat.

'Tired?' Jeff gave her a sideways smile. 'Not long now.'

'Longing for a cup of tea,' said Claudia evasively. 'It'll be good to be home.'

A few weeks later, she began to put her theory to the test. The weather had been too cold and wet for people to want to go out in the evening. In late January, however, Jenny had a birthday and she decided to give a party. Jeff had been very quiet since his return from Sussex and Claudia longed more and more to bring the whole thing to some conclusion. If he had fallen in love with Jenny then something must be done about it. She wasn't prepared to sit by, watching and waiting, for another moment. She dressed carefully for the party and her heart beat nervously. The trouble with the Gavins of this world was that they were unpredictable. She'd half hoped that he might turn up again at the house but, so far, she'd only seen him at the pub. He'd smiled at her from behind the bar, a secret, knowing smile, that made her feel oddly breathless and, each time she glanced in his direction, she caught him watching her. She felt completely unsettled and wondered, as they walked the short distance to Jenny's flat, how he'd behave towards her this evening.

Claudia was quite unprepared for the success of her plan. Gavin might have been forewarned, his reaction was so perfect. He kissed her hand and made much of her, waited on her every whim and treated her as if she were a princess and he a devoted subject. And beneath it all ran an electric current of excitement. Luckily, his compliments weren't so obvious as to attract everyone's notice because Jenny's younger brother, Andy, had come for a holiday and he made a third in their little group. Gavin and this boy – who was barely out of his teens – pretended to vie for Claudia's attentions, pushing each other, laughing and generally behaving like two children, which nicely masked Gavin's more personal remarks made under the cover of the noise and fun.

Claudia entered into it all and even allowed Gavin to kiss her – very briefly – while they were dancing in the small crowded space. The two men had pretended to fight over her when it came to dancing and they suddenly burst into an impromptu dance together which made everyone laugh before Gavin broke away, seized Claudia in his arms and swept her on to the floor. As they gyrated breathlessly, she caught a glimpse of Jeff's face. It was closed and grim as he watched them from across the room, oblivious of everything around him. Her heart gave a great leap of triumph and, as if Gavin knew what was in her mind, he held her more tightly and kissed her quickly and fiercely. Breathlessly, she stood quite still at the end of it and waited for her cheeks to cool before she approached Jeff. She made her way across to him just as Jenny appeared with the light buffet that she'd prepared and, having filled their plates, they perched together on one chair to eat it. Jeff barely spoke to her and Claudia smiled secretly to herself. She had no intention of soothing his anger just yet. She glanced across at Gavin but he was sitting on the floor with Andy, talking quite seriously whilst he ate his supper, and only once did he glance very quickly in their direction.

Jeff made no reference to her behaviour but that night he made love to her for the first time for weeks. It was a rather hurried, desperate affair, almost violent, and Claudia felt another surge of triumph. She'd been right, after all. What a fool she'd been in the past! It didn't occur to her that it might be rather difficult keeping Jeff's somewhat sluggish physical desire at this level. She just knew that she'd hit on a formula that worked. Added to which, she'd rather enjoyed her first efforts at serious flirting. She found herself looking forward to her next meeting with Gavin and once, rather to her horror, she found herself imagining how he would have performed in Jeff's place. She pushed that thought away quickly. There was no question of that. She was quite certain, now, that all that was needed was to give Jeff a short sharp shock which would make him see her in a different light. She'd been too eager, too ready. Next morning, as she washed up the breakfast things, she tried to remember a French proverb she'd heard once. How did it go? 'In each relationship there is always one who kisses and one who extends the cheek.' Something like that. Anyway, she was fed up with being the one who did the kissing!

She was still in a mood of pleasurable defiance when Phyllida arrived.

'Come on in. It's ages since I saw you.' Claudia looked more closely at her as she took off her coat. She looked tired and thinner and even somehow older. 'Did you have a good Christmas?'

'Better than I hoped.' Phyllida followed her into the kitchen and watched her fill the kettle. 'How about you?'

'It was fine.' Claudia prepared the coffee carefully. 'Nice to see the families.'

'Mmm.' Perching on a stool, Phyllida glanced round the kitchen. No single item was out of place; the working surfaces were clean and bare, the cooker – looking as if it had never cooked a meal in its life – twinkled brightly, even the taps sparkled aggressively. Phyllida, thinking of the muddle of her own kitchen, felt inadequate.

'It must have been awful all on your own.' Claudia put the cups and saucers on a tray. 'You didn't go home to your mum and dad?'

'No.' Phyllida had deliberately avoided that, knowing that she might not be able to hide her misery from her mother's sharp eyes. She hesitated. 'I didn't feel up to it.'

In the dustless drawing room, Claudia put the tray on a low table and lit the gas fire.

'That's better,' she said. 'More cheerful. Now.'

She poured the coffee, passed Phyllida a cup and sat back in her chair. The coffee was delicious and Phyllida felt even more depressed. She longed to tell Claudia her problems but something held her back. So far there had been no need to tell anyone about Alistair's unfaithfulness. The news had been passed round for her and she couldn't quite bring herself to blurt it out. She sipped her coffee and cast about for something to say.

'You always make me feel ashamed when I come to see you,' she said at random. 'Everything's so beautifully clean and tidy and you always look so pretty.' She looked down ruefully at her old cords. 'Lucy couldn't find her plimsolls this morning and we turned the place upside down.' She laughed a little. 'It looks like the council tip. I dread going back.'

'Well, I haven't got anything else to do, have I?' Claudia shrugged and smiled at her. 'I have to keep myself busy or I'd go mad.'

'Have you thought of trying to get a job?' Phyllida wondered just how frustrating it must be for her, alone all day.

'There's nothing going round here. I'd have to go further afield.' Claudia looked rather wistful. 'I must say it was very hard to turn down the job I was offered just before we moved. It was a well-known London design group and the salary meant I could afford to commute. It was a real boost to my confidence but Jeff wanted to move down . . .' She was silent, remembering her own reasons for wanting to leave Sussex.

They both sat for a moment, each longing to unburden herself to the other. Phyllida spoke first.

'I had a letter this morning from the agents. We've been given notice to quit.'

'Oh, no!' Claudia looked sympathetic. 'What rotten luck. You really love that house, don't you? Still, last time we spoke you were thinking of moving up to be near Alistair, weren't you?'

There was a long silence.

'The thing is,' said Phyllida at last, 'well, things have changed a bit.'

Claudia frowned a little. 'How d'you mean?'

'Alistair's been playing around.' Phyllida looked directly at her. 'He . . . slept with an old girlfriend of his when he was at Greenwich.'

Claudia could think of nothing to say and Phyllida finished her coffee abruptly and put her cup back on the tray.

'I'm really sorry. God! That's awful . . .' Claudia found her voice at last and, for want of something positive to do, refilled Phyllida's cup. 'That must have been a terrible shock for you. And it seems so unbelievable. I suppose . . . it seems silly to say it but are you absolutely certain? I mean, it's not just idle gossip?'

Phyllida shook her head and took her cup. 'No. He's admitted to it. He said it was just one night. He said he was upset about the baby, too, and when he came home I used to drain down all over him . . .'

The cup shook a little in its saucer and Claudia's heart contracted with sympathy. Her fears about Jeff and Jenny seemed to crystallise into an identification with Phyllida's pain and she put down her own cup and went to sit beside her on the sofa.

'Well, why shouldn't you? It was a dreadful thing to happen and you were on your own all through those weeks. It's only natural you should turn to him for support.'

Claudia sounded so indignant that Phyllida smiled.

'I know but I can't help feeling a bit guilty. If only I'd thought about his own disappointment as well as mine . . . That sort of thing. And it's more than that. When you're separated as much as we are you feel a sort of obligation to make the times you do have together as good as possible. It's silly, really, but you feel each weekend or leave is a holiday. I know other naval wives feel the same as I do. You feel guilty when they go back to sea if you've had a row or been a bit off. It's hell. You go over and over it in your mind and curse yourself for wasting precious time.' She shrugged. 'Anyway, it's over between him and Janie, what there was, and we're going to carry on. It's just difficult to come to terms with.'

'I should think so! And the whole situation is unreal, isn't it? It means you have to spend all your time together on your best behaviour, just in case, and then weeks and weeks all on your own again. It must be a terrible strain. And then he goes and cheats on you! I don't know how you can be so reasonable about it.'

'I'm not really reasonable.' Phyllida looked miserable. 'And now this about the house has come as a bit of a blow. I wanted to stay put, you see, while he's in Scotland. Gives me time to think things out and adjust. But I know he'll pressure me to go to Scotland now.' She grimaced. 'Oh hell! Why does everything come at once?'

'But you could find somewhere else round here, couldn't you?'

'It looks more pointed, you see. It's one thing just staying put, it's another deliberately moving to another house down here when I could be with him in Scotland. He was prepared to give in when I told him I wanted to stay but I know he wants us up there with him. He'll expect that now and it will make everything that much more difficult.' She looked despondent.

'You don't think it might be a good idea to be near him?' Claudia asked tentatively.

'It would be hell,' said Phyllida at once. 'Everyone will have heard about it in the Mess and everywhere I went I'd know people were talking about me.'

Claudia felt a shudder of horror at the thought of it. 'Do you have to tell him?' she asked. 'Couldn't you just move and tell him afterwards?'

Phyllida smiled at her. She felt a sense of ease at having unburdened herself and she was touched by Claudia's wholehearted response.

'I've thought about that,' she admitted. 'I shall have to think it all through carefully. I must be off. I've got masses to do. Come and have lunch soon. Tomorrow?'

'Lovely,' said Claudia. 'But you don't have to go. Stay and have some lunch here.'

138

'No, I really must go and sort the house out.' Reluctantly Phyllida got to her feet. 'Thanks though. And thanks for listening.'

'Don't be silly. I'll come over tomorrow then.'

Claudia waved her off and went back to the drawing room. The restraint that had crept into the relationship when she'd discovered that Phyllida had penetrated the magic circle of friends, which was still closed to her, had vanished completely. Her preoccupation with Jeff and Gavin had somewhat distracted her from her determined friendship with Abby but she still felt hurt by her exclusion. Poor Phyllida! What a terrible shock, especially so soon after losing the baby. It just showed that you shouldn't trust anyone. Her own fears, which had surfaced even as she listened to Phyllida, began to undermine her confidence and, as she was staring sightlessly at the logs which never burned or dissolved into soft plumy ash, the telephone rang.

'Hello.' It was Jeff.

'Oh. Hello.' She was aware of a slight tension between them after the unusual excesses of the previous night. 'Everything OK?'

'Yes. Fine. It's just that everyone's going to the pub for lunch and I wondered if you'd like to join us?' For a moment Phyllida was forgotten and Claudia felt a surge of pure triumph. She was on the right track at last. Never before had he invited her to the pub at lunch time. 'When you say everyone . . . ?'

'Oh.' He sounded confused. 'Well, Liz is coming. And Jenny. Sue and Jerry. Oh, and Andy's meeting us there. And Gavin will be there, of course.'

'Goodness!' Her voice was light and social. 'What a gathering. I'd love to. See you there, then. One o'clock? Fine. 'Bye.'

She replaced the receiver, her heart beating with excitement. This was exactly what she'd hoped for: a chance to be flirtatious, witty, light-hearted; another opportunity to show Jeff what he was risking if he continued to take her for granted. Claudia ran upstairs to touch up her make-up, spray herself with scent and redo her hair. Cheeks flushed, head held high, she put on her coat, seized her bag and hurried out.

Chapter Thirteen

The winter drew on and Phyllida, finishing a late breakfast after the school run, realised that it was nearly a year since she'd been pregnant with her ill-fated baby. How long ago it seemed! That happy-go-lucky, confident, trusting life she'd lived was worlds away. She experienced a tiny thrill of fear that their lives were hurrying by and they were wasting time but, when she thought about it calmly, she knew it wouldn't have made too much difference if she'd been in Scotland with Alistair away at sea. After all, he would spend every leave at home and it was the quality of their time together which was important. She still felt that she'd been right to stay put and think things through, letting time heal the wounds at a distance rather than exposing their hurts to the interested gaze of the married patch and the Wardroom. Her jealousy and pride, she was quite certain, would have had much more to feed on in that small social circle and the dangers of prolonging the rupture were not to be underestimated.

The three months' notice to quit had upset all her plans. Where would they go? To Alistair, the obvious solution would be to join him in Scotland. Or he might press his suggestion that they buy and settle down, which would put an end to the question of her leaving him. Did she really have any idea of leaving him? She examined her feelings carefully. She would have liked longer; at least the next year, whilst Alistair was away in Scotland. Perhaps it was foolish but it would have given her the time needed to test her love for him and make herself strong again. She didn't want the complication of choosing houses with all the attendant problems and commitments and decided not to tell him just yet that they must leave.

With a heavy heart, Phyllida cleared up the breakfast things. She was going to the Halliwells' for lunch and she could talk the problem over with them.

It was with Clemmie that Phyllida walked through the woods and down to the bridge after lunch. Quentin had volunteered to do the washing-up and they'd accepted his offer and set off in the pale afternoon sunshine. The light, capricious breeze was cold and Clemmie moved rather more slowly than of late. Her joints were stiffer than ever and she huddled deep into her tweed coat. Down in the wood it was more sheltered but the icy beech mast crackled beneath their feet and, where the sun had not penetrated, the twigs were rimed with frost. The water was clear and the low slanting beams of late winter sunlight lent it a cold sparkle as it raced past. The blackthorn beside the bridge was afoam with white blossom. So pure a white was it that the tree seemed to be covered with soft snow and great drifts of it covered the hedgerow that bounded the meadow. The delicate flower was at odds with the black branches and long, sharp thorns and

Phyllida and Clemmie were enchanted by the spectacle of its lavish beauty.

They stood on the bridge with the sun on their shoulders and stared into the chilly depths beneath.

'You won't go to Faslane then?' asked Clemmie.

They'd talked through lunch about her need to find somewhere to live and discussed the option of joining Alistair. Phyllida had said that she didn't want to move Lucy, who was settling in so well at Meavy but, even in her own ears, it had sounded more like an excuse than a good reason.

'I don't want to go.' Phyllida continued to stare down into the water. 'You know why really, don't you? Abby told you about Alistair and his Wren, didn't she?'

'Yes,' said Clemmie after a pause. 'Yes, she did. Only because she didn't want anything said that might hurt you. Not to gossip.'

'I realise that. I'm glad she told you. It makes it easier, not to have to pretend. But that's why I don't want to go to Scotland. I need more time and it would be so much more difficult up there. Everyone would know, you see, and I'd have to be much more social. I can be quiet here.'

'I can understand that.' Clemmie remembered with vivid clarity how she'd hated social occasions once she'd known about Quentin; each woman had been a threat, every conversation a possible flirtation. Her heart ached for Phyllida. She longed to sympathise, warn, comfort, all at the same time and, in her inadequacy, remained silent.

'I feel very extreme about it, you see.' Phyllida perched on the bridge, turned sideways. 'I feel if I can't love him enough for it not to matter then it's best we split up. I don't believe that you could ever quite forgive or forget something like that, do you?'

'No,' said Clemmie, after an even longer pause. 'No, I don't think so.'

'No. Well then. That means I have to be certain that I love him so much it doesn't matter.'

'That would be a great deal of love.'

'I know.' Phyllida pushed her cold hands deep into her pockets. 'And sometimes I think that I *do* love him that much and sometimes I'm not sure.' She looked up at Clemmie. 'I imagine them together.'

Her face looked stiff with a kind of horror and Clemmie involuntarily touched her arm.

'Oh, my dear.'

'I try not to,' said Phyllida defensively, as if Clemmie had accused her of something. 'I can't help it. It just comes. Do you know what I mean?'

'And you don't think it would be easier if you were together?' Clemmie ignored the question, not ready to commit herself, to admit how very well she understood.

'Not in Faslane.' Phyllida shook her head decisively. 'It's too small and claustrophobic. I feel that this is the right way. I just wish we didn't have to move. It will be easy enough to find something to rent, I expect. It just makes an opportunity for pressure.'

Clemmie looked away, an idea crystallising at the back of her mind, and gave a little cry as the dipper sped out from under the bridge and up river.

'What is it?' asked Phyllida, startled.

'It was the dipper,' said Clemmie. She looked surprised,

almost excited, and she suddenly shivered.

Phyllida gave an exclamation of concern.

'You're frozen,' she said remorsefully. 'I've kept you standing about in the cold while I droned on. Come on. Let's go back.'

After Phyllida had left, hurrying away to fetch Lucy from school, Quentin set off with Punch at his heels to walk on the moor above the wood. He rarely walked there these days except in the warmest weather but the clear blue sky and the setting sun drew him up on the slopes where he looked out at the eternally satisfying scene: at the stony, majestic tors high above the river valleys; at the inky blue pine woods like dark shadows in the folds of hills whose grassy spaces glowed red-gold in the dazzling light from the west. The fitful breeze was like ice in his nostrils, his breath hung in clouds on the frosty air and his skin seemed to shrivel from his old bones but he was seized with a great exhilaration and his heart swelled with joy. Another winter was nearly past and he was still here; walking in this beloved landscape. They were both here, still together, but Clemmie's increasing frailty was an anxiety to both of them and he wondered how she would manage should anything happen to him.

Gerard had paid a brief visit after Christmas and his shock at the way they'd aged since he'd last seen them was undisguised. He was insistent that they should sell The Grange and move into Tavistock. Quentin knew that Clemmie was disappointed that Gerard obviously hadn't, even for a moment, considered keeping The Grange for himself and his family. She was hurt that he was content to let the house which had been in her family for generations pass to strangers without a second thought. She'd said nothing but Quentin had seen the shadow in her eyes and, to cover her silence, he'd laughed off the idea, saying that they were good for a few more years yet. Gerard's lifted brows suggested that he thought otherwise and, just before he left, he took his father aside and urged his point.

'What if one of you fell?' he asked reasonably. 'Or there was an accident? Neither of you is strong enough to look after the other. Mother couldn't lift you or look after herself. Wouldn't it be wise to move now? Choose something together while you're both fit and enjoy making a new home? It's much worse, you know, when one's left and has to do it all alone, along with the shock and grief.'

Wise words and Quentin remembered them as he walked on the hills in the sunset. In his heart he knew that Gerard was right and began to frame sentences with which to prepare Clemmie for his capitulation. How on earth would she manage if he died and she had to cope with a move, all alone to a strange, unfriendly place? At no point had Gerard suggested that both or either of them would be welcome in his own home. Quentin was slowly coming to the conclusion that they must make the most of this spring and summer and try to get things organised before next winter.

The sun looked as if it were balancing on the farthest hills. It would disappear quickly now, the glow fading, the shadows deepening and the dusk advancing swiftly. Quentin watched the stars appearing in the eastern sky and turned for home. At least this last year had been a truly happy one. Since the advent of Phyllida and Lucy into their lives, the shadow was almost gone. Quentin felt that he could show his very real affection for them both, knowing that Clemmie's reaction would be one of genuine pleasure. How good it was to feel Lucy's childish warmth in his arms and to respond naturally to Phyllida's farewell hug! What ease and comfort it brought to tease and talk naturally to them both, without fearing that it might be misunderstood by the listening Clemmie.

He remembered Clemmie's words and he, too, had the oddest sensation that Pippa had been suddenly restored to them; both as the child she'd been and as the woman she would have become. The friendship had deepened so quickly and, although it was almost impossible for him to believe, Phyllida and Lucy seemed to extract a similar benefit from the relationship. It was wonderful, too wonderful to question or analyse. And a move need not mean a cessation of this ever-growing love.

Unless, warned a cautious voice, they move away.

Quentin sighed and stopped a moment for Punch, plodding behind, to catch him up.

'Come on, old chap,' he said. 'You're not really up to it either, are you? Not much further.' He stooped to pat the elderly dog, who wagged his tail valiantly before they set forth again.

The kitchen was warm and welcoming and Clemmie turned from the Esse, her cheeks flushed like a girl's, her eyes happy, her smile warm. He pressed his cold cheek to hers and she held him tightly for a moment.

'You're both much too old to go walking about on the moor in the dark,' she said lightly.

He sighed as he took off his coat, remembering his resolve. 'You're right, I'm afraid,' he said ruefully. 'I wondered whether old Punch was going to make it back. At one point I had a dreadful fear that I might have to carry him.' He watched her as she drew a tray of scones from the oven and summoned all his willpower. 'In fact, it made me think a bit. I've had an idea . . .'

'So have I,' she said and her voice was excited, full of enthusiasm. 'A really wonderful one.'

She turned the scones on to a cooling rack as he stared at her in surprise and she smiled at him.

'Whatever can it be?' he asked and felt strangely apprehensive.

'I thought that we could offer Phyllida a home with us. Just until Alistair finishes in Scotland. She's got nowhere to go and she doesn't want to have to make any irrevocable decisions yet. Oh, Quentin, it would be so lovely, wouldn't it? Lucy's such a darling and Phyllida's almost like my own daughter to me. What d'you say?'

The idea was so extraordinary that Quentin was dumbfounded. Never could he have imagined a situation in which Clemmie would suggest opening her home to another woman. Well, two women! She took his silence for disapproval and stretched out her hands to him.

'Would you hate it?' she asked pleadingly. 'It's such a big house. That little suite that we did for Gerard when he started to come home with the children is almost completely self-contained. They needn't be too much under our feet.' Some of the happiness faded out of her face. 'Is it such a crazy idea?'

'No.' He took her hands. 'Not crazy at all, if it's really

what you want. And what she wants. Have you . . . ? Did you . . . ?'

'No.' Clemmie shook her head. 'Not without talking to you first. It came to me on the bridge. Just flashed into my mind and as I thought it . . . Oh, Quentin, the dipper flew out from underneath the bridge.'

She stared up at him and he drew her closer, touched by her faith and knowing with a deep certainty that the shadow so long between them had passed away.

'In that case there's no question,' he said. 'The dipper has always known what's best for us but we've got to be certain that it's right for them, too. Alistair may have something to say to it. We'll think it through very carefully and then you can speak to her.'

Clemmie reached up to kiss him.

'Bless you, my darling. I feel so sure that it's the right thing to do. And it's only for a year. Hardly that.' She began to make tea and then turned. 'Oh. You said that you had something to tell me.' She shook her head, smiling. 'I was too excited by my idea. Tell me now.'

'I don't think it really matters now,' said Quentin slowly. 'It was just a thought I had when I was out walking. Somehow it's no longer important.'

Chapter Fourteen

Claudia sat on her paved terrace in the warm March sunshine reviewing her situation. She'd begun to realise that, in attempting to deal with Jeff's infatuation with Jenny by arousing his jealousy, she was complicating the problem rather than solving it. The real trouble lay in the fact that, in encouraging Gavin, she'd bitten off rather more than she could chew. She had no power over him and he seemed unaware of the rules that govern polite society. She remembered the image she'd had of him the first time she'd seen him at her party: a tiger amongst well-behaved domestic cats.

Claudia stretched thoughtfully. He'd turned up at the house one afternoon recently with Andy and they'd both still been there when Jeff arrived back from the office. Gavin and Andy were in a merry mood; paying Claudia extravagant compliments, pretending to fight over her and generally playing the fool. Claudia enjoyed this sort of thing. They kissed her hand and nuzzled her neck, complimented her on her clothes and excitingly, underneath it all, was the smouldering reminder of Gavin's real desires. He let her know it without rousing Andy's suspicions, which made it all the more delicious, and Jeff arrived to find her flushed and rather silly and all of them well into their second bottle. In his dark suit, with his neat, short hair, polished shoes and his serious face, he'd made a noticeable contrast to the other two and Claudia felt rather irritated by his taciturnity, his unwillingness to join in. He was always willing enough to fool around with Jenny, she reminded herself. He'd said he had some work to finish and closed himself in the little study whilst Gavin and Andy made faces at each other, pretending to be chastened, and said they'd better go.

Reluctantly she saw them out and went to prepare some supper. Jeff reappeared, more in command of himself, and Claudia – not unpleased with the situation – had been a little cool.

'Do they often turn up?' he asked and his voice still held a certain irritation.

'Not often,' she replied evasively. 'Why?'

But he'd shrugged at that and muttered something about Gavin drinking too much at the pub and that Andy was a bad influence. Claudia smiled to herself.

'Oh, they're OK,' she said tolerantly. 'Don't be so stuffy. Andy's trying to find a job. He's decided to stay down here for a bit.'

'Poor Jenny told me that she's finding it a bit cramped in her little flat,' he said unguardedly. 'She's got hardly any privacy at all with him there.'

Claudia felt a stab of jealousy. Why should he be worrying about Jenny's privacy? Had he ever been invited back to Jenny's flat after work? All the old fears came rushing back and she took refuge in a rather haughty silence which

Jeff could interpret how he chose.

Now, Claudia gave a sigh of dissatisfaction. Her confidence – boosted by Gavin and Andy's behaviour – had been dented by Jeff's remark about Jenny's privacy and, unable to enjoy her power derived from the boys' visit, she found herself feeling insecure. Nevertheless, that night they'd made love again and Claudia was able to convince herself that making Jeff jealous worked. How to keep it up? That was the real problem. It was becoming clear that Gavin wouldn't be prepared to let himself be used indefinitely.

The previous afternoon, he'd arrived at the house alone and behaved very badly. Claudia frowned a little at the rather unpleasant memory. She'd started by being rather distant but hinting that she wasn't averse to a flirtatious few moments. He'd seized her and kissed her rather roughly and she'd been aware of the claws and the teeth, and the muscles rippling with lazy power beneath the tiger's fur. Frightened, she'd tried to draw back and quite a tussle had followed. She'd been forced to cry out and had seen, as he released her, a look almost of contempt and something else in his eyes. Closing her own eyes against the sun, Claudia tried to interpret the expression. It was almost a look of boredom; as if he wouldn't continue to waste his time if something more rewarding than giggles and a few daring caresses wasn't forthcoming.

He'd backed off and apologised – well, as good as – but she couldn't forget what she'd seen in his face. There had been a strained atmosphere and he'd left quite quickly and now, today, sitting in the sunshine, Claudia tried to make sense of things. Clearly, Gavin wasn't a man to flirt with if you weren't prepared to deliver the goodies. She was getting out of her depth and, although Jeff had been much more passionate in the past weeks, she had no conviction that, without a certain amount of competition, he'd be able to sustain it. She felt frustrated and upset. Even when she'd fought Gavin off, she hadn't felt virtuous and justified in her action. She'd felt prudish and immature and rather foolish and knew that his opinion of her was roughly the same as her own: hence the expression of boredom.

Feeling sorry for herself, Claudia got up and went into the house. Nothing ever worked out right for her. Not even the friendship with Abby and her friends had materialised, yet everyone had welcomed Phyllida with open arms. At the thought of it she was almost tempted to pour herself a gin and tonic or a glass of wine but, somehow, she'd never grown accustomed to having a drink just because she felt like one. She'd been brought up to look upon alcohol as an adjunct to a meal or to do with celebrations and when she was alone she could never quite overcome the feeling that it was rather wrong to turn to the bottle in emergencies.

Instead, she went upstairs to the little boxroom with the intention of finding some photographs which she'd promised to send to her mother. The boxroom was still – to Claudia's eyes – in rather a muddle. Some old clothes, on their way to the charity shop, lay in a pile on the single bed and there were several boxes of photographs and odds and ends beside them. She looked through the folders in a rather desultory way, selected a few to be gone through more carefully and glanced around the room. It occurred to her, standing there in the quiet sunny room, that it would make a charming nursery. In a flash, she had it redecorated, with a cot in place of the bed and saw herself sitting on a low nursing chair with a baby in her arms, and in that same moment she knew the answer to her dilemma.

It was quite simple. What she and Jeff needed was a child. Never mind his convictions that he'd be an indifferent father. She knew now that she should never have listened to him for so long. A child would bring them close, give her thoughts a new healthy direction and protect them both from temptation. She looked around again at the little room. It was perfect. She thought of the fun of all the preparations, her heart beat fast with excitement and she smiled to herself. As she made her way back downstairs she decided that she would say nothing to Jeff just yet. She'd stop taking the pill and see what happened. It would be much better to present him with a *fait accompli* and carry him along in her own enthusiasm and joy. Meanwhile, she must continue to keep Gavin interested. Jeff's new passion must be sustained until she'd achieved her goal.

Claudia stood in the hall for a moment and breathed a great sigh of relief. She felt quite certain that her problems were nearly over and that she and Jeff were on the brink of a new and happy phase of married life. Why on earth had she waited so long? Claudia shook her head at her own stupidity and went into the kitchen. Perhaps a drink – just a small one – wasn't such a bad idea after all!

Abby heaved the dirty clothes into the washing machine, added the plastic ball containing the detergent and slammed the door. She twiddled the knobs with a dexterity born of practice and remembered, as the machine burst into life, that she hadn't put any softener into its little drawer.

'Hell and damnation!' she muttered and turning her back on the utility room went back to the kitchen.

She took out some apple cake and cut a generous slice. Breaking off a corner, she put a large piece into her mouth, swung round and gave a loud squawk of alarm as she came face to face with Oliver. She choked, coughing violently and waving Oliver away as he tried to thump her on the back.

'My God, Oliver! Don't do that!' she cried, as soon as she could speak. 'Creeping up on me like that! You frightened me to death.'

She scrabbled amongst the muddle on the table and Oliver watched, amused, as she took a cigarette from a crumpled packet and lit up. She inhaled deeply and sat down at the table, reaching for the ashtray and, suddenly, Oliver had a clear mental image of her as a girl. Definitely café society, old Abby, he thought as he sat down opposite and grinned at her. He saw her in his mind's eye: straight black hair cut short, black stockings on thin legs, huge shapeless jersey, elbows on a beer-stained table, her eyes narrowed, peering through wreaths of cigarette smoke. And in the background, a jazz quartet, the swish of the brush, the strum of the bass. And a singer, also black, crooning softly. Yes, that was Abby; very fifties; very Audrey Hepburn.

'How on earth did you meet William, Abby?' he asked.

Abby smiled reminiscently. 'He was at school with my brother,' she said. 'And one day he invited me to the Sandhurst Ball. All those uniforms. I couldn't resist! What are you grinning at?'

'What an incestuous class you are! Same nannies, same

schools, same regiments! I see you as a bit of a rebel, to tell you the truth. I'm surprised you should have settled so readily for country life.'

'So was I!' said Abby frankly. 'But I was an Army wife for a few years before William's pa died and he inherited.'

'And now it's all dinners with the High Sheriff and the Pony Club.' Oliver shook his head. 'What a con it all is.'

'I'd like to point out that William *is* the High Sheriff, but never mind all that. To what do I owe the pleasure of this visit?'

'I'm in serious trouble.' Oliver smiled at her across the table and Abby was reminded again of his grandfather. 'I need some advice.'

'Good Lord!' said Abby. 'Whatever can it be? Have you told Cass? My God! You haven't got Sophie pregnant, have you?'

'Certainly not,' said Oliver indignantly. 'What an idea. I've fallen in love with a married woman and I don't know what to do about it.'

Abby stared at him, momentarily bereft of speech. Of all the children – her own, her friends' and her relations' – Oliver had always seemed the least likely to do anything foolish and she was taken aback at his confession. He was watching her quizzically as she stubbed out her cigarette and pulled herself together.

'Do I know her?' she asked and he nodded.

'It's Phyllida,' he said. 'Silly, isn't it? But I can't seem to help myself. There's something about her that's got right under my skin. I know there's something wrong with her marriage but I don't know what it is. Can you tell me?'

'Oh, Oliver,' said Abby anxiously. 'Oh, honestly, love. You mustn't. You simply mustn't. It's all too messy. Alistair's been unfaithful to her and she was terribly hurt and upset but I don't think she really wants to leave him. And there's Lucy. Honestly, love. You mustn't rock the boat.'

'Don't panic.' Oliver smiled reassuringly at her. 'She hasn't got a clue how I feel. I just wanted to find out how things stand with her. Nobody else knows.'

'Of course not and I shan't say a word, naturally. Oh, how awful for you.' Distressed, Abby lit another cigarette. 'I do agree that she's an absolute sweetie but you mustn't poach. Not until she's decided, anyway . . .'

'Fair enough. I just wondered, that's all. Let's forget it. How about some coffee?'

'Of course,' agreed Abby, relieved at his ready capitulation. 'Sorry. I wasn't thinking. I haven't seen you for ages, have I? So what's the latest news? How's life in London? Did you get invited to that job interview?'

After he'd gone, Abby sat on at the table thinking about him. Despite his good looks and charming ways, he'd had very few love affairs. She remembered that there'd been a girl at Cambridge he'd brought home once or twice. She was very young and it was obviously a case of first love for both of them. It lasted most of his time at university but seemed to die a natural death once he'd graduated and, as far as she knew, there'd been no sign of anyone since. It would be a pity if he really fell in love with Phyllida but Abby suspected that his emotions were those of the knight errant; she roused his protectiveness and her situation made him want to care for her.

158

Abby sighed and got to her feet. Phyllida wasn't the sort to play tit for tat and it was unlikely to come to anything. Even so, she couldn't quite put it out of her mind as she went to hang the washing out.

Chapter Fifteen

Phyllida was completely taken aback at Clemmie's invitation to make The Grange her home whilst she was looking for something more suitable and trying to get her feelings sorted out. She simply didn't know how to answer and Clemmie, understanding her dilemma, told her to go away and think about it. She showed her the suite of rooms that had been made into self-contained accommodation when Gerard got married and started to come home with a family. It was very pleasant but, after her roomy Victorian villa, Phyllida could see that it would feel rather cramped.

'Of course, you can use the rest of the house,' said Clemmie quickly, reading her expression accurately. 'In fact we hope you would want to. The idea of young people about the place is lovely. We've missed the family dreadfully. I can quite see it wouldn't do permanently but while Alistair's away so much . . .' She hesitated. She didn't want to force Phyllida into anything. 'We always hoped that, when we were too old to cope, we'd get someone to live in,' she said, looking round the apartment. 'This would have been just right for a housekeeper. Sadly, we can't afford it. Never mind. You could look on it as a bolt hole.' She smiled at Phyllida, keeping her voice light. 'A place to tide you over, so that you don't have to be pushed into something you don't want. Think about it.'

Phyllida thought about it. When she was alone, with Lucy in bed, she thought how nice it would be to wander down for a chat with Clemmie or a game of Scrabble with Quentin; to have the occasional meal with them instead of eating alone so regularly. The thought, too, of having immediate access to the moor and the woods was a very attractive one, especially with summer close at hand. Phyllida sighed and shook her head. She knew, too, how difficult it could be to share a house with another set of people once you were used to running your own home. Even with her mother, she found things reached straining point very quickly these days. Clemmie might say that she'd love to have them around but she and Quentin must be very set in their ways by now. Would it be fair to them; or to Lucy?

Phyllida wandered out into the garden. The evenings were drawing out but it was too cold to do anything more than stroll round, looking at the early blooms that had survived frost and biting winds. In a few days Alistair would be home and she could put Clemmie's idea to him. She had very little doubt that he would reject it. Even if he were not to see the advantage that imminent homelessness gave him in their own private struggle, he wouldn't be happy at the idea of sharing a house, even a big one with his own apartments. Phyllida turned back across the lawn. The fact remained that Alistair would be rarely there and she felt that his behaviour had given her the right to take a few decisions for herself.

Even so, she told herself, they must be the right ones for

all of us. I mustn't get carried away by a sense of grievance or cut off my nose to spite my face.

Nevertheless, the thought of a few months at The Grange was a tempting one and, as Phyllida reasoned to herself, it was for a short time only. As soon as Alistair came ashore they must make other arrangements. It began to take shape in her mind as a kind of extended holiday, a shelving of one or two responsibilities. She was not aware just how much she looked upon Clemmie and Quentin as substitute parents who were without the irritating habits and rights of the genuine article. As the days passed and Alistair's leave drew nearer, Phyllida grew more nervous. The time for thinking was past and the testing time of action and decision was upon her.

She was not prepared for Alistair's absolute rejection of the idea. He was not predisposed to consider it for a moment and Phyllida felt a sense of injustice beginning to stir. He immediately saw the advantage he'd been handed and, rather unwisely, began to push for the solution which would be the happiest for himself. He wanted Phyllida and Lucy to join him in Scotland, postponing a decision as to where to settle permanently until he'd finished with his present appointment. He overestimated Phyllida's softening towards him at the end of his Christmas leave and the effect his card had upon her. Her letters had given him hope and his welcome home had been much warmer than he had dared to imagine during the long weeks at sea.

Consequently, when the suggestion of a temporary move to The Grange was raised, he rejected it with a finality – and a lack of sensitivity – which raised Phyllida's partially smoothed hackles. Since these conversations only took place when Lucy – who was on holiday – was in bed, they tended to drag themselves out in a fragmented and unsatisfactory manner. During the day, Phyllida, who was determined that Lucy should have no suspicion of the discord between her parents, made such efforts that Alistair felt confident that he'd made his point but, as the time approached for his return to Faslane, they were no nearer a solution. Anxiety made Alistair brutally realistic and Phyllida's warmth and evident desire to make the marriage work made him overconfident. The combination was unfortunate.

'Honestly, Phylly,' he said, on their last night, as he carried their after-supper coffee into the sitting room, 'you don't seriously imagine that we could shake down happily with a couple of old dears who are obviously far too set in their ways to cope with such an invasion? We'd all drive each other mad within a week.'

'You'd hardly be there anyway. We're talking about two lots of leaves at the most. Four weeks, that's all, as far as you're concerned,' said Phyllida. 'And Clemmie and Quentin aren't like that. They're very sweet and easy-going.'

Alistair gave a short laugh. 'So you keep saying. Wait till they've had Lucy roaring round at half-past six in the morning or screaming the place down when she falls over.'

'Lucy's very quiet for her age,' said Phyllida defensively. 'And they love her. They lost their own little girl at about that age.'

'So you've told me,' said Alistair. '*Ad nauseam*,' he added, rather unwisely and Phyllida stiffened, hurt. 'That doesn't mean that we could all live together happily. Look how strained it gets with your mother when we go back. You can't wait to get away.'

'It's not at all the same. And it's only for a few months till you finish driving. It would be lovely for Lucy and me to have some company while you're away.'

'Then come to Scotland.' Alistair saw his chance and grabbed it. 'If you were up there at least we'd be together when the boat's in. And there are lots of our friends up there.'

'I don't want to come to Scotland!' cried Phyllida, setting her mug down with a bang. 'You know I don't! I'd hate it. Everyone gossiping and looking knowing. And what about Lucy? She's settled so happily at school. Why drag her away and make her start another new one for nine months at the most? Why don't you think about us for a change?'

Alistair stared with alarm at her flushed angry face and realised that he'd handled things very badly.

'I'm sorry, Phylly. Don't be cross,' he said remorsefully. 'I miss you both so much, you see. I know you don't want to come to Scotland and I can see why. I realise I'm being selfish and I honestly don't want to push you but that doesn't mean that I want to become some sort of lodger to a couple of old crumblies who can see the advantage of a strong young couple around the place! Don't get too carried away by the generosity of this wonderful offer. I'm sure they've sized you up and realised how very useful you'd be.'

Phyllida, who had begun to soften at the beginning of this speech, was on her feet by the end of it.

'That's a horrid thing to say.' Her voice shook and she gazed at him almost with dislike. 'It's a genuine offer made to help me out and give me time to sort out my own mind—'

'Oh, I see,' Alistair stood up, thrusting his hands into his pockets and with something very like a sneer on his face. 'So you've opened your heart to the dear old things and told them what a shit I am and they're offering you a shelter from the cold hard world. How very touching.'

'You . . . you pig!' said Phyllida, inadequately. 'You think of no one but yourself, do you? If you hadn't been so selfish we wouldn't be in this position at all. I'm doing my best to come to terms with it . . .'

'Oh God.' Alistair turned away, his eyes rolled heavenward. 'Here we go again.' Rage at his own stupidity and an element of self-pity drove him on. 'One bloody night, for Christ's sake! Does it really warrant all this drama? I almost wish I'd done it more often. At least it would make all this penance worthwhile!'

'Well, go on, then. Why don't you?' Phyllida's face was white. 'I don't think I care any more. I shall go to The Grange and you can stay in Scotland with all your wonderful friends. That will give me all the time I need and you needn't bother to come down. We'll discuss it again in nine months. No! Don't touch me! You can't get round me again. Go and find another Wren to spend your last night with!'

She fled upstairs and Alistair stood silently, head bent, cursing himself. He realised that, with a few stupid words, he'd destroyed all that they'd achieved in the last few months and he had just nine hours to put things right.

It wasn't nearly long enough. Phyllida drove him to the station next morning, after a night locked in the spare bedroom and deaf to his whispered pleadings, and if Lucy thought her parents' manner odd she put it down to the earliness of the hour. Alistair caught his train feeling desperate, remorseful and aggrieved in equal parts and Phyllida drove home feeling hurt, defiant and thoroughly miserable. She was almost relieved when Lucy went back to school so that she could relax into her unhappiness, but still she delayed in giving Clemmie an answer. Part of her wanted desperately to put things right. But how?

On a warm morning in early April she came out of Crebers and saw Oliver crossing the road towards her. His face lit up with such genuine pleasure when he saw her that her unhappy heart was eased a little and she smiled at him.

'What are you doing here?' she asked. 'Are you on holiday?'

'I am.' Oliver took in her pale face and the shadows under the huge grey eyes. 'Giles, that's the chap I work with in London, has come down to see his mum. We're taking a bit of a break. Just a week or two. So how are things with you?'

'All right.' She made a little face and wondered how much Oliver knew. He looked so nice, standing there, watching her thoughtfully, that she slipped her arm in his. 'I'm miserable,' she admitted. 'Fed up.'

'Now there I can help you,' he said promptly. 'But you'll have to tell me what sort of person you are first. Each of us requires a different form of cheering up. Giles's mum, for instance, would want to commune with nature, undisturbed by other influences. My ma would immediately set out on a huge shopping spree but my sister, Gemma, would demand to be taken to the pub so that she could pour out all her troubles whilst getting pleasantly pissed. There are other treatments for the condition, of course. Do any of these appeal?'

Phyllida gazed around her, frowned a little and looked up at him. 'I'd like to do all of them,' she said simply.

Oliver burst out laughing. 'All of the above,' he said. 'So what we'll do is this. We'll drop your car back at Yelverton and I'll drive you slowly across the moor so that you can drink in all that nature. We'll go on down into Exeter and do the shopping bit and then I'll take you into Coolings and you can do the telling of troubles, and the drinking. What about it?'

'Oh, Oliver. I should love it,' she sighed. 'It sounds terribly decadent and very appealing. I've got to be back for Lucy, though. She's having tea with a friend but I mustn't be late.'

'Plenty of time,' said Oliver comfortably. 'It's early yet. Had coffee?'

'Not yet.' Phyllida realised that she was still clutching his arm and let it go rather reluctantly. There was something strangely comforting about him and the thought of spending the day in his company was both exciting and relaxing.

'We'll have one at the Bedford and then I'll follow you back home.'

Oliver jumped to no presumptuous conclusions about her friendliness. He knew very well that she looked upon him much as Gemma did and that the way she'd taken his arm had no significance. Oliver liked women, knew their ways and enjoyed their company. If there was any danger in the proposed outing it was to himself. The painful, foolish, ecstatic phenomenon, known as infatuation, had him in its grip and he could only endure it in silence until it was over. This day together was a delightful and unexpected bonus and he intended to make the most of it.

They made their way across Bedford Square, Phyllida's spirits rising at the prospect of such a jolly outing.

'You're rather like Uncle Eustace,' she said, somewhat irrelevantly as they waited for the traffic.

'Now is that a compliment?' mused Oliver.

'Definitely!' Phyllida laughed a little. 'You have the same breadth of vision. You both think big. I love him.'

'Lucky chap,' said Oliver lightly, hurrying her across between a coach and a taxi. 'Somehow I don't think Liz feels the same way about him.'

'I know.' Phyllida chuckled. 'He can be rather naughty. He's coming down again soon, she tells me. He likes to come before the great holiday trek starts. Tell you what! I'll take you both out to lunch. What about it? Don't you think it would be fun?'

Oliver smiled at her as they went up the steps and his heart beat a little faster at the thought of more time in Phyllida's company. 'I can think of nothing I should like better,' he assured her and followed her into the bar.

Chapter Sixteen

Claudia was surprised at how relieved she was once she knew that Phyllida was not going to be moving away. It occurred to her that this was the first really close friend she'd had for some years, since she'd become afraid of people getting too close and finding out her secrets. It was a tremendous relief to have someone to talk to, to have little jollies with and, although she never breathed a word about her own problems, she felt deep down that she might be able to if it were to become necessary.

It had come as rather a shock to hear Phyllida talk quite openly about her fears. She was never afraid to show her weaknesses or listen to advice or discuss how she felt. Claudia imagined that people would despise her if they realised that she had problems and Phyllida's approach helped her to see that this need not be the case. On the other hand, she never pried, never pressed Claudia to discuss her private life. She was a relaxing companion and Claudia was more than ready to encourage her in the move to The Grange.

'I'm a bit worried about Lucy,' Phyllida confided one afternoon as they sat in her garden. 'It's going to be a bit of a culture shock for Clemmie and Quentin having a five-year-old in the house after all these years, don't you think?'

'Don't see why.' Claudia shook her head. 'After all, she's not rowdy is she? Or precocious? She's such a funny little thing. So old-fashioned, I always think.'

'Is she?' Phyllida looked anxious. 'Perhaps that's because we've been on our own together so much. Alistair's friends are that much older than me and their children are round about ten and eleven. Too old for Lucy. She's made some friends at school, of course.'

'It wasn't meant to be a criticism. I think it's nice,' protested Claudia. 'Children are so pushy these days.'

She smiled a secret smile to herself, nearly certain that she was pregnant.

'Oh, well.' Phyllida looked resigned. 'It's too late to do anything about it now.'

'About what?' asked Claudia. 'Lucy or the move?'

'Oh, the move. It's far too late to do anything about Lucy!'

'It'll be fine, you'll see,' said Claudia comfortingly. 'Stop worrying.'

'You must come over and meet Clemmie and Quentin. I'm sure you'll love them. They've told me to invite my friends and not to be inhibited by the fact that they're around.'

Claudia was silent. It seemed, after all, as if she were to be introduced to the magic circle of friends she'd so longed to meet and she wondered briefly how Abby would react to find her there. At least Phyllida wasn't ashamed to have her for a friend!

'I'd love to,' she said. 'It sounds rather fun.'

'Well, it is. Our bit is quite self-contained but it's not that big. It's the sort of place that's fine all the time you're alone but a man in it will make it seem sort of overcrowded. D'you know what I mean? It'll be fine for a short while. And, after all, Alistair will only be there for two weeks at a time.' She hesitated. 'If he comes at all, that is.'

Claudia looked at her sharply. 'How d'you mean?'

Phyllida made a face. 'He's going to be very cross about it,' she admitted. 'I've gone against what he wanted. I've never done that before and he won't like it.'

'But it hardly affects him, does it?' asked Claudia. 'Not while he's at sea. Surely he can put up with it for short bursts? Perhaps you could go away together while he's on leave?'

'He wouldn't like that either. When he's on leave he likes to be in his own home.'

'Well, he can't have everything, can he?' retorted Claudia. 'He shouldn't have played about.'

Phyllida smiled. Claudia's indignation on her behalf was always very touching.

'You're right,' she said. 'He'll have to lump it.' She glanced at her watch. 'I must go and get Lucy. Coming?'

'OK.' Claudia hauled herself out of the old basketwork chair. 'I must admit I love to see all the little ones coming out.'

Phyllida glanced at her and raised her eyebrows. 'Getting broody?'

'Why not?' asked Claudia casually.

'I'll lend you Lucy for a weekend.' Phyllida grinned. 'That'll put you off. Now where on earth did I leave my keys? You go round to the car and I'll lock up and come out the front.'

Claudia strolled through the garden and along the side of

the house. She felt contented and confident. Part of her longed to confide in Phyllida but part hung back, unwilling to commit herself until she knew for sure. She thought about being pregnant and excitement swelled through her. If only it were so! She was quite certain now that it would solve the problems that had arisen. She'd been a fool to be swayed by Jeff's feelings on the subject of parenthood, too ready to fall in with his wishes, to push down her own needs. Sometimes it was right to take decisions for other people and, after all, something had to be done. It was intolerable, going on as she and Jeff were now. The baby would weld them back together and banish other distractions.

She watched Phyllida come hurrying out of the front door and felt a surge of affection for her. Things were turning out right after all!

Uncle Eustace was very happy to be back in Devon. On his return to Shropshire, his round of gardening and reading and the regular meetings with his friends seemed strangely pointless for, without Monica's acerbic wit, these little gatherings – shrinking now as death claimed one or two of them or illness made activities less possible – became rather depressing. He wasn't one to sit about discussing diseases and the latest treatments or pulling a long face over the diagnosis of this one or that. He still felt young enough to be making a positive contribution to life and his holidays with Liz underlined it. His circle seemed so hidebound and gloomy when compared to the more youthful friendships he'd been cultivating and, after four months of it, he was very ready to make another visit to the West Country.

True to her word, Phyllida took him and Oliver out to lunch which proved to be great fun. Uncle Eustace described how increasingly difficult it was to settle down every time he returned to Shropshire and Oliver told them how, after nearly three years of sending hundreds of letters, he'd been unable to find a sensible job and that having a degree from Cambridge University seemed to mean less than nothing. He made jokes about the endless interviews he'd attended and the hundreds of application forms he'd filled in but Uncle Eustace was shocked. He knew how very difficult it was for the young to find employment in the present economic climate but he'd never met the problem so close before.

'So what d'you actually want to do?' he asked him.

'To be honest, I don't really know.' Oliver folded his arms on the table and shook his head. 'I've tried several things but there's nothing particular that I have an overwhelming passion for. I'd like something different, something challenging. And fun, too.'

'Oh, my dear boy, so would I!' Uncle Eustace finished his cheese and sighed. 'I must admit that I don't really find retirement any fun at all.'

'Why don't you move down here?' suggested Phyllida. She made eyes at him across the table. 'Think what fun you'd have then!'

'Shameless wench!' He grinned at her. 'See me settling in with Liz, do you?'

'Heavens!' said Oliver involuntarily.

'Quite!' Uncle Eustace lit a cigarette.

'You don't have to live with Liz,' protested Phyllida. 'You live on your own now, don't you? You could buy a little place but we'd all be around if you needed us. And if you're bored, you and Oliver can go into business together.'

Uncle Eustace drew on his cigarette and his gaze drifted round to meet Oliver's. There was a tiny silence.

'Say the word, Unk!' Oliver grinned at him. 'I'm yours to command.'

He and Phyllida began to think up schemes, each one wilder than the last, but Uncle Eustace's eyes were thoughtful and, as he drank his brandy, his mind was busy.

Perhaps if everyone hadn't been so helpful when the time came for Phyllida to move to The Grange, even at the last moment she might well have changed her mind. As the days passed it became more difficult to whip up the feelings of resentment and hurt. The cool voice of reason told her that Alistair had spoken out of impatience and disappointment. After all, it said, he's been very understanding, trying to put things right. He won't wait for ever. This sent a little chill of fear down her spine. For a week or so she'd nursed her anger to her heart but now, as the days lengthened into weeks, she imagined how grey life would be without him.

She was torn between two conflicting emotions. She longed to put the clock back and reconsider where she and Alistair might live together but, at the same time, she knew that she couldn't draw back from the move to The Grange. Quentin and Clemmie had made such efforts to make their quarters cosy and welcoming and Lucy was thrilled at the prospect. Night after night during the week prior to the move, Phyllida paced the floor wondering how she could either get out of it or put it right with Alistair. It was all so silly. It could have been such a pleasant interlude and, after all, Alistair would have been there for such a short time. At this point, some of the resentment returned. Why shouldn't she and Lucy have this period without all this anguish? Was it so great a price for him to pay? If he hadn't been unfaithful the situation would never have arisen in the first place.

Confused, unhappy, Phyllida took the only course left open to her. She compromised. She underlined the fact to the Halliwells that she and Lucy could only stay until Alistair came ashore, and wrote to Alistair saying that the arrangements had gone too far to be able to withdraw but that she hoped that he would feel he could come for his leave when they would discuss what should be done when he left the boat. He wouldn't receive this letter until he returned from sea in two months' time and during that time he would not be allowed to communicate with her at all. She could send him a familygram but these forms of communication were vetted lest they should contain news deemed to unsettle the men at a time when they were unable to take action of any sort to help their families and she had no intention of allowing their personal affairs to be read by the censors.

She knew that she was more or less telling him that she wanted them to be together and that the past must be forgotten but, when she thought of life without him, she knew in her heart that there was really no choice. The sacrifice of pride was not too high a price to pay. She loved him and instinctively recognised that the time for prevarication was past. Either that love was enough or it wasn't.

Meanwhile, the move went ahead. Since Alistair and Phyllida had never owned their own home there wasn't too much to be packed and The Grange was big enough to absorb their belongings. Having posted her letter to Alistair, Phyllida was visited with a lightness of heart and began to enjoy herself. In making her commitment to their marriage it seemed easier to put the whole dreadful business of Alistair's night with the Wren away from her. She concentrated once more on his love for her and Lucy and felt confident that she could be strong enough to resist jealousy and resentment. If a small voice whispered that it might be different when he was home again, she ignored it. Whether they liked it or not, she'd been given this moratorium and it would be foolish – and ungrateful to Clemmie and Quentin – not to make the most of it.

To Clemmie, it was if she too had made a commitment. For her, the gesture was showing Quentin that, at last, she too had put everything to do with that terrible time of grief and betrayal away from her for ever.

'And not a bit too soon,' she told herself as she walked by the river on the morning that Phyllida was due to arrive. 'What an old fool I've been. How ridiculous passion is in the elderly! Yet Quentin's been my life for nearly fifty years. Was it foolish to fear that I might lose him to someone more attractive, more clever, more amusing than I am? Why should it be that a man can continue to be sexy and desirable long after a woman's become saggy? Why is an elderly man, making the best of himself, described as "distinguished" and a woman in a similar condition, as "mutton dressed as lamb"?'

She shook her head as though to free it of all negative thoughts and looked about her. It was a bright morning with white fleecy clouds racing before the warm westerly wind. The wood was full of birdsong and the branches of the tall beech trees swayed and the leaves rustled high above her. Deep in, under the trees, the bluebells made a spreading pool of deep soft colour and, nearer to the path, the white flowers of the wild garlic had broken through their green sheaths. She touched one gently with the ferrule of her stick and, sighing with pleasure, turned back to the river.

The dipper flashed upstream and perched on a low branch that swung above the water and she almost cried out in her delight. She'd hardly dared to believe that she might see him on such an auspicious morning but there he sat, dark against the pale gleaming wood, his bib a startling white. She watched him until he flew down to the rocks below, alternately bobbing and preening himself, and at last turned away. It was time to go back. She left the wood and climbed to the stile, the wind buffeting her in a friendly almost playful manner, the sun warm and comforting. She opened the garden door and went into the courtyard and, through the open kitchen door, she heard Quentin's voice. He sounded excited and happy and then Phyllida's voice chimed with his and they laughed together. Clemmie stood quite still, testing for the old feelings: fear, insecurity, jealousy. All she felt was a joyful, grateful excitement and, propping her stick by the door, she hurried in to them.

Chapter Seventeen

Towards the end of June, Claudia was quite certain she was pregnant. She was gratified by the speed at which she'd conceived and deeply relieved. Now she could relax. The past few months of flirting and playing up to Gavin had paid off but now she could draw back and take things quietly again. She'd achieved her purpose and that was all that mattered. Once she'd decided to have a baby, the relationship growing between her and Gavin seemed tasteless to her and the initial attraction waned. Claudia had begun to weary of it all and the mere thought of having a child lifted her above Jenny's foolish antics and enabled her to view them with a kind of patronising pity. It appeared that Jeff was much more concerned with her own flirtation with Gavin – and Andy – than his own with Jenny and, of late, he'd been very quiet and withdrawn. Their lovemaking was still spasmodic and hurried – as though Jeff feared that if he didn't get it over quickly he'd never make it – and it would be a relief to be pregnant. It was a shield against life and she felt confident and happy. Soon she would get it confirmed and then she would tell Jeff. This was the last small cloud in her otherwise blue sky and she spent hours planning how she would do it.

Surely, she reasoned to herself, he would be delighted and relieved. Not the least because it would be the end of her flirting which had obviously made him very unhappy.

She was still making plans as she arrived home from shopping on a still, overcast morning in late June. A man was standing on the pavement at the front door. He'd obviously rung the bell and now stood waiting, head lowered, hands hooked into the back pockets of his jeans. For one second she thought it was Gavin and her heart gave a little lurch but he turned his head towards her as she approached and she saw that he was a stranger. He gave her an indifferent glance and rang the bell again. Claudia stepped up beside him and raised her eyebrows.

'Can I help you?' she asked coolly. 'Are you looking for someone?'

He looked at her appraisingly and his eyes narrowed a little as if he were weighing her up.

'I'm looking for Jeff Maynard,' he said. 'I'm an old friend. I understand he lives here.'

'That's quite right.'

Claudia couldn't resist letting her eyes drift critically over the well-worn jeans and T-shirt before she looked at his face again. This time a smile touched his lips.

'You must be Mrs Maynard.'

'I am. I'm afraid Jeff's at the office. Can I take a message?'

The young man looked at her, as though summing up the situation, then he nodded.

'Why not? Shall we go inside? I'd rather not deliver it on the doorstep. You needn't worry. I've no intention of mugging or raping you.'

His eyes travelled over her almost with contempt as he spoke and she felt hot with embarrassment. Without a word she took out her key and unlocked the door and the young man followed her inside. She hesitated for a moment, torn with the desire to take him into the kitchen so as to show him his proper place and the urge to let him see the drawing room so as to squash any pretensions he may have. The latter won. He strolled after her and looked round the elegant room.

'Nice lounge,' he said casually and looked at her again, smiling a little as though he knew exactly what she'd intended.

'Drawing room!' she snapped and bit her lip as he laughed outright.

'Beg your pardon, ma'am,' he said and bowed ironically. 'Well, I've seen it and it's very nice. Any chance of a cup of coffee and I'll write my message to Jeff.'

She stalked ahead of him into the kitchen and filled the kettle. He watched her but she ignored him until the coffee was made and she pushed the sugar bowl and a jug of milk ungraciously towards him.

'Have you something to write with?' she asked rather curtly.

He stood for a moment, his hands resting on the back of a chair, his head bent.

'I should like to see him,' he said at last and Claudia shrugged a little as if to imply that the desire would necessarily be all on his side.

'He won't be home until after six,' she said. 'Are you staying in Tavistock?'

'No.' The young man seemed to be trying to come to a decision. 'No. I'm going back to Sussex tonight. OK. If you've got some paper, I'll leave him a note.'

'Sussex? Is that where you knew Jeff?' Claudia pushed a notepad towards him and a Biro. 'We came down here from Sussex.' Claudia sat down at the table and he followed suit. 'Our families are still there.'

'And are you happy?'

It was an odd question and, had it not been asked in such a serious tone, Claudia might have resented it more.

'D'you mean, do we like Devon? Yes, we do.'

'No, I didn't mean that,' he said. 'I meant are you happy with Jeff? Is Jeff happy?'

'Perfectly,' she said with a rather brittle smile that implied that she found the question impertinent. Again he looked at her with narrowed eyes and she felt an odd need to defend herself and their marriage. 'I'm expecting a baby,' she said and immediately regretted it.

He stared at her, his brows drawn together.

'Jeff always said he wouldn't have kids,' he said flatly and she stared at him with cold surprise.

'He changed his mind,' she said and, as if guessing the truth, his eyes slid away from hers and he took up his cup and drank some coffee, still frowning. 'Hadn't you better write your note?' she reminded him.

He continued to frown, turning the notepad round and round between his fingers.

'Were you at school together?' she asked, to fill the silence, allowing a disbelieving note to creep into her voice. 'Jeff was at grammar school, of course.'

'Of course,' he said and looked at her with open dislike. 'No. We weren't at school together.' He hesitated for a moment. 'I think I ought to see him.'

'Suit yourself.' Claudia sounded indifferent. 'But he's got a very busy day today so I doubt he'll be here much before six. I don't know your name.'

'I'll be back about then. Thanks.' He ignored her hint. 'See you. Thanks for the coffee.'

Claudia shut the door behind him and went to clear up, feeling indignant that he should have invited himself in so coolly. She realised that she had no proof at all that he was an old friend and that he could have hit her on the head and gone off with all their valuables. Somehow, though, she instinctively believed what he'd said; his remark, for instance, that Jeff didn't want children had rung true, though what business it was of his she couldn't imagine. Now she came to think of it, she didn't know many of Jeff's friends. She'd met him through one of her own friends and they'd tended to mix with the young married couples who lived around them. He was so reserved and quiet that it hadn't seemed surprising that he was a bit of a loner. Perhaps the young man wanted some financial advice but it was an awfully long way to come for it. Claudia had the impression that he was in trouble of some kind and she hoped Jeff wouldn't get involved.

The man was back before Jeff arrived home and Claudia, who had just made a pot of tea, was obliged to offer him a cup. He sat down at the kitchen table. She could feel his eyes on her, summing her up again, but this time she looked him squarely in the eye.

'You didn't tell me your name,' she said as she passed him his cup.

'It's Mike,' he said. 'I don't suppose Jeff's mentioned me.'

'I'm afraid not.' Claudia felt he needed to be put in his place after his cool approach earlier. 'You weren't at the wedding, were you?'

'No,' he said shortly.

'Well.' She allowed a pause to develop. 'We couldn't invite everybody.'

She managed to imply that it would have been presumptuous of him to have expected an invitation and he shot a glance of dislike at her.

'I'd have probably been an embarrassment to him.'

He sounded almost provocative, as though he were calling her bluff, challenging her. Claudia's eyes ranged over his shabby clothes once more and she sipped her tea as though declining to give an answer which must be, inevitably, insulting. Mike stared at her and his expression grew ugly.

'I'm glad he's happy,' he said but his voice was almost spiteful. 'I never thought he'd make it.'

'What d'you mean?' Claudia managed to sound both annoyed and surprised. 'Make what?'

'Well.' He shrugged. 'You know . . . be able to keep it up.' He drank his tea and his eyes were frankly malicious as he watched her puzzlement increase.

'I've no idea what you're talking about,' she said dismissively.

'D'you mean you've never guessed that Jeff's gay?' He watched her disbelief slowly give way to a kind of appalled enlightenment and he smiled and nodded to her. 'All makes sense? I thought it might. Jeff and I were lovers. Before he

186

got married. Like a fool I broke it up and he decided to try it straight. By the time I realised how much of a fool I'd been, it was too late. He was always determined he could be bisexual but he swore he'd never have children.'

The silence stretched out and out until it became unbearable whilst inside Claudia's head the pieces of the puzzle clicked into place and presented a horrifying picture.

'No!' She shook her head. She wanted to stand up but feared that her legs wouldn't support her. 'How disgusting. How dare you suggest—'

'Oh, it's all quite true. You know it is really. You might not have guessed it but you believe me. I can tell. But if you want proof . . .' He took a wallet from the pocket of his shirt and extracted a much-thumbed photograph. 'That's my Jeff. That's how I remember him.'

He held it out to her and after a moment she took it. The shock was cataclysmic. The scene was a sunny one, with mountains in the background. On a low wall, Jeff and Mike sat together, his arms circling Jeff's waist, Jeff hugging him round the neck, their cheeks pressed together. They were laughing out at the camera, their tanned, entwined legs sprawling easily, their feet bare. Jeff's hair was long and flopped over his forehead, his flowered shirt was open to the waist and his neck was hung about with chains of gold. His happiness and vitality positively blazed out of the picture. It came at her like a physical blow which caught her under the heart and drove the breath from her lungs and she pressed the back of one hand unconsciously to her lips.

'Ever seen Jeff look like that?' Mike was watching her and, as she glanced up at him, she saw that he hated her.

She shook her head but whether in answer to his question or in complete rejection, or simple disbelief, he didn't know and suddenly he didn't care.

'We were so happy.' His voice was barely audible. 'So bloody happy. But I got distracted by another boy and Jeff couldn't cope. He never could, really. He was a terribly jealous person and he was always so frightened people would find out.' He looked at her and his dislike seemed to flick out at her across the table. 'Can you imagine what hell it is to be . . .' he hesitated, '"abnormal" in a "normal" society? What it's like to really love someone but never be able to show it? Look at your ordinary couple. Watch how often they touch each other, hold hands, have a little kiss, call each other darling. When Jeff and I went out together we hardly dared look at one another we loved each other so much. I called him darling by mistake once at a party. It was just a slip of the tongue but I had to turn it into a joke, camping it up as though we were those ghastly stage versions of "the queer". You know? Jeff was furious. He didn't speak to me for days.'

'Please don't.' Her lips felt stiff and strange.

'He'd get into that bloody collar and tie and the dark suit and it was like he was nailing himself into a box. It's like a straitjacket to help him keep on the straight and narrow. I begged him to give it all up, come abroad with me. That's why he left Sussex. I hounded him. I wanted him back. I couldn't leave him alone, you see. We were so bloody happy. I knew we could be again if he'd give it a chance. He refused because he was married. I got silly, threatened to tell people. Next thing, he'd moved down here.'

Claudia continued to stare at the photograph.

In a minute, she told herself, this will all stop and it will be over. It can't be true . . .

Jeff – a Jeff she'd never seen, never known, never suspected existed – glowed out of the photograph at her. She saw the way Jeff's right hand was cupping Mike's ear, pressing his head close to his own, while his left hand rested on the knee hooked so negligently over his own. She looked at the other hands, Mike's clasped fingers resting against the dark hair on Jeff's stomach as they held him close. She noticed Jeff's long, carelessly disposed legs, the brief shorts . . .

'I'm HIV positive.' The words were like hammer blows on her mind, echoing in the silence of the room, and she looked at him now, terror in her eyes. He nodded at her. His eyes were bleak. 'That's why I came. I wanted to see him. Warn him. I couldn't just write. When I saw you I decided that perhaps I'd better leave a note. It's too late to rock boats, I thought. But when you said about the baby . . .' He shook his head. 'He had no right to risk a child but I don't think he did, did he? He wouldn't. Not Jeff.'

She stared at him her face twitching with fear.

'D'you mean . . . ? D'you mean Jeff might be . . . ? Oh Christ . . .' She stood up, clutching at the table as though she were drunk and he jumped up and came round to her. 'Don't touch me!' she screamed. 'Oh God. You disgusting animal. You might have given him AIDS. All of us. Me and the baby. Oh Christ! Get away from me,' she choked and struck his outstretched hand down. 'Get out. Oh God! What shall I do?'

'You should've left him alone in the first place.' His face

was pale. 'He didn't love you. He told me. You chased him until he gave in and married you. You've asked for it. If you hadn't worn him down, he'd've come back to me. He loved me.' He snatched up the photograph and shook it at her. 'You've only got to look at this.'

'Oh God,' whispered Claudia and sank back on to her chair. 'I shall have to tell the doctor.' She buried her face in her hands. 'What will he say? I shall have to tell him . . . Oh God.' She sounded as if she were going to be sick. 'Supposing people find out . . . ?'

He watched her with a strange expression on his face. Pity, fear, shame, dislike, all passed across it fleetingly.

'You'll be OK, I expect,' he said, almost reluctantly. 'Jeff was clear when he married you. He had a test first.'

She stared up at him with such hope in her face that he hadn't the brutality to disillusion her, to tell her all the facts.

'He's all right, then?'

'If he hasn't messed about since.' He couldn't resist frightening her just a little. She was so indifferent to the terrifying towering shadow of death which loomed over him. 'No young chap he's got his eye on? A bit rough perhaps? He always liked a little bit of rough trade. Not too much. Just enough to make him uninhibited.' He watched the colour drain out of her cheeks as another piece of the puzzle clicked smoothly into place and he felt a jab of jealousy. 'So there is!' He gave a short ugly laugh. 'Better get yourself tested then, dear.'

She hardly heard him. She was remembering Jeff at their party, staring across the room, not at Jenny but at Gavin who was just behind her; realising that his flirtations with Jenny were simply a form of showing off before Gavin, and that his jealousy was, in fact, of Andy. She felt as if she were disintegrating until she took in what the young man had just said.

'What d'you mean?' She leaped up and then stood still as she heard the sound of the front door being opened.

Quick as light the young man moved round so that he was facing the door and his was the face Jeff first saw when he opened it. Claudia watched his look of amazement slowly transform into a tender, aching look of love that she'd never seen and the longing in his voice when he simply said, 'Mike,' struck her dumb.

'Hello, Jeff.' He held out his arms and Jeff moved into them almost automatically, his eyes still fixed on Mike's face.

'Don't mind me!'

Claudia's icy voice cut through the dreamlike quality of the moment and spun Jeff round to face her. She stared at him, letting all her disgust show so as to hide her own pain and jealousy, and his face changed, closing down, the light dying away from it. Mike watched, looking spiteful.

'Sorry, Jeff. I spilled the beans.' His voice was light but there was a tender note underlying it as he looked at Jeff. 'It just came out, I'm afraid.'

'I see.' Jeff looked as though he were reeling from a heavy blow and he carefully kept his eyes away from the scornful horror on Claudia's face.

'You bastard!' she hissed at him, ignoring Mike and coming close to Jeff. 'You've tricked and cheated and lied and you'd have gone on doing it. You'd got no right to marry me. You . . . you . . .' She cast about for something despicable enough and her eye fell on the photograph. 'Look at this. Look at it! God, it makes me want to vomit!'

She held it out in a hand that vibrated with shock and rage and fear and he took it almost fearfully. When he saw what it was, his face softened involuntarily and Mike smiled triumphantly. Claudia gave an exclamation.

'You're quite right.' Jeff's hand closed over the photograph as though it were a talisman. 'I had no right. I wanted to try to be . . . to be "normal". I really thought I could. And you seemed to want it.'

'Oh, yes. Of course, it was all my fault, wasn't it? I forced you into it, didn't I? Next you'll be saying it was a shotgun wedding . . .'

Her voice trailed away and there was an odd silence. Mike saw his chance and smiled.

'Do you know you're shortly to become a father, Jeff?'

'No!' It was a plea rather than anything else and Claudia stared at him defiantly. 'You can't be. You told me that you'd take the pill. *Are* you pregnant?' he asked and Claudia nodded. 'But we agreed. You absolutely promised.'

'Then you should have told me why,' she burst out. 'If you'd told me the truth . . .'

'Then what?' he asked when she paused. 'What would you have done?'

'I'd have chucked you out,' she said, between clenched teeth. 'Before you had time to kill me as well as the baby.' She jerked her head at Mike. 'He's got AIDS.'

'Oh, Mike!' It was a cry of love and compassion and Claudia stared with disbelief as Jeff took Mike in his arms and held him close. 'Mike.'

'I came to warn you. Just in case.' Mike's face was tragic and stamped with terror. 'And I wanted to see you once again before . . . you know.'

'You told me Jeff was clear when we got married. You didn't need to warn him about anything. You came to make trouble. And while I'm thinking about it . . .' She picked up the cup Mike had used on both occasions and smashed it on the tap.

The two men stared at one another for a long moment and then Jeff turned to Claudia.

'What do you want to do,' he asked, 'now that you know?'

'I want you to get out,' she said, feeling that she might fall to pieces. 'Just go! I don't care where. I don't want you here.'

She burst into tears and Jeff went to her. 'I can't just leave you like this,' he said. 'This is dreadful. Please, Claudia—'

'Go away!' She caught sight of Mike's expression, compounded of pity, shame and triumph, and she turned away, her humiliation complete.

'I'll come back later.' Jeff touched her shoulder but she shook him off. 'We'll have to talk . . .'

Claudia fled out of the kitchen and raced up the stairs and presently the front door shut behind Jeff and Mike and she was left alone.

Chapter Eighteen

Phyllida was beginning to feel twinges of apprehension. For one wonderful month she'd put her problems on hold and had simply set out to enjoy those early weeks at The Grange. The four of them had settled down together and they had all been happy. Now there would be changes. For a start, Lucy would shortly be on holiday from school and that in itself might make complications. The second thing was that the boat would soon be in and Alistair would find her letter waiting for him. All through the two months since he'd sailed, he'd been unaware of her final decision. Although she could have made this news innocent-sounding enough to pass the censors, still she preferred to wait. She knew that he would be very upset to hear that she'd actually gone against his wishes and moved to The Grange. The letter which he'd written after that disastrous leave, and posted as soon as the train had arrived at Glasgow, told her that. Despite their last row, she could read enough between the lines to see that he didn't expect her to take this step and she didn't want him brooding whilst he was at sea and in no position to do anything about it. She even hoped that those eight weeks may have calmed him and shown him that there really was nothing so terrible in what she was doing. Meanwhile, before she moved, she sent a routine 'we are all well' type of familygram and left it at that.

Nevertheless, she waited with growing anxiety for the date the boat was due in. Unlike any other branch of the Submarine Service, the Polaris boats sail and dock exactly in accordance with their ETDs and ETAs and Phyllida watched the calendar uneasily. There was no question of Alistair coming down on leave. She knew that he was going on a course as soon as the boat docked and after that he would be in the command team trainer before going back to sea. He wasn't due for leave until September. The question was, would he then come down to see them?

If the Halliwells sensed the change in Phyllida as the days passed, they didn't mention it. Phyllida had told them rather vaguely that Alistair wanted her to move to Faslane but that she didn't want to disrupt Lucy's schooling and that the final decision as to where they made their home must wait until Alistair was ashore and knew his next appointment. Clemmie guessed that Phyllida was struggling to come to terms with her own fears and did what she could to provide a sounding board for Phyllida to try her theories against. Although she made every effort not to impose on the elderly couple's time together, it was clear that they enjoyed her company and loved to have her with them. Little routines sprang up and very soon all awkwardness fell away and they were easy and natural together.

In the middle of July a letter arrived from Alistair. Phyllida disappeared upstairs with it and read it with growing alarm. It was a cool, well-thought-out letter containing phrases which chilled her heart:

whilst I can appreciate your dilemma, I regret the move you've ultimately decided on . . . Since I consider nine months more than enough time to come to a decision, I find it difficult to accept that you're still unable to make up your mind as to whether your pride is more important than our marriage . . . I note your invitation to join you for my leave but have decided that your first idea was the best one and we should have a complete break for the time being . . .

It was Alistair at his most pompous and unlikable and she felt real fear battling with anger in her breast. Her letter had been conciliatory and loving and she felt as if he'd slapped her. She couldn't know that he'd spent the eight weeks at sea listening to his engineer officer trying to come to terms with a very painful divorce and whose advice to Alistair had been to 'get tough and stay tough', confident that if he'd been more so himself his marriage might have survived. Alistair had brooded on these things but kept an open mind, still convinced that Phyllida would come round to his way of thinking. The row at Easter had been most unfortunate and due to his own insensitive handling; he knew this, accepted it and said so in his first letter. Perhaps he was unconsciously relying on this letter having the same effect on her that his card had had for, when he opened her letter and saw that she'd gone, after all, to The Grange, he'd been absolutely shocked and then very angry. He'd written this second letter, bringing all his superiority of age and experience to bear on it and posted it before he could change his mind. At that moment he'd decided that his engineer officer was right and

Phyllida needed to be put in her place. If he regretted his action, he wouldn't admit it but waited to see what her reaction would be. For a considerable time, he waited in vain.

This was simply because Phyllida didn't know how to reply. Sometimes she longed to push aside all these foolish accusations and desires to hurt and just get back to how they'd been before. Sometimes her own hurt was so great, she felt as if she never wanted to see him again. In her present situation it was tempting to imagine that she could live without him. She had company, love, approval and it was easy to imagine this as reality. There was another danger. The Navy teaches wives to live without their husbands so it's not terribly surprising that, occasionally, some women find that they can do just that and actually grow to prefer it. Phyllida was not yet in this situation but Alistair was taking a far greater risk than he knew.

Whilst Phyllida was dithering, Oliver came down for the weekend. Her delight when she arrived downstairs and found him in the kitchen with Clemmie and Lucy was so great that it should have warned her how vulnerable she was. He received her hug with great pleasure and accepted Clemmie's suggestion that he should stay to tea. Lucy monopolised him, flirted with him outrageously and insisted that he read her a bedtime story.

'The one great blessing,' confided Phyllida, as they trailed upstairs, 'is that Lucy needs her sleep. Even in the summer, with the light evenings, she goes out like a light. On schooldays she can barely stay awake to eat her tea.'

By the time she was bathed and in bed they were all

exhausted and Lucy, having selected her story, sat in bed watching Oliver over her thumb.

'*Percy the Parrot and the Robber Rats*,' he read, seating himself at the foot of the bed. 'Aha! Good old Percy.'

'We both love the Percy books,' said Phyllida, who was pottering around, tidying up. 'And we're always glued to the television programme, aren't we, Lucy?'

Lucy nodded and bounced up and down in excitement. 'I like Polly,' she said. '"Pretty Polly". That's what Percy calls her. "Pretty Polly. Pretty Polly",' she crowed and bounced up and down again, enchanted by all this attention at bedtime.

'That's the presenter,' explained Phyllida, lest Oliver should be puzzled. 'She's so pretty and so funny. She makes Lucy laugh till she cries. And Percy sidles up close and tries to kiss her.'

'He does this!' cried Lucy, exploding from the bed and creeping up to Oliver and butting his cheek with her nose several times.

'All Lucy's schoolfriends are fans of Percy,' said Phyllida. 'It's a really super programme and the mums seem to like it as much as the children.'

'Tell you what,' said Oliver, tucking Lucy back beneath her quilt. 'If you're a good quiet girl, I'll bring you a Percy the Parrot soft toy from London. Just like the one on the television. How about that?'

Lucy gazed at him, hardly daring to believe her ears, and Phyllida lifted her eyebrows.

'Are they being made now? How wonderful. Oh, Lucy! Wouldn't that be fantastic? What do you say?'

Lucy mouthed, 'Thank you, Oliver,' without making a

sound, shot under her quilt and lay quite still and silent, obviously determined to be a 'good quiet girl' in earnest. Laughing, Phyllida bent to kiss her and Oliver winked at her as she went out.

'One morning,' she heard him say as she shut the door, 'Percy the Parrot woke up to find that all his special breakfast peanuts had disappeared in the night . . .'

A little later, Phyllida and Oliver strolled together by the river. The sun was still quite high and the river, low in its bed after a protracted period of dry weather, flowed slowly, meandering between mossy rocks that were rarely exposed.

'Are you down for long?' asked Phyllida hopefully, going first along the well-worn path.

'Just the weekend.' Oliver watched the small figure, glad that she couldn't see him. 'But I'm down at the beginning of August.'

'Oh, good!' She turned suddenly to look at him, her face alight with pleasure and he only just managed to control his face and smile back at her.

'Has Alistair got leave?' His voice was commendably casual.

'No.' She turned back. It was her turn to hide her expression. 'Not till autumn at the earliest. If then. You know the Navy.'

Oliver was silent. He did indeed know the Navy. His father was a naval captain and Oliver knew very well that, as a captain of a Polaris submarine, Alistair would know exactly when his leaves were due and was obviously prevaricating.

'Look.' Phyllida paused and caught his arm. 'See the wagtails?'

They watched the two birds, flying from boulder to boulder, their tails wagging as they strutted about on the rocks. A dragonfly skimmed above a quiet pool, hovering for a moment, before swooping away only to return and hover again over the still water. The sun sent long fingers of dazzling light through the trees, turning the water to the colour of molten gold.

'I keep hoping to see the dipper,' said Phyllida as they moved away. 'I think I have once or twice but he flies so fast. I'm too noisy, that's the trouble.'

They reached the bridge and stopped by unspoken mutual consent to gaze down into the water. Phyllida perched sideways on the sun-warmed stone and Oliver looked down at her.

'Everything OK?' he asked lightly.

'Not really,' she said, at last.

Her face was so downcast that he was obliged to put his hands in his pockets lest he should pull her up and take her in his arms.

'Anything I can do?'

'No.' She managed to control herself and smile up at him. 'Just being silly. Sorry. So have you got a busy weekend?'

'Nothing special. Unless . . .' He hesitated and frowned a little, fighting an inner battle.

'Unless?' She looked up at him questioningly and he weakened as she smiled at him again.

'I wondered if you'd like to come out to the pub tonight. Just for a drink and a sandwich?' He shrugged a little as though it were of no real moment, praying she'd accept.

'Oh, I'd love to,' she said at once. 'And it will give

Clemmie and Quentin a break. Super! Let's get back and warn Clemmie so that she doesn't start preparing something for us.'

'Perhaps it will help to cheer you up a bit,' said Oliver as they started back and felt his heart lift as she smiled gratefully at him.

At the end of a long hot day in the office, Liz was irritated to find a message from Uncle Eustace on her answering machine when she arrived home. He was thinking of another little trip to Devon, he said, to see Christina whilst she was on holiday. Just for a day or two. He'd ring again later. Liz snorted as she wiped the message. What a cunning old devil he was! He often left messages as a way of imparting information that he didn't want to tell her directly. Next time he telephoned he would behave as though everything were arranged and there would be no question about his coming.

She went into her kitchen, poured a long cold orange juice and took it out on to the back lawn. She kicked off her shoes and walked barefoot on the grass, the dry stems warm and prickly to her tender soles. She had an intuition that Uncle Eustace was working up to a suggestion that he should move down and she didn't know how to deal with it. She knew that he and she could never share a house. They drew too many sparks from each other and, despite their underlying attachment, to live together would be a disaster. She knew, too, that he was lonely and bored and that he liked to have young people about him.

Liz sat down on a little bench under the plum tree and dropped her head forward in an attempt to ease her aching neck. With Jeff going off in such a hurry to see his mother they'd been shorthanded in the office all week and she was hot and tired and looking forward to a shower before going over to the Manor for supper with Abby and William. Uncle Eustace was simply an added problem that she didn't have the energy to solve. The best thing would be for him to buy a flat in Tavistock where he was close at hand but without being under her feet all the time. She knew quite certainly that he would come, whatever she might say, so the best thing was to accept it gracefully. At least Christina would be delighted. She could send them off house-hunting and get them both out of her hair. With this encouraging thought, Liz finished her drink and hauled herself to her feet.

She wandered back to the cottage and heard the telephone bell as she reached the kitchen door. It was Uncle Eustace. His gravelly old voice was determinedly cheerful.

'Got my message? Good! I was wondering if the first week in August would be suitable?' he asked, giving her no chance to protest.

Liz discerned the barely disguised note of anxiety and swallowed her sarcastic retort.

'I should think so,' she said. 'Why not? Look, I've got to dash but we'll talk again later. The first week in August's fine with me.'

'Wonderful, my darling.' His voice was jubilant now. 'I won't keep you if you're busy. Love to you both.'

Liz sighed. So that was that. At least he and Christina could have some time together before she went off to stay with Tony's parents. Liz's face grew grim as she went upstairs. She'd tried everything within her power to detach

Christina's affections from Tony but to no avail. As Christina grew older Liz had made no pretence of her feelings, even going so far as to tell her how badly Tony had behaved within months of Christina's birth.

This had been greeted by a silence that was part shock and part loyalty to the father she was so fond of, and Liz had been hurt even more. Stung by Christina's partisanship, she descended to sneers and gibes at Tony's expense but the child stood firm. She remained loving to Liz but would not be deflected from her affection for her father.

She'd gone so far as to invite him to the Easter play and Liz, used to Tony being at sea and looking upon school as her preserve and not his, had been taken aback at the sight of him.

I still love him, she'd thought, staring at him across the crowded hall packed with enthusiastic parents. Oh, hell! I can't cope with this.

He'd made his way to her side and they'd talked in a brittle, silly way whilst her heart hammered and thumped and she cursed Christina for not warning her. Afterwards she'd watched him talking to another child's mother – had seen the charm in action – and felt as she had always felt, the knife of jealousy twisting in her gut. She'd hardly taken in one word of the play and left as quickly as she could but not before he'd come to say goodbye and suggested a sandwich and pint before they set off back to their respective homes. Longing to accept, she'd refused pleasantly, kissed Christina and hurried away, cursing all the way home that she hadn't accepted.

Liz went slowly upstairs and turned on the shower. It was

ten years since she'd divorced Tony and the pain was still as fresh as if it had been yesterday. She threw off her clothes and stepped into the cubicle, allowing the needle-fine jets of water to wash away the stress and memories along with the grime of the day. Feeling refreshed, she wrapped herself in a towel and began to think about the evening ahead.

Chapter Nineteen

After Jeff's departure, Claudia kept to the house like an injured animal in its lair, afraid to cross the threshold. She was quite certain that everyone must, by now, know her shameful secret and she felt dizzy with shock and humiliation. Once he knew that she really wanted him to leave, Jeff acted with a promptness and discretion that was almost insulting. He gave in his notice at the office, saying that his mother was ill and he wanted to be near her and that Claudia was staying behind to sell the house. He also managed to infer that they'd had several rows over it, hinting that his mother disliked Claudia intensely and that Claudia hated the idea of moving back. Subtly he gave the impression that he was more than a bit of a mother's boy and that her wishes came a long way before Claudia's and added – just in case he'd been seen with Mike – that a cousin of his had been sent down to urge his speedy return.

Everyone was taken in and most of them had a sneaking sympathy for Claudia.

'I did it,' he told her, 'so that if you decided to stay on after all, people won't be too surprised.'

'I'd no idea you were such an accomplished liar,' she sneered.

His face took on the shuttered, secret look and his eyes were bleak.

'Oh, yes,' he said quietly. 'When you're an untouchable you get to be very good at lying.'

He'd turned away and gone upstairs to finish his packing, not waiting to see the flush that mounted her cheeks. He was taking very little, packing his belongings into Mike's car and his own as the days passed. He'd been allowed to leave the office as soon as his affairs were in order although no one had yet been found to take his place and Claudia, terrified that someone might notice his absence, had agreed that he should spend the nights at home in the spare bedroom.

'We've found a cottage down in Cornwall,' he told her on the night before he was due to go for good. 'Mike's organised it. He's been back to Sussex and collected his own stuff and taken everything down with mine. He'll be back tomorrow for the last things.'

Claudia listened, her face averted as usual. She could rarely bring herself to look at him. He watched her for a moment, his expression sad.

'I know that marrying you was quite unforgivable,' he said. 'I had absolutely no right. I wanted so terribly to be "normal", you see, and you seemed to . . . to love me so much.' He brought the words out in a rush. 'I thought it would work. That your love would make me . . . "normal".'

She sent him a scalding glance. 'Even I'm not capable of miracles,' she said bitterly.

'No,' he said sadly. 'It would have been a miracle. I see

that now. I couldn't forget Mike—'

'Please!' she cried and stood up abruptly. 'Must you welter in self-pity? You've got what you want, haven't you? You used me and risked my life and made me feel that your inadequacies were my fault. I shall never forgive you for that! Isn't that enough? If you want sympathy or forgiveness you'll have to wait a very long time.'

'I'm sorry.' He stood up, too. 'I've left my solicitor's name and number. You can divorce me on whatever grounds you like. I shan't contest it. Also,' he hesitated and then went on without looking at her, 'I've had another blood test. I'm quite clear. So you have nothing to fear. Nor the baby. I just thought I'd mention it in case you wanted to change your mind.' He paused and when he spoke again his voice was infinitely sad. 'All my life I've lived a lie and I wasn't prepared to extend that into fatherhood.'

'How can you give up everything?' She simply had to ask him. 'How can you risk your own life to be with him. Even if we separate, you could carry on as you are. You're taking a terrible risk.'

He smiled at her then as though she were an ignorant child. 'I love him, you see,' he said. 'There's never been anyone else. I love him so much and I can't bear the thought of what's ahead for him. My God! To have to go through all that alone.' He shook his head and his eyes were dark with the horror of it. 'And anyway, you make it sound as if my life's worth living. I've spent it pretending to be someone I'm not. I never had the guts to stand up and be counted and, even with you, I couldn't make it. And I do love you, Claudia. But it wasn't enough. It only ever worked with Mike and now we might have a short time together to make up for everything else. I'll settle for that.'

She turned away from him and he saw that her shoulders were shaking and that she was crying soundlessly. He stood, helplessly watching her, and then went out and upstairs. When he'd gone, Claudia wrapped her arms around herself and bent herself double with pain and unhappiness. How could she go on living, with her life smashed to pieces?

Now, after he'd been gone for nearly a week, Claudia felt no better. She'd had time for other fears and humiliations to make themselves known to her and she seemed to exist from one terror to the next. Although she'd seized at once on Jeff's infatuation for Gavin, it was only much later that she realised that Gavin, too, must be gay and had probably pursued her in an attempt to undermine her marriage and encourage Jeff. Jeff swore that he'd never succumbed to Gavin's suggestions and that it was only because he bore a resemblance to Mike that he'd been thrown off balance in the first place. Later still, it occurred to her that Gavin might also be HIV positive and that she'd let him kiss her. She remembered, with a shock wave of pure terror, his tongue touching hers. She sat quite rigid, sick with fear, unable to think of anything else and knowing that she'd never feel entirely safe ever again. She'd almost decided to keep the baby. When Jeff told her that he was clear, she knew that she'd rather risk having it than go and explain to the doctor why she wanted an abortion. But if Gavin . . . ?

The telephone rang. She willed herself to answer it, making her voice as near normal as she could. It was Phyllida to say that she and Lucy were just off for their two weeks with her parents. Claudia was overwhelmed by a desire to tell her everything but the words simply wouldn't come and she couldn't bring herself to pour it all out on the telephone. She laid the receiver down with a sense of loss at Phyllida's departure but thankful that it was the school holidays which meant that most people were preoccupied with their own affairs. Tomorrow she'd have to go shopping. No, not tomorrow. Tomorrow was Friday, market day. Everyone would be out tomorrow. She began to cry, weakly, helplessly, and realised that she hadn't eaten all day and felt quite faint. She dragged herself to the kitchen and stopped short as the doorbell pealed. She stood quite still, praying that whoever it was might go away. The bell pealed out again, however, and Claudia suddenly took a grip on herself and went to answer it.

Gavin stood outside. They stared at each other for a second and then, with a sharp movement, Claudia made to slam the door. He was much too quick. He forced it back and the next minute was in the hall, shutting the door behind him.

'So what goes on here?' he asked softly and his eyes gleamed in the gloom of the hall.

'Nothing.' She stared up at him, trying to control her face.

He caught her by the shoulders and pushed her into the kitchen where he spun her round so that he could scrutinise her face.

'I've heard rumours that Jeff's gone back to Mummy,' he said, watching her, 'leaving you to pack and follow. Don't tell me you're missing him that much already. You've been crying, haven't you?'

'No!' she cried, twisting free from his grasp. 'No, I haven't. Leave me alone.'

'Oh.' His eyebrows shot up and he pursed his lips. 'Like that, is it? Bit of a change, wouldn't you say?'

'Please,' she said and her voice shook. 'Please go, Gavin. I don't feel very well. I haven't ever since Jeff went.' She swallowed.

'Poor old Claudia.' She knew she hadn't fooled him. 'Sit down and I'll make you a cuppa.'

'Don't touch them!' It was out before she could stop herself as he made to take her pretty cups from the dresser. 'Leave them alone.' Her voice changed to despair. 'Oh God.' She subsided into a chair and began to weep.

'Come on.' His voice above her head was quite gentle. 'Are you going to tell me what's happened. Or shall I tell you?' She stared up at him fearfully and his mouth twisted a little as he stood looking down at her. 'Found out he's gay, haven't you? What's he done? Gone off with his boyfriend?'

The brutality of the remark stiffened her spine and a wave of rage engulfed her.

'You bastard!' she screamed at him. 'How dare you talk to me like that! You tried to ruin my marriage and you lied to me all the way along. It was Jeff you were after all the time.'

The shame of the whole sordid situation struck her afresh and she closed her eyes. The fight went out of her and she began to cry again.

'Get a grip!' His voice was still gentle. 'Poor old Claudia. You've had a basinful, haven't you? All of us leading you up the garden path. Poor kid. I'm sorry, I really am. Part of it was because of Jeff, it's no good denying that. But part of it was you. I'm like Jeff, confused and wanting to be straight and you're beautiful enough to make me think it might have worked.' He paused. 'So the long-lost boyfriend turned up, did he? I thought he might.'

'How did you know?' Claudia's voice was barely audible and she couldn't look at him.

'I guessed.' Gavin leaned against the dresser and stuck his hands in his pockets. 'Takes one to know one, they say, don't they? He couldn't help himself, however much he fought it. I just recognised the signs. I guessed he'd had a great romance and never got over it. I wondered if I reminded him of whoever it was.'

'He's got AIDS.'

'Christ!' Gavin took his hands from his pockets and stood up. 'Poor bloody Jeff—'

'Not Jeff. Mike. The boyfriend.' Claudia listened to her voice saying these private disgusting things with surprise. 'He came to tell him and Jeff went with him. He's going to look after him until . . . Until.'

'And what about you?'

Claudia struggled to think of some fiction and found that she couldn't be bothered.

'I threw him out. I said he should never have married me in the first place knowing that he was . . . Knowing.'

'That's fair.'

'I think I'm pregnant.'

'Oh Christ!'

'Yes. I'm afraid it might be . . . that I might be . . .' Claudia looked at him at last. 'You kissed me and I don't know now whether . . .' Her face crumpled again and she cried with her head in her arms, resting on the table.

He stared at her for a long, long moment and went to fill the kettle.

'Come on, Claudia,' he said at last. 'Surely you don't believe that old myth! You can't catch AIDS from kissing. Anyway, if it makes you feel happier, I'm clear at the moment. And I haven't been with anyone for a bit and then it was only safe sex. I'm not the suicidal type. But you've got to have a test, Claudia. You must.'

'I can't.' She stared at him in terror. 'I can't. What would I say to the doctor? It's such a small place. Oh, I can't . . .'

She began to cry again and Gavin made some coffee, heaped sugar into it and pushed it towards her.

'Drink. Look. You don't have to have it done locally. There are hospitals you can go to. All perfectly official and above board. Just confidential and no one will know you. You've got to, Claudia.'

'But if Jeff's OK and you're OK, I don't need to, surely?' Her voice was pleading as she picked up the coffee. Her hand shook and she held the cup with both hands and raised it to her lips.

'Look, love, it's not quite that straightforward.' He slipped into the chair opposite and looked at her compassionately. 'It simply means it may not have shown up yet, see?'

Her hands shook so violently that the coffee spilled and she set it down again.

'D'you mean . . . ? What d'you mean?'

'Look,' he said. 'I talked to Jeff quite a bit and I'm absolutely certain he was telling the truth when he said that he'd stayed straight since he married you. I'm sure you've nothing to fear but it doesn't necessarily show up immediately.'

'But he told me that he had another test in the last few weeks.' Her eyes were wide with fear. 'He said he was clear.'

'Well, then.' He shrugged. 'He must be OK. Still. Don't you think you'd feel better if you had it confirmed? It's only a blood test, you know. I'll take you up to Exeter. You can be quite anonymous there. No one here will ever know.'

He smiled at her, coaxingly, caringly, and she felt her lips tremble.

'No one would know?'

'I promise. Just me. You can trust me.'

She felt quite suddenly that she could and she nodded. 'All right then.' She looked exhausted.

'Good girl.' He looked at her thoughtfully. 'What do you know about AIDS?'

'Nothing.' She shook her head. 'Not really. You can be infected by bodily fluids and blood and things.' She looked at him defiantly. 'I smashed the cup he used.'

'Oh, Claudia.' Gavin shook his head. 'We'll go and get that test done and straighten you out a bit. I'm very sure you have nothing to fear. Jeff was very honest and very honourable, poor sod. He was so screwed up it was painful.'

'I thought it was me. Because he didn't fancy me. I loved him. I really did . . .' She began to cry again and Gavin sighed and pushed back his chair.

'Go and get yourself tidied up,' he said. 'We're going out. Oh, yes we are. Somewhere quiet out in the country where no one will see you and you can eat something sensible. I shall stand here till you're ready, so you might as well hurry up.'

She got up and went out and he wandered round the kitchen. A photograph on the dresser caught his eye and he picked it up. He stared at it for a long moment, studying it closely, wondering how long Mike's skin would remain so smooth and unblemished. A shiver crawled over his own flesh as he thought of the risks he'd taken in the past and he brooded on how much Jeff must love Mike to throw everything up for him.

'Poor sods,' he murmured. 'Poor bloody sods,' and turned quickly as he heard a sound behind him.

Claudia stood staring at the photograph, her face screwed up in pain, and he felt another stab of remorse as he remembered how he'd used her and deceived her in his pursuit of Jeff.

'I never saw him look like that,' she said. 'I can see now that he never loved me at all. Neither did you. It was all a pretence. What a fool I've been.'

She stifled a little sob and he gave an exclamation and tore the photograph across. She gasped and he looked at her and nodded, his face grim.

'That's all over,' he said. 'Done with. But we're still friends, aren't we?'

Chapter Twenty

Clemmie stood at her bedroom window watching Quentin climbing up from the woods with Punch labouring faithfully at his heels and she smiled sadly to herself. How terrible it was to be old – stiff, slow, clumsy – when inside she still felt the same pulsings of life and love that she'd always known; the urge to go for a long brisk walk or dig a flowerbed and then hoe a row or two in the kitchen garden. It was still a shock to see the age-mottled wrinkled face in the bathroom mirror and know it for her own or to catch a glimpse of a bent, mouselike creature in a plate-glass window and recognise it as herself.

The sky was grey, the heavy clouds bulging with the weight of water, and more rain was forecast. It seemed to have been raining for months and Clemmie woke each morning longing to see the sun shining in through the bedroom window. Now Phyllida had taken Lucy to stay with her parents, Clemmie missed them terribly. They'd become part of the household so quickly. She knew that Phyllida had gone, as much as anything, to give the Halliwells a break from Lucy's chatter and an opportunity to be peaceful for a while.

But we don't want to be peaceful, thought Clemmie, climbing back into bed. We've had plenty of years of peace and she won't be here for long. We want to make the most of both of them. But then what?

She sighed and pulled the quilt higher round her shoulders. It might be August but it was dank and chill and Clemmie's joints ached. She knew that when Phyllida and Lucy left them, she and Quentin would have to face up to the fact of their old age. They must look about for a small place in Tavistock, perhaps sheltered accommodation. She grimaced but turned it into a smile as Quentin arrived with her morning tea. There was a bunch of oxeye daisies on the tray with a few scarlet poppies and she raised her eyebrows at him.

'I crossed the bridge,' he admitted, 'and went a little way down the lane. The wood's very wet and it's dark under the trees with all the leaves dripping. Very melancholy some-how.'

His voice was sad and she wondered if he, too, were missing the girls. She felt no pang of jealousy at the thought but instead a glow of relief and gratitude spread through her that, at long last, she could react normally to any thought she might have about Quentin in relation with another woman.

And it's got nothing to do with being old or loving him less, she told herself firmly. If anything, I love him more than ever.

She poured their tea, passed his cup and wondered whether to broach the subject of the move from The Grange.

'Tavistock morning?' she began. 'Library and the bank

and some lunch at the Bedford? What d'you think

He brightened a little as he sipped.

'Good idea. Cheer us up a bit. I miss—' he caugh
up quickly out of habit. 'I miss the sunshine,' he
can't get on in the garden.'

Her heart ached as she thought of how often
watched his words and controlled his feelings – even per
natural harmless ones – lest he should hurt her mo
sensitivity or arouse her jealousy. She smiled at him o
her cup.

'It's so quiet without them, isn't it? I miss them both
What shall we do when they leave us?' She pretended to
ponder this question. 'Perhaps we should think of moving
after all, Quentin. It might be quite fun in Tavistock. More to
do and people around. We'll be able to manage less and less
here, won't we? We should look upon it as a new venture;
the start of a new life.'

He didn't answer and she watched him anxiously out of
the corner of her eye.

'It's inevitable, I suppose,' he said at last. 'I've thought
of it, of course. Phyllida coming to stay postponed it for a
while but I've thought about it and wondered where we
might go.'

'Let's be positive,' she said, placing her cup back on the
tray, and her voice was almost pleading. 'Let's accept it and
try to make it fun. Looking for somewhere to live and so on
and deciding where we want to be.'

He saw the misery at the back of her eyes and reached for
her hand and held it tightly. 'As long as we're together,' he
said, 'it doesn't matter where we are. Not really. Does it?

t's be glad that we've still got each other. You're quite
ght. We'll make it fun.'

She squeezed his hand gratefully. 'Phyllida will be with
s until the beginning of March,' she said. 'We'll have next
spring and summer to look about and then we can move in
the autumn. Gives us plenty of time.'

Her words seemed to hang in the air; plenty of time. Both
remained silent, aware that the one thing they might not have
was plenty of time, knowing that each was frail and vulnerable
and that, at any moment, one of them might be taken and the
other required to go on alone.

Alistair stood at the window of his cabin and stared out over
Gare Loch, watching the rain sweeping in from the west. His
thoughts were far away in Devon and he was trying to come
to a decision. He knew now that he'd been a fool to be
influenced by another person's experience and to write that
pompous letter he'd sent to Phyllida in July. He shook his
head, embarrassed at the thought of it now that his temper
had cooled, but he really hadn't imagined that she would
flout his wishes quite like that. She'd always been so pliable
and ready to be persuaded. Even taking her resentment and
hurt into consideration, he hadn't expected her to be so
defiant.

Alistair took his hands out of his pockets and crossed his
arms. It had come as such a shock that his reaction had been
too extreme. He'd waited for a reply to that letter and the
days had stretched into weeks and nothing had arrived. Since
he'd be going back to sea in a few weeks' time, this would
mean another two months of enforced silence and he shook

his head involuntarily at the thought of it. He considered
going down to see her at The Grange but rejected the idea
almost at once. How on earth could they have any sensible
conversation with two old people hovering about? Alistair
balled his fists into his armpits. It was all so bloody
frustrating! The one thing of which he was quite certain was
that he wanted Phyllida and nobody else. That at least was
clear. He'd been a fool to refuse to go down for his leave in
September and he was busy trying to decide how he could
put that right without losing too much face.

At one point, he'd swallowed his pride and telephoned
The Grange only to be told that Phyllida was with her parents
and wouldn't be back for another week. He'd hung up as
quickly as possible without seeming rude, unwilling to get
into a conversation with the old lady at the other end, and
then wondered if he should telephone Phyllida upcountry. He
wondered if his mother-in-law knew the truth and his courage
failed him. She'd fought against the marriage in the first
place, learning of his reputation from Phyllida's brother,
Matthew, who'd been appointed to Washington eighteen
months ago and who, with luck, mightn't have heard the
rumours and informed his family. Surely Phyllida wouldn't
have told her! Since that silly letter, he couldn't be certain
any more.

He turned back into the cabin and his eye fell on the
photograph by his bed. Phyllida smiled sunnily out at him,
her arm round Lucy who stood on a low wall beside her.
Their happy trusting faces brought a lump to his throat and,
for a moment, the picture blurred before his eyes. He
swallowed furiously and jumped at a knock on the door. He

glanced at his watch and swore under his breath.

'Just coming,' he said to the head that poked round the door. 'See you down on the court.'

The head vanished and Alistair began to drag out his squash kit. He'd made up his mind. This evening he would write a sensible letter and put things right between them for good. Phyllida had tried to achieve that in her letter to him. He saw that now. She'd found it difficult to let the old couple down and back out of her arrangement to stay with them but had made it quite clear that she was open to discussion as to where they should go when he left the boat next March. This was as good as saying that she was prepared to start again and, if he hadn't been so pig-headed, he would have accepted the compromise and they wouldn't be in this foolish situation.

He simply couldn't believe that there was any real danger to their marriage. Phyllida wasn't the sort to take up with another man or try any tit for tat measures; nevertheless it was madness to take chances or waste any more time on top of the enforced separation that the Navy imposed upon them. Her silence was making him nervous. If only she'd written, he could have replied at once. The trouble was that the longer you let a thing drag on the more difficult it became to put right. Well, this had dragged on quite long enough. He wouldn't risk a telephone call which might get off on the wrong note but he'd write as soon as he'd finished his game of squash. He wanted to see her during his next leave even if it had to be at The Grange with the old biddies in attendance.

His heart felt lighter at this decision and confidence in

Phyllida's love surged over him so that when he looked again at the photograph there were no more tears in his eyes. He smiled back at them as he lifted his racquet from the bed and gave a little wink.

'See you soon, girls,' he said and hurried out.

Uncle Eustace and Oliver faced each other across Liz's kitchen table. Liz was at the office but Christina was privy to their plans and part of the team.

'You see the problem,' Uncle Eustace was saying. 'We've got to think of something really exciting. Something new and different, never done before but that people will want.'

'The snag is,' said Oliver reflectively, 'everything I think of has been done before. It's difficult to come up with something really new.'

'Difficult but not impossible,' insisted Uncle Eustace. He glanced at Christina who sat, chin in hand, watching Oliver. 'Any ideas? If you can't think, put the kettle on. Better still, get us a drink. It'll help us to concentrate. What with my money and brains and your youth and education we should be able to think of something.' He looked with pleasure at the whisky Christina had poured for him – she had no idea about spirits and it was a treble at least – and beamed up at her. 'A widget. That's what we need.'

She took a can of beer from the fridge, pouring some for Oliver and putting the rest into her own glass. He winked at her and she grinned back, her heart all over the place. This was almost as good as any fantasies she'd made up. That Oliver and Unk should decide to go into business together was amazing enough, that their meetings should take place in her own home was nothing short of miraculous!

'Here's to us and Unk's widget,' she said and went to open the window wider so that the smell of his cigarettes shouldn't be too apparent when Liz came home.

The telephone rang and she disappeared to answer it.

'Got a crush on you,' announced Uncle Eustace.

'I know.' Oliver's tone was a nice blend of desperate resignation. 'Crazy! She's known me all her life.'

'She hasn't been a woman all her life.'

'She's hardly one now,' protested Oliver. 'She's only sixteen.'

'Old enough,' observed Uncle Eustace. 'Females develop quicker than males. You'd better watch it. Don't want to hurt her.'

'Of course I don't,' returned Oliver crossly. 'And I don't want to encourage her, either.'

They fell silent as Christina could be heard returning.

'It was Daddy,' she said. 'To arrange the holiday. He's down here seeing friends so he's going to pick me up. That's nice, isn't it?'

Uncle Eustace looked at her sharply. 'Coming here?' he asked, undeceived by her innocent tone. 'Does Mum know?'

'Not yet.' Christina sounded defensive. 'I shall tell her, don't worry.'

They stared at each other for a moment and Uncle Eustace shook his head.

'Be very careful, my darling, that's all. People who play with fire sometimes get burned.'

'I'll be careful,' said Christina. 'No need to worry. Concentrate on your widget, Unk, and leave the rest to me.'

Chapter Twenty-one

The ten days that had to be survived before the result of her test was known seemed the longest that Claudia had ever lived through. She realised how precious her life was to her and how everything, even the shock of Jeff's betrayal, faded into insignificance once she knew that she might be facing a death sentence. She'd been missing Phyllida terribly and longing for her return so that she could share her unhappiness. Phyllida was the one person she knew who would understand what she was suffering and whom she could trust with her awful secret.

One thing was made clear, however. She wasn't pregnant. She'd jumped to conclusions far too rapidly, loss of periods being fairly natural when newly off the pill after five years. Her relief was enormous and she clung to this in the days that followed as the one bright spot amongst the fear and desperation. As she wandered round the house – up and down the stairs and into rooms to stare unseeingly from their windows – she saw how much of her life had been wasted on futile passions and desires and she knew that, if only she could be delivered from this dreadful uncertainty, she would live very differently in the future.

This noble, but sadly impractical, resolution was put severely to the test when Jenny called to see her on the evening before she was due to return to the clinic to hear the results. All the old resentments flared up at the sight of her, waiting on the doorstep, and it was some seconds before she remembered that all her jealousies had been totally unfounded and that Jenny had never been a threat to her at all. Nevertheless, it was an effort to smile at her and invite her in whilst maintaining a dignified front to cover her anxiety lest she should mention Jeff. Jenny did so at once.

'I just wondered how you're getting on with Jeff gone,' she said, dropping her bag on a kitchen chair. 'Perhaps you'd like to come and have some supper at the pub? Gavin's on this evening and he said he'll look out for us.'

'Oh.' Claudia was taken aback. She hadn't expected such an invitation and, quite suddenly, she knew that she'd love to go out, to be amongst happy carefree human beings and simply pretend that all was well for a few hours. 'I'd like that,' she said and hesitated.

It occurred to her that there would be a terrible strain in maintaining the fiction that Jeff had merely gone back to Sussex ahead of her and that all was well between them. Since Liz was away on holiday, Claudia had no idea what was being said at the office. Jenny was watching her, her bright little face sympathetic.

'I know all about it, if that helps,' she said bluntly. 'I hope you won't be cross but Gavin told me everything. I'm ever so sorry. It must've been a terrible shock.'

Claudia stared at her with horror that bordered on anger. How dare Gavin tell her! How could he! And he'd sworn that he could be trusted. Colour rushed into her face and she grasped the back of a chair.

'He had no right. He promised—'

'Don't be upset.' Jenny went swiftly round the table and laid a hand on Claudia's tense arm. 'He thought you should have a woman friend to talk to. I shan't tell anyone.'

'That's what Gavin said.' Claudia sounded mortified and she pressed her lips together to stop them trembling with fear and rage.

'I guessed, you see,' said Jenny simply. 'I knew about Gavin from the beginning. I was a sort of a cover for him. And then I began to wonder about Jeff . . .'

'But how? Oh God!'

Claudia sat down at the table and covered her face with her hands. She had no energy to brazen it out or freeze Jenny off. She felt helpless and humiliated. If Jenny had guessed perhaps other people had, too. She thought about it and gave a little sob of misery. Jenny touched her shoulder.

'Don't, love. No one else will know. Don't be upset. I promise you, no one else would've guessed anything. Come on. We've all got our secrets. Why d'you think I left Bristol in a hurry? I got pregnant and had to have an abortion. He was married and there was a hell of a row. Gavin knows but nobody else. I needed a bit of support myself when I got here. That's why Gavin told me about you. He thought you might like some moral support.'

Helplessly, Claudia began to cry. Tears welled up from some deep spring and forced themselves from under her screwed-up eyelids. She crossed her arms and, laying her head upon them, wept as though she would never stop.

'I'm so afraid,' she gasped. 'I'm frightened I might have AIDS.'

She sobbed out her fear, whilst Jenny stood gently stroking her shoulder and murmuring comfortingly to her. Presently her sobs lessened and she raised her head, fumbling for her handkerchief. Jenny stepped across and ripped several sheets of kitchen towel from the roll.

'Here, love. Mop yourself up with this. Can I get you anything?'

Claudia shook her head, keeping her eyes carefully down and Jenny bit her lip consideringly.

'I'll go if you want me to. I don't want to interfere, honestly. It's just I could imagine how frightened you must be. I'd be out of my mind. Christ! And I couldn't bear the thought of you sitting here all alone, that's all. I expect you've got friends to talk to and you don't need me.' Jenny picked up her bag.

'Don't go!' Claudia summoned up all her courage and looked full at her. 'I haven't got anyone else at the moment. Only Gavin. I couldn't . . .' She shook her head. 'I couldn't talk about it to anyone else. Do they . . . ?' She swallowed and tears threatened again. 'Do they know at the office about . . . ? You know?'

'Course not!' Jenny sounded cheerful. 'Too dense most of 'em to notice anything that isn't stuck under their noses. And Jeff played it perfectly. Talked about his mother as if she was a right old bat but like he was under her thumb, if you know what I mean. He was very clever. Everyone's on your side. Indignant, like. You know? "Why should poor old Claudia have to sell that lovely house and go back just 'cause he's a mummy's boy?" That sort of thing. No one would be a bit surprised if you stayed put. And it would be a miracle, let's face it, if you could sell the house, anyway.'

'I feel such a fool.' Claudia stared at her hands. 'That I never guessed anything. I just thought . . .' She paused. She'd already gone too far and felt the need to keep some pride intact.

'I don't think anyone would, unless they were that way themselves. Or very close to it. Like me with Gavin. Jeff was so buttoned-up, wasn't he? So proper? No, you needn't worry. Nobody'll suspect anything.'

She stood by the door, watching the other woman and wondering whether to go or stay. Claudia was so prickly and, after all, they'd never liked each other. She wouldn't have come if Gavin hadn't pushed her into it; bullied her, almost. Now she was here, though, she felt really sorry for her. Her glance wandered round the immaculate kitchen and she gave a tiny grimace. Beautiful, expensive things weren't quite so important when the executioner's blade was poised a few inches from the back of your neck. She looked at Claudia again and was moved, despite herself, by the expression of despair on her blotched face.

'Come on, love,' she said impulsively. 'Don't let it get to you. I'm sure you're OK. Jeff wasn't the sort to mess around. Too scared. Do your face and come and have a drink. Why not, eh?'

Claudia nodded and smiled waveringly. 'I think you're right. It'll do me good to get out. I'll go and get tidied up.'

'You do that,' said Jenny encouragingly. 'Put the old warpaint on and we'll show 'em.'

She mooched round the kitchen as Claudia went upstairs, wondering what on earth they'd talk about all evening. She couldn't think of a single thing they had in common and her heart sank a little at the prospect of it. Never mind. It need only be the once. Claudia wouldn't want her when she'd pulled herself together.

She'll probably hate my guts, Jenny thought, 'cause I saw her with her defences down, poor cow.

'Ready.'

Claudia was standing in the doorway and Jenny felt a very genuine sympathy for her, sensing how difficult it was for someone of Claudia's temperament to have to climb down from her superior position to be an object of pity. For a brief – a very brief – second, Jenny remembered the put-downs, the barely concealed sneers, the glances of contempt and her own pride raised its head a little and she realised how tempting it was to use the very weapons that had once been used against oneself. She made an effort and smiled naturally.

'You look great.'

They went out together, exchanging only a comment or two before they arrived at the pub. Jenny waved to Gavin behind the bar. He nodded to her and raised his eyebrows interrogatively at Claudia, an expression of pretended fear on his face which didn't altogether disguise the real anxiety beneath it. She gazed at him unsmilingly, still not quite able to forgive him for exposing her so readily, but when he looked seriously concerned she smiled a little before sitting down in the corner. She didn't feel up to talking to him. She fumbled for her purse but Jenny shook her head.

'I'll get these,' she offered. 'What would you like?'

'Um.' Claudia gathered her wits together. She felt almost light-headed after her bout of weeping and wondered whether she should be drinking anything at all. 'Some wine, I think. A glass of medium white would be nice. Thanks.'

She sat still, staring at nothing, not wanting to see Gavin and Jenny discussing what had happened without appearing to be talking about her. She turned her head away and felt strangely lonely. She wondered quite suddenly whether Andy, too, knew all about it and her heart sank. He would surely be the sort who would whisper it, in confidence, to anyone who might take his fancy. Was there no end to this fear of discovery and shame? She glanced up as Jenny set a glass beside her.

'Thanks. I was just thinking. I haven't seen Andy around for a bit. Is he OK?'

'Oh, he's gone back to Bristol,' said Jenny, sitting opposite. 'Thank goodness. There simply wasn't room for both of us.'

She smiled at Claudia and raised her glass and Claudia smiled back, relief lifting her heart.

'Yes, you must have been cramped.'

Claudia took a great gulp of wine and closed her eyes for a moment. When she opened them again, Jenny was watching her concernedly.

'You OK?'

'I think so.' Claudia tried to look more cheerful. 'Tired, really. And I haven't been eating properly.'

'Too frightened, I should think,' said Jenny with her characteristic frankness. 'I would be. Tomorrow, isn't it?'

Claudia nodded and looked at her with a kind of horrified amazement.

'I can hardly believe it sometimes. It all happened so quickly and . . .' She took another drink. 'I can't think straight.'

'I can believe it.' Jenny looked thoughtful. 'It would push everything out of your head, I expect. Nothing else would matter but what the man's going to say tomorrow.'

'That's it.' Claudia looked at her curiously. It surprised her that the light-hearted Jenny should be able to understand these sensations. 'I feel guilty, to tell you the truth.' She took another sip to give her courage. 'I loved Jeff, you see, really loved him. But now it's like it never happened. I don't care about him. All I'm worried about is me.'

She sat back and watched how Jenny would react to this but Jenny was looking at her in perfect accord.

''Course you are. Christ! Why not? It's bound to knock you for six. It's bad enough if it's another woman but this . . .' She shook her head and blew out her lips. 'Bit much, isn't it, trying to be normal at your expense? And then dashing off with the old boyfriend the minute he shows up! Enough to kill anything, I should think.'

Claudia finished her drink. Her head felt light and swimmy and she couldn't quite focus. Jenny giggled suddenly and then looked guilty.

'Sorry. Not trying to make a joke of it or anything but you look a bit squiffy.'

'I think I am.' Claudia chuckled too and suddenly felt certain that all would be well. 'I haven't eaten since . . . well, I can't remember when.'

'Let's order. Gavin'll see you get extra. Is he going with you tomorrow?'

Claudia nodded, a tiny icicle of fear sliding through the warmth of her new-found courage.

'He's been very kind.'

'He's a nice guy.' Jenny studied the menu. 'Mixed up, of course, poor thing. And he's very worried about you. I'm glad you're not going alone.' She looked up rather shyly. 'I could come too, if you thought it might do any good. I'm sure you don't need both of us but I just thought I'd offer.'

She looked back at the menu and Claudia experienced a sense of real liking for her. It was so surprising that she needed time to assimilate it and wondered whether it was simply that she was a tiny bit drunk.

'That's really kind but I shall be fine. Really. But thanks for offering.'

'That's OK. What will you have? You need something plain if you haven't eaten for ages. Don't want you throwing up in the loo!'

Even this remark, which a few weeks previously would have made Claudia curl a lip in disgust, had no power to shock. Instead, she nodded agreement.

'You're so right. I think I'll have the chicken.'

'OK. Good idea. No, don't get up. I'll order and we'll sort the bill out later.'

Claudia watched her go and this time smiled at Gavin with genuine warmth which drew an answering grin and a wink. Somehow it no longer mattered that he'd never cared about her except as a pawn in his game with Jeff. She knew that he felt ashamed and that he'd tried to make up for it since by his kindness. She thought of Jeff and saw the two pictures in her mind. On the one side was the image of the

Jeff she'd known: tall and good-looking, smart in his dark suit and wearing his habitually watchful expression. On the other was the Jeff of the photograph – the image of which was now burned into her mind and returned regularly with clear and painful clarity – with Mike. How could she have competed successfully against such odds?

Before the feelings of inadequacy and despair could engulf Claudia, Jenny stood at her elbow again. She put a full glass beside her and grinned.

'Drink up,' she said. 'This one's on Gavin.'

Chapter Twenty-two

Lucy sat at Clemmie's kitchen table with her crayons and her colouring book. The door stood open to the courtyard, where Punch was stretched out in the sunshine, and the lazy sounds of summer filtered in soothingly: the coo of pigeons in the trees, the sleepy drone of a bumblebee collecting pollen amongst the flowers, the mewing cry of the buzzard circling high above. Lucy worked quietly, her tongue clenched firmly between her teeth, her chubby fingers clasping the crayon tightly. Clemmie moved round her, making a jelly for tea and gathering together the ingredients for a cake. Occasionally they would look at each other and smile, each content, each absorbed in her own task, yet each glad of the other's company.

Lucy liked Clemmie's kitchen with its flagged floors, whitewashed walls and the great beams that crossed the white ceiling. A pot full of sweet williams stood on the deep window-sill and their scent drifted to mingle with the sharp lime of the jelly and the herbs that had been chopped earlier. She liked the old bentwood rocking chair and the round mahogany-framed clock which hung on the wall next to the dresser and whose deep, regular ticking added to the peacefulness of the hour. Lucy stopped for a moment to watch Clemmie break an egg into the mixture and sighed in pure satisfaction.

'I like it here,' she told Clemmie earnestly. 'Better than anywhere I've ever lived. Can we stay with you for ever?'

Clemmie's hands, beating in the egg, were stilled for a moment and her heart jumped with a mixture of joy and anxiety.

'I wish you could, darling,' she said. 'Wouldn't it be lovely? But we have to think about your daddy, too, don't we?'

Lucy thought about her father. She leaned back in the chair and put her thumb into her mouth, the better to concentrate.

'He can come here, too.' She nodded and beamed blindingly at Clemmie, glad to have solved the problem so simply. 'He'll like it here.'

Clemmie began to pour the mixture into a baking tin and prayed for guidance. 'It's not quite as easy as that,' she began cautiously. 'Daddy may not be given an appointment near enough for him to be able to live here. It would be too far for him to travel. Do you see?'

'You mean like now? He's in Scotland,' said Lucy, proud of her knowledge. 'That's a long, long way to go. And then he goes to sea in the submarine. That's why we never see him.'

'Yes,' agreed Clemmie. 'That's why. But when he stops going to sea you could see him more often. You and Mummy could go and live with him. That would be nice, wouldn't it?'

'Mmm.' Lucy thought about it. She couldn't remember a time when they'd all three lived together. 'I think I'll stay here,' she said, 'with you and Mummy. Daddy can come and visit us if he can't live here, too.'

'Oh, dear,' said Clemmie, feeling the situation slipping from her grasp. 'Poor Daddy. Think how he'd miss you.'

'Oh, he's used to that,' Lucy reassured her. 'He's always missing us. That's because his job is so important.'

Words hovered on Clemmie's tongue but each sentence that she formed was followed by a pitfall that she couldn't quite handle and she remained silent.

'Oh, look!' Lucy, feeling that the subject had been dealt with quite satisfactorily, had returned to her colouring but now she dropped her crayon and sat quite still.

A robin had hopped just within the door and was watching them, his head cocked, his beady eye expectant.

'He's come for his breakfast,' said Clemmie, not without relief at the distraction. 'Where did we put his crumbs?'

Keeping an eye on the robin, Lucy edged herself off her chair and Clemmie passed her the bowl from the dresser. Slowly, slowly, Lucy crept towards him, pausing as he gave a little flutter of alarm, and threw a few crumbs at his feet. He pecked them up and she threw another fistful, this time beyond him so that he hopped after them out of the door, and she followed him into the sunshine. Punch raised his heavy head and rolled his eye at the crumbs, decided that the result wasn't worth the effort and resumed his slumbers.

Clemmie put her cake tin into the oven and went to the door. The robin was pecking up the last of the crumbs and Lucy had sat down beside Punch, insinuating her legs under his head so that it now rested on her lap. Thumb in mouth, her own head now lolled against his black one, she sucked drowsily, her eyes on the robin, her back against the sun-warmed wall. Clemmie knew that her heart would break all over again when Phyllida and Lucy went away but she also knew that the pain would be a just payment for these months that were making a perfect ending to their lives at The Grange. If only she could be as certain that it was just as right for Phyllida. She'd noticed that there had been no letters from Alistair recently, although she was convinced that it was he who had telephoned when Phyllida was away with her parents, and she feared that the rift might be widening. It would be too terrible if she and Quentin were taking this joy at Phyllida's expense.

Clemmie raised a finger to her lips as the door opened and Quentin came into the courtyard. He nodded, smiling, as she indicated the now sleeping Lucy and followed his wife into the kitchen. They smiled at each other and instinctively and wordlessly embraced. Lately, it was as if they knew that time was passing so quickly for them that outward expressions of their love were terribly important, especially now that the presence of Phyllida and Lucy had removed the shadow and enabled them to show it without reservations of any kind. The relief to Quentin was so enormous that his joy and gratitude seemed to mount up on wings. To be absolved of the guilt he had hugged to himself for forty years was like the removal of a growth, whose poison had tainted all his actions and whose presence had pressed heavily on his heart.

'Where's Phyllida?' he asked.

'She's walked down to the bridge,' she told him. 'Oliver

rang up. He's coming to lunch and she's gone down to meet him. He can park down by the bridge and they can come back together.'

'I suppose everything's all right.'

It was a statement rather than a question but Clemmie glanced at him anxiously.

'I'm a bit worried that she hasn't heard from Alistair,' she admitted. 'I know he's away at sea for some of the time but I should have thought that he's ashore again by now.'

'She told me that he goes on courses between patrols.' Quentin went to wash his hands at the sink. 'And she might have heard from him when she was at her mother's.'

'Yes.' Clemmie piled the dirty pots and pans on the draining board. 'She seems quite happy and I don't want to interfere but . . .' She shook her head and bit her lip. 'Oh, Quentin. I hope that their coming here hasn't rocked the boat. He may have preferred them to be on their own somewhere.'

'Obviously, I can't deny that that might well be so.' Quentin dried his hands on the towel behind the door. 'But as far as I can see, it makes hardly any difference to him where they are, given that he accepts that Phyllida refuses to go to Scotland. He'll come down for leave, won't he?'

'I hope so,' said Clemmie dubiously. 'It might put him off, us being around. That's what worries me.'

Quentin looked thoughtful but, before he could answer, a noise from behind made them exchange a warning glance. Outside, Lucy was waking up. She crawled out from under Punch's head and smiled sleepily at them.

'I winked,' she confided and held up her arms.

Quentin picked her up and held her close and she put her arms round his neck and gave his cheek one of her smacking kisses.

'How are you, my sweetheart?' he asked and she beamed at him.

'I'm going to live with you for ever,' she told him and looked to see his delight at this treat in store for him. 'Clemmie says I can.'

'Well,' he said heartily, after the tiniest pause, 'that sounds splendid.'

He looked questioningly at Clemmie, who made a face, shrugged her shoulders helplessly and sought for some distraction. Lucy supplied it quite naturally.

'I've done you a picture,' she said and he put her down so that she could fetch her book. 'It's you and Punch going for a walk,' she told him, hopping to and fro over the joins in the flagstones as he admired it. 'Shall we go and find Mummy now?'

Clemmie, who could see that Quentin was tired from his morning's exertions in the garden, intervened.

'Will you help me hang the washing out first, Lucy?' she asked. 'You can bring the pegs.'

Quentin watched them go and sank down in relief in the rocking chair. His legs and back ached so much he wondered how he'd kept upright and he sat quite still in an attempt to relax and ease his painful joints. He, too, wondered and worried about Phyllida and suspected, from one or two things that she'd let drop, that Alistair was not very happy at their temporary move to The Grange. Having rid himself of one guilt, he couldn't bear the thought of having to shoulder another. Yet Phyllida and Lucy were so dear to him that he hated the idea that he might be responsible for any trouble between them and Alistair. Wondering why life had to be so complicated, he dropped his head back on the cushion and presently he dozed.

Phyllida was already waiting on the bridge when Oliver came down the lane in his little Fiat. She waved and he pulled in on the other side and came to meet her. He carried a large carrier bag in one hand but he slipped his other arm round her shoulder and gave her a hug.

'How are you?' she asked, surprised as usual at how pleased she was to see him and hugging him in return.

'Fine.' They fell into step together as they left the bridge. 'How's everyone?'

'We're all fine. Well . . .' She hesitated. 'Clemmie and Quentin look pretty frail, some days more than others. Thank goodness the sun's shining again. It helps when you're old and creaky.' She frowned a little. 'I worry about them. It's OK while I'm here to keep an eye on them but what will they do when I go? I'm sure they shouldn't be stuck out here miles from anywhere, all on their own.' She looked at him anxiously. 'I hope you don't think I'm interfering. I know I haven't known them long but it's like it's been for ever. Lucy adores them.'

Oliver let her go in front along the narrow path, the mere sight of her causing his heart to beat fast and giving him a lightness of spirit.

'I don't think you're interfering at all,' he told her. 'We all worry about them. The trouble is that it's going to break their hearts to leave The Grange and none of us can bear to broach the subject. It's cowardly really. We keep hoping that something will happen to take it out of our hands, thus absolving us of making the decision about what should be done.'

Phyllida was silent. She knew exactly what he meant. She was in the same situation regarding Alistair and their marriage. Several times she'd attempted to frame a reply to his pompous, blighting letter and each time she'd failed. It was easier to do nothing, hoping that fate would take a hand and solve the problem for her. When Clemmie told her that she thought it was Alistair who had telephoned, her heart had leaped up with relief. The silence would now be broken and they could move forward. But he didn't telephone again and when Phyllida, taking all her courage in her hands, telephoned the naval base she was told that Commander Makepeace had gone ashore for the evening. Immediately imagining Alistair enjoying himself at some party, Phyllida hardened her heart and refused to leave a message. So the impasse continued. Her life seemed to be in some sort of limbo and there was a peace about it that was seductive.

'You're very quiet.' Oliver spoke at last and Phyllida was once again aware of the rushing of the river and the clamour of the birdsong.

She turned suddenly and the love on his face startled her out of her preoccupation and silenced the words that she'd started to speak. She stared at him and he looked away from her.

'Oliver?' she said gently and halted, wondering if she could have been mistaken.

'It doesn't matter,' he said rapidly, still staring out across the river. 'Can't seem to help myself, somehow, but I don't want to be a nuisance. Can we just pretend it hasn't happened?'

He looked at her at last and the expression on his face touched her heart and moved her strangely. Coming at the end of nearly a year of unhappiness and insecurity, his love was comforting balm to her pride and the novelty of discovering it caught her off balance. The mixture of surprise and gratitude as she looked back at him caused him to stretch out a hand to her quite involuntarily and she took it and held it tightly.

'But I like it,' she said childishly and he laughed.

'Then that's all right. It needn't hurt anyone. I know you're a happily married woman so you're in no danger from me.'

Phyllida opened her mouth to correct his image of her and wisely shut it again. It was bad enough to blurt out her gratitude for his love but there was no need to be too foolish. She continued to hold his hand though and they went on slowly together in silence until they reached the stile.

Lucy, who was helping Clemmie to lay the table whilst Quentin carved the cold beef, gave a cry of joy when she saw Oliver. She ran to greet him and Oliver bent to hug her, smiling at the Halliwells over her head.

'Present,' he said, giving her the carrier bag and everyone stood still to watch her open it.

She put it on the floor, plunged her hands inside and drew out a gorgeous grey felt parrot. His white comb was jauntily erect, his black eye had a saucy look and his talons were arranged so that he could stand unaided. He was soft and cuddly and an exact replica of Percy the Parrot who appeared with Polly on children's television. Lucy gazed at him speechlessly, touching his beak with a gentle finger, and Phyllida looked at Oliver and there were tears in her eyes. He knew that if they'd been alone she would have thrown her arms round him and let him kiss her and he thanked God that the scene had taken place in the Halliwells' kitchen. He might not have been able to control himself quite so well as he had in the wood.

'Oh, Lucy,' said Phyllida and her voice was not quite steady. 'What a lovely, lovely present.'

'It's Percy,' said Lucy, as though she couldn't quite believe it. 'It's Percy the Parrot.'

'It is indeed,' said Oliver cheerfully. 'All the way from London, especially for you. Just like the one on the television except this one doesn't speak, I'm afraid. You'll have to do that bit yourself.'

' "Pretty Polly, Pretty Polly," ' crowed Lucy and jumping up she ran to Oliver.

He sat down in the rocking chair and pulled her on to his lap and she held the parrot close to him, butting its beak gently on his cheek. Quentin returned to his carving and Clemmie to her knives and forks but Phyllida watched with softened eyes the two in the rocking chair and Oliver winked at her over Lucy's head. She smiled back at him and pulled herself together.

'I didn't hear you say thank you, Lucy,' she said, picking up the bag. 'Look. There's something else here. It's a badge and there's a booklet. "Join the Percy the Parrot Club",' she read and began to laugh. 'What fun. It's the latest craze, isn't it? They'll be doing T-shirts next, I suppose. You'd like one of those, wouldn't you, Lucy?'

Oliver sat up straight so suddenly that Lucy and Phyllida, who was pinning the badge to Lucy's T-shirt, stared at him.

'Of course!' he said softly and his eyes blazed with inspiration. 'Why ever didn't I think of it before? It's brilliant!'

'What is it?' Phyllida looked at him curiously whilst Lucy hugged Percy to her breast, her eyes wide.

He smiled at Phyllida and she felt a tiny twinge of jealousy that his newly expressed love for her seemed to have been so completely forgotten in this more recent excitement.

'You're a clever girl,' he said. 'You've just discovered Uncle Eustace's widget.'

He set Lucy gently on her feet and stood up, smiling at their puzzled faces. 'I'm not really mad,' he said apologetically, 'and I'll explain it over lunch. But do you think I could use your telephone, Quentin? It's so terrific, I simply can't wait to tell Uncle Eustace that our problems are over and we've got a whole new career!'

Chapter Twenty-three

Despite the fact that her test had proved negative, Claudia was still living in the limbo that seems to paralyse the minds of those who are forced to wait for some major result or decision which will ultimately affect their lives quite drastically. Her brief euphoric relief was almost immediately tempered by the knowledge that she must return in three months for another test and, although she tried hard to keep her spirits up, she could never quite banish it from her thoughts. It was merely a precaution, they'd assured her, just to be on the safe side, and with that she had to be content.

Her secret knowledge had effectively isolated her from most of her previous activities and she had far too much time in which to brood and become depressed. Sometimes she felt that, if only she could be uninfected by this terrible disease, she would be so grateful and happy that nothing else would matter but, at other times, she wondered what on earth she would do with herself now that Jeff was gone. She'd begun to miss him dreadfully but, even had it been an option, she knew that she would never have him back. She shivered at the thought of it. Never again would she put herself at risk, and this added to her isolation. She suspected that she'd never feel safe again in a physical relationship; every male that approached would be suspect as far as she was concerned. Nobody would be exempt. After all, who would have thought of suspecting Jeff?

She was unable to tell the truth to Liz and certainly not to Abby. Pouring out the whole sordid tale to one or other of them was out of the question and she felt herself shrivel up inside at the mere thought of exposing herself so far. Apart from anything else, the fewer people who knew about it the better. Excepting Phyllida, only Gavin and Jenny were trustworthy and then simply because they had their own secrets. She began to long for Phyllida's return, persuading herself that the relief of having someone to talk to would outweigh the shame of describing what had happened.

Once Phyllida was back from her holiday with her parents, however, Claudia was seized with nerves at the thought of telling her and, right up to the moment when they were sitting together on Claudia's little terrace after lunch, she doubted she had the courage to do it. Phyllida pushed her into it quite unwittingly.

'You've lost weight,' she said, studying Claudia thoughtfully. 'Don't think me rude if I say that you're too thin. Have you been dieting or has something been going on I don't know about?'

She spoke quite lightly but Claudia felt the treacherous tears fill her eyes and she stared blindly down the garden. Phyllida looked at her more closely and knew that something had indeed been going on. She was aware of several simultaneous reactions. The strongest was to persuade Claudia to talk about the problem, another was to respect her pride and pretend she hadn't noticed anything. Phyllida dithered. Affection elbowed tact aside and she reached out her hand and touched Claudia's arm.

'I really don't want to interfere,' she said awkwardly, 'but if there's anything I can do . . .'

She paused and Claudia swallowed several times. Now that the moment was here, the thought of exposing herself, her marriage, the awful sordidness of it all to Phyllida's gaze was appalling to her and she wondered how she could have ever thought it possible. How would she react? Desperation came to her rescue; she simply couldn't go on hiding behind a façade any longer. Surely she could trust her to understand! After all, Phyllida had been ready to share her own secrets, to discuss them and accept comfort and advice.

'Jeff's left me.' She said it quickly before she could change her mind and bit her lips to stop them trembling.

'Left you?' Phyllida's voice seemed to come from a great distance away and after a long silence. 'But why?' She hesitated. 'I'm sorry. I really don't want to pry but you seemed so happy.'

'We were in a way but we had . . . there was . . . Oh, hell!' Claudia shook her head. There was no way round it. 'Jeff's a homosexual. I didn't realise. I know that sounds really unbelievable but I didn't.' She gave a dry little sob and pressed her lips tightly together again. Phyllida was quite silent. 'He seemed normal enough except that he didn't have much interest in . . . you know . . . well, lovemaking. I thought it was me. That he didn't fancy me.'

'How perfectly awful for you.' A thousand questions knocked at Phyllida's lips but, guessing just how much courage it had cost Claudia to tell her the bare facts, she asked none of them. 'It must have been the most appalling shock.'

'I can still hardly believe it. It was just before you went away.' Claudia clenched her fingers and then crossed her arms, tucking her hands out of sight.

'I'm sorry.' Phyllida sounded genuinely remorseful. 'What rotten timing. And after you were so good to me about Alistair.'

This made Claudia feel a little better; rather as though Phyllida thought their positions were equal.

'It's not the same though, is it? What Alistair did was, well, normal, wasn't it? I don't mean it made it easier for you, just that lots of men do it. I feel such a fool because I never realised. I can't come to grips with the fact that he preferred another man to me.'

'I can imagine that,' said Phyllida thoughtfully. 'You know what you're up against when it's another woman.'

'That's what I mean.' Claudia turned to her eagerly, her shame forgotten in a desire to be understood. 'I always felt inadequate and I never knew what to do about it. Whatever I did, it never worked.'

Phyllida looked at her, carefully keeping any pity out of her voice and face and continuing to consider the matter as unemotionally as possible.

'It must have been terribly frustrating,' she mused. 'And he's such an attractive man.'

'It was humiliating,' Claudia looked away again, remembering.

'Awful,' said Phyllida quickly, trying to spare her from

other embarrassing revelations. 'Why do women always feel guilty when they have physical needs?'

'Do you feel that, too?' Claudia stared at her.

'Of course I do. It seems perfectly reasonable for men to feel like it but for women it's rather shameful, isn't it? Even though it's just as natural.'

'I thought it was just me,' mumbled Claudia.

Phyllida watched her sympathetically and decided to go one step further.

'At least you can have confidence now knowing that it wasn't because Jeff didn't want you but that he didn't want women at all. You don't have to feel inadequate any more. I always feel I'm being compared to women like Janie.'

'I tell myself that but I can't forget his face when he looked at Mike.'

'Mike?'

'Mike was his boyfriend before we got married. He turned up on the doorstep and that's when it all came out. Mike told me about him and Jeff.'

Phyllida gazed at her in horror, shocked into silence, and Claudia nodded as though accepting the horror.

'But that's . . . You mean he just turned up out of the blue and then told you . . . ? Good God! I don't believe it.' Phyllida found her voice at last.

'Neither did I. He showed me a photograph of them together. No.' She shook her head at Phyllida's expression. 'It wasn't . . . disgusting or anything like that. It was almost worse, in a way. They were on holiday, sitting together on a wall in the sun. They had their arms round each other and they looked so happy. I'd never seen Jeff look like that.'

Her voice was almost inaudible and Phyllida felt the urge to put her arms round her and hug her tightly.

'I think you're being terribly brave,' she said. 'When I found out about Alistair I just hid away. It took me ages to be able to talk about it. The trouble is, you feel that somehow it's all your fault. That it's your weaknesses that are to blame, not theirs. And you feel ashamed telling people, especially when they seem to have managed so much better than you have.'

Claudia remembered her own feeling of superiority in the face of Phyllida's troubles and felt a deep sense of regret and a new level of understanding and courage.

'Mike's got AIDS,' she said baldly. 'He came to tell Jeff and when Jeff heard that, he decided he wanted to be with him and see him through it. He went off with him.' She struggled to be fair. 'I told him to go. I couldn't have carried on, once I knew.' She hesitated and when she continued her voice shook. 'I've been to have a blood test just in case, although Jeff said he was clear and hadn't . . . done anything since before we were married.'

This time Phyllida got up and went to crouch beside Claudia's chair. She put an arm round her shoulders and gave her a little hug.

'Oh, Claudia,' she said and Claudia smiled at her gratefully.

'I'm clear,' she said. 'It's OK. But I've got to go back for another one in three months' time. Just to be on the safe side. I'm sure it'll be all right really . . .' and she put her face in her hands and burst into tears.

The great release of telling it all and sharing her shame

and fears was so overwhelming that she simply couldn't help herself. Phyllida hugged her tightly and waited for the storm to pass. She felt as though they'd negotiated a dangerous minefield and emerged the other side successfully. When Claudia became calmer, Phyllida stood up.

'I'm going to make us some tea,' she said, certain that Claudia would prefer to have a moment or two to pull herself together and regain some composure. 'Shan't be long.'

Claudia sat quite still. She knew that something important and valuable had happened between her and Phyllida and, though she felt drained of energy and emotion, she was aware of a new sense of peace. There was much more to say but, for the moment, it could all be put aside and she could enjoy this feeling of respite. She smiled when Phyllida appeared with the tray – despite the fact that she'd used odd saucers and had forgotten the sugar spoon – guessing that there might be some awkwardness at picking up the threads of conversation again.

'So how was your holiday?' she asked, accepting a cup of tea. 'Did your mum give you the third degree? I've been wondering how it went. Take my mind off my worries and tell me all about it.'

It was Christina who'd had the idea of the mail-order catalogue for Percy the Parrot children's clothes.

'I think she's right, Unk,' said Oliver after a moment. 'We've already got a captive market with the Percy the Parrot Club and we could use mail order to create more members.'

Unk smoked thoughtfully whilst the other two watched

him. Percy the Parrot's creator was a friend of Oliver's parents and she'd been very willing to listen to their ideas. Nevertheless, just thinking of designing the clothes wasn't nearly enough.

'They've got to be fun,' said Christina, leaning both elbows on the table. 'Not just boring old T-shirts. Fun clothes that'll turn the kids on so they nag and nag till they've got them.'

'Are small children that interested in clothes?' Uncle Eustace looked surprised.

''Course they are! If there's a gimmick. You'll have to get kids wearing them on to the programme. You know? A sort of *Clothes Show* for teeny-weenies!'

'That's absolutely brilliant, Christina,' said Oliver slowly. 'Then every child who watches the programme will want a Percy the Parrot something or other. Aren't you clever? I think you should leave school and join the team.'

'And I think you should stop putting ideas in her head.' Liz was standing behind them. 'And we need the table for supper. Did you remember to do the vegetables, Christina, or were you too taken up with the Think Tank?'

'They're all done.' Christina, exalted by Oliver's praise, twisted round on her chair. 'What d'you think, Mum? A mail-order catalogue for Percy the Parrot clothes. Good, isn't it?'

'I should have thought our society was quite weighed down enough already with consumer products. It sounds to me like another way of putting pressure on hard-working mothers to buy yet more unnecessary luxury items for spoiled children.'

'Well.' Uncle Eustace pushed back his chair with a tiny wink for Christina and Oliver. 'That certainly puts us in our place. No chance, I suppose, of putting the case for creating employment?'

But Liz was back in the kitchen and they started to clear the table, still preoccupied with the new idea.

'There's an awful lot to think about,' said Oliver. 'To begin with, who does the designs? Do we advertise?'

'Have to,' said Uncle Eustace. 'The making of the clothes will be subcontracted out, of course. But we need someone with a flair for colour and material. We'd need to show the garments, I think, not just the designs. Got to make 'em sit up and take notice!'

'Prudence!' exclaimed Christina. 'She's brilliant at making things. Honestly she is. They look really professional.'

The two men gazed at her and Uncle Eustace wrinkled his brow. 'I think I've met her,' he said.

'We went to her party last year,' confirmed Christina. 'Thin woman with specs. She's really sweet but a bit nervous. You'd have to break it to her gently. Oliver can do it. He's good at chatting up the women.'

'Who are you talking about?' asked Liz sharply, back again with plates and dishes.

'Oliver chatting up Prudence.' Christina smiled at her mother. 'She'd be really good at making the clothes, wouldn't she? You know. The samples to show these people?'

'She's a first-class tailor.' Liz put the things on the table. 'She's not just the little woman round the corner. She was properly trained and she's extremely professional.'

'Could she design them, too?' asked Oliver.

Liz pursed her lips and shook her head slowly. 'Most unlikely, I should think. I've known her for years and she's never volunteered to make anything without a pattern.' She turned to Christina. 'Scoot upstairs and get that dress she made for you last winter.'

Surprised and delighted to see her mother taking an interest, Christina raced upstairs. The others looked at each other.

'It's a start,' said Uncle Eustace. 'Would you phone her, Liz? If she's nervous we don't want to frighten her off. Perhaps she could come over for coffee or something and we could take it from there?'

'Why not?' Liz shrugged. 'If it's going to take off then Prudence may as well be in on it. She's always desperate for money. We'll have supper and I'll phone her afterwards. And the sooner you get on with laying the table, instead of standing there with your hands in your pockets, the quicker I'll be able to speak to her!'

Quentin, walking on the slopes above the house a few weeks later, felt the quiet satisfaction of a man whose hunch has played off. It was not coincidence that he and Clemmie had arranged to visit an old friend in north Devon the very week that Alistair was due on leave so that he and Phyllida, with Lucy, should have the place to themselves. Phyllida's delight when his letter arrived was a relief to Quentin. She'd been so taken up with Claudia's problems and Oliver's new project that he'd begun to be afraid but her reaction to Alistair's proposal that he come down for his leave had filled him with delight. He'd already primed Clemmie, so that when he'd asked casually when Alistair would be arriving, and Phyllida read out the dates of his leave, Clemmie had said with wonderful naturalness, 'Oh, isn't that the week we're going to Barnstaple?'

Phyllida had been quite taken in. They both were aware of a flash of relief in her eyes but her pleasure when she knew that they would be back in time to meet Alistair was very genuine. Quentin had taken to him at once. He had great charm and was easy to talk to and it was quite obvious that things had been sorted out between him and Phyllida. Looking out over the heather that covered the higher slopes, Quentin took a great breath deep into his lungs and paused to give Punch an encouraging pat. As he straightened he saw someone climbing up from below and knew at once that it was Alistair. He waited, Punch sitting gratefully at his feet, whilst he approached.

'It's wonderful up here,' he declared as he arrived at Quentin's side. 'Quite breathtaking, I envy you.'

'Well, you needn't.' Quentin told him as they strolled forward together. 'I rarely make it up here these days. Too old and breathless. And it's going to break both our hearts to leave it.'

'I can imagine that. Do you feel that you must?'

'Getting too old to cope with it all.' Quentin sounded quite cheerful but Alistair was not deceived. 'We'll be looking about next spring for something small in Tavistock. Might get one more summer in, if we're lucky.'

'Phyllida says Clemmie's family have lived at The Grange for generations.'

'Perfectly true. She feels it very keenly that Gerard, our

son, doesn't want to take it on. It'll break her heart to see it go out of the family.'

Quentin was glad when Alistair paused to light a cigarette so that he could seize the opportunity to regain his breath although they'd barely been more than sauntering along.

'I should have thought that Gerard would want to hold on to it, if possible.'

Quentin shook his head. 'Too far away from the centre of his world and his own family's all gone. Very urban chap, Gerard. Likes the bright lights and so on. And why not? Very few people want to be buried out here, miles from anywhere.'

They stood gazing out past the great granite outcrops to the misty blue hills in the far distance and Alistair shrugged.

'Looks all right to me.'

Quentin smiled at him. His heart soared suddenly upwards, rather like the lark singing high above them, and he felt a strange affinity with the younger man who stood, drawing quietly on his cigarette, drinking in the magnificence that was spread before him.

'It's not an acquired taste,' he said. 'It has to be bred in the bone. That's my opinion. I'm glad you made it down.'

Alistair turned surprisingly shrewd eyes upon him. 'Did you think I wouldn't?'

Quentin pursed his lips and raised his eyebrows and then nodded. 'I wondered a little, that's all. None of my business.'

Alistair took another lungful of smoke and glanced up at the skylark. 'I've been a bit of a fool,' he admitted at last. 'But Phyllida seems prepared to overlook it.'

'Your Phyllida,' said Quentin after a moment, 'has a great gift. It's the gift of love. It pours out of her and embraces us all quite freely and without any self-seeking. It's very rare.'

Alistair looked at him curiously. 'I'm glad,' he said at last. 'I mean I'm glad you've benefited from it. That is . . .' He hesitated.

'Oh, we have,' said Quentin at once. 'Beyond anything we could have imagined. Phyllida's coming to The Grange has been the greatest thing that could possibly have happened to us.'

'Well!' Alistair laughed a little to cover his embarrassment at Quentin's intensity. 'That's – that's good. I'm glad,' he repeated, somewhat inadequately.

'She's healed us, you see.' Quentin wanted him to understand, feeling it to be, somehow, terribly important. 'We lost a child when she was your Lucy's age and . . .' He swallowed a little and then looked directly at Alistair. 'I was unfaithful to Clemmie at that time. She found it impossible to forgive me completely and it cast a shadow over our lives until Phyllida and Lucy came. Clemmie's jealousy was tied up with her grief which was why it went so deep, I think. We both took so strongly to your wife and child, you see. It was as though Pippa had returned to us, both as a child again and as the woman she would have been and she took away the shadow and the pain.'

He stopped and Alistair took him by the arm, concerned by the pallor of his face and the shortness of his breath, and seeing the tears on his cheeks continued to hold the spare bony arm whilst looking away from the emotion still visible on the tired old face.

'I didn't know,' he muttered. 'I knew about the child but not about . . . not the other. I'm sorry.'

'Don't be sorry.' Quentin was feeling for his handkerchief whilst keeping Alistair's hand pressed close to his side. 'How should you know? And you've generously spared us your family. It's meant so much to us both. We can never repay you for it.'

'Not generously,' Alistair glanced at Quentin who was mopping his face. 'I fought it. I nearly didn't come down. I didn't want her to come here and I wanted to punish her.'

'But you didn't.' Quentin watched him almost tenderly.

Alistair shook his head and gave a short explosive laugh. 'I love her too much. I missed her terribly – and Lucy, of course – but it's been a difficult time.' He stopped but Quentin continued to regard him steadily, in silence, and presently Alistair went on again. 'I was unfaithful, too, you see. Over a year ago. It was nothing, just a silly moment with an old girlfriend, no real excuse like you had although we'd just lost the baby. Phylly found out and all hell was let loose.' He paused again, struggling to be just. 'Even then, she wanted it to work, though. She's always tried. I got impatient with her and things went wrong and I behaved badly when they moved in with you.' He looked at Quentin. 'I'm sorry. I thought . . . I misjudged the situation quite selfishly.'

'All's well, though, now?'

'All's very well, now.' Alistair smiled at him, squeezed his arm and let it go. 'It's been a magic week. Perfect. And to think I might not have come!'

With one accord they turned and began to make their way back down the hill. 'Have you decided where you'll go in the spring? If they stay till then?'

Alistair heard the note of anxiety in Quentin's voice and smiled reassuringly.

'Oh, they'll stay till then,' he said. 'And after that it depends where I go. I hope you don't mind if I come down for Christmas? Just a few days. Not a proper leave.'

'My dear boy,' said Quentin with heartfelt thankfulness, 'I can think of nothing that would give us both greater pleasure. Our last real family Christmas at The Grange.'

They smiled at each other with genuine affection before descending the last few yards and Phyllida, watching their approach from her bedroom window, felt a surge of pleasure at their evident companionship and hurried down to meet them.

Chapter Twenty-four

Oliver, driving over to see Uncle Eustace, negotiated Meavy bridge, drove into the village, past the school and thought of Lucy and of Phyllida. How hard it was to love with no hope of its being returned! Even in his wildest imaginings, he knew that she would never love him, at least, not in the way in which he desired to be loved by her. To begin with she'd regarded him as she might her brothers, with an easy friendly affection which had developed with the friendship, but there had been a moment between his presenting the parrot to Lucy and before she'd received Alistair's letter when she'd been wavering. Aware of his feelings for her, she'd become charmingly shy, almost as if she were grateful, and the excitement surrounding the new venture had given an edge to these emotions and shown them how dangerous they could be.

Oliver crossed the Yelverton-Princetown road and dropped down into Walkhampton. He knew that she loved him now in the way that she loved Clemmie and Quentin, Prudence, Uncle Eustace; with that generous, uncalculating warmth that drew people to her. Would it ever have become more than that? At the end of his holiday, they'd walked through the wood together to the bridge where he'd left his car and she'd hugged him goodbye and then on a mutual impulse they'd kissed; a long, long kiss from which he'd drawn back, shaken, and she'd stared up at him, her eyes dark with anxiety and guilt. He'd smiled at her, lest she should imagine that he'd read more into it than she wished and he'd seen the quick relief and felt his heart plummet like a stone. He knew that she would love him if she could and he'd hugged her tightly once more before turning away to his car and driving off.

He turned out of Horrabridge on the Whitchurch road and his heart was heavy again with remembrance. The next time he'd seen her, she'd received a letter from Alistair suggesting that he come down for his leave and he knew at once that this was what she really wanted. After all, it was obvious that she must try to make a go of things. Lucy loved her father and, despite all that he'd done, Oliver knew that Phyllida loved him too. He remembered Abby's advice and wished that he'd never met her that day in the Bedford, standing a little shyly behind Liz, waiting to be introduced.

He sighed and tried to concentrate on Uncle Eustace and this tremendous opportunity that was now being offered to him. Despite the ache in his heart, Oliver smiled to himself. Luck had certainly been on their side so far. Prudence had come over and had been persuaded that she was more than equal to the task of making the prototype. The idea of Percy the Parrot clothes by mail order had been discussed with the London agent and he'd approved the idea and, later, they'd all met to discuss the way forward.

Still smiling, Oliver parked the car outside Liz's cottage.

It had been a most productive meeting and it was agreed that some designs must be produced, after which further discussions would take place. He and Uncle Eustace had gone home, borne up on a wave of euphoric bliss, and he'd dropped Uncle Eustace off and driven on to report the outcome of the meeting to Phyllida. The smile faded from his face as he recalled how she'd hugged him with joy and how much he loved her and, as he went up the path to Liz's door, he was glad that he had something now in which he could immerse himself.

At that moment, Phyllida was walking in the wood. She was watching for the dipper who always managed to elude her but her mind was on Alistair and the leave they'd shared. His letter had come at exactly the right moment. Oliver's love had thrown her off balance, a welcome flattery to set against Alistair's silence, and she was very attracted to him. It boosted her confidence and she'd been swung along by it, accompanied by the excitement surrounding the Percy the Parrot catalogue and Uncle Eustace. She remembered the kiss on the bridge and she put her hands to her hot cheeks. How easy it would have been to go further, much further!

It was almost in the same spot that she'd stood with Alistair a few weeks later on his return home. She'd gone to meet him from the station and, despite the way he'd taken her in his arms and held her tightly to him, there was still a formality between them as he drove out of Plymouth and up on to the moor. She felt strangely shy although her heart was hammering with love for him and she was so happy that they were together. Alistair was too experienced to make too much of it. He talked easily of mutual friends and asked about Lucy but, when they arrived at Blackthorn Bridge and she told him they were nearly at The Grange, he pulled in at the side of the lane and switched the engine off.

'Let's get out,' he suggested. 'Give me a chance to stretch my legs and have a cigarette.'

She'd slipped out of her seat and walked ahead of him up on to the bridge where she stood looking down the river, still paralysed by shyness.

'How beautiful it is.' Alistair lit a cigarette and looked around him. 'Where does the road go on to? Well, it's hardly more than a track, is it?'

'It only goes to The Grange,' said Phyllida. She felt oddly breathless. 'The lane swings round to the right before the bridge, you see. Clemmie's great-grandfather had the bridge built when he bought a jingle and didn't want to take it through the ford. He was very rich so he had a bridge built just for him.'

He leaned beside her, their hands almost touching, but as he started to speak she gave a cry. His eyes followed her pointing finger and he saw a bird speeding out from beneath the bridge, skimming downstream and vanishing round the bend in the river.

'It was the dipper!' She turned to him, her eyes shining. 'I've never seen him before. Not properly. Clemmie says he always brings her good luck.'

Before she could remember her shyness, he put his arms round her and smiled down at her.

'Let's hope that it applies to us, too. I think I need a bit. I hope you read my letter very carefully, Phylly. I meant every word. I'm sorry I was such a boor. I love you so much. Can we put things right?'

He looked so anxious that her shyness vanished and she held him tight.

'I'm sure we can,' she said. 'I love you, too. I always have. It's got to be right, though.'

'I know that,' he said gently. 'And nothing I can say can put back the clock. I just wish you could understand how stupidly unimportant it was. You can be fond of someone but . . .'

He stopped, fearing that he was getting into deep waters and she answered quickly, still hugging him.

'I know. I mean, I can imagine how it might be . . .' It was her turn to flounder to a halt and she flushed brightly and buried her face in his jacket.

Alistair stood holding her and his face was grim. He knew quite certainly in that moment that some other love had touched Phyllida's heart and he felt a brief murderous rage. Could she possibly have been unfaithful to him? Was that why she was now ready to be understanding about him and Janie? Jealousy held him in its painful grip and, as he struggled with himself, he had a clear vision of how it must have been for her all these months. The violence in him died and he put a finger beneath her chin and turned up her face and kissed her.

'Let's go home,' he said.

Now, weeks later, Phyllida stood on the bridge and remembered her feelings of guilt. They'd receded as Alistair took possession of her all over again and the week had progressed. It had been lovely to have The Grange to themselves, making it seem much more like home, but Alistair had been very happy to meet Quentin and Clemmie on their return and the whole leave had passed like a dream.

She perched sideways on the bridge and sighed with happiness. Surely now all would be well and no more misunderstandings would occur? Her feelings for Oliver had given her an insight into Alistair's behaviour and she was determined to give her marriage every chance. Alistair would be home for Christmas. Home! Phyllida smiled to herself. Well, The Grange seemed like home! She wondered where they'd go in the spring and knew that, though she would be sad to leave this magic place, nothing mattered as long as the three of them were together. She remembered Lucy's joy at her first sight of Alistair, when she'd come out from school and seen them waiting for her, and felt a deep contentment. She looked around at the tall beeches, whose leaves were turning to gold, and at the bright berries of the rowan tree and gave a sigh of satisfaction. After all, Christmas wasn't so very far away.

Liz went up the steps of the Bedford Hotel, into the bar and looked about her. Abby was sitting at a corner table, sipping at a glass of wine and reading a leaflet which she waved at Liz in greeting.

'So there you are. I decided to put my time to good use and read about this wonderful new skin cream that's going to make me look twenty years younger.'

Liz dropped her coat and bag on the chair and shook her head in disgust.

'Surely you don't believe all that rubbish,' she said derisively.

'I certainly do!' said Abby. 'Anything that might make me look more like I used to and less like an ordnance survey map must be worth a try.'

Liz shrugged and went to order a drink and Abby watched her, a half-smile on her lips. It was a pity that Liz had become so bitter and anti-men. It made inconsequential conversation much more difficult. Even the most light-hearted remarks she took seriously and became very intense. Abby slipped the leaflet into her bag and settled back in her chair.

'Sorry I'm late.' Liz was back. 'It's hectic at the office this morning and I thought I'd never get away.'

'I suppose you're missing Jeff Maynard,' suggested Abby. 'What's happened there? Claudia phoned weeks ago and said that they were having to go back to Sussex. Has she gone? I thought I saw her a week or so back. I waved but she fled into Boots and I'm still not sure whether it was her or not.'

'Yes, she's still about.' Liz frowned a little. 'The house is up for sale, apparently, and she's hanging on till it sells. Not very satisfactory. Could take years in this market.'

'Oh, well.' Abby shook her head, still puzzled. 'I was surprised at the speed with which she resigned from my committee. I thought she was off that minute. Perhaps I ought to give her a buzz or something.'

Liz picked up the menu. 'She seems a bit anti-social at the moment. I've phoned several times and asked to meet her but she's very evasive. Said she wasn't too well at one point and then there was something else. All very vague.'

'I see.' Abby looked thoughtful. She had no desire to become entangled again with Claudia but she felt a little guilty. If she was ill perhaps something should be done. 'I'd better phone her, then.'

'I don't know.' Liz put the menu down and picked up her glass. 'I wonder if there's more to it than that. It was all very sudden. Jeff having to rush off because his mother was ill or something. Sounded fishy to me.'

Abby, who always enjoyed a gossip, looked interested. 'How d'you mean?'

Liz hesitated for a moment. 'I think it's a smokescreen,' she said at last. 'I think they've split up.'

'Heavens!' Abby sat up, her eyes bright and interested. 'Has Claudia been playing around?'

'No.' Liz looked almost cross. 'No, it's not Claudia. It's Jeff. I think he's gone off with someone else.'

'Goodness!' Abby took a sip at her wine. 'But he seemed so strait-laced. You said so yourself. Almost too perfect, you said! Anyway, how can you be sure? You would blame him, of course.' She grinned at Liz. 'It couldn't possibly be the woman's fault, could it?'

'If it were, I hardly imagine Claudia would still be sitting in that big house all on her own,' said Liz, somewhat acidly. 'Since it's Jeff that's rushed off leaving everything behind, I think it's more likely to be him than her. I must order or I shan't be back on time. What are you having?'

She went to order at the bar and Abby lit a cigarette. The trouble was that Liz had never had much of a sense of humour to begin with and, of late, it seemed to have disappeared altogether. She was heavy-going, these days, and it was almost an effort to have lunch with her.

Abby sighed and tapped ash into the ashtray. The older

one became the more vital it was to be able to laugh at life although, on reflection, it wasn't particularly amusing for Claudia if Jeff had gone bolting off into the blue. Love caused more problems than all the other emotions put together. This thought made Abby think of Oliver and his unrequited love for Phyllida. Certainly she had no desire to laugh at that. She'd seen Phyllida recently and been almost taken aback by the glow of joy that enveloped her. Alistair had been down to The Grange for his leave and they'd had a wonderful time. A private word with Clemmie had assured Abby that all was well between Phyllida and Alistair and she'd been much relieved, though her heart had ached for Oliver. Why couldn't he fall for someone available who would love him in return? Sophie, for instance? Abby smiled to herself. She was getting old, after all; matchmaking for the children and wanting to see them happily settled. Liz rejoined her and Abby put such thoughts away from her. She wouldn't be interested in such notions and was trying to bring up Christina along strictly feminist lines although she wasn't sure that she was having much success.

'So,' she said, determined to make an effort, 'how's everything? Has Unk found a place to live yet? I hear he's put his own house up for sale. And what's all this excitement about a mail-order catalogue?'

'He and Oliver have started some idea.' Liz shook her head. 'I wasn't very enthusiastic, to tell you the truth, but actually it looks quite interesting. If they can get it off the ground it might go quite well. It needs a lot of working out but Unk's got his head screwed on.'

'Christina must find it all very exciting.'

'She does.' Liz looked bleak and Abby watched her thoughtfully. 'She's got a crush on Oliver which adds to her excitement. It was a relief to send her back to school.'

'Oh dear.' Abby decided not to interfere. 'Well, we all did it, didn't we? It'll pass.'

Chapter Twenty-five

Claudia left the clinic, made her way to the car park and got into her car. She'd gone alone knowing that, if the news were bad, she'd need time to attempt to come to terms with it and she sat for some moments staring through the windscreen. Once again the result was negative. She was clear, uninfected, free to continue with her life as before; except that Claudia knew that nothing could ever be as it was before the morning that she'd walked along the road and seen Mike standing at the front door.

How much we take for granted, thought Claudia. So much we never think about at all until we know it's going to be taken from us.

She sat quite still, her hands holding the car keys in her lap. She'd been quite certain that this second test was going to prove positive and, as each day passed, she'd begun to realise how very much there was to lose. Once the conviction had taken hold, she noticed all the tiny pleasures that would be so terribly, impossibly difficult to relinquish. How could anything ever be the same again once you knew that sentence had been passed and the expectancy of death was to be your constant companion? When she saw clearly how it would be, she'd tried to rationalise the terror that took her by the throat. After all, we all live with the knowledge that, at any moment, by accident, illness, violence, our lives could be cut short. Surely, then, each moment should be precious and lived to the full? Why should it be different simply because one was more aware of how much time was left?

Claudia had made a vow then that, should the test prove negative, she would never again squander the precious distillation of life but treasure it and approach every day as though it might be her last. Even as she made it she knew that it was an impossible resolution. Nevertheless, she was changed and nothing could be quite the same again. She saw how shallow her values had been and how fear can cripple and destroy. She was moved by Gavin's anxiety for her and Jenny's offer of friendship and saw how easy it was to judge and condemn.

How strange that it should be in these two unlikely people she'd found strength and even companionship. How much she and Jenny had to clear away before they could accept each other! Now, she liked to see Jenny's bright little face, hear her perky voice with its urchin slang. As for Gavin . . . Claudia staring out over the rows of gleaming metal, wet with the afternoon rain, shook her head. She'd seen beyond the tiger to a kind man, frightened by the risks he took and by the tendencies which tore him in two and allowed him to be neither one thing nor the other. Jeff's situation, Claudia's fears, and the realities of it all, had looked him grimly in the face and his life had been touched by it. He and Jenny had moved closer together, an odd relationship but one that worked.

Claudia started the engine, drove out of the car park and headed towards Tavistock. The October afternoon was wet and windy, the rain driving against the windscreen. Claudia, who found the moor too elemental and wild unless she was in the company of others, stayed on the A38. She had a terror of breaking down in the empty wastes with no one to rescue her and with miles of lonely road to cross in order to find help. She was just getting used to the trip over the moor to The Grange but she had no intention of traversing its whole length on such a day as this. As she drove, vigour flowed back into her veins, beating and swelling within her, so that the terrible apathy of the last few weeks receded and she began to feel happy. She was clear, she was free and life could be taken up again.

As soon as she was indoors she telephoned Phyllida.

'I'm OK! All clear! Isn't it great?' Suddenly she was crying, hardly able to hear Phyllida's gasps of relief.

'I wish you'd have let me come with you!' she exclaimed. 'Oh, thank God! Now look, are you capable of coming over? Or shall I come to you? Whichever. Just say which you'd prefer.'

Claudia looked round her. The house was still, empty, indifferent.

'I'd like to come,' she said. 'Oh, but do Clemmie and Quentin know . . . ?'

'Of course not! Don't be daft! They're in Tavistock this morning but I said you might be over for lunch. They'd love to see you but we can have it upstairs if you'd rather.'

'Yes. No. I don't know.' Claudia burst out laughing and Phyllida laughed with her, realising how seldom, if ever, she'd heard Claudia really laugh.

'Decide when you get here,' advised Phyllida. 'Come now and we'll have a good old chat and then you can see if you're up to facing them. Crack on! I'll put the kettle on. Or perhaps we need something stronger. Oh, Claudia! I'm so pleased!'

'Oh, Phyllida. So am I. I'm on my way.'

As she drove down the lane and over Blackthorn Bridge, the clouds parted and the sun shone through and she saw Phyllida waiting at the door. She flew to the car and hugged Claudia as she emerged. Both talking and laughing at once, they went inside and up to Phyllida's quarters. In her little kitchen they made coffee and Claudia talked and talked until she was weak with relief.

'I've told Quentin and Clemmie,' said Phyllida, when Claudia was calmer, 'that you and Jeff have separated. It was best that they knew or it might have become embarrassing. But they're far too well-mannered to bring the subject up so you needn't ever worry.'

'They've been so kind to me,' said Claudia, following her into the sitting room whose sash window looked over the moors and sitting down in a comfortable, if ancient, armchair. 'What a lovely house this is. It's got such an atmosphere of, oh, I don't know, peace. And friendliness. Sounds a bit fanciful.'

'I don't think so,' said Phyllida. 'I felt it at once. I love the thought that Clemmie's family have lived here right down through two hundred and fifty years.'

'Heavens! That's a fair old time.'

'It's going to break her heart to leave it.' Phyllida looked sad. 'So what about lunch? Here or downstairs?'

'Oh, downstairs. Why not? No more hiding. I shall start as I mean to go on. I've got someone coming to view the house at four o'clock and then I shall really have to make some decisions, find a job. There's a design company in Exeter, apparently, and I've seen an advert I shall answer. I feel like a reprieved woman!'

'It's wonderful. But you mustn't go too far away. Maybe we'll persuade Clemmie to offer you another wing of The Grange.'

'No, no.' Claudia shook her head. 'It means a lot to me being able to come but I wouldn't want to live here permanently. I want my own little place. Ideally I'd like to stay in Tavistock. I've come to love it and I've made a few friends. Of course, people would find out that Jeff's left me but I don't mind that too much now as long as nothing else gets out.'

'I'm sure it won't.' Phyllida looked at her compassionately. 'I just know things are going to work out for you. Look! I've got some wine here. I thought we'd have a little private celebration before we go downstairs. Finished your coffee? Right. Grab a glass and we'll have a toast!'

Lucy had never been so happy. The weeks had rushed by, the holidays begun and she could barely contain herself with excitement.

'And Father Christmas can get down your chimney easily,' she told Clemmie, pausing in her work on Phyllida's Christmas card at the kitchen table.

'He's managed for the last few hundred years,' Clemmie

agreed somewhat absently as she iced the Christmas cake. 'I think he'll make it this year.'

'He's very old, isn't he?' Lucy looked awed. 'Why isn't he creaky like you?'

Clemmie laughed to herself. She often used that word to Lucy about herself and Quentin.

'All that port he drinks, I should think,' she said. Lucy had already put in her request for his repast on Christmas Eve. 'Keeps his joints oiled.'

'Oliver says he's magic,' said Lucy, colouring busily again. 'What's magic?'

Clemmie sat down at the table and looked at the child's absorbed face. Several answers occurred to her. 'It's something that's usually beyond our experience and often outside our imagination,' she said at last. 'Which is why so few of us believe in it.' She shook her head. 'I don't quite know, Lucy.'

'Or like being happy?'

Clemmie pursed her lips thoughtfully and nodded. 'I suppose so.'

'When Prudence asked if we'd enjoyed our leave with Daddy, that's what Mummy said.' Lucy rolled her eyes and made an ecstatic face in faithful imitation and breathed the word as Phyllida might have done. 'Magic!'

'Yes, I see.' Clemmie smiled to herself. 'Well, it was, wasn't it? And he'll be home for Christmas, too. Have you done his card?'

'Not yet. He's having a snowman.'

Lucy sorted through her pile of cards which had yet to be coloured in and held one up, Clemmie nodded her approval.

'Very nice. He'll like that.'

'I've got lots to do yet.' Lucy sighed deeply and picked up her crayon. 'I must crack on.'

Alistair's phrase sounded oddly on her lips and Clemmie burst out laughing and got up painfully. Lucy watched her anxiously as she straightened up and went to put the kettle on.

'How about a cup of tea to help you along?' she asked. 'And perhaps a bun.'

'That would be nice.' Lucy's voice was serious. 'What are you having?'

'Tea.' Clemmie looked at her in surprise.

'Do you think you should have some port instead?'

'Port! Why ever should I want port? Ah!'

She looked at Lucy's anxious face and went to her and hugged her. The child looked up at her and Clemmie's heart contracted with love. She kissed the rosy cheek and smiled at her.

'The trouble is, it wouldn't really help. You have to be magic for it to have the same effect as it would on Father Christmas. I'm afraid, my darling, that I'm not magic.'

Lucy looked disappointed but at that moment the door opened and Phyllida and Quentin came in followed by Punch, and she slipped from her chair to put her arms round the old dog's neck.

'What a picture of industry,' observed Quentin as he took off his coat. 'Lovely walk. It's surprisingly mild. No white Christmas for us!'

'I suppose Punch isn't magic either,' sighed Lucy wistfully, as he sank gratefully on to his beanbag by the Esse. She kneeled beside him, stroking him gently.

''Fraid not!' said Clemmie cheerfully, shaking her head a little at the others' enquiring glances. 'Just a poor old mortal like the rest of us. You can give him a biscuit and we'll stick to tea. Never mind. Tea has been known to have marvellous restorative properties. Here, give him this and then come and have your bun. No time to waste. You've got to crack on, remember!'

Alistair was looking forward to Christmas. His last leave had been wonderful and he'd felt strongly that all the obstacles between himself and Phyllida had been completely swept away. Why, then, did he have an odd nagging fear at the back of his mind? Now, back from patrol, he let himself concentrate on his doubts and suspicions. The answer was really quite simple. He feared that Phyllida had forgiven him because she'd had an experience which helped her to understand his own betrayal and which had made her feel guilty. There had been no mistaking her expression when they'd stood on Blackthorn Bridge and he'd tried to explain to her the possibility of being fond of someone other than your partner. How quickly she'd picked him up and agreed with him and how consciously she'd blushed and been unable to look at him! Even now his heart hammered with rage at the thought that she might have been unfaithful. Desperately he sought to rationalise it. Supposing it were true, she'd done no more than he had. He had no right to criticise or complain.

This, he told himself, is what Phylly's been going through for twelve months.

He remembered his words to her; 'One bloody night . . .

Does it really warrant all this drama? I almost wish I'd done it more often . . .' and squirmed inwardly. He'd been insensitive and impatient, expecting her to understand and forgive. So why should it be different with the shoe on the other foot? The answer to that one, of course, was that he knew his own reactions to his night with Janie. It meant very little and certainly had no effect on the way he felt about Phyllida or his marriage. If he hadn't been found out, nothing would have changed. He couldn't say the same for Phyllida. He didn't know what she felt or how it had affected her. He couldn't imagine her entering into a physical act with another man unless she really cared about him.

He clenched his teeth until the muscles stood out on his cheeks. It was no good pretending that it was the same for both of them. It wasn't the same for women; everybody said so, at least not for women like Phyllida. She wasn't the casual sort; and she loved him. Alistair shut his eyes to blot out the thought of what he'd risked. Slowly, painfully, he forced his brain to work. If Phyllida had met another man and fallen in love with him enough to sleep with him, she could never have behaved with Alistair as she had during his leave. Her love had been wholehearted, generous, authentic. He would have known the difference. If she had felt anything at all for someone else, it must have been a flash in the pan.

Even so . . . Alistair struck the palm of one hand with the clenched fist of the other. He was overwhelmed by the depth of his jealousy. Never had he experienced anything like this before. It was always he who'd done the backing off, the letting down; kindly, carefully but with finality. It had never been his experience to be the one rejected or deceived. He couldn't forget her look on the bridge nor her sudden wholehearted forgiveness.

Now he understood her own reservations and terrors when she'd learned of his unfaithfulness. It was his turn to realise that when trust was smashed it might be mended but it would always be vulnerable. There would be weak places and its bright sheen could never be replaced. If only he could ask her outright! He'd already forfeited that right and all for one stupid night, a moment's pleasure. He remembered how she had explained to him that if her love wasn't enough to put his infidelity to one side then they should separate.

'I couldn't live a life of suspicion,' she'd told him. 'Wondering what you were up to, who you were with. My eyes having to follow you about at parties, my ears straining to hear your conversations. I've seen women like that. I couldn't bear it.'

He'd been touched by her desire to love him so much but faintly scornful that she should make such a song and dance about it in the first place and slightly patronising about the whole thing. Now he saw clearly what she meant. He knew that his eyes would be watching, examining new friends or old ones, noticing how she behaved, listening to what she might say. It was what she'd feared. Surely if her love could overcome that, then so could his?

It's different, his brain repeated stubbornly, quite different. If Phyllida's been unfaithful, it's more than just a flash in the pan. In that case, he argued with himself, she hasn't been unfaithful. She couldn't have been like she was on leave if she had.

Unless, his brain said coldly, unless she was sorry for

you. Unless she felt guilty and has decided she must go on with the marriage despite the fact that she's met someone else.

Alistair sat down at his desk and dropped his head into his hands. He struggled with this new thought. It would be like her to do the thing wholeheartedly. Certainly the guilt had been there. Once again he saw her face, the blood mounting to her cheeks, and he groaned in despair. If she'd decided to stay with him then there would be no half-measures. It wasn't her style. His spirit writhed beneath the humiliating thought of Phyllida's pity and once again, despite himself, he realised what a hell she must have lived through during the last year. She'd struggled with her jealousy and misery all alone. No wonder she'd wanted to go to The Grange. Well, he had no intention of giving her up. She was still there, still wanting it to work, still – he was certain of it deep inside – loving him. Soon he would be back for Christmas and it was madness to keep going over and over it like this.

Alistair picked up his most recent letter from her and held it in his hands, rather as he might hold a talisman. It would be all right. He glanced at his watch. Thank God the bar was open! He put the letter back, looked for a long moment at the two happy faces in the photograph beside his bed, and went out shutting the door gently behind him.

Chapter Twenty-six

Liz pushed through the Christmas shoppers that crowded Exeter's busy pavements and hurried into Dingles. Even Christina had never guessed just how much her mother loathed the festive season. Liz, in moments of self-honesty, could never decide whether her dislike stemmed from the materialistic excesses this particular holiday encouraged or the fact that it was a time that pointed up her own loneliness. When Christina was small she'd tried to do different special things that depended less on presents and food and more on one's own resources and initiative.

Liz gave a cynical snort as the escalator bore her up-wards. It had worked during the early years but pressure from the television, shops and her peer group had soon influenced Christina and, in the end, it was easier to give in and become like everyone else. Also, Liz had feared that she may lose her to Tony and his family who celebrated the nativity with the more traditional customs: overeating, overspending, overindulging generally. Tony never insisted that Christina should visit until after Christmas – guessing perhaps how lonely Liz would be on her own – and she usually went off for the New Year to her grandparents where

Tony, unless he was at sea, would join her.

Searching through the racks of clothes for the long tunic that Christina – with a kind of indifferent anxiousness – had carefully pointed out to her on her last exeat, Liz wondered why Tony had never remarried. Her lip curled, as she found the tunic and pulled it out. Why should he tie himself to one woman, after all? He hadn't found it sufficient the first time, why should he bother to try again? She located the leggings that Christina had coveted and took her purchases to a pay desk. She paid by cheque and then took the escalator up to the restaurant, queued for a pot of tea and sat down gratefully. How she hated shopping! And now she had Uncle Eustace to cater for as well!

Liz poured her tea and relaxed back in her chair, looking round the busy restaurant. She'd found it impossible to leave him on his own at Christmas and he'd accepted her invitation eagerly. She knew that he would arrive loaded with presents and she'd bought him a Marks and Spencer's jersey and, in a moment of extreme weakness, two hundred cigarettes. She couldn't decide if she were indeed weak or merely stupid. At least he had no intention of making a permanent home with her. He and Christina had enjoyed themselves enormously choosing and discarding the details of properties in between all the excitements over the mail-order catalogue. Secretly, Liz was very proud that the catalogue had been Christina's idea but she was anxious that she was spending so much time in Oliver's company. It *would* be Oliver Wivenhoe that Christina would fall for!

As she poured a second cup of tea, she found herself thinking about Tony again and remembering how she'd felt when he'd come to collect Christina in the summer. It was years since he'd done that and Liz had begun to wonder if Christina was plotting; first the Easter play, then the summer holiday. Surely she couldn't imagine that she and Tony would be likely to get together again after ten years? Liz grew hot at the thought. Had she implied to Tony that Mum was lonely? Missing him? Liz shut her eyes. The idea was intolerable.

A passer-by bumped against the second chair, on to which Liz had loaded her shopping, and apologised. She smiled automatically but she was still thinking of Tony; the shock of seeing him in an old shirt and his jeans. He seemed hardly to have aged at all whilst she . . . Liz gritted her teeth lightly together when she recalled how much she minded that her hair had so much grey in it and that she had deliberately dressed in her frumpiest clothes, refusing to make an effort for him. How she had regretted that afterwards! Why should she let him see her at a disadvantage after all? But it was too late then. He'd seemed so much at ease, so friendly, as if all those fights and bitter recriminations had never taken place. She remembered how much she'd loved him, through his affair with Cass Wivenhoe, and afterwards, when they'd married because Christina was on the way, and he'd continued to have affairs, she'd gone on loving him.

Liz swallowed her tepid tea. How she'd hated those women! She could visualise each one clearly, even ten years on, and still hated them. When she'd looked into Tony's eyes and he'd smiled at her, the pain had flooded through her as if the years between simply hadn't existed. She knew, then, how close hate and love could be and had been grateful for

Christina, chattering away. After they'd gone, it had taken her hours to recover.

A woman was standing at the table asking if the other chair was taken and Liz pulled herself together. Glancing at her watch she realised that she would only just make it back to the car park in time and, collecting up her belongings, she hurried away.

Claudia was preparing for her interview. She stared at herself in the looking glass, remembering how she'd despaired at Jeff's lack of interest in her, his lack of response. Even now, she was unable to assess her own attraction. Her smooth fair hair shone silkily, and her skin was clear and soft. She'd lost weight, with all her fears and shocks, and she was quite thin but careful dressing made her look simply elegant and her confidence rose a little as she stared.

The interview was being held in Tavistock at an address only a few minutes away. She could walk it easily and was relieved that the day was dry and bright, with very little wind, so that she wouldn't arrive blown about or soaked through. She picked up her bag and went downstairs feeling terribly nervous. The advertisement hadn't been particularly explicit, nor had the person who had arranged the interview, but it was worth exploring. She shut the front door behind her and set off down the road trying to remain calm. The address turned out to be a room upstairs in an estate agent's office and she knocked quietly on the door and turned the handle when she heard a voice call, 'Come in.'

Oliver, who had reached the door just as it started to open was taken aback to find himself face to face with one of the most attractive women he'd ever seen.

'How d'you do?' he said and held out his hand. 'Have you come in answer to the advertisement for a designer?' He smiled at her as she nodded and they shook hands. 'I'm Oliver Wivenhoe. And you're Claudia Maynard?'

'Yes,' she said almost fearfully.

She still lived with the terror that someone might recognise the name and know about Jeff but, as Oliver stared at her intently, a memory slipped into her mind and suddenly she remembered Liz talking about the Wivenhoes. They were friends of Abby's and there was something else . . .

'Do you know Phyllida Makepeace?' she asked diffidently. 'I'm sure—'

'I certainly do!'

'And it was you who gave Lucy the parrot?'

'That's right.' Oliver decided not to repeat what he knew of Claudia through Abby and Liz, apart from which he was still rather stunned by her delicate loveliness. 'How amazing! Do you mean to tell me that we had this designer right under our noses and nobody realised?'

She smiled at him and his heart did peculiar somersaults in his breast.

'I haven't talked about it much since I moved down here, you see. Phyllida knows but I've only worked on wedding dresses and ball gowns and things like that. I'm not sure what it is you want?'

Oliver thought of several responses and hastily pulled himself together.

'Could you design children's clothes?' he asked. 'We want to produce a mail-order catalogue of Percy the Parrot garments. We've been offered the chance to show what we can do but we're still putting the team together. Uncle Eustace, that's the chap with the brains and the money, is hoping to keep it a local effort. That's why we advertised in the local papers to start with. We've got Prudence Appleby who's a marvel at making the clothes as samples, if you see what I mean . . .'

He stopped. All through his speech she'd looked happier and happier and now she laughed. 'This is ridiculous,' she said. 'I've heard all about Uncle Eustace and I know Prudence . . .'

'Good grief!' Oliver clutched his brow. 'Then why did no one mention you to us?'

'I've been in retirement for a bit,' she explained. 'I can quite imagine that nobody would have given me a thought.'

'Well, I can't!'

He grinned at her and, after a second, she responded to his intended compliment with a smile.

'So what would I have to do?' She brought things back to a serious level. 'Do you want me to have a try at some designs and let you see them? Have you got anything particular in mind?'

'We're aiming at the three- to six-year-olds,' Oliver explained. 'We thought the parrot motif could be used. You know, the cartoon character from the books?'

'I've seen Lucy's books,' she said thoughtfully. 'But I'd like to look at them properly. So it would be things like dungarees and pinafores and jerseys and so on?'

'That's right? Think you could do it?'

'I don't see why not.' She was beginning to feel excited. 'I haven't worked much with those sorts of garments but I'm sure I could learn.'

'Would it help you to talk to Prudence? She's been making children's clothes for years although she's useless on the design side.'

'It certainly would.' She hesitated. 'Are there lots of people after the position?'

Oliver shook his head. 'Designers seem to be thin on the ground down here. We've had a few people like Prudence who feel sure that they could do it, given a chance, but if this takes off it'll be nationwide and probably on television. It's got to be good.'

'Golly!' Claudia grimaced. 'Sounds terrifying! Although I can show you all my qualifications and references . . .'

'I'd like to see them sometime but we'll take them as read for the moment. The thing is to get you going and see what you can do. Where would you like to start?'

Claudia looked round the office. 'Is this your headquarters?'

'No.' Oliver shook his head. 'It's part of the estate agency downstairs. The owner's a friend of ours and is lending the office for interviews. We haven't got a headquarters yet. It depends where people will want to be. You might want to work at home. Prudence does. Or you might like a studio.'

'I'd prefer to work at home,' said Claudia thoughtfully. 'I'm hoping to move soon, so I could look for a place with a suitable workroom. I could always liaise with Prudence at her place if she prefers.'

'Or she can come to you,' agreed Oliver. 'But what I really meant was, where do you want to start with your ideas? Do you want Lucy's books? Or a chat with Prudence?'

'Books first,' decided Claudia. 'Then a chat. And Phyllida can show me the sort of things Lucy likes to wear . . .'

He smiled at her, seeing that she was already preoccupied with ideas.

'Tell you what,' he said. 'How about coming to meet the big chief first? He's waiting at the Bedford, all agog! Mustn't keep him in suspense.'

Claudia had a sudden *frisson* of horror. Supposing Abby was at the Bedford? She'd already wondered if she'd heard of the developing friendship with the Halliwells. Would she think that she'd been sneaking in through the back door, as it were? She was aware of Oliver watching her and she tried to smile.

'Is he on his own?' she asked and blushed scarlet. What a fool he'd think her! But Oliver, with the sixth sense he'd inherited from his grandfather, remembered Abby's unkind observations and knew exactly what she feared.

'Quite alone,' he assured her. 'Nothing to worry about.'

'OK.' She smiled at him gratefully. 'I'd like that.'

'Wonderful!' Oliver opened the door for her. 'We can tell you all about it and then it's up to you.'

'Quite!' she said, her terror returning, and followed him down the stairs.

Uncle Eustace could barely believe his eyes when he saw Oliver arrive with an extraordinarily beautiful young woman. Could it be possible that he was to spend his declining years in close liaison with this gorgeous creature?

'Forgive me, Lord, for I have sinned,' he murmured devoutly. 'And now I can remember why!'

'This is Claudia Maynard,' Oliver was saying. 'You simply won't believe this, Unk. She knows Prudence and Phyllida. She's even heard of you!'

'Now none of that, dear boy.' He shook Claudia's hand. 'He's jealous of my reputation,' he explained. 'It takes years, you know, to get a really good one.'

'I believe you.'

She smiled at him as she sat down and was suddenly engulfed with happiness. Both men, young and old, were looking at her as if she were a rare and desirable woman and she felt a burst of confidence in herself.

'And you're a designer of children's clothes?' Uncle Eustace asked her, as Oliver went off to get drinks.

'Not as such,' she said and explained her position.

By the time Oliver returned, Uncle Eustace was studying her qualifications and her CV and he winked at her as he passed her a glass. She smiled back at him, praying that this wasn't all some wonderful dream, and looked nervously at Uncle Eustace as he returned her papers.

'Very impressive,' he said and she gasped with relief. 'Now drink up and I'll explain the whole situation to you and then you can tell me your thoughts. I take it you can stay to lunch?'

They were both looking at her with such anxiety that she felt one gloriously heady moment of power.

'Thank you very much,' said Claudia demurely. 'I should love to.'

Chapter Twenty-seven

It took Alistair less than forty-eight hours to discover the identity of Phyllida's admirer. He refused to use the word 'lover', having nearly convinced himself that this was simply inconceivable. Her welcome, when he arrived late on Christmas Eve, was too genuine to admit any such thing. Yet, to his heightened perception, she seemed different. There was a suppressed excitement about her, a gaiety which was new, and he found his senses tingling to a sharp awareness. His rational self put it down to the general excitement of Christmas and the fact that their own relationship was back on its old footing for the first time for over a year. Indeed it was on a whole new footing, deeper than before and doubly precious, yet even with that so forcibly before him, Alistair wasn't satisfied. There was something he couldn't quite define; a lilt to her voice, the proud carriage of her head, the secret smile that touched her lips when she thought no one was watching . . .

At the Halliwells' Boxing Day party he met Oliver Wivenhoe and several pieces of the puzzle fell into place. He saw the look on Oliver's face when Phyllida came into the room and noticed the tenderness on hers when she greeted him and a great wave of jealousy engulfed him and receded, leaving him watchful and sensitive. After he'd summed Oliver up as best he could from a distance, he introduced himself. He thought he detected an antagonism in the younger man's eyes but he was friendly enough and they talked about the Navy and submarines and Alistair realised that he knew Oliver's father, Tom, who was a four-ringer. He hadn't been talking to Oliver for very long when he realised that he was in great danger of liking him and he brought the conversation to a halt and turned away to talk to Quentin.

Without appearing to, Alistair observed Phyllida's behaviour even more closely but could detect none of the sleekness and posturing that was usually apparent in these cases. Women, he'd noticed, and men too, seemed unable to resist the temptation to flaunt a little on such occasions. They either displayed themselves to the admirer from the shelter of the partner in possession or teased the partner by acting flirtatiously with the admirer and Alistair was relieved to see that Phyllida showed neither of these tendencies. There was no doubt in his mind, however, that Oliver had a *tendresse* for her and Phyllida's attitude to him suggested that she knew it. If there had been anything on her side it was over, so much was plain, but what might there have been between them during those long summer months when he'd been behaving like a stiff-necked fool?

Try as he might, Alistair couldn't put it out of his mind. He knew that this was exactly what he'd expected Phyllida to be able to do – and a great deal more – but, to his shame, he was quite unable to practise what he'd preached. If only he knew the truth, he told himself, then it would be possible to forget it all; it was the not knowing that was the problem. Even as he thought it, he knew it to be specious and he cursed himself in disgust. But what else could account for that little air of contentment that Phyllida wore like a garment? It was nothing so crude as the prancings of a female with two males in attendance. She seemed to have a very special secret which only she knew and to which, it seemed, he was not going to be made privy.

On his last morning they went for a walk in the woods. It was a mild day and there were snowdrops growing amongst the great roots of the beeches. The sky was high and pearly white and the river seemed little more than a diffusion of silver light between the grey trunks of the tall bare trees.

'How very different the woods are in winter,' mused Phyllida as they wandered along hand in hand. 'So empty and quiet. The river's noisier because there's more water, of course, but there's no birdsong and no leaves rustling.'

'Seen any more dippers?' asked Alistair when the silence had lengthened unbearably and he could think of nothing else to say.

'No.' Phyllida shook her head and made a face much like Lucy's when she was thwarted. 'Not since that last one with you.'

She smiled at him and squeezed his hand and suddenly Alistair could bear it no longer.

'Oliver Wivenhoe's in love with you,' he began and stopped, aghast at himself and the accusing tone of his voice.

Phyllida looked at him quickly and he was horrified to see the flush mount in her cheeks and to feel the now familiar surge of jealousy. She, in turn, saw that his face was closed, his eyes suspicious, and her inclination to make light of it vanished and resentment took its place.

'I know he is,' she said.

There was a certain defiance about her reply, a 'so what?' implied, that antagonised him further.

'And from what I could see, you feel the same about him,' he said unforgivably.

She stared at him indignantly, dropping his hand with a gesture that rather threw it from her than just released it.

'That's a beastly thing to say,' she cried and her voice echoed round the wood. 'How can you? And when we've been so happy? And when—'

She stopped and shook her head, biting her lips as though to stop herself from speaking or from crying. He couldn't tell which and was visited with a terrible remorse.

'I'm sorry, Phylly. Really sorry. Please wait.' He caught her arm. 'I'm behaving like a fool. Only I thought there was something when I was here last . . .'

She stared back at him and he saw the guilt creep into her eyes. 'It was nothing,' she said.

'Nothing?' he repeated and a great terror filled his breast. 'How d'you mean? Please, Phylly. I don't want to go back to sea with any more misunderstandings between us. Do you mean that there was something between you which is now over?'

Phyllida hesitated so long that he began to feel quite weak at the knees and he took out his cigarettes and lit one, keeping his eyes on her face.

'I didn't realise to begin with,' she said at last. 'I found out by mistake and he never made any attempt to . . . to . . .

you know. It was just that you'd sent that horrid letter . . .' Alistair let out an exclamation and she glanced at him and away again. '. . . And it was just nice having someone around who . . . loved,' she stumbled a little over the word, 'who loved me.'

'So then what happened?' asked Alistair, when it seemed that she'd finished.

'We got carried away,' said Phyllida and Alistair flung his half-smoked cigarette down and ground it viciously under his heel. 'Just after we'd heard that Prudence might be able to make these clothes. We were so carried away with it all and we kissed each other. It was so exciting and it just seemed natural somehow.'

Alistair stared out over the river, his arms folded across his chest, trying not to see the picture in his mind of Phyllida and Oliver making love.

'Where were you?' he asked, unable to meet her eyes. 'When this . . . excitement took place?'

'On the bridge,' said Phyllida simply and sighed. 'Poor Oliver.'

'On the *bridge*!' Alistair uncrossed his arms and looked at her at last. 'On the bridge?'

'Why not?' Phyllida looked slightly defiant. 'It was only a kiss and there was no one about. Oliver went straight off afterwards and I felt terribly guilty. It wasn't fair to him.'

'Wait a minute!' Alistair began to feel laughter and a great relief building in his breast like a bubble. 'D'you mean that's all there was to it? Just a kiss?'

'Of course that's all,' said Phyllida, affronted. 'Isn't it enough? I've felt guilty ever since. Not just because of us but because it was mean to Oliver.' She stared at him and her eyebrows rushed together in a frown. 'What d'you mean, "that's all"? I suppose it would be nothing to you, of course. You think nothing of going to bed with your old girlfriends . . .'

'Please, Phylly. Don't!' He captured her hands and dragged her close to him. 'I was wrong to be suspicious and I know I have no right at all to criticise or complain. But I was really worried. You looked so guilty. And ever since I've been home you've been behaving oddly. Like you've got a secret or something.'

He stared down at her and the frown slowly vanished and she began to smile.

'I have,' she said. 'Were you jealous? About Oliver?'

'Terribly,' he admitted at once. He owed her that much. 'I realise now how you must have felt and how difficult it's been for you. I don't know what to say. I know I wanted to kill him.'

Her smile widened. 'Don't do that,' she said. 'He's really nice but it wasn't the same at all. I love you.'

'I'm a bloody idiot!' he said and bent to kiss her.

They kissed for a long time but when reluctantly he let her go, he still retained her hands.

'So what's this secret?' he asked and she laughed at his doggedness.

'How dense you are!' She shook her head. 'I'm pregnant. That's my secret. Just three months. I wanted to wait a few days more, just to be certain. It must've been seeing the dipper when we were on the bridge. Clemmie says it's a lucky bird and I've never seen him before or since.' She glanced at him rather shyly. 'That's if you think it's lucky.'

He put his arms round her and held her close, 'I think it's the most wonderful thing,' he said unsteadily. 'Oh, Phylly. Can we just forget everything and start all over again?'

'It's what I want,' she said. 'More than anything.'

They kissed again and strolled on, holding hands, closer than they'd ever been before. Already a new problem was presenting itself, however, and both of them were thinking about it. Alistair's next appointment was to the Ministry of Defence in May and neither of them wanted a permanent home in London. They'd discussed it a little but now Alistair felt more sure of his ground. To begin with he'd been afraid of suggesting that Phyllida should stay in Devon, lest she might feel that he wanted his freedom in London, and he'd been wondering how to phrase it in a way that wouldn't upset her. Later, he'd been afraid for himself and what might happen if Oliver was at hand whilst he was away.

'Would you like to stay around here?' he asked her as they strolled on to the bridge. 'I can't imagine that you would want to come to London now that you're expecting a baby. I know how you feel about children in big cities. We could buy a house in Yelverton. How d'you feel about it?'

'I don't want to come to London,' she said at once. 'I'm just not a city person and Lucy's so happy at Meavy. Would you mind?'

'I want what's right for you,' he answered. 'I can get down for weekends and I'd rather our base was around here. I just don't want you to feel . . .' He hesitated and she slipped an arm round him. 'I love you,' he said, 'but I'll be a long way away and people like to gossip.'

'I know.' She hugged him and they stared down into the water. 'I'll have to take that chance. It's not that I don't want us to be together. I do. I shall hate you going back this time, but I can't see us in London.'

'I know that.' He sighed. 'I don't want to go to London either. I'm a countryman, too, remember. Sometimes I have dreams about coming outside. My driving career is over now and the thought of sitting at a desk in London for the rest of my life fills me with horror.'

Phyllida turned to look at him, 'D'you really mean it? That you'd come outside?'

'Why not?' He shrugged. 'I'm old enough to retire. I've done my eighteen years. The problem is what I'd find to do. Especially with the recession.'

'Oh, wouldn't it be wonderful?' Phyllida's eyes shone. 'I do wish you could.'

'I'm working on it.' Alistair sighed and glanced at his watch. 'We must be getting back. I've got a train to catch.'

After lunch, Phyllida and Lucy went with Alistair to the station and when Phyllida kissed him goodbye she saw that there were tears in his eyes.

'I'll write from the train,' he said as he bent to wave to Lucy through the car window. 'Take care, my darling. Only three months to go. Two. I'll try to get down for a weekend when the boat comes in.'

'Oh, darling.' She held him tightly. 'Perhaps we'll come to London after all. I can't bear us going on like this.'

'Weekending would seem bliss after this,' he said, trying

to smile. 'Let's just not waste any more time. I love you so much.'

He walked quickly into the station and Phyllida got back into the car, trying to swallow her tears and fighting down the longing to rush after him.

'Well,' she said with an attempt at brightness. 'Home to tea.'

'Are you crying?' Lucy sounded anxious.

'I am a bit,' admitted Phyllida. 'Sorry.'

She wiped her eyes, blew her nose and started the engine, glancing round to smile reassuringly before she pulled out. Lucy looked at her, Percy clutched tightly in her arms.

'Because of Daddy going?'

'That's right. Silly, aren't I? I ought to be used to it by now but . . . well, I shall miss him.'

'So shall I.' Lucy stared out of the window as they drove away from the station. 'Is he ever going to live with us properly, like other daddies?'

'Of course he is!' Phyllida sounded more cheerful now. 'And he'll be back in no time. When the boat comes in he'll be able to get home every weekend. That will be much better, won't it?'

'Mmm.' Lucy nodded. 'Will he come to The Grange?'

'We'll see.'

Phyllida didn't feel strong enough to deal with this particular question. She felt bereft, as if an important limb had been amputated and she was incomplete. Her heart was heavy and talking was an effort. She wondered how she would get through the next three months without him. Why on earth had they wasted so much time? She loved him so much that she knew she would forgive him anything if only they could be together. And now there was the baby. A measure of joy penetrated her misery and she took a deep breath and felt stronger.

'Tell you what!' she said and her voice was back to normal and Lucy relaxed. 'Shall we drop in and see Unk on the way home? He'll be able to tell us the latest news about the clothes and things and he'll cheer us up. What do you say?'

'Yes, please,' said Lucy eagerly.

Feeling happier, she held Percy up to the window so that he could look out over the misty moorland that stretched away, mile upon mile, as far as the eye could see.

Chapter Twenty-eight

Claudia went back to Sussex for Christmas. The temptation to remain at home and accept the invitations tendered by her friends was great but she knew her mother would be hurt if she continued to stay away. She was dreading the ordeal ahead of her. Her mother would require all the details that related to the break-up of the marriage and Claudia was still trying to decide exactly what she should say even as she was arriving at the door.

It turned out to be as bad as she'd feared. Her mother, whilst sympathetic, couldn't help insisting that she was certain that Jeff would come back, her father maintained a reproachful silence and her younger sister – who'd always had a very soft spot for Jeff – managed to imply that Claudia was to be pitied for not being able to hold him. By the time the holiday was over, Claudia was exhausted and very relieved to be travelling back to Tavistock. She had so much to look forward to and, during the long drive, tried to rebuild her battered confidence by thinking of the positive aspects of her life: the designs that were slowly coming to life, Phyllida's unwavering friendship and support, the excitement of looking for a new home. Last but not least, she allowed the obvious admiration shown by

Oliver and Uncle Eustace to soothe her dented pride.

She'd made up her mind not to leave Tavistock. Jeff had paved the way for it and now she decided to let it be known that they'd split up. Those that mattered most knew it already and her newly growing confidence enabled her to bear the embarrassment of telling those who hadn't guessed. She longed to be out of the house, where the terrible shock had taken place and where she'd been so unhappy, and she spent hours poring over house particulars sent by the local agents. There was a trickle of interest in her own property and, in February, a couple over from Hong Kong on leave made an offer for it. Claudia accepted it gladly and began her own house-hunting with renewed vigour.

The designs that she'd drawn, with advice from Prudence and help from Phyllida, were now finished and Prudence was turning them into charming garments from Claudia's patterns. They'd decided to use Lucy as a model and things began to move a little faster. Oliver had taken Claudia to meet the author of the Percy the Parrot books, who lived in an old station house just beyond Tavistock, and who'd been delighted with the designs. Her agent would be down for a few days at Easter, she told them, and by then it was hoped that the clothes themselves would be ready to be shown.

Claudia's relief that her designs were acceptable was so great that when Oliver suggested they go out to celebrate she accepted without a second thought. Afterwards, she couldn't remember when she'd enjoyed herself so much. Although during the previous weeks both he and Uncle Eustace had flirted with her outrageously, Oliver made no attempt to do so when they were alone. During dinner, he allowed her to talk and talk until her nerves were talked away and then they chatted easily about the project, Uncle Eustace, her own house-hunting, until the evening was over and he took her home. She asked him in for coffee and to show him the details of a property she'd received only that morning from Barrett-Thompson's estate agency.

'I love the look of it,' she said as she made the coffee and he sat at the kitchen table reading the description. 'It's a converted coach house in the grounds of a big house. It's got a tiny courtyard but I'd have the use of some of the grounds. I'm not really a gardener so this is like having the best of both worlds.'

'It's very convenient for the town.' Oliver turned a page. 'It's just on the edge.'

'That's what I mean.' Claudia stood the coffee pot beside him. 'It's a marvellous compromise all round but the best thing is this. Look.' She leaned beside him to point to the page. 'See. "Attic room stretching the whole length of the property." It'd make a perfect workroom.'

It was borne in upon her that he was sitting unnaturally still and she glanced down at him. At the same moment he looked up at her and the expression on his face caused her to look quickly away. She blushed scarlet and drew back, her heart rocking.

'It looks great,' said Oliver rapidly, his eyes fixed once again on the pages before him. 'Just the job. Have you viewed it yet?'

'No.' She shook her head, trying to keep her voice steady. 'I thought I'd ask Phyllida to go with me. Help yourself to coffee.'

She tucked her trembling hands into the pockets of her skirt, praying that he'd pour hers, too. He did so and she sat down and pretended to study the papers with renewed interest.

'Is the price about right?'

'Oh, yes.' She couldn't look at him. 'I'll go and see it and if I like it I'll make an offer.' She laughed a little awkwardly. 'It'll be odd doing it all on my own. Still, it's good practice.'

'Well, if you have any problems you know where I am.'

'Yes. Thanks.' She made herself look at him again. 'I mustn't be feeble, though. Look at Phyllida. She has to do nearly everything on her own.'

Oliver thought about Phyllida and felt a whole series of conflicting emotions.

'Yes,' he said at last. 'Naval wives are very capable people on the whole.'

For a moment there was a silence and then, subtly, the atmosphere changed. Claudia realised that he was as shaken and nervous as she was and a new sense of confidence grew within her.

'Thanks for this evening, Oliver,' she said and looked at him properly. 'I can't tell you how much I've enjoyed it.'

'I'm glad.' He smiled at her and it was as if they drew more closely together. 'Maybe we can do it again?'

'I'd love to.' Her tone was so sincere that he took a great breath of relief.

'It's been quite a time, hasn't it?' he asked. 'So much going on.' He shook his head. 'I can hardly believe it.'

'Oh, I know,' said Claudia at once. 'My whole life has changed overnight. I never know what might happen next. When Uncle Eustace saw my designs he proposed marriage to me and I was so distraught I nearly accepted him.'

'You dare!' said Oliver lightly. 'Good God! You simply can't trust that man. I hope he sells his house soon and can buy something. He's driving poor Liz out of her mind!'

Claudia laughed. 'Talk about chalk and cheese! I really love him, though. He makes me feel capable of anything.'

'Good heavens!' Oliver looked shocked. 'Worse and worse!'

'I didn't mean that.' She felt shy again and a look passed between them that made the colour rise in her cheeks and Oliver push his chair back and stand up.

'I must be on my way,' he said. 'I'm off north tomorrow to interview clothing manufacturers. Thanks for a wonderful evening.'

'It was great.'

She wished suddenly that he would take hold of her and kiss her and, as if he'd read her thoughts, he slipped an arm around her and turned her face up to his. It was a few seconds before Claudia remembered the terrors that had dogged her during the past months and she pushed him away suddenly, fear in her face. Oliver looked down at her, puzzled, and began to apologise.

'No, don't apologise.' She gave a breathless little laugh as if deprecating her foolishness. 'It's just . . .' She sought for something realistic to say that would reassure him without actually telling the truth. 'It's just a bit of a hang up I've got. I've been in the same safe relationship so long that I feel a bit nervous, if you see what I mean. You know?' She held on to his arm lest he should feel hurt. 'You read about things, don't you? Catching things. And I'm completely out of touch . . . I don't want to lead you on . . .'

Her voice trailed away and she blushed scarlet. She looked so distressed that Oliver smiled reassuringly at her.

'I can quite understand that,' he said gently. 'I wasn't trying to be pushy.' His brain leaped hither and thither as he guessed at her dilemma and wondered how to dispose of her fears. 'I'm just as nervous as you are. I've only had one relationship with a girl at university and it was her first, too. So we're in the same boat.' He wondered how far he should go. Was she actually implying that they might make love and how could he find out without sounding overconfident? 'Everyone takes precautions these days, don't they? I know I always would. I wouldn't want to take any risks of any sort.'

She looked so relieved that he felt certain he'd guessed right but he suspected that it was best to draw right back for the moment.

'I'm sorry,' she said. 'I just wanted you to understand.'

'I understand perfectly. Much better to get it out of the way. And now I really must be off.'

He hesitated on the doorstep, touched her cheek lightly with his lips and went off down the street. Claudia closed the door behind him and stood in the hall trying to calm her confused emotions. It had been a dreadfully embarrassing few moments but at least they both knew where they stood. She was almost alarmed at the way she felt about Oliver and told herself that her reactions were due to the fact that it was such a change to be treated like a highly desirable woman who nevertheless deserved respect. Jeff had been caring and thoughtful but he'd been like a brother and other men had been frankly lecherous, which had frightened her. Oliver seemed to combine caring, passion and fun all in one and it was a completely new experience.

She went back to look again at the picture of the coach house in an attempt to take her mind off her thoughts about him. It was really most attractive.

Tomorrow I'll make an appointment to view it, she decided and suddenly felt quite euphorically happy.

Driving north, Oliver felt quite as confused as Claudia. Coming so soon upon his infatuation with Phyllida, this new passion for Claudia made him feel as though he were being unfaithful. He knew that this was foolish, not least because Phyllida was married to someone else. Since that moment on the bridge, she'd made it clear that the brief moment of romance was over. It was obvious that everything had been put right between her and Alistair and she had no intention of keeping Oliver dangling on a string no matter how flattering it might be to her ego. She made certain that they were never alone together and, though he knew she was very fond of him, it would have needed a vainer man than Oliver to read anything more into her affection for him.

Nevertheless, this sudden transfer of his love unnerved him. Part of it must be put down to the fact that Claudia was a very attractive girl but it was more than that. As he got to know her he grew to like her more and more. He realised that she had moments of insecurity, which sometimes took the form of a prickly offhandedness, and he longed to know the true facts that surrounded the breakdown of her marriage. He had no intention of harassing her, however. The last thing he wanted was to cause any problems in the tight-knit little team that they were building.

Oliver groaned as he turned off the motorway. It seemed that whilst he was developing a penchant for married women, which could be unfortunate to say the least, he also had Christina's ongoing youthful passion with which to contend. He'd been aware of some indefinable change in her this Christmas. Hitherto he'd always thought of her as a young version of Liz – a small brown girl – but when she'd come to greet him dressed in the new leggings and tunic she looked taller, certainly taller than Liz, and he realised for the first time that her eyes were a greyish hazel and not brown at all. She'd let her hair grow – unlike Liz's short crop – and he could see that she was growing into a very attractive young woman. Her legs were long and straight and when she laughed she reminded him of Tony. She was quick to notice that he was looking at her in a new light and her happiness and pride were delightful to behold. Unfortunately, her new-found confidence was unable to withstand the arrival of Claudia and Phyllida who dropped by en route to see Prudence. Beside Claudia's elegant beauty and the ease with which they teased Oliver, not to mention his obvious fondness for them, her happiness was obliterated by a black wave of jealousy and she disappeared upstairs muttering that she had some work to do.

'Why is love such a nightmare, Unk?' he'd asked, after Claudia and Phyllida had gone and Christina was still in her bedroom.

The older man had cocked an eyebrow at him. 'Sure it's love you're talking about?'

Oliver had looked at him in surprise.

'How d'you mean?'

'Perfectly possible to confuse an ordinary biological urge with the authentic fire, dear boy. Easiest thing in the world and causes the most trouble.'

'How do you know the difference?'

Uncle Eustace had shaken his head and reached for his cigarettes. 'Now you're asking. Try it and see if it lasts. If it does then it's probably the real thing. If not, well,' he shrugged, 'gets it out of the system.'

'You make it sound so easy,' said Oliver.

Uncle Eustace looked at him. He opened his mouth, remembered what it was like to be young and shut it again.

'It isn't easy,' he agreed. 'It's the same as anything else. Driving a car, for instance. Comes with practice.'

'I'm sure you're right.' Oliver looked depressed.

'Cheer up. Tell you what. It's nearly lunchtime. Let's go round the pub! Go and call that child down and make a fuss of her. She can come too.'

Now, watching for signs to the industrial estate, Oliver sighed. It was all too complicated and it had been quite a relief when Christina had returned to school although he hadn't let his feelings show and had even promised, in a fit of weakness, to take her out for lunch one weekend. At least his love for Phyllida was becoming more manageable and a good thing too; but what about Claudia? He shook his head. There was simply no time to think about it now. He pulled into the factory's car park, reached for his briefcase and concentrated his mind firmly on his work.

At the same moment, Claudia and Phyllida were viewing the

coach house. They'd fallen in love with it at once and went from room to room imagining Claudia's furniture and hangings in situ and getting thoroughly excited about it. The owner watched them warily, having heard it all before, and was gratified when Claudia told her that she would be contacting the estate agent and making an offer.

'D'you think I should offer the full price?' she asked Phyllida, when they were back at home and Claudia was making them some tea.

'Certainly not!' said Phyllida promptly. 'It's a buyers' market. Everyone keeps saying that. Make an offer. If she refuses it you can always increase it.'

'That's true. But I wouldn't want to lose it and she said she'd had lots of people round.'

'They always say that,' said Phyllida dismissively. 'That's just to get you going. But I agree, you don't want to take chances. Talk to the agent. They might give you a clue.'

'I just love that attic room!' Claudia clasped her hands as she remembered it.

'Oh, it was just lovely! And that view across the park from the bedroom. All those wonderful old trees!'

'And the sitting room with the woodburning stove!'

They grinned at each other excitedly.

'Your stuff will look great there. And that dear little courtyard is a real suntrap.'

'I just wish I knew what to offer.' Claudia looked anxious. 'I can't afford to give money away.'

'Would you feel happier if someone else saw it and could give you advice?'

'But who?' They stared at each other, perplexed.

'What about Unk?' suggested Phyllida. 'He's selling and buying at the moment. He ought to know. Or Oliver.'

Claudia turned away and began to make the tea. 'What would he know about it?' Her voice sounded rather muffled. 'He's never bought or sold a house.'

'No, I suppose not but he'd probably be quite a tough cookie when it comes to business. He's really nice but he's got all his marbles.'

'He is nice, isn't he?' Claudia's voice was casual now.

'He's a sweetie,' said Phyllida warmly. She was about to divulge their tiny moment of romance when some sixth sense alerted her to the oddness in Claudia's behaviour. She looked at her sharply. 'He's one of the kindest people I know.'

'We went out to dinner last night.' Claudia turned to look at her, the teapot clutched in both hands. 'It was really great. I can't remember when I enjoyed myself so much.'

At the look on her face, Phyllida experienced a sharp twinge of jealousy. Oliver's love had been a source of comfort and she hadn't expected to lose it so soon. She thought of Alistair and the new baby and took a deep breath.

'I'm glad. You deserve a break. Did you . . . ? Was it . . . ? Where did you go?'

'The Horn of Plenty. It was such fun. He makes me laugh and he's got lovely manners but he doesn't . . . well, he isn't pushy. You know what I mean?'

'Yes.' Phyllida remembered the kiss on the bridge. 'I know what you mean. Well, why don't you show him the coach house? See what he says. It never hurts to get a second opinion.'

'No. That's true. I might just do that.' Claudia glowed a little at the thought.

'And it'll be a good idea for you to see it again.' Phyllida smiled a little sadly. So that was that and very right, too! No point in being a dog in the manger.

Chapter Twenty-nine

As the winter closed in, Clemmie became aware of the fact that Phyllida was enjoying every moment of it. For the first time, she was experiencing the extremes that real country living force upon those who live in isolated or remote areas. January and February were very wet and it was necessary to put on gumboots if any of them ventured anywhere outside the house. The lawn was waterlogged, the drive was a river of mud and even the courtyard was full of puddles. Merely hurrying out to the car was a cold wet miserable business and bringing anything in, without its being soaked or mud-spattered in the process, was a miracle in itself.

Inside, however, a different world existed. The oil-fired Esse made sure that the kitchen was always a warm cosy place and, in the sitting room, the wide granite fireplace held great logs of wood that burned day and night, for here the fire was never allowed to go out until summer had well and truly arrived. Each morning, as they drank their first cup of tea together, Phyllida watched, fascinated, as Quentin drew the remains of the logs together in their bed of hot ash and, pumping gently with the bellows, blew new life into the smouldering wood until a good blaze was going and more logs could be piled on top.

Each afternoon, she and Lucy arriving back from school chilled and damp would hurry into the sitting room to find Clemmie toasting crumpets or bread; honey or home-made jam waited in little pots on the tray beside a cake or some buns, whilst the teapot, in its woolly jacket, stood in the grate. The mulberry velvet curtains would be drawn across the windows, shutting out the bleak twilight, the soft lamplight casting its intimate glow, gleaming on the worn, polished wood of Clemmie's bureau and glinting on the glass of the bookcase doors. The clink of china and the clatter of spoons mingled with Lucy's clear voice relating the history of her day, the murmur and hiss of the flames and the slow thump of Punch's tail on the carpet as he was given the crusts to finish up.

After tea was cleared, Lucy would sit at the low table on a little stool to do a jigsaw puzzle or she would climb up with Quentin in his large armchair to listen, thumb in mouth, one hand stroking Punch's smooth head, whilst he read her a story. Clemmie and Phyllida took it in turns, night and night about, to put her to bed whilst the other prepared the supper. Central heating had been installed when the self-contained apartment had been converted but a hot water bottle was essential and Lucy was tucked into her warm bed with Percy beside her and a night-light left burning on the chest of drawers.

The three of them ate supper in the kitchen and, when the washing-up was finished, they'd go back to the sitting room, make up the fire and settle down to listen to a concert or play

Scrabble, to read or simply talk. It was a different world to Phyllida who, during the long and countless evenings she'd spent alone during her married life, tended to resort to the television for company. She felt that she was living in a past, almost forgotten, world and she loved it. She didn't mind the dusting that the ash from the fire made a daily task or hoovering up the mud left by Punch's paws on the carpet. The carrying of logs and the extra thought for stocking up the larder – since they were so far from the shops – were no hardships to her but she could see how difficult these things were becoming for Clemmie and Quentin.

Walking in the woods was simply not possible now. The river, swollen with the heavy rains, ran high and fast, bursting its banks and flooding the woodland. Branches and leaves were whirled along on its restless, hurrying surface and the trees on the edge of its banks stood deep in the brown swirling water. The paths, when they were passable, were covered with dank wet leaves and sodden beech mast whilst the rhododendron leaves clattered and shivered in the cold searching wind. Sometimes they were granted a dry sunny morning and then Quentin and Phyllida, wrapped in scarves and hats and thick coats, walked on the moors above the house; bent against the roaring powerful south-westerly winds, tears stinging their eyes as they gazed out on the wild wet lands from which water gushed and spouted and ran down rocky gullies whilst the drowned earth reflected back the weak glimmerings of a pale sun.

In early March the weather changed. It grew colder but drier. The winds backed round to the north-east and slowly the floods abated and the earth began to dry. Quentin was laid low with a bad attack of bronchitis and the sound of his agonised coughing seemed to fill the house. Alistair travelled down for a weekend and told them that he'd be leaving the boat officially at the end of April and would be able to take some leave.

'Have you been finding us a home?' he asked Phyllida. 'We ought to be thinking about it seriously.'

'I'm on the mailing lists with all the agents,' she told him. 'I just haven't seen anything I like yet.'

'What did Lucy say about the baby?' he asked.

'I told you when I wrote. Thrilled to bits.' Phyllida chuckled. 'She says it's to be called Polly if it's a girl.'

Alistair laughed too. 'Let's hope she doesn't insist on Percy if it's a boy,' he said. 'Quentin doesn't look too good.'

The smile died from Phyllida's face. 'He was very ill,' she said. 'They almost took him into hospital. He's so weak. I wanted to ask you a favour but after what you said I don't like to.'

'What did I say?' Alistair looked surprised.

'You know. About them looking on us as a strong young couple to help them out or whatever.'

'Oh, for goodness' sake!' He looked embarrassed. 'Don't bring that up. I didn't know them, then. What d'you want me to do?'

'It's the logs. We've nearly run out of the sawn-up ones. There are plenty in the woodshed but they're huge.'

'No problem. Anything else?'

'That's the main thing. Clemmie and I can deal with everything else. Oh, Alistair, it's going to be so dreadful

322

when they have to leave this place. Can you imagine them in a little bungalow in a town? Or in a flat?'

'It's hard.' He shook his head sympathetically. 'But it comes to us all in the end. Come on. Show me these logs.'

In early April a warm spell took the West Country by surprise. The wind blew gently from the south-west, tumbling small fluffy white clouds in a soft blue sky, and the sun was warm.

Clemmie had suffered an unusually restless night and, having seen Phyllida off on the school run with Lucy, Quentin put on his coat, took up his stick and strolled down to the wood. He still felt weak, much weaker than he admitted to Clemmie, but the day breathed new hope and energy into him and he stood for some moments, his eyes closed, the sun warm on his face, and gave thanks that they'd survived yet another winter.

'We're into the straight, Punch, old lad,' he said, letting them both out through the wicket gate he'd built beside the stile. 'Spring's here, thanks be to God. We've made it.'

He paused at the entrance to the wood, feeling the weakness flood over him again. It was the first time he'd been out for a walk since his illness and he realised that he must take it gently. He felt a spasm of fear at the thought of the climb back to the house and wondered if he should go any further.

But after all, he told himself, I'm on the level now. No harm in a quiet stroll by the river.

His keen old eyes darted hither and thither, noting the primroses under the trees and in the meadow opposite and the patches of violets beside the path. Slowly and carefully he bent to pick Clemmie's first spring posy and, as he straightened up and turned to go on, he saw the blackthorn blossom and caught his breath in delight. The thick, massed, white flowers foamed over the hedge in a wave of unearthly beauty and, as if this were not enough, the cuckoo's poignant, evocative call sounded suddenly from a nearby copse.

Quentin stood quite still, his senses drowning in the presence of an English spring; the birdsong filling his ears, his eyes dazzled by the glory of the blackthorn and, in his nostrils, the delicate scent of wet earth and blossom. When he came to himself, his eyes were wet and his heart banged erratically in his breast.

'Old fool,' he told himself and Punch, waiting patiently a little further on, wagged his tail in sympathy.

Something spurred him on as far as the bridge, as though it were a kind of goal which he must attain before he could turn for home. Anyway, he wanted to see the blackthorn tree in all its springtime glory. He stood for a while in the sun, leaning against the parapet, inhaling the scent of the flowers on the black branches which curved beside the warm stone. The water ran clear and bright and two wagtails played on a boulder downstream but there was no sign of the dipper.

He pushed himself upright, called to Punch who was fossicking up the lane, and descended on to the path, pausing to break a spray of pussy willow from a trailing branch. Holding the little posy, he set off again. The pain struck quite suddenly, causing him to stagger in the path, and struck again before he could recover. He fell amongst the primroses, his anguished cry stilled on his lips, the flowers scattering from his outstretched hand. Punch pushed his nose against the unresponsive hand that lay amongst the pale delicate blooms, and licked the face that was turned with open sightless eyes to the pale blue sky above. He whined a little and sat down, sniffing at the inert form, and presently stretched himself out, nose on paws, waiting for Quentin to wake.

Clemmie woke suddenly and lay still, listening. Had she heard a cry or had it been part of the dream she'd been having; something about Phyllida having the baby . . . ? She tried to recall the sensations and images but they faded as she grasped at them, eluding her until she woke up properly, realising that the sun was shining in and it must be late. She peered at her watch on the bedside table and took it up, frowning. Surely it couldn't be so late! She remembered Quentin kissing her earlier, murmuring about letting her sleep on, but even so . . .

She climbed stiffly out of bed and went to the window; no sign of activity in the courtyard or in the garden beyond. She wondered if Quentin had been tempted to go further afield and anxiety gnawed at her heart. He really wasn't strong enough for any proper exercise yet. Clemmie, undeceived by the soft spring morning, pulled on her warm clothes and hurried downstairs. The house was deserted, not even Punch was in his usual place by the Esse. She opened the door and looked into the courtyard. No signs of life, apart from the robin who was pecking at some crumbs. She shut the door, saw that Quentin's coat and stick were gone and clicked her tongue in reproof.

Pushing the kettle over to boil, she tried not to feel cross. He'd been so patient since his bronchitis, resisting the urge to do the tasks that were beyond his strength; an undemanding, cheerful invalid. A walk in the sun would do him no harm, after all. She made her tea and toast, still feeling anxious, and was halfway through her first slice when it occurred to her that he might find the climb back to the house more than he'd bargained for. Taking a gulp at her tea and, leaving her toast half eaten, she took her own coat from behind the door, collected her stick and set off down the garden. She let herself through the little gate Quentin had made for her, giving thanks that she no longer had to attempt the undignified clamber over the stile, and crossed the open grass to the wood below.

'It'll be the halt leading the blind,' she muttered to herself, remembering how once she had run across the sunlit spaces into the shadowy woods beyond; supple, strong, without pain. She grimaced at the memory of that young, uncaring Clemmie and hobbled slowly on to the woodland path. A smile touched her lips at the glory that spread out before her and she moved forward, her heart thrilling to the magic of the morning.

The sight of Punch struggling to his feet beside the path made her frown but, as she saw the dark form that lay beyond him, the bright beauty of the day turned dark and the blood seemed to drain from her heart. She called his name but no sound came and she ran on trembling legs and fell to her knees beside him. She stared into his upturned face and seized his cold hand.

'Quentin.' It was a whisper, barely a breath.

She held the hand tightly between her own, using it to blot the hot tears that filled her eyes.

'Quentin.' This time it was a plea and the tears came fast. She bowed herself forward so that her brow touched his breast. 'My darling.'

Her agony was too much to bear and she cried aloud and Punch came to stand beside her, whining and pressing close to her side. His warmth was reassuring and she held him close, within her arm, as she touched Quentin's cheek and smoothed back his hair. She reached for his other hand, flung out, and saw the posy scattered beyond it. Weeping silently, she gathered up his last gift to her, kissed his icy lips and pressed her cheek to his.

As she kneeled beside him, the sounds of the woodland were borne slowly in on her numbed senses; the river splashing over the sun-warmed rocks, the whispering of the breeze in the tree-tops and, in the woods above the bridge, the mocking laughter of the yaffingale.

Chapter Thirty

Abby stood in the old walled kitchen garden – which had been laid to turf and generally allowed to run wild – hanging out the washing. It was warm and sheltered here, protected from the gales that shook the trees beyond the old stone walls but with enough breeze to dry the clothes, and Abby was enjoying the feel of the sun on her back as she took the garments from the basket and pegged them on the line. A friend, down from London to stay, had gone into fits of laughter at the idea of hanging the washing out to dry and asked if Abby had heard of tumble dryers. Now, as she saw the sparrows darting in and out of the ivy that grew thick on the walls where, year after year, they made their nests, and as her eyes were drawn again and again to the primroses and polyanthus that studded the emerald turf, Abby realised how time-saving conveniences had removed so many of the small pleasures of life.

She dropped the peg-bag into the basket and stared down the valley, across the village roof-tops and the church tower to the humped shoulders of the moor beyond, and knew how very lucky she was. Lucky, not only to live in such a place – even if it were falling down around them and so much of the grounds run wild – but to be alive on such a morning. She thought of Quentin, remembering his joy in the countryside and the passing seasons, and her heart mourned. The burial service in the small moorland church had been moving and simple, a fitting end for such a man.

Abby sighed and thought of Clemmie. She appeared to have shrunk even more, dwarfed by Gerard's height beside her in the pew. Phyllida and Alistair had kept well back but it had been for Phyllida that Clemmie had looked as she turned from the graveside and it was Phyllida, with a half apologetic glance at Gerard and his wife, who had stepped forward to take her arm and lead her to the car; Phyllida, seven months pregnant, who had seen to everything but stayed well in the background.

Abby took her cigarettes from her jeans pocket and felt for her lighter. Afterwards, Gerard had taken her on one side and asked for her support in persuading Clemmie to sell and move into more suitable accommodation. His second wife had nodded her approval, trying to hide her yawns and surreptitious glances at her watch. Although it would be almost impossible for Clemmie to manage alone at The Grange, Abby had found herself quite unable to agree with him; probably because she suspected that his suggestions were not really for Clemmie's wellbeing and happiness but simply because he wouldn't have to worry about her any more. She'd be tidied away, swept under the carpet and he could continue his own life with a sigh of relief.

'It will break Clemmie's heart to leave. And how terribly sad for The Grange to be sold!' she'd said. 'Don't you want to keep it in the family?'

Gerard's wife had shot him a look of pure horror, quickly disguised, and he'd pretended a very real regret whilst putting forward a well-reasoned argument as to why it would be foolish to do so. That he was right merely made it more irritating. Nevertheless, Abby had shrugged regretfully and said that she was quite sure that Clemmie wouldn't listen to her anyway. Gerard was also extremely keen to find out on exactly what terms the Makepeaces were staying at The Grange and Abby found herself being uncharitably amused by his anxiety. Her amusement had been short-lived. She only had to watch Clemmie trying to be brave to feel that life wasn't terribly funny after all. Quentin had been such a kindly gentle man but with an in-built strength that made him approachable: easy to turn to in times of trouble. He would be deeply mourned and greatly missed by more than Clemmie. It had been a comfort simply to know that he was there and they would all be so much the poorer without him.

Abby drew in a lungful of smoke and glanced up as she heard a familiar trilling cry. The swallows were back. She stared up, watching in delight as they wheeled above her and then swooped beyond the high walls to the field below, where the remains of last year's nests still clung to the old beams in the derelict barns. She couldn't prevent an uprush of joy and was feeling a little more cheerful as she left the kitchen garden and came face to face with Oliver outside the high wooden door. She smiled with all the deep affection she felt for him and slipped an arm in his.

'If you say a word about giving up smoking you can turn round and leave,' she warned him. 'Have you brought the stuff your mama promised for my charity coffee morning?'

'I have indeed,' he said as they strolled up to the house. 'I dropped the bags in the kitchen. I think they contain the best part of her wardrobe. She was about to set off for Exeter with all her credit cards and a well-known gleam in her eye. Pa'll kill her when he gets home.'

'He's used to it.' Abby chuckled. 'She's always been the same. It's wonderful to find someone who doesn't change. So comforting to find a constant point of reference in a rapidly changing world.'

'Goodness!' Oliver arched his brows in admiration. 'I do believe you've been reading, Abby. That sounds almost like a quote.'

'It is,' admitted Abby, with a rather touching pride. 'It was in the newspaper. I committed it to memory but I didn't imagine I'd be able to use it so quickly. But I meant it. There's something about your mother that raises the spirits and gladdens the heart. Quite the opposite of someone like Liz who's always droning on, complaining about life or men or whatever.'

'That's known as existential angst,' said Oliver as they reached the kitchen. 'You'll have to bone up on the modern idiom now you've started to read. I should write it down and learn it by heart so you can use it at your next committee meeting.'

'I wouldn't know how to spell it.' Abby pushed the kettle on to the hot plate. 'So how's things?'

'All over.' He didn't pretend to misunderstand the anxiety that lay beneath the casual question. 'Not that it ever got going. You were right. It was just a blip for her, I think.

Anyway, they're back together and, as you saw for yourself, she's pregnant.'

'Yes. I'm sorry, love. And about Quentin, too. I always wondered about him being your godfather. He seemed rather old.'

'He was my grandfather's aide during the war and grandfather used to come down to stay with the Halliwells when it was all over. They were one of the reasons he settled here when he retired. Apart from which, he'd really got to love this part of Devon. I'm going to miss Quentin.'

'We all are.' Abby put sadness to one side and tried for a lighter note. 'I hear you're about to plunge into the big business scene.'

'Looks like it. There's a lot to be done before it's up and running but we're getting there.'

'We're all thrilled,' said Abby. 'So tell us the details . . .'

By Easter the sale of Claudia's house was completed. The new owners – who had returned to Hong Kong and wouldn't be moving in for some time – had allowed her a few extra weeks at the house to sell some of her furniture whilst it was in situ and she was in the last stages of packing when a ring at the doorbell disturbed her. Sighing, she put some half-wrapped china on the floor beside a packing case and went to open the door. It was Jeff.

She stood, clutching the door handle, whilst a whole host of emotions shook her. He looked younger, more the Jeff of the photograph, and the old resentment began to burn in her.

'You'd better come in,' she said and held the door wider.

He passed her and walked down the hall into the kitchen. He wore jeans and a roll-necked jersey and his hair had grown long, though it was clean and shining. She felt a sickening thrust of longing for him and, as he turned to look at her, she went to the cupboard so that he shouldn't see her face.

'Looks like I was just in time,' he said.

'In time for what?' she asked coolly, as she took out a jar of coffee and some sugar in its bag. 'Want some? It's all I've got.'

'That'd be nice.' He watched her, as he lent against the sink. 'So when are you off?'

'Day after tomorrow.' She wasn't going to help him out.

'You didn't write.'

'What was there to say?' The kettle boiled and switched itself off and she spooned coffee into two mugs.

'Goodbye?' he suggested, taking the mug she held out to him.

'We said that last time.' She looked at him at last. 'No point in repeating ourselves.'

He stared at her and she felt the treacherous throb of desire that sent colour flowing into her cheeks.

'Oh, Claudia.' He held out a hand to her. 'I'm really sorry. It was such a brutal thing to do to you.'

She turned away from him, furious that he should see her weakness, humiliated that he should pity her. She picked up her coffee and perched on the kitchen stool.

'It's over. Forget it. I have. So what do you want?'

Jeff stared down into his mug for a long moment and then he pursed his lips and shrugged a little.

'It's not going to sound too good, I'm afraid. I wondered if you could spare some money from the sale of the house?'

Instantly, Claudia was cold and wary, all soft weakening passions vanished.

'How did you know it was up for sale?'

'I saw it in the paper.' He looked at her. 'Mike's been hospitalised.'

Claudia felt a chill creep over her flesh. On that dreadful visit to the hospital she'd been given pre-test counselling and she'd heard for the first time the facts about AIDS. She felt a terrible pity for them both and when she spoke her voice was gentle.

'I'm sorry, Jeff. I really am. Is he . . . very ill?'

'Not too bad, yet. He's home again now. But it's the beginning of the end. We both know it. Maybe nine months.'

She swallowed, longing to question him, but she restrained herself and tried to be rational.

'The thing is, I've bought a little cottage on the edge of Tavistock and I think I've got myself a job.' She didn't want him to know the whole truth. 'I can earn a living and I've got a roof over my head. But there's nothing spare, I'm afraid. I couldn't risk taking on a mortgage.'

He nodded and turned to stare out into the garden. 'I know I shouldn't have asked. We agreed. It's just I didn't know the end would come so quickly. I've managed to get some work, just casual. I'm sorry there wasn't any extra to send you.'

'Don't be silly.' She stared at him, seeing the droop in his shoulders, the way his hands gripped the sink. 'How much did you want?'

'Oh.' He shrugged. 'I hadn't got that far. It's just I'd like the last few months to be . . . to be . . . bearable.'

His lips shook and she watched the cords on his neck stand out as he swallowed.

'Never mind.' He turned back and his mouth twisted as he tried to smile at her. 'Just a thought. I shouldn't have asked. Thanks for the coffee.' He put the half-full mug down.

'Wait a minute.' Claudia bit her lip. 'I might be able to squeeze a bit.'

'I don't want to make things difficult . . .'

'No, it's OK.' She smiled at him. 'I've got a slush fund. You know? Just in case of an emergency.'

'But I can't take that,' he protested. 'You might need it. Forget it.'

'No. I want you to have it.' She nodded at him and he saw that she was quite sincere. 'It's only five thousand pounds. You could have four.'

He gave a short laugh. 'You can't possibly imagine what a fortune four thousand pounds would mean to us – to me – at the moment.' He shook his head, lost for words. 'Honestly . . .'

'Well then. Don't go on. Look. I've got a home, a job, friends.' She nearly added 'a future'. 'I don't need a slush fund. It was my own personal safety net.'

Jeff smiled properly for the first time since he'd entered the house. 'I'm sure your bank manager would be furious with you for giving it away.' He hesitated. 'I suppose you've managed to cope with the financial side of life?'

'Oh yes,' she answered quickly. 'Don't worry. You taught me enough to know what I'm doing.'

'Well. If you ever need any help you know where I am. Or

rather . . . you don't. We're moving.'

'Oh?' she raised her eyebrows.

'Someone found out,' he said at last. 'About Mike. We've been given a month's notice.'

'Oh, Jeff . . .'

'That's how it goes,' he said quickly. 'We don't want to stay. The whole village is talking. A friend's offered us a cottage, fairly isolated. On the edge of Bodmin Moor. It's very beautiful, actually, and the cottage is really nice. Small but very pretty. Trouble is, he needs three months' rent in advance.' He smiled wryly. 'He's not that much of a friend.'

'I'll write you a cheque. Will that be OK?'

'It will be so wonderful that I can't ever thank you enough, but not four thousand. Let's split it. Half would be plenty.' He hesitated. 'I probably shan't be able to pay you back, you know.'

They stared at each other. Claudia remembered those dreadful weeks she'd lived through when she'd imagined the threat of death at her elbow and her eyes filled with tears. She wondered how life would be for Jeff when Mike had died and he was all alone.

'I don't want it back,' she whispered, 'it's as much yours as mine. I wish there was more.'

He shook his head. 'We'll get through now. You're giving us the chance of a home, a lovely one, and those few things that take the edge off poverty. We'll be able to keep the car going now. We get allowances and things. Don't worry.'

She opened her bag which was standing on the draining board and took out her cheque book. He turned away, swallowing down his tepid coffee, as she wrote out the cheque. She tore it from the book and held it out to him and, after a moment, he took it and held it between his fingers, staring at it.

'Thanks,' he said at last and, having folded it in half, he tucked it in the back pocket of his jeans.

'Stay in touch, Jeff,' she pleaded. 'You know. Afterwards. Look. This is my new address.' She gave him a change of address postcard. 'Keep it safe and drop me a line when you move. Promise?'

He put it in his pocket with the cheque and nodded. 'I will, I promise. Bless you, Claudia.' He held out his arms as if to give her a farewell embrace and for a second she hesitated, fear in her eyes, and his face grew bleak. 'Perhaps you're right,' he said, with an attempt at lightness, and she ran to him and hugged him.

They held each other, both trying not to cry and then, with one last hug, he was gone. The door slammed and she was alone. She cried in earnest then, her arms over her face, like a child, abandoned and uninhibited, until she was exhausted and her sobs ceased. Presently she got up and went to the sink. She held his mug and remembered how, in her ignorance and fear, she'd smashed Mike's cup on the tap. For a moment she saw the photograph clearly in her mind's eye; their happy, laughing faces, the love that glowed between them, a love which she had never known.

Before she could cry again, the telephone rang. She went to answer it, making an effort to keep her voice light.

'Hi, there. How's it going?' It was Phyllida.

'Oh. Phyllida.' Claudia felt weak with gratitude at the sound of the cheerful voice. 'It's fine.'

'Sure? You sound exhausted to me? So what time are you coming round?'

'Oh . . .' Claudia hesitated.

'Don't tell me you'd forgotten? And Clemmie and I cooking a great big casserole!'

'No, I hadn't forgotten. Oh God, Phyllida. Jeff's just been here.'

'Oh, no!' She sounded horrified. 'Whatever for? Was he alone?'

'Yes, all alone. Mike's very ill. He's dying and Jeff needed some money.'

'Oh, honestly! Did you give him any?'

'I had to . . . No.' She shook her head at Phyllida's expostulations. 'He's got nothing and I've got everything. I couldn't just turn him away.'

'You're an old softy.' Phyllida's voice was gentle. 'What an awful shock for you.'

'It brought it all back.' Claudia's voice wavered and she swallowed.

'Just drop everything and come straight over. You need a good meal and a long night's sleep. We can finish the last bits together in the morning. There's plenty of time before the van arrives. No excuses.'

Claudia began to laugh. 'It'll be wonderful. The place is empty and depressing and I'm starving. It sounds great.'

'OK. I'll expect you in twenty minutes.'

She hung up and Claudia went back into the kitchen. She picked up her bag, stared for a moment at Jeff's mug, and then hurried out, slamming the door behind her.

Chapter Thirty-one

Clemmie sat in the summerhouse with Punch at her feet and watched the robin pecking at toast crumbs. The sun was comfortingly warm on her aching bones, the lilac's scent was intoxicatingly heavy, and the bluetit was building as usual in a hole high up in the wall. One of the terrible things about death, she reflected, was that life carried on so callously regardless of it. Nothing had changed or stopped.

Except, thought Clemmie, my own will to carry on living.

She tried to imagine herself leaving The Grange, and all that was familiar and beloved, and settling in a small bungalow or flat in Tavistock or an old people's home where she could be looked after properly.

How sensible and reasonable, she thought. And how totally pointless. What should I do with myself all day long? How can I go on without him? Why should I?

Her hands clutched each other, as if seeking his strong warm clasp, and as the realisation that she would never touch his hands again assaulted her – stabbing new and fresh each time – the tears overflowed, coursing down her withered old cheeks. Try as she would to recall the long happy years, she could only remember the months of estrangement and anger; the rejections and recriminations that had lasted for years after that one act of betrayal following Pippa's death. Why had she wasted so much time? Reason told her that no couple could expect to live in perfect love and harmony for nearly sixty years, with no cross words or displays of anger, but all she could feel was remorse. In her heart she knew that on many occasions she'd seized the opportunity to punish him for that act which had caused her so much pain and humiliation. All the time he was repentant she'd been able to be loving and generous, assuring him that it was over, forgotten. When he'd taken her at her word, however, and got off his knees – figuratively speaking – she'd felt resentment slinking back and, at the first opportunity, she'd given the knife a little twist and enjoyed his guilty despair.

Sitting in the summerhouse, which he had converted so lovingly to her comfort, fresh tears fell and she groaned at the pain in her heart. Thank God this last year had been so happy, so free of shadows, with everything finally forgotten and forgiven. What miracle had sent Phyllida with Abby that day, to be the instrument which brought about the final release from it all? Clemmie wiped her eyes and strove for a rational outlook, remembering the happy times, the peaceful hours, spent in this old house.

Her heart grew heavy again at the thought of leaving it. Gerard had been right to advise them to go whilst they were both together. Now, wherever she went, it would be to a place that had never known Quentin. There would be no memories of him; staring out at the moonlight before he climbed in to bed beside her, bending thoughtfully over the Scrabble board before the fire, dozing in the courtyard with his straw hat over his eyes, crossing the moor below the garden with Punch at his heels. Clemmie swallowed back the tears and bent to stroke Punch. He, too, would soon be gone and she'd be truly alone. She thought about Gerard hurrying away, as soon as was decently possible after the funeral, to his own life and family, urging her to sell The Grange. He would be back soon to sort things out, he'd told her, meanwhile she must think about moving. She couldn't stay at The Grange alone.

Well, he was right. She couldn't. She tilted back her head to feel the sun on her face and experienced a moment of clear headedness, as if someone had spoken to her, presenting her with an idea, a solution. She knew very well that Phyllida and Alistair couldn't afford to buy The Grange but supposing she sold it to them at a much reduced price with the proviso that she lived on there until she died or became ill? Clemmie thought about it carefully. Was it fair to them? She might be around for years yet. Phyllida and Lucy loved the house, of that much she was certain, and they needed somewhere to live. Would getting the house at a bargain price be worth putting up with her in it with them? And what on earth would Gerard say? She must be fair to him.

Clemmie sat up straight and tried to reason sensibly. If she went into a home then the proceeds from the sale of The Grange would be eaten up in no time whereas, if she stayed at The Grange, the sum that the Makepcaces paid could be set aside for Gerard's inheritance. She could pay her way with what Quentin had left her and her pension. Naturally she'd want to pull her weight with the bills but she needed little else apart from that. Phyllida had discussed their own situation with the Halliwells when she'd been looking at details of houses sent by local agents. Having lived for all those years in the Mess before he got married, Alistair had set aside a good portion of his salary and now had nearly twenty thousand pounds invested. He'd also taken out an insurance policy which would mature on his forty-fifth birthday to help pay off any mortgage he might have. Added to which, if he decided to come outside, there would be his gratuity to take into consideration. Clemmie took a deep breath. It was definitely a possibility – if they would only consider it.

'The problem is,' Phyllida had said, 'if he comes outside we've got a bigger lump sum but less chance of a mortgage. If he stays in we've got a reasonable deposit and we'd get a good mortgage.'

'I'm surprised that he's thinking of coming out into such a depressed economic market,' Quentin had said. 'Terribly difficult to get a job.'

'I know.' Phyllida had looked worried. 'He always vowed to himself that he'd come out and do something completely different as soon as he'd finished driving, you see. He'd hate to be deskbound. That's why he took out the insurance policy. It was to give him a bit of a start. But in those days no one was imagining a depression.'

Quentin had shaken his head. 'He must think carefully,' he'd said. 'Especially now that you have to plan for another child.'

'I know.' Phyllida shuffled the pages about and stared at the glossy photographs. 'Why is being sensible so difficult and so boring? We just want to be together. Perhaps we could run a guesthouse.'

Clemmie, remembering that conversation, felt hopeful. Certainly The Grange could be run as a guesthouse after she'd gone. Meanwhile, the financial side needed careful consideration. She wondered if Phyllida would be tempted to do it simply so that Clemmie could remain in her old home. That was certainly a possibility, thought Clemmie anxiously. She didn't want anyone to be sacrificed on this particular altar. She relaxed suddenly and shook her head. Even if Phyllida was prepared to make sacrifices, Alistair wouldn't let her. She knew with an exquisite relief that Alistair would do what was right for Phyllida and his family and, if that was to buy The Grange and let her stay in it with them, then she could accept it thankfully and without guilt. Sometimes, selfish people were so much less tiring to deal with than the unselfish. The fact that you knew they were doing exactly what they wanted to do was so restful. Not that Alistair was selfish, he had no obligation towards her, but it would be comforting to know that he was taking the decisions. Gerard was much the same. She knew that he would just be glad to get it settled although he might be concerned to ensure that it was done to her – and ultimately his – financial benefit.

Clemmie lay back in her chair feeling slightly happier. At least there was a faint hope that she might not have to leave The Grange, that she could stay with all she held dear. She determined to put her plan to Alistair when he next came down. Exhausted with grief, wakeful miserable nights and worries as to her future, she relaxed at last in the hot May sunshine.

Lucy stood at the school gate waiting for Phyllida and

brooding on life and death. She missed Quentin dreadfully. It was her first experience of death and she was having some difficulty in coming to terms with it. For one thing, she couldn't imagine where Quentin might be. People talked of heaven but it became quickly apparent, when questioned closely, that none of them knew exactly where it was or of what it consisted. Why, after all, should Quentin want to go to heaven in the first place? He was very happy at The Grange. That he was tired and his joints ached and his heart was all worn out wasn't much of a reason. She knew that God was all-powerful and she'd heard the stories of the miracles Jesus had performed. Very well. Why should one not be performed on Quentin?

'Please God,' prayed Lucy, clinging to the railings and squeezing her eyes tight shut, 'please give Quentin a new heart and send him back. Clemmie needs him,' she added as an afterthought. She didn't want to appear selfish or to imply that Quentin should be sent back solely for her benefit. Anyway, heaven must be crammed with jolly people; surely he could be spared! Of course, there was the faint possibility that Quentin might be enjoying heaven but Lucy felt confident that he'd probably had quite enough of it by now and would be ready to come back where he belonged. He could look on it as a kind of holiday. Surely he'd hurry back if he knew just how unhappy Clemmie was.

Lucy opened her eyes as fear gripped her heart. Ever since Quentin had gone, Clemmie had had that look on her face and that tone in her voice that Mummy sometimes had when Daddy was at sea. It made Lucy feel that the world wasn't so safe and happy as she supposed, especially now Mummy was looking for somewhere else to live. She'd imagined that they would live at The Grange for ever and now, it seemed, they had to find another house. She'd argued that they couldn't possibly leave Clemmie until Quentin came back and Mummy had looked so miserable that Lucy had climbed on to what remained of her lap and hugged her breathless.

Lucy swung on the railings thoughtfully. She couldn't understand why grown-ups were sometimes so stupid. Why must they leave The Grange? There was plenty of room for them all, even the new baby, and Clemmie didn't want them to go. She could tell that, no matter how often Clemmie might insist that it was right for them to have their own home. And what would Quentin think when he got back with his new heart and his new joints and found they'd gone, leaving Clemmie all alone? He wouldn't want them to go. She closed her eyes again.

'Please God,' she prayed, 'could you tell Quentin to crack on? If he comes back soon perhaps we shan't have to find a new home.' She deliberated, her eyes still shut, wondering if it sounded rather selfish but before she could rephrase her request she felt a nudge in her ribs.

'What're you doing?' Hugh Barrett-Thompson stood beside her. He was seven, more than a year older than she.

'I'm praying.' Lucy liked Hugh. 'Quentin's dead and I'm praying that he'll come back.'

'Who's Quentin?' asked Hugh.

Lucy hesitated. She wasn't too certain of Quentin's status. 'A friend,' she said at last. 'His heart wore out and he went to heaven to get a new one.' She frowned a little as she told him, suspecting inaccuracies in her explanation.

'Max did that,' said Hugh unexpectedly and Lucy stared at him agog with excitement.

'How long did it take?' she asked breathlessly.

'How long did what take?' he asked, waving to his mother who'd just arrived and preparing to hurry off.

'To come back with his new one?'

'He didn't. They don't come back. We've got Ozzy, though, so it's not too bad.'

He ran out of the gate and climbed into a car and Lucy was left to ponder this extraordinary statement. Before she could unravel it, Phyllida arrived.

'Hugh's Max went to heaven,' she said, hardly waiting to get in to the car before communicating this amazing coincidence. 'His heart was old, too.'

'Really?' said Phyllida cautiously.

'Yes. But he didn't come back.' Lucy frowned again, puzzled. 'He said they've got Ozzy so it's not too bad.'

'Ah.' Phyllida felt she was entering deep waters.

'I wonder what an Ozzy is?' mused Lucy. 'Anyway. We want Quentin back, don't we?'

'I think Max was their dog,' Phyllida told her. 'So is Ozzy, I expect.'

'Perhaps that's why Max didn't come back,' suggested Lucy. 'People are different, aren't they?'

Phyllida drove through Dousland in silence, feeling quite unable to grapple with this problem yet again. The baby was due in less than six weeks and she still hadn't found a place to live. Even if she did, they'd never move in time before the baby came. She felt exhausted and dispirited. Quentin's death had been a terrible shock. She'd arrived back at The

Grange on that glorious morning to an empty house and, eventually, had found Quentin dead on the river path and Clemmie kneeling beside him. At that moment another Phyllida had taken over – cool, calm, organised – and had remained in charge until well after the funeral. Now, this veneer was beginning to wear thin. She was tired and frightened, worried about Clemmie, missing Quentin and concerned that Lucy was expecting him back at any moment, as if he'd just popped out for a walk. She simply couldn't find the words to acquaint her with the finality of death without it seeming brutal and frightening.

She turned off into the lane that led down to The Grange, offering up a prayer of thankfulness that Alistair was due on leave in a few weeks. She could put everything in to his hands and let him deal with it all. What a luxury that would be.

'I wonder if he's back.' Lucy was wrestling impatiently with her seat belt as soon as the car stopped.

'Oh, Lucy.' Phyllida turned her bulk awkwardly. 'Wait a minute. Look.' She hesitated but decided to continue with the easy option. 'Don't go rushing in asking Clemmie if he's back. If he isn't, she'll just be more upset. Do you see? It sort of rubs it in and makes it harder.'

'I know.' Lucy was watching her intently. 'Like when people ask you if Daddy's due back from sea and you have to say, "No, it's another month yet," and your face goes funny, just for a minute, like you're trying not to cry.'

'Yes,' said Phyllida after a minute. She stared through the windscreen, blinking back tears. 'Just like that.'

'It probably takes ages, anyway,' said Lucy thoughtfully.

'Months and months.' Phyllida seized her chance. 'We mustn't make it hard for her.'

'All right then. But that means we'll have to stay here. We can't leave Clemmie on her own, just waiting, can we?'

'We'll talk to Daddy about it,' promised Phyllida, guiltily passing the buck. She opened the door and let her out. 'Let's go and have some tea.'

Chapter Thirty-two

Liz sat at her desk staring sightlessly at her computer, her thoughts a million miles away from VAT returns. Only that morning she'd received a letter from Tony asking if they could meet; he had something rather important he wanted to discuss with her. Each time she thought about the letter, her heart hammered and her cheeks felt hot. During the past year there had been a subtle change in his approach to her and, when he'd dropped Christina back home after the New Year, she'd been certain that he wanted to say something particular. They'd communicated at a distance for such a long time that it was most peculiar to have him there beside her, chatting about old friends, recent promotions, the latest scandals. She'd been so busy condemning him, hating him, that she'd forgotten what fun he could be and she'd begun to enjoy herself a little. Once Christina had disappeared upstairs and she was alone with him, however, her own feelings made her brittle and she'd been quite incapable of assisting him in his obvious difficulties in coming to the point she guessed that he was trying to make. He'd abandoned the air of defensive cheerfulness with which he normally dealt with any form of communication between them and had really seemed to want to know how she was coping and whether she was happy.

It had unnerved her. Once he'd gone she had the usual feelings of regret that she'd been so unforthcoming. When Christina reappeared, her face innocent, Liz was certain that she'd left them alone together deliberately and she wondered if Tony had prompted it before they'd arrived. She couldn't bring herself to ask and was noncommittal when Christina asked a few probing questions but, inside, she felt edgy. Her carefully frozen emotions were beginning to melt through her icy composure and she didn't know how to handle them.

And now this letter! He'd enjoyed their chat, he wrote, but he'd like to have time to talk properly and suggested that he came down one weekend. He left it to her to fix a date and a time. The idea of this meeting and what he might wish to discuss had obsessed her all day.

'Working late? You mustn't show us all up, you know!'

Liz glanced up as Jenny paused beside her. 'Heavens!' She glanced at her watch. 'I had no idea of the time. No, I can finish this on Monday.' She tidied her desk and switched off her computer. 'Thank God it's Friday.'

'And so say all of us. Coming to Claudia's house-warming tomorrow?' asked Jenny as they left the office.

'I am, indeed. I'm really pleased things have worked out for her.' They stood together on the pavement and Liz gave a little sigh and smiled quickly to hide her strange feeling of sadness.

'I love her new cottage,' said Jenny. Liz's mood seemed, somehow, to infect her and she felt seized by a sudden apathy. 'Come and have a drink,' she said impulsively, unable to face her empty flat. 'I haven't seen you to talk to properly for ages. Go on!'

Liz looked at the bright little face and nodded and Jenny grinned gratefully. They walked along together amicably, talking about work until they reached the pub and, going in, waved to Gavin who was collecting up ashtrays.

'I'll get them,' said Liz as they reached the bar.

It occurred to her that, close though Jenny and Gavin were, their relationship didn't seem to be going anywhere. They seemed easy and relaxed but not what she would have described as being in love. Yet they were never seen publicly with other partners and rarely alone. Well, perhaps it was the best way to be; so much less painful.

'Does anyone actually know what happened to Jeff?' she asked suddenly, when they had their drinks and were sitting on the high stools with Gavin leaning beside them on the other side of the bar. 'I never believed all that about his mother, somehow. Was there someone else?'

There was an odd silence and Gavin and Jenny seemed to draw imperceptibly closer together. Liz glanced at them and, as the silence lengthened, she raised her eyebrows.

'Not as far as I know.' Jenny's tone was negligent, almost disinterested. 'Never heard anything. I always thought he was a bit of a mother's boy myself. I wasn't that surprised.'

'That's right.' Gavin hauled himself upright and gathered up a few empty glasses. 'Claudia seems happy enough, anyway.'

Liz gave a mental shrug and returned to her drink. Ever since the break-up of her own marriage she'd tended to be oversensitive about other people's relationships. Perhaps she was imagining things.

'What a stroke of luck,' Jenny was saying, 'to get a job like that. I think she's found it a bit of a culture shock after what she was doing before but she's really enjoying it. Is your Uncle Eustace coming tomorrow night?'

'Catch Unk missing a party!' Liz snorted. 'He's been upcountry for a week or two. His house has sold at last although he's had to drop the price a bit. Anyway, he's been getting all the ends tied up. He's travelling down tomorrow. He'll be there.'

'I wish my uncles were like him,' said Jenny rather wistfully. 'He's just like a big kid, really, isn't he?'

'Just like,' said Liz grimly.

Gavin laughed at her expression and Liz grinned unwillingly. She remembered Tony's letter and suddenly felt a rush of excitement. Supposing . . . She pushed the thought swiftly away.

'Let's have another drink,' she said abruptly. 'And what about some food, Jenny? I haven't got anything planned. Shall we stay and have a bite of supper?'

'Great idea!' said Jenny with relief. 'Same again, Gavin and have one yourself. Thank goodness we've got a party to look forward to! I feel really cheesed off, somehow. All on edge with myself.'

Liz knew exactly how she felt. She simply couldn't get the phrases of Tony's letter out of her mind and she, too, felt on edge and nervous. She'd write back agreeing to the meeting, she decided, and felt another surge of excitement. It could be that Tony had grown up at last and realised that he'd been a fool. Even so, could she possibly take him back? Her excitement turned to panic and for the hundredth time she pushed the thought away.

'Pass the menu,' she said. 'And hurry up with that drink!'

The party was a tremendous success. Each of Claudia's friends was determined to help make it a memorable occasion and, as she looked round at their faces, she felt quite overwhelmed with amazed gratitude. She could hardly take in all that had happened in the past year and certainly wouldn't have believed in the happiness she now felt to be possible. She realised how buttoned-up, how restricted, her life had been with Jeff. He'd been her first serious boyfriend and her love for him, and its rejection which had so distorted her own emotions, had blinded her to her own capabilities and passions.

It was lovely to feel admiring glances and to banter and joke and to simply enjoy being young and beautiful. She knew she was looking at her best; her skin carefully tanned to a warm honey colour, her strappy silk dress clinging to her slim body and flowing round her slender bare ankles. Everyone was generous with their compliments for her and the new house and she felt buoyed up by their friendship.

When the guests had gone, however, and she was left with Oliver, who had stayed to help clear up, she was attacked by shyness and found that she hardly dared look at him. Oliver felt much the same. The love and affection that he had for Phyllida was rather different to this overwhelming desire and he felt confused. His limited physical experience and the fact that Claudia was several years older made it more difficult.

She was, after all, an experienced married woman and, even now, he didn't know how her marriage stood.

He piled glasses and plates on to the draining board in her delightful kitchen and, taking his courage in both hands, turned to smile at her.

'What an evening!' he said. 'Best party I've been to for years.'

She smiled too as she stacked things into the sink, not looking at him, and suddenly remembered that last awful party with Jeff. A spasm of pain crossed her face, her old insecurity overwhelming her, and Oliver instinctively put an arm about her.

'Why don't you sit down,' he said, 'and I'll make us some coffee? It'll give us the energy to tackle the washing-up.'

'Thanks.' She sounded rather breathless and his heart jumped about uncomfortably.

She sat down in the corner of the sofa, looking at the house-warming presents she'd received. Liz had given her a cookery book and she pretended to lose herself in it while he put a cassette in the tape deck and went to make the coffee. When he disappeared into the kitchen, she rested her head back against the cushion and felt a piercing longing for him. She'd had enough to drink to feel pleasantly relaxed and that conversation with him about safe sex had subdued her fears and enabled her to overcome her ingrained inhibitions. To be admired was a heady sensation but she suspected that what she felt for Oliver was sheer lust and part of her was shocked by it. She was extremely fond of him but her overwhelming need was for pure physical release although she didn't analyse it in quite that way. She just knew that she wanted to touch him and, even more important, to have him touch her and she knew, also, that she could trust him and feel safe with him. Her body seemed to expand with desire and, when she heard him returning, she seized the book again and pretended to be immersed in its contents.

Oliver, hardly knowing what he was doing, had put on an Ella Fitzgerald tape and the old-fashioned purely romantic music somehow relaxed him a little as he returned with the coffee. He stood her cup on the table at the end of the sofa and she thanked him. He sat down, turning sideways so that he could look at her, and the curve of her body under the silk dress and the long line of her legs undid him.

'You really are so beautiful,' he said and his voice was unsteady. 'Perhaps, after all, I ought to go before I do something I might regret.'

She looked at him then. 'Don't go,' she said quickly.

They stared at each other and their mutual desires were quite unmistakable. He saw her need and, throwing caution to the wind, pulled her into his arms and kissed her. All the pent-up emotion, the suppressed passion of years, was released within her and she clung to him. Jubilation, desire and terror, in equal measure, swept over him. He knew, without any doubt, that he must show no hesitation, that he must take the initiative before she lost her nerve and, as he kissed her, he pushed her back into the corner of the huge comfortable sofa and slipped the straps of her dress from her smooth shoulders.

His overwhelming desire for her was like a drug to Claudia. He made her feel beautiful, passionate, special, and his hands and lips and tongue electrified her into a response that was almost wild. Oliver's experience was only just up to it but her own had been so limited that she was quite unaware of his limitations. Together they soared to greater and yet greater heights until, rolling to the floor, the final climax caused Oliver to cry out and Claudia to burst into tears. They clung together, he gasping, she weeping, until the storm was passed and they lay quietly, her head cradled on his breast, his lips against her hair. He sought for words and, finding none that were adequate, merely tightened his arms about her. She pressed her cheek against his skin and wanted to weep again from pure happiness.

Presently Oliver lifted her back into the corner of the sofa, put his shirt round her shoulders, collected a half-full bottle of wine and two tumblers and carried them back to the sofa. He made no attempt to cover himself up and his naturalness allowed her to remain as she was. She looked at him with a kind of shy pride as he passed her a tumbler and he touched his glass to hers before he drank.

Her reaction had shown him that his own inexperience had gone unnoticed and with a deep thankfulness he leaned forward and gently kissed her hand as it clutched the glass and then bent lower and kissed her breast. Her hand shook, spilling the wine, and he felt desire rising in him all over again. He stood his tumbler on the table, removed hers from her unresisting hand and placed it beside his, then slipping his arms beneath her he licked the wine from her belly.

'Mustn't waste it,' he murmured. 'Mmm. Tastes better this way.' And, feeling her desire rising to match his own, he began to make love to her all over again.

* * *

Christina lay in her narrow bed at the end of the dormitory and stared into the darkness; ideas, memories, imaginings crowded out sleep. The most exciting of all these was the suggestion that she should channel her future in a direction which would enable her, once qualified, to join Uncle Eustace and his team. Her jealousy of Claudia was gradually becoming admiration and she'd gathered up the courage to ask her about designing and how she'd trained. Claudia was encouraging and helpful but once she'd gone, Christina had sighed.

'Even if I were good enough, you wouldn't want another designer on the team, would you?' she asked.

Detecting a wistful note, Oliver glanced up from the figures he was working on with Uncle Eustace.

'We shall want all types of people,' he said seriously. 'We shan't just stop at this, you know. Once it's really going we shall be doing all sorts of things. By the time you've finished your A levels you'll be able to judge whether or not we're worth joining and we shall know what openings there are. You don't have to narrow yourself down to design just yet.'

'Perfectly true.' Uncle Eustace peered at her over his spectacles. 'Remember it was you who thought of the mail-order idea. Always room for an ideas person within this sort of organisation. There's advertising to be thought up and marketing. All sorts of things.'

She gazed at them, thrilled to be taken so seriously.

'So what's the most important thing to have?' she asked eagerly.

'Enthusiasm,' replied Uncle Eustace promptly. 'Worth a

dozen degrees. Keep interested in life, keep learning, keep listening.'

'Gosh!' She looked excited. 'I really meant what A levels I should go for.'

'Whatever turns you on most. What you're good at.' Oliver smiled at her. 'Do what you like best.'

Now, in the darkness, Christina grinned with pure joy. Imagine working with Oliver every day! Maybe she needn't bother about a degree but could join the team as soon as she'd done her A levels. She wondered what Mum would have to say about that. Or Dad . . . On top of all this excitement, she was sure that Dad was thinking of getting back together with Mum. He was making all sorts of odd little hints that she couldn't quite understand but which could be interpreted as a desire to settle down and stop playing the field. It would be good if he did. She was beginning to find the way he looked at her friends a bit embarrassing, almost creepy, as if he fancied them. After all, he was too old for them. It was all right with women of his own age but with girls . . . She felt a little pang of pity for him. It must be awful to be old.

But how would Mum feel? Even after all these years it was difficult to know exactly what she thought about Dad. She always gave the impression that she hated him but, deep down, there was something else. Christina wondered how much of her hate was just hurt. She could sympathise with that, he'd been pretty awful to her, but would Mum want to risk it again? Was it possible that, secretly, she might still love him?

Christina's thoughts carried her back to Oliver and how

the other girls had envied her when he'd arrived to take her out to lunch. She relived it all in her mind, revelling in how he'd looked and what he'd said. Even her GCSEs held no terrors for her with the promise of the long summer holidays stretching ahead. Wrapped in memories, she sighed with pleasure, turned on to her side and composed herself for sleep.

Chapter Thirty-three

Alistair, travelling to the West Country by train, watched the familiar landmarks sliding by without really seeing them, so immersed was he in his thoughts. It was clear to him that there was no possible chance of buying a house, or even renting one, before the baby was due. In itself, this wasn't too much of a problem. With all the trauma of Quentin's death, Phyllida was in no fit state to be house-hunting. Alistair lit a cigarette, ignoring the glares of a fellow traveller who should have found a seat in a 'no smoking' compartment. He inhaled deeply as he stared out over the flat Somerset countryside. He was worried that Phyllida was doing too much, wearing herself out. At the same time he could see that she was extremely happy at The Grange and that she would be very sad to leave it. She and Clemmie had forged a strong bond, almost like mother and daughter except that Clemmie was old enough to be Phyllida's grandmother. Perhaps the fact that this was no blood relationship made it easier. There were none of the natural animosities, jealousies or criticisms that seemed to be present amongst the members of the happiest families. Alistair tapped ash into the inadequate ashtray and wondered whatever Clemmie would do when they moved out. She couldn't hope to manage alone and he frowned a little as he imagined the trouble he might have in persuading Phyllida that they must leave her to it. They had their own lives to live and, sweet though Clemmie was, they couldn't live in the guest wing at The Grange indefinitely, especially with a new baby. Alistair sighed and tried to stretch his legs without kicking his fellow passenger.

He wished he could come to some decision about his own future. How many times he'd gone over and over it; weighing things up, trying to decide what was best. He knew that it would be wise to buy a house now, whilst prices were still low, in which case it would be sensible to stay in the Navy so as to be able to get a good mortgage. That meant that he would be able to take advantage of the school fees allowance. If he came outside he might not be able to get a job and then what would they do? He'd always decided that he'd start a new career at forty but now he could see the bars closing round him. He stubbed out his cigarette and folded his arms across his chest. If only he and Phyllida could be together! Well, that might not be out of the question. He could be offered Commander SM at *Drake* or be given an appointment where Phyllida and the children could join him. It wasn't quite the same, however, as being together as one family on a permanent basis. It was obvious, too, that early retirement would be out of the question. One of the disadvantages to an extended bachelor's career was that you had your children late in life. He'd be in his middle fifties when this new baby would be leaving school to embark on university and nearly sixty before it was self-supporting. Alistair grimaced and glanced up as a fellow officer, making his way along the carriage, hailed him.

'Skiving off early, too, I see!' he said.

Alistair nodded. 'Friday afternoon,' he said and shrugged. 'Made the earlier train by a gnat's whisker.'

'Got a lift the other end?'

'No, as it happens I haven't. Didn't have time to let Phyllida know. I thought I'd phone from the buffet car.'

'We'll give you a lift. No problem. Come and have a drink.'

'Why not?' Alistair followed him along the swaying train. 'We're not at Yelverton, now. We're out in the sticks towards Sheepstor.'

'Fair enough. So how's life treating you?'

The car turned in the lane and disappeared, leaving Alistair standing on Blackthorn Bridge. He leaned on the parapet for a while, watching the river meandering below him. Marsh marigolds grew on the exposed rocks, their deep gold reflected in the slow-moving water. He'd marvelled to see them completely submerged after a night of heavy rain, swaying in the depths in ghostly fashion, and imagined that they'd be dead the next day. As the water retreated, however, they'd been left none the worse for their drowning, standing erect once more and lifting their golden petals to the welcome sunshine. He looked for the dipper, smiling a little shamefacedly at his superstition, and made his way along the track and up the drive. The front door stood open and he dropped his grip on the hall floor but, before he could give a shout to announce his presence, he heard voices in the sitting room. The door was ajar and he paused for a moment, wondering whose voice was speaking. As he looked in from the hall, his heart gave a jolt. A tall figure moved across his line of vision and, for a breathtaking moment, he thought that Quentin had returned; a more upright, younger Quentin, whose hair was only just greying and whose voice was more flexible. It was Gerard. Alistair shook his head at his moment of fear and moved in to the doorway. Clemmie was sitting bolt upright in an armchair with Phyllida, big with child, standing beside her. Alistair felt his heart move with love to see her, clasping Clemmie's hand, the big grey eyes fixed on Gerard.

'Just a little more time, darling,' Clemmie was pleading. 'Just the summer. I'm sure I shall have reached a decision then, one way or the other.'

'And what if you go falling over in the wood like Father did?' he asked.

Alistair saw Clemmie flinch and Phyllida jerk up her chin in anger at his thoughtless words. He looked at Gerard as he turned away from them and paced across to the window and he knew that the man was cursing himself for his tactlessness but determined to bring things to a satisfactory conclusion. Alistair sympathised with him but he was moved by the sight of the two women, fighting for their own futures. He saw, in one moment of insight, the ineluctable passage of time, the inexorable advance of death; childhood, motherhood, old age, all were before his eyes, motionless as in a tableau, and then the moment passed and he saw Clemmie smile up at Phyllida and squeeze her hand. He stepped into the room and Gerard turned quickly as Phyllida gave a little cry of welcome.

'Sorry to take you by surprise.' He smiled at them and gave Phyllida a quick kiss. 'Caught an early train and got a lift up. How are you?'

He shook hands with Gerard, sensing his wariness.

'How lovely.' Clemmie was rising from her chair. 'I'm sure you'd like some tea.'

'I don't want to interrupt anything.' Alistair could feel the older man's frustration. 'I can make my own tea.'

'No, no—' began Clemmie, only too grateful for the interruption, but Gerard cut her short.

'We're trying to get things sorted out here, Commander,' he said – and the formality in his tone warned Alistair that this was no friendly chat. 'I understand you and your wife are about to move on and I'm trying to persuade my mother that she really mustn't be alone here.'

'I absolutely agree with you,' said Alistair cheerfully and saw both women's faces flash round at him, alarmed, shocked at his ready betrayal.

'I thought you would.' Gerard's relief was palpable. 'She's a wonderful woman,' he tried very hard not to sound patronising, 'but it's much too remote here and I simply cannot see how she could cope all on her own.'

'Quite right,' agreed Alistair. 'But she won't be all on her own, will she?' Once again the women's eyes were on him, still wary but hopeful now, too.

'I don't understand.' Gerard looked mistrustful.

'We shall be here with her for as long as she needs us,' he replied and his heart sank into his boots as he made the commitment. He smiled at Clemmie and Phyllida who were gazing at him in growing delight, tinged with disbelief.

'We're in no hurry to go anywhere. Clemmie can have as long as she needs.'

'I understand that you're a serving officer?' Gerard's voice was smooth. 'You would feel quite happy in leaving these two women alone here with your wife about to give birth? How will she manage when her time comes? And my mother might need physical assistance at any moment.' His glance took in Phyllida's bump and he raised his eyebrows. 'Do you really imagine that your wife's in a fit state to supply it?'

Alistair grinned. Gerard could be even more pompous than he could himself! 'My dear chap,' he said with the utmost friendliness. 'I think you underestimate women. Especially these two. I'd be prepared to back them against nearly any eventuality. As you say, Clemmie's a wonderful woman and Phyllida's a naval wife. She's used to coping alone. But let's not get too morbid. I'm due a month's leave which I'm saving so as to be on hand when the baby arrives. Let's deal with that first, shall we? If Clemmie wants us, we'll stay. If or when she wants to sell, we'll go.'

'How very accommodating of you.' Gerard made no attempt to hide his displeasure. 'My mother's most fortunate to have such friends.'

'We love her.' It was Phyllida who spoke up. She stared at Gerard defiantly and Alistair saw the flash of discomfiture on his face before he pulled himself together.

'So do I,' he said gravely. 'Which is why I'm trying to do my best for her.'

'I know that, darling. Of course I do! I'm just a difficult old woman who doesn't want to leave her home.' Clemmie looked at Alistair and her brown eyes were bright. 'Thank you, Alistair. I accept your very generous offer. We'll go into details later but meanwhile I think we all need some refreshment.'

Gerard shrugged and Alistair sympathised yet again but the two women had escaped and all he could do was to smile at him. Gerard did not return the smile: he left the room abruptly. Alistair heard his footsteps on the stairs and, after a moment, he followed Clemmie and Phyllida into the kitchen.

On an overcast June morning three weeks later, Alistair walked along the river bank with Punch at his heels, his thoughts in turmoil. He was still trying to come to terms with Clemmie's generous offer which he was trying to weigh up sensibly and unemotionally, just as Clemmie had known he would. The whole issue was complicated by the fact that Phyllida desperately wanted to accept and was now in the maternity unit of a Plymouth hospital. She was having a rather hard labour and it was with difficulty that she'd persuaded him to leave her so as to be back in time to put Lucy to bed and reassure her that all was well. He'd tried to plead that Clemmie was more than capable but Phyllida had been adamant. She knew that Lucy had a private fear that Phyllida might be whisked off to heaven, too, and she wanted to make quite certain that she wasn't frightened.

'Come back in the morning,' she told him. 'It'll all be over then. I'll be OK. I shall be happier if I know you're with Lucy.'

He'd kissed her, his heart heavy with anxiety as he looked into her shadowed eyes, knowing that he'd give her anything she desired if only she came through this quite safely.

Something had held him back, however, from making the final commitment, from accepting Clemmie's amazing offer. Now, as he walked by the river, he knew that he was trying to be quite certain about what was right for Phyllida. Would they all live together quite happily? Old people could become difficult and demanding and there would be no way that either of them would be prepared to bundle Clemmie into a home unless she needed regular nursing. Alistair reached for his cigarettes. Financially speaking it was a once-in-a-lifetime offer. If they accepted it, however, he would certainly have to stay in for the time being, at least until his policy matured and the mortgage could be paid off. Four more years! Alistair sighed. By then he'd probably be in the school fees allowance trap.

Phyllida had repudiated this idea. 'They can go to the local schools,' she'd said. 'Come out when your policy matures, darling. We can pay the mortgage off and run The Grange as a guesthouse. It would be such fun!'

Her face had glowed with enthusiasm and his heart had beat a little faster at the thought. It would be hard work but fun, being together all the time.

'I must think about it,' he'd said and her face had fallen a little. 'We've no experience,' he'd explained. 'It's probably not as easy as it sounds.'

'It's our widget. I just know it!' she'd retorted and he was reminded of Uncle Eustace and had laughed and then grown serious. Uncle Eustace was seizing his new opportunity with both hands and he was seventy-odd! Alistair strolled on, his eyes not yet attuned to the minutiae of the countryside about him, but nevertheless aware of a glow of wellbeing despite his anxieties. He felt, as Phyllida did, a sense of belonging. If only he could be certain . . . !

'Come on, Quentin, old chap!' he muttered, pausing to finish his cigarette. 'Give me a sign.'

He remembered Phyllida on the bridge and smiled to himself.

'OK,' he said to Quentin's spirit. 'If we're supposed to accept Clemmie's offer and stay here, let's have a glimpse of this famous dipper.'

He stood for a moment, waiting, and realised that his heart was beating rather quicker and his eyes were straining along the bank. He'd started to turn away, aware of a tremendous disappointment, when a flash of white beneath the further bank caught his attention. The dipper was sitting on the rock, half turned away, so that only the smallest glimpse of his white breast was visible. Alistair held his breath as the bird dipped with its regular motion, noticing how well camouflaged it was against the rocks and the tumbling water. It must have been there all the time and yet he might so easily have missed it.

As he stared, he heard a voice. It was Clemmie calling to him and his heart contracted with a new fear as he ran to meet her, Punch blundering just ahead of him. He saw her on the path ahead, hobbling as quickly as she could, and when they met she held out her hand to him, her eyes shining.

'She's had a boy!' she cried. 'She's perfectly fine. Very tired and no wonder! A big boy, nine and a half pounds. Poor Phylly. No wonder she was having difficulty. Oh, Alistair. Many congratulations, my dear boy.'

He was clutching her hand and nodding, blinking back his

tears and laughing at the same time.

'A boy, Clemmie!'

He hugged her, holding her frail frame close, and quite suddenly all his anxieties vanished as though they'd never been. 'How will you like having a baby at The Grange again, Clemmie?'

She peered up at him quickly and he smiled down at her and nodded. 'I should like to accept your amazing offer,' he said. 'Thank you.'

'Oh, Alistair.' Her lips trembled and her grip tightened on his hand. 'Are you quite, quite certain? For the right reasons?'

He understood her perfectly. 'All the right reasons,' he reassured her. 'I'm absolutely sure, now, that it's right for all of us as a family. Let's hope that you don't regret it.'

'Most unlikely.' She had control of herself now and they turned for home together.

'You'll come in with me?' he asked. 'To see Phylly and the baby?'

She shook her head firmly. 'You must go alone for the first visit,' she said. 'And Phyllida will be too tired to cope with anyone else. I'll go tomorrow if she's ready for visitors.'

She took his arm and they climbed slowly to the gate.

'Lucy can come in this evening,' said Alistair. He felt so happy he would have liked to run and shout but he walked slowly, Clemmie's arm in his. 'I hope to God she doesn' insist on "Percy".'

Clemmie smiled and stopped to catch her breath. She looked up at him, her eyes serious. 'What made you decide to accept?' she asked.

He hesitated, knowing how important it was to her tha

the decision was based on good sound sense, with his family's wellbeing at its heart. He thought of all the excellent reasons, all the advantages, and finally spoke the truth. 'I asked for a sign that we should stay,' he said. 'And I saw the dipper.' He looked at her, worried that she would think he'd taken too light-hearted a view of such a momentous undertaking, but to his surprise he saw that her face was full of joy and relief and her eyes shone with happy tears.

'Thank God!' said Clemmie and turned with him to make the last ascent to the gate. 'Now I can sleep easy in my bed!'

Chapter Thirty-four

Uncle Eustace's housewarming party was, if possible, even more fun than Claudia's. By the time he was settled in a large Victorian villa, not far from the Bedford Hotel, Percy the Parrot Clothes Limited was a going concern and an autumn catalogue was nearly finished. The party wasn't simply a housewarming; it was a celebration. Uncle Eustace had offered Oliver rooms in the house which he gladly accepted. He had been living at home for most of the summer but he was delighted to be offered his own quarters – bedroom, bathroom and study – until such time that the business was doing well enough for him to be able to afford his own place.

It hadn't occurred to either Claudia or Oliver that he should move in with her. Both of them instinctively recognised that this was not going to be a long-lasting relationship. Each knew that it was an invaluable experience and were grateful for it but that somehow it was bound up with the excitement of the new venture and the changes in both their lives. They accepted that it would have its natural end, rather like a shipboard romance or a holiday affair, and took what the other had to offer without fear or guilt.

For Claudia it was a minor miracle. The realisation that she was desirable, beautiful, irresistible, brought her a confidence that was increased by her achievement with her designs. For the first time she felt strong, happy, fulfilled, and those dark days of misery and shame were put behind her. Nevertheless, she needed the privacy and peace that her cottage brought her and, although she still loved her visits to The Grange, she no longer envied Phyllida her sense of belonging. Claudia realised that she liked her own company – and the freedom she'd discovered – and was revelling in her new beginning.

Oliver, too, could hardly believe his luck. To have found a career and a ravishingly exciting lover at one stroke was almost too good to be true. As Claudia's confidence grew, however, the difference in their ages became more marked and Oliver knew that the end of their love affair could not be far away. He suspected that it would be she who would bring the relationship to a conclusion and could only hope that he'd have the maturity to accept her decision gracefully when that time came. The fact that they would have to go on working together showed them how essential it was that they should remain friends but since their work made up a good part of their lives together, he felt that this would not be too difficult to achieve. Their affair roused very little interest. Everyone knew that they were both involved in the new business and, for the rest, they were very discreet. Only Uncle Eustace and Phyllida guessed the truth. Claudia and Oliver knew that they could relax and be themselves in Unk's company although, even then, some in-built reticence restrained them. Phyllida simply knew it. Her intuition had informed her long before Claudia, overwhelmed and too happy to keep it to herself any longer, confided in her.

'I can't believe it,' she kept repeating. 'Me, of all people! I was so strait-laced and starchy.'

'I think it was Jeff who was strait-laced and starchy,' observed Phyllida. 'You've never had the chance to be anything else. You're simply making up for lost time.'

'Isn't it frightening?' Claudia looked thoughtful. 'I wonder how many people live under the shadow of others?'

'Millions!' said Phyllida at once. 'Through love, fear, jealousy.' She shrugged. 'You name it.' She hesitated. 'Does Oliver know? About Jeff, I mean.'

'Oh, no!' Claudia grimaced. 'I just couldn't bring myself to tell him, somehow. He thinks the same as everyone else. I don't want him to know. I can cope with it now but I don't want to dwell on it, if you know what I mean.'

'I know exactly what you mean,' said Phyllida in a heart-felt tone.

'You're happy now, though, aren't you?' Claudia looked at her anxiously. In her new-found joy she couldn't bear to think that Phyllida was still unhappy.

'Oh, yes! I think I feel a bit like you do. I can hardly take it all in. I've come to terms with Alistair's . . . fling. Well.' She gave a tiny shrug. 'More or less. I still get the odd twinge but I can accept it. And James is a duck. Which reminds me.' She glanced at her watch. 'I must crack on. I don't like to leave him with Clemmie for too long.'

'Don't you worry that she might be taken ill or something while she's looking after him?'

Phyllida paused at Claudia's front door, gazing across the

parkland to the big house which was almost obscured by the trees.

'You can't legislate for everything, can you?' she said at last. 'Fear can rule your life if you're not careful. I agree with Alistair. You can become so fearful about life, so anxious to preserve it at all costs, that you forget how to live it. Clemmie loves to have James and he's very happy with her. We have to assume that they'll be OK. I would hate her to feel that she's too old to cope with a baby and he only lies in his pram, after all.'

'I'm sure you're right.' Claudia gave her a quick hug. 'Is Sunday still OK?'

'You bet it is! Your godson will be waiting for you and Clemmie is already planning your favourite pudding. Lucy is going to deck herself out in her designer clothes!'

Claudia sighed contentedly. 'She did look great in them,' she admitted. 'Prudence is a marvel. She's incredibly professional.'

'I'm so pleased for her,' said Phyllida, pausing by her car. 'She's so thrilled to be involved and to be doing something really exciting, not to mention the money, of course! Take care. See you on Sunday.'

Claudia waved until the car vanished round the bend in the drive, and then went back inside. She climbed the stairs to her loft room which had designs pinned to wall-boards and a huge table covered in more drawings and swatches of materials. She wandered round the room, picking up samples and studying her recent work until finally, with a sigh of happiness, she settled down to work.

* * *

On the morning after the party, Oliver came yawning downstairs to find Uncle Eustace surveying the remains somewhat disconsolately.

'No such thing as a free lunch, Unk,' he said cheerfully as he went to fill the kettle. 'Don't worry. I'll do the washing-up.'

'I knew that I wouldn't regret sharing my home with you, dear boy.' Uncle Eustace brightened a little. 'I suggested that Christina might like to pop round this morning to lend a hand.'

'And what did she say?' Oliver rooted about for two clean mugs.

Uncle Eustace snorted indignantly. 'Suggested I went out first thing and bought a dishwasher.'

Oliver chuckled as he made the coffee.

'Not a bad idea,' he said. 'I'm not sure that you or I are sufficiently house-trained to live together without help, Unk.'

'It's funny you should say that.' He took his coffee and wandered into the sitting room which looked marginally less depressing. 'I was thinking that we should get someone in to look after us.'

Oliver pursed his lips and nodded. 'Sounds a good idea to me. Shall we advertise?'

'Well, we could.' Uncle Eustace sipped his black coffee appreciatively. 'Now, how should we phrase it? "Bachelor household needs young willing girl . . ."'

'Now you're talking, Unk! Don't hold back. "Needs young willing nubile blonde girl . . ."'

'Nothing against dark girls,' protested Uncle Eustace. 'Or

redheads for that matter. Must have a sense of humour, though. Don't want some sour-faced female tutting at me simply because I've dropped my socks on the floor.'

'Of course it's quite likely that we might get some chaps answering the advert. Can't specify that we need a girl. It's sexist.'

'Well, of course it is.' Uncle Eustace stared at him in surprise. 'I *am* sexist. I want a woman looking after me. It's what I'm used to. I like women.'

'Don't we all.' Oliver sighed regretfully. 'I'm just saying that it might not be that easy. We'll have to advertise privately. You'd shock the Job Centre rigid.'

'The trouble is that it's such a risk. Could get anybody. We need someone who understands our ways.'

'Nobody would understand your ways these days, Unk.' Oliver grinned at him. 'You're an old dinosaur.'

'Cheeky young beggar,' grumbled Uncle Eustace. 'No respect.'

The ring at the doorbell startled them both and, after a moment, Oliver hauled himself from his chair and went out. Uncle Eustace stared mournfully round at the detritus and then stiffened as he heard a well-known voice in the hall. Oliver reappeared, followed by Christina.

'My dear girl.' The older man was obviously moved. 'You've come to help us after all. This is very kind. Oliver will get you some coffee so as to set you on your way.'

'I've already had breakfast *and* coffee,' said Christina contemptuously. 'The trouble is that I felt guilty thinking of you two, sitting here, and I thought I'd cycle in and see how you were getting on. Honestly!' She stared round. 'You haven't even started yet! How on earth are you going to manage on your own?'

'Now, no criticism, please,' begged Oliver. 'We were just discussing that very thing. Do you know anyone who would like to look after us, Christina?'

'Someone amusing?' asked Uncle Eustace hopefully. 'I can't stand a nagging woman. Brings out the worst in me.'

'I'll have to think about it.' Christina began to gather up glasses, unable to bear the thought of anyone looking after them but herself. 'You could advertise at the Job Centre.'

'We've thought about that,' said Oliver. 'We were just composing our advertisement.'

'I bet you were!' Christina glanced at them sharply. 'I bet the words "young" and "beautiful" came in to it.'

'We're hardly likely to ask for someone who's old and ugly!' protested Uncle Eustace. 'Anyway, Oliver keeps telling me that I'm not allowed to call people old or ugly any more.'

'Perfectly right, too!' Briefly, Christina looked and sounded like Liz.

'Oliver's got a book about it.' He followed her into the kitchen. 'I'm learning it by heart. Bet you can't guess what a housewife's called these days.'

Christina piled dishes into the sink and delved for the washing-up liquid.

'No, I can't,' she said reluctantly, after some thought. 'What is it?'

'Domestic incarceration survivor!' he cried triumphantly and she burst out laughing. 'I try to learn a few each day. You know, like the White Queen in Alice. Six impossible things before breakfast. I learned "bald", this morning.'

Oliver, leaning against the door jamb, grinned.

'"Follicularly challenging"?' he hazarded.

'"Differently hirsute",' said Unk with simple pride. 'Good, eh?'

Christina shook her head, still laughing, and ran hot water on to the plates.

'Honestly! You two aren't safe out. I'll see if Mum knows of anyone who would be prepared to take you on.'

'And how is my dear niece, this morning? Recovered from the excesses of last night?'

'She's OK.' Christina plunged her hands into the soapy water. 'She's a bit twitchy, actually. Dad's coming down tomorrow to see her. They've got things to discuss.'

Involuntarily, Uncle Eustace and Oliver exchanged a look behind Christina's back.

'Ah,' said Uncle Eustace, noncommittally. 'Well, there must be plenty to discuss about your future and so on.'

'I s'pose so. I wondered if I could come over to you. It might be a bit embarrassing for them if I'm just hanging around. You know? I could say you've invited me for tea.'

'Well, of course you can come. You don't need invitations. You should know that.' Uncle Eustace squeezed her shoulder. 'Certainly come to tea. Oliver will go out and buy a cake.'

They were aware, now, of a certain tension in the way she spoke and stood and they exchanged another longer look.

'Absolutely,' said Oliver easily. 'Why not lunch? We can go round to the pub. After all, that's why Unk bought this house, because it's two minutes' walk from the nearest watering hole. May as well make use of the amenities.'

'No, thanks,' said Christina, after a moment. 'I won't do

that. Mum's a bit worked up about him coming. I won't leave her on her own. He's arriving after lunch, so I'll stop long enough to say Hi and then leave them to it.'

'Just as you like,' agreed Uncle Eustace. 'Come when you're ready. We'll be here. And now I think I'll just pop out for the newspaper while you two finish off. Don't let me get in your way!'

He disappeared and Oliver picked up a tea towel.

'What an old fraud he is,' he said lightly. 'Thanks for coming round.'

'It's OK.' She shrugged off his thanks. 'I was glad to get out. Mum's roaring round like the white tornado. I've never seen her like this before.'

Oliver wiped dishes silently. He felt ill-equipped to comment on Liz's behaviour. They worked together for a little longer and then Christina spoke again.

'D'you think she might have him back if he asks her?'

'Oh, honestly, Chrissie, I've no idea.' Oliver made no pretence of misunderstanding. 'They've been apart for quite some time, haven't they?'

'Ten years.' Christina pulled out the plug and wiped round the sink as the water went swirling down. 'She always says he never loved her and they only got married because I was on the way. She says he was in love with your mum.' She wrung out the cloth and turned to look at him.

'I've heard that rumour,' he said reluctantly. 'But that was over twenty years ago and it stopped after he and Liz married.'

'But you can go on loving people, can't you?' she asked. 'Even if they're married to someone else?'

Oliver thought of Phyllida. 'Sadly, yes,' he said. 'Perhaps Tony regrets the divorce and would like to start again.'

'He's been hinting things for ages,' she said as she helped him put the crockery away.

'And what do you want?' Oliver smiled at her. 'D'you think it would work?'

'I'd like it to,' she admitted. 'But I couldn't bear it if they tried and it didn't. Mum still loves him, I'm sure of it, whatever she says.'

Oliver thought about Liz with her biting tongue and bitter expression, the way her face fell into unhappy lines.

'Yes,' he agreed. 'I think you might be right.'

'I only hope she doesn't chuck the chance away through pride,' said poor Christina anxiously. 'Surely she couldn't be so daft!'

'You mustn't get worked up about it,' said Oliver gently. 'They ought to know what's right for them after all this time. You must be prepared to accept whatever Liz decides. It will be harder for her.'

'I know that really. I've tried to see it from her point of view. He's just been enjoying himself all these years and now he's getting old he wants to come back to her to be looked after in his old age.'

'Hang on a minute.' Oliver tried to inject a note of humour. 'How old's Tony? Forty-five? Hardly ready for a Bath chair just yet!'

'You know what I mean, though.'

Christina grinned unwillingly and Oliver saw how very nervous she was at the thought of the meeting. He slipped an arm round her shoulders and gave her a little shake and, as she looked up at him and he saw her love for him, he bent his head to hers and kissed her gently on the cheek. It was hardly an earth-shattering embrace but when he released her, he saw that her eyes were tight shut and he drew her back to him and held her closely.

'You see, you've got all your life before you,' he told her. 'So many things will happen to you, wonderful things. And even though you'll go on loving them, your parents' lives will become separate from yours. They must do what's right for them and you must be brave about it.'

'I don't really mind,' said Christina, muffled. She held him tightly, unwilling to let this dreamed-of moment come to an end. 'I just want Mum to be happy.'

'If only life were that simple.' Oliver's face was sombre and presently he loosened her clasp and smiled down at her. 'Come on. I'm going to take you out and buy you a drink.'

'What about Unk?' she asked, reluctant to break the spell. 'Won't he wonder where we are?'

'He'll know,' said Oliver grimly. 'All that rubbish about buying papers! He'll be in the pub with a pint in front of him! We'll join him.'

Christina suddenly accepted that she must behave like an adult. Her joy at the kiss still burst and exploded like a fountain of fireworks in her breast but she instinctively knew that the best thing now was action. It would be fun to go to the pub and have a drink. She grinned at him as they went down the path and he knew that the dangerous moment had passed.

Chapter Thirty-five

Liz barely slept on Saturday night and rose up on Sunday morning, heavy-eyed and with an incipient headache. She was now quite sure that Tony was coming down with the intention of suggesting that they should try again and she had finally allowed herself to believe that she should swallow her pride and give their relationship another chance. Once she'd accepted the idea her excitement steadily mounted. The love that she'd continued to feel for him through all the years since she'd first met him began to surface, bursting through her sealed-up emotions and coming painfully to the surface. She knew that she'd probably never be able to trust him but, after all, he was not far off fifty now. Surely he must be ready for a quieter life!

She suspected that he was thinking of retiring from the Navy and that to get back together with the woman who had always loved him and the daughter of whom he was so fond was really not such a foolish plan. Ever since he'd written asking that they should talk, Liz had thought of little else. In the long watches of the night she'd sat huddled in the corner of the sofa, wide-eyed in the darkness, wondering if it could possibly work. There was so much pride to swallow. Her jealousy of the women he'd betrayed her with was as fresh as if it had happened yesterday. Even now she could sometimes hardly bear to look at Oliver. His expressions, his colouring, were Cass's and she still felt the stab of pain when she remembered how Tony had used her as a front whilst he and Cass continued their affair. When he'd made love to her, she knew quite well that it was Cass whom he imagined in his arms and humiliation swept over her anew as she recalled her misery.

Could she really put it all behind her and start again? She reflected on the surprise of her friends, the gossip, the speculation, and she felt hot with embarrassment. Against it she set her loneliness, the love she still felt for him and Christina's needs. There was no doubt that Christina wanted it but Christina was a child still and had no idea of how much sacrifice would be called for if it were to be given a real chance.

Liz dressed carefully. She had no intention of looking too keen nor did she want to undervalue her attractions. She was very slim and, although she'd never been pretty, she looked better now at forty than she had at eighteen. She noticed that Christina looked her over when she arrived downstairs and gave her an approving grin. She'd already warned her that she'd be dashing off just after lunch and Liz had felt a deep relief. She couldn't bear the thought of Christina being party to the discussion or of having to conduct it with the anxiety that she might burst in at any moment.

By the time Tony arrived they were both ready to fly apart with nerves. When he came in with Christina, Liz noticed that he looked equally nervous and her spirits rose a little. She could only bear it if he approached the business of his visit in a serious vein; if he were flippant she knew that she would be simply unable to cope. There seemed no danger of it. Never had she seen Tony so ill at ease. He and Christina chatted whilst Liz made tea but their talk was brittle and fragmented and she could see that Christina was relieved to go and leave them together. Tony got up to kiss her goodbye and then stood looking down at Liz who'd curled back in an armchair, her legs drawn up under her, her hands wrapped round her mug.

'Well, this is quite like old times.' He attempted a laugh. 'It must be years since we were alone together.'

'Yes.' Despite her determination to make it easy for him, her heart was pounding so hard that she could barely speak. 'Years and years.'

The sudden treacherous wave of tenderness, which she experienced as she watched him, unbalanced her completely. Just ask, she begged him silently. I love you, you fool. I always have. Just ask.

'I wondered if you might guess what it is I want to say,' he said at last. He made no attempt to sit down. 'It really is very difficult to come to the point but I suppose I shall just have to spit it out.'

He walked away to the window and stared down the garden whilst she watched him, willing him to speak, unable to utter a sound.

'I know I've always been a fool,' he said. 'I threw away your love and behaved like an idiot and I don't expect you to overlook it. I've behaved badly to you from the very first moment we met. I can't tell you how sorry I am or how deeply I regret it.'

He paused and she made an inarticulate little sound. He

turned and glanced at her but she couldn't meet his glance and, instead, sipped quickly at her tea. After a moment he turned back to the window.

'I'm trying to say that I think I may have learned some sense at last. I suppose the thing is that I'm getting old and I don't want to fritter the rest of my life away. I get lonely these days and I'm thinking of coming outside and doing something different while I'm young enough to adjust.' He took a deep breath and gave another little laugh. 'Oh hell! This is just as bad as I thought it would be. I'm sure you've guessed by now what it is I'm trying to say to you. I know you'll have your doubts but I want to get married again. To have another try at it.'

He was silent for a moment and she felt an exquisite relief seep through her and hot tears filled her eyes. He was going on speaking, still with his back to her.

'I know you'll think I'm the most fearful fool and I can't expect you to approve but it was important that you were the first to know so that you could prepare Christina.'

As he spoke, Liz suddenly had the beginnings of a terrible fear.

'What . . . How d'you mean? The first . . . ?'

He looked at her at last. He'd cleared his fences and he was into the straight. His face looked young again and his eyes shone.

'I've decided to take the plunge. I've made up my mind. She's quite a bit younger than I am but I don't think it matters. It's Christina I'm really worried about. She's had this crazy idea that you and I might get back together.' He laughed and this time the laugh was genuine and unforced. '

thought she ought to know you better than that but it's understandable, I suppose. Anyway, this is going to come as a bit of a shock to her and I thought it was only right that you should hear it from me first.'

'Who . . . who is she?' The brutal shock had the effect, after the first cruel pain, of numbing her senses a little.

'Oh, you'll never believe it.' He was glossy with success and relief. 'It's Lizzie Mallinson. I know!' He accepted her uncontrollable gesture of shocked disbelief as mere surprise. 'Isn't it incredible? Even got your name. She's twenty-eight years old, would you believe! She remembers the first time we met, so she says, at a barbecue her parents gave when they had a cottage down here. I remember that it was the hot summer of '76.' He paused then, remembering, too, that it was when he'd resumed his affair with Cass and first met Liz. He shrugged aside his embarrassment and smiled at her. 'Anyway, I've got it off my chest. I know you'll think I'm the most awful fool but they say there's no fool like an old fool, don't they? I felt I couldn't just put it in a letter but it took some courage to spit it out, I can tell you.'

He looked as though he expected her to congratulate him and she forced her shaking legs from beneath her and got to her feet.

'I didn't realise that you looked upon me as quite such an ogre.' Her voice was brittle, her tone contemptuous and she prayed that she could keep it up until he left.

'Of course you aren't.' She thought for one terrible moment that he might embrace her. 'But I know your opinion of me and very well justified it is, too. You'll do your best for me with Christina?'

'Of course I will. She'll adapt to it in time. You'll just have to be patient with her for a while. It might be a bit of a shock. Especially as Lizzie is nearer her age than yours.' She bit her lip, regretting the jibe but unable to resist it.

'Oh, hardly,' he protested laughingly. 'Well, only just. I'm a lucky devil, I know that . . .'

Go, she begged silently, just go. Don't stand there like a cock on its dunghill bragging about its conquests.

'. . . and of course Christina will love her when she gets to know her, she's such a sweetie . . .'

'I'm sorry to hurry you along.' Liz spoke rapidly and at random. 'But if there's nothing else, I'm going out myself in a minute . . .'

'Oh, of course.' He looked slightly hurt. 'Having come all this way I thought we might have dinner or something just for old times' sake. Still.' He shrugged.

She stared in disbelief at his insensitive, self-satisfied face and realised that her self-control must be more effective than she imagined. At least she was spared the degradation of his guessing the truth. She summoned all her courage.

'A bit of a problem with a friend of mine cropped up this morning. She's on her own so . . .'

'Oh well.' He knew he was lucky to be let off the hook without any more sarcastic or cutting remarks and accepted his dismissal in good part and with relief. He hadn't really wanted to take her out to dinner; he just felt he owed her something. After all, she was going to have the dirty work with Christina. 'I'll get off then.'

'Good luck.' Her pride kept her upright. 'When's the happy day?'

'Quite soon, we thought. Nothing to wait for, after all. I'll let you know. I'd like Christina to be there if possible.'

They kissed perfunctorily and she went back inside and closed the door. Her life seemed to lie in ruins round her and she felt so shocked and humiliated that she was incapable of speech or action. She sat down again in the armchair and stared at nothing, willing up the hatred and disgust for him that had supported her through all the long years and which held the pain at bay. She thought of telling Christina and her heart quailed and she knew a fierce longing to unburden herself to someone, to sob out her foolish hopes and describe her hurt and disappointment; Unk, perhaps, or Abby. Slowly her spine stiffened and she raised her chin. No one should know of her stupidity, no one at all. That way it might just be bearable. She sat on, preparing herself for Christina's return and the disappointment she, too, would suffer and, when she'd won a sufficient measure of self-control, she got up and went to the telephone to tell Uncle Eustace that the coast was clear and Christina could come home.

Abby packed eggs and cream into her basket and made her way out of the crowded pannier market. Autumn was on its way, the visitors were gone and the town was quiet again. She turned into Crebers to buy cheese and coffee and, coming out, met Claudia on the doorstep.

'Well, hello.' Abby looked slightly embarrassed. 'I've been meaning to get in touch with you. First of all I thought you'd gone and then I heard you were still here but you'd moved. And now I've been told all about your clever designs.'

Claudia smiled at her. To her surprise she no longer felt

awe or that numbing sense of inferiority; she didn't even feel the longing to be accepted. She realised that she didn't care one way or the other about what Abby thought of her. She had her own life now and she didn't need anyone else's approval as to how to live it.

'It's all been quite unbelievable,' she said and wondered how Abby would react if she knew about her and Oliver. 'Fantastic luck for me.'

'I'm glad.' Seeing that Claudia was obviously so content, Abby felt more relaxed. 'I can see that you won't have time for my committee, though. I was very sorry when you resigned.'

'I really thought I was going back to Sussex.' Claudia shrugged. 'It just didn't work out that way. But I'm afraid I simply haven't got a spare moment any more. Uncle Eustace is a terrible slave driver and Oliver' – she couldn't quite resist mentioning his name – 'has been wonderful.'

Abby raised her eyebrows. Claudia had, after all, achieved just what she wanted without Abby's help. Clemmie and Phyllida had already sung her praises and now it seemed that she had won Oliver and Unk over, too. Abby felt a flicker of irritation and then suddenly it didn't seem to matter any more.

'Come and have a cup of coffee,' she suggested impulsively. 'I'm just going round to the Bedford. Got the time?'

For a moment, Claudia had the urge to throw the invitation back in Abby's face, to tell her she was too busy, that she didn't need her friendship, but something held her back. Perhaps it was simply that she'd learned that friendship was too rare a commodity to be squandered for the sake of a cheap victory.

'Why not?' she agreed and they turned their steps towards Bedford Square. 'I haven't seen Liz for ages. Is she OK?'

'I think so.' Abby frowned a little. 'Her ex-husband is about to get married again and she says that Christina's taking it rather hard. I can't think why. He and Liz have been divorced for years. Perhaps it's because the girl's rather young, not much older than Christina, Liz says. Anyway, she was having such a difficult time with her that she decided to take her off for a couple of weeks' holiday before school started.'

'I'm sorry about that,' said Claudia. 'Christina's such a nice girl. She seemed OK when I saw her recently.'

'Well, I was a bit surprised,' admitted Abby. 'Didn't sound like Christina at all.'

'Perhaps it was a shock to Liz, too,' suggested Claudia. 'Must be, well . . . hurtful.'

'Could be,' said Abby. 'These men! You simply can't trust 'em!'

'You're so right!' said Claudia and they laughed together as they went up the steps and into the bar.

Chapter Thirty-six

Clemmie stood at her bedroom window watching Phyllida crossing the open ground above the wood. She was walking quite slowly, the baby held against her heart in his canvas sling and Clemmie watched until she was lost from sight in the trees. She remembered the times she'd seen Quentin coming back to her, some small offering in his hand, and her eyes filled with tears. Far from becoming used to his absence, the pain and loneliness grew worse and she wondered how on earth she would manage without the presence of Phyllida and the children in the house.

After the initial shock, Gerard had taken defeat gracefully enough. He'd sorted out the legal situation and cleared up matters relating to tax, insisting that all he wanted was her happiness. At least she was in good hands; even he could accept that. As far as sharing the house went, there were no problems. Clemmie had taken Quentin's study as her private room, whilst the Makepeaces used the breakfast room as a family room. The sitting room was common to all, as was the kitchen, and Phyllida and Alistair had moved into one of the larger bedrooms leaving the self-contained suite as the nursery wing.

It was working and Clemmie was grateful and relieved. She loved to hear Lucy's voice, calling in the hall when she returned from school, and to see James kicking in his pram in the courtyard. The pattern was being repeated and life was going on in the house, renewing itself, as it had for the past two centuries. She knew that Phyllida had been obliged to endure criticism from her family. Why, they must have asked her, must you buy a house with a sitting tenant? Her parents had come down to see her when James was born and Clemmie had tried to make herself scarce. It was only natural that they should feel worried and possibly resentful.

Certainly Phyllida seemed completely happy. James's birth had taken the focus away from Quentin's death and that was how it should be. It had distracted Lucy from her determination that Quentin should rise from the dead and come back amongst them, as good as new, and she was delighted with her new brother. She sat for hours by his pram, reading her Percy the Parrot books aloud to him, and entered into every stage of his development with enthusiasm.

Clemmie left the window and made her way downstairs. How deeply she missed Quentin's arrival with the tea tray, and their morning chats. Wisely, Phyllida had made no attempt to take over the role. Instead, they bought tea-making equipment to put beside her bed and she was very glad of it. Now, during the long wakeful nights, she could make herself a comforting cup whilst she put on the earphones that Phyllida had bought for her so that she could listen to music or the new talking book cassettes. Lulled, she would often drift back to sleep, only to wake suddenly, reaching out a hand for the warm beloved body that no longer slept beside her.

Punch was lying beside the Esse but he wagged his tail as she entered the kitchen and came to greet her. She patted him, wondering how much he missed Quentin, and went to make some toast. She noticed that the old dog rarely accompanied Phyllida on her walks, although he invariably went with Alistair. She doubted that he would survive the winter but knew that, once he was gone, Phyllida would bring a puppy to The Grange and the cycle would go on. Whilst she ate her toast she thought of the life going back into the past and forward into the future and was comforted. How could she have borne to have left The Grange? Quentin's presence was everywhere, he felt so close on occasions that she could barely believe that she would never see him again on this earth.

She'd just put the butter away and her plate in the sink when she heard a voice calling in the hall and, opening the door, came face to face with Oliver.

'My dear boy.' She put a hand to her heart. 'You quite startled me. How nice to see you. Come in, come in.'

He followed her in to the kitchen and crouched beside Punch, stroking his head and talking to him. Oliver had been to see her several times since Quentin's death and, although she knew that he'd left Oliver a small bequest, she wanted to offer him some memento of his godfather. He smiled at her and stood up and she decided that now was the moment to broach the matter.

'I know Quentin left you a little something,' she said, 'but I think it might be nice for you to have some rather more tangible reminder of him. Is there anything you'd like? The really special things have to go to Gerard, of course, but if there were some small thing . . . ? Think about it.'

'That's a very kind offer.' Oliver was touched that Clemmie should have thought of him. 'There is something, actually, if no one else wants it. I'd like his walking stick.'

Clemmie's eyes involuntarily went to the stand by the door. Quentin's ancient ash stick stood where Phyllida had gently placed it on that terrible morning six months before when she'd brought it back from the wood. Clemmie had seen the stick in Quentin's hands on countless occasions – striking back some brambles, its ferrule tenderly lifting the drooping head of a flower, testing marshy ground for a safe foothold – and tears filled her eyes and overflowed in a crystal stream down her cheeks.

She put her face in her hands and sobbed and Oliver went to comfort her.

'I'm so sorry,' he said, putting his arm round her and passing her his handkerchief. 'I wasn't thinking. It's just so much part of him that I should like it more than anything. You must feel the same.'

Clemmie shook her head, mopping her face with his handkerchief, and attempting to staunch the flow.

'I'm like this about so many things,' she said. 'Forgive me. It just took me off guard. I should love you to have the stick and I know that Quentin would feel the same.'

'Thank you.' He continued to crouch beside her for a moment, gently patting her shoulder, and presently he dropped a kiss on her white hair and stood up. 'Quentin taught me nearly all I know about the countryside,' he said. 'I shall treasure it as a reminder of many happy walks.'

Clemmie nodded, unable to trust her voice. They sat for

moments in a companionable silence whilst Clemmie regained her self-control.

'Phyllida's down in the woods,' she said. 'Can you stay to lunch?'

'No, no. Just a flying visit to make sure that all's well. Must be on my way.'

'It's lovely to see you. Come for longer next time. Oh. Don't forget the stick.' She took it from the stand and held it for a moment before passing it to him. 'Take care of it.'

He hesitated. 'Are you absolutely certain? You could cut it down to your own size, you know.'

She shook her head, smiling. 'I want you to have it. You'll appreciate it and think of him sometimes when you use it.'

Oliver took it and held it. 'It was Quentin who taught me the usefulness of a walking stick,' he said. 'But then he taught me so many things.'

He left her standing at the front door and she waited for him to put the stick in the car, and to turn and wave, before she went back inside.

Oliver drove down the track and over the bridge and, on an impulse, he pulled in at the side of the lane and switched off the engine. He got out and wandered back to lean on the parapet. Quentin was still very much in his mind and he felt that, at any moment, he might see the tall figure strolling between the trees with Punch at his heels. The October sunshine was mellow and the air was soft. The beech leaves, burnished and fiery, cast a golden haze over the wood and the river ran low in its rocky bed after the long dry spell.

Oliver straightened up and paused. Phyllida was standing on the path, staring out over the river. She stood quite still, gazing at something he couldn't see, her arms cradling the baby in his sling. His heart beat a little faster at the sight of her and he was surprised at how much he still cared about her. He'd hoped that, with the passing months, Quentin's death, the birth of her child, his own new exciting career and his passionate affair with Claudia, his love for her would die a natural death but, as he watched her, he knew that she would always have a very special place in his heart. He wondered whether he should call to her but something held him back and presently he turned away and went back to the car.

Phyllida heard the engine and turned to see who it might be. No car crossed the bridge, however, and she concluded that whoever it was had gone on up the lane. She resumed her walk towards the bridge, deeply content, enjoying the bright day. Occasionally she talked softly to James, who watched her, his eyes fixed on her face. She stood on the bridge and looked far downstream, remembering how she had kissed Oliver here. She remembered how she and Alistair had stood together here and how she'd seen the dipper fly out and had known everything would work out. Of course, part of it had worked out because of Quentin's death and that was very sad. If he'd lived, then she and Alistair would have found another home and he and Clemmie would have sold up and moved. It felt as if they were taking some happiness at his expense.

Perhaps we all have our turn, she thought, and we must

take care to make the most of the good bits.

She remembered the summer evening, after Alistair had gone back and the children were in bed, when she and Clemmie had sat talking in the summerhouse. It had been a hot, still night, with the moon rising and the bats fluttering about the eaves, and Clemmie had told her how Quentin had been unfaithful to her after Pippa had died. Phyllida had sat in shocked silence, glad of the darkness, and listened to Clemmie's story. She recognised now the link between the two of them as the tale unfolded and, imagining how she would have felt if Alistair's betrayal had come on top of Lucy's death rather than the unknown baby's, her heart went out to Clemmie.

As the story continued she suffered, too, for Quentin and she vowed silently never to let any bitterness creep back into her relationship with Alistair. She understood now why the dipper had become a symbol of hope and good fortune and how much faith Clemmie placed in it. When Clemmie told her how she and Lucy had dispelled the shadow and how wonderful the last year had been, Phyllida had been obliged to swallow back her tears until Clemmie stood up quite suddenly, said good night, and disappeared into the house. They'd never referred to it again but there'd been a new understanding between them, a deeper tenderness, and Phyllida felt her blessings even more strongly than before.

She cast a last look down the river and passed from the bridge on to the path. James crowed suddenly and she smiled down at him, all sadness vanished.

'You were very nearly called Percy,' she told him. 'Laugh that one off!'

She smiled as she recalled Lucy's bitter disappointment when she discovered that, not only was there no chance of a Polly, her parents also refused to consider Percy as a name for her new brother. She was too excited to bear any resentment for long, however, and she couldn't wait for him to come home from hospital and crack on with real life.

Phyllida watched a mallard, disturbed by her presence, paddle hastily away from the bank. She could still hardly take in that The Grange was to be her permanent home. It was the most amazing miracle and even more amazing that the pragmatic Alistair had finally made the decision on the sighting of the dipper. She shook her head. At one point she'd been terrified that he'd decline Clemmie's wonderful offer but her pleadings had seemed to carry no weight. He was determined to do what was right for all of them.

She remembered how he'd come in to visit her and to see James at the hospital and he'd told her then that he'd decided to accept if she still wanted to live at The Grange. She'd wept with joy but it was only later that he'd told her how he'd come to the decision. Of course, it meant postponing his departure from the Navy but he'd heard a buzz that he might be appointed to Devonport after Christmas, as Commander SM.

Phyllida screwed up her eyes and hugged James tightly at the mere thought that such luck should be theirs, coming on top of all the other joys.

'We must make a wish,' she told him. 'We must wish that Daddy gets the appointment. Oh, imagine it! He'd be home every night.' She shook her head at the idea of so much joy and then nodded at him. 'I know. We must watch for the dipper,' she said. 'If we see him, then Daddy will get the job. How about that?'

James crooned softly and Phyllida stood on the bank gazing intently up the river but there was no sign of the elusive bird. After a while she turned away, disappointed, and wandered on. She thought of Quentin and how much he had loved these woods and her heart seemed to twist with grief. How terribly they missed him and how glad she was that, in the end, all had been well for him and Clemmie and the shadows dispelled. She knew how much Clemmie repented of all that wasted time and, once again, she vowed that she and Alistair would never fall into the trap of fear and give way to recrimination and jealousy. If only they could be together!

Phyllida clutched at James as she felt a thrill of fear. In accepting Clemmie's offer, they'd postponed precious time together. Supposing something happened to one or other of them in the meantime? James weighed heavily, suddenly, and Phyllida sank down on a fallen trunk beside the path. Supposing they'd made a dreadful mistake in staying at The Grange? She screwed her eyes up, looking just like Lucy.

'Please, God,' she prayed, 'let it be right. Don't let it all be a mistake. Please let Alistair come down to *Drake*.'

She sat for a moment, rocking James, and feeling soothed by the sun on her back and the peaceful murmuring of the water. Presently she glanced at her watch and gave a little cry. It was nearly lunchtime and Clemmie would be wondering wherever they'd got to. The wood and the river had done their work, however, and Phyllida was calm again and her naturally cheerful spirits stilled her panic. As she braced herself to rise, a flash of white and brown caught her eye and she saw a bird fly upstream, straight as an arrow, a few inches above the water, to alight on a rock near the opposite bank. It preened for a few moments and then bobbed rhythmically, hardly distinguishable from the rock and the water.

It was the dipper.

Looking Forward

Marcia Willett

Life at The Keep changes forever when Fliss, Mole and Susannah arrive in the summer of 1957. Their parents and elder brother have been killed in Kenya so the children are sent to their grandmother, Freddy, in Devon.

Freddy is no stranger to grief, but she would be lost without her devoted helpers, Ellen and Fox, who enable her to cope with this latest tragedy. And, above all, she looks to her brother-in-law, Theo, to guide her while the children heal their wounds and embark on the treacherous journey to adulthood.

Looking Forward is a magnificent novel, introducing us to the unforgettable Chadwick family.

'A genuine voice of our times' *The Times*

'A fascinating study of character' *Publishing News*

'Very readable' *Prima*

'Rich characterisation here, and not a little humour, too' *Manchester Evening News*

0 7472 5996 8

HEADLINE

Thea's Parrot

Marcia Willett

As soon as George Lampeter, a submarine commander, sets eyes on Thea, twenty years his junior, he's found his partner for life.

Just about everyone knows of George's long-standing affair with the intimidating Felicity Mainwaring. Her husband's death had prompted many to speculate that George would end up marrying his formidable mistress. No one expected this outcome more than Felicity herself and as her phone calls to George go unanswered she becomes increasingly anxious.

George somehow manages to duck Felicity's attempts to contact him long enough to marry Thea, and the couple embark on a harmonious life together in the heart of rural Devon. Then, in Thea's opinion, George begins acting strangely. If she had been more aware of her husband's past, she might have noticed his behaviour changing from the day that she told him an old friend of his had dropped in for a chat while he was in London – Felicity Mainwaring . . .

0 7472 4904 0

HEADLINE

Now you can buy any of these other books
by **Marcia Willett** from your bookshop or
direct from her publisher.

FREE P&P AND UK DELIVERY
(Overseas and Ireland £3.50 per book)

Winning Through	£5.99
Starting Over	£6.99
Hattie's Mill	£5.99
Looking Forward	£6.99
Second Time Around	£5.99
The Dipper	£6.99
The Courtyard	£5.99
Thea's Parrot	£5.99
Those Who Serve	£5.99

TO ORDER SIMPLY CALL THIS NUMBER

01235 400 414

or e-mail orders@bookpoint.co.uk

Prices and availability subject to change without notice.